Peking man—evolutionary ancestor or revolutionary concept?

When the remains of Peking man were unearthed from the limestone hills outside the quaint Chinese village of Choukoutien, in the 1920's and 1930's, anthropoligists realized that the discovery of this link in the evolutionary chain was of profound importance. Fossil evidence indicated that the hidden secrets of mankind's beginnings were about to unfold.

Before studies of the site could be completed, however, Japanese expansionism loomed threateningly on the horizon. When Japanese soldiers invaded the Chinese mainland they brought with them a reign of terror, and took away cultural treasures and works of art valued as priceless. In late 1941, with occupation only days away, the Chinese decided that the Peking man remains would be safer in the United States. Preparations for shipment were made.

Then came the day of infamy—for the peace of the world as well as for the enlightenment hoped for by the scientific community. The fossils disappeared. During the war years no word of their whereabouts was heard. Afterward, no sign of them was seen. They were history. Gone, but not forgotten.

Half a century passed—a blink in the eyes of geological process but generations to the human species. The passage of time changes everything regardless of the scale of events. New and abrupt intelligence brought Peking man out of the past and into the unsettled world of international intrigue. The search for the fossil remains was reincarnated with vigor— only this time with guns, grenades, bombs, and rockets.

When anthropologist and underwater archaeologist William Waldo Hutchison III was "enlisted" to lead the search, he had no idea what he was getting into. He waded into the conflict with seven league boots that were so full of leaks he was soon drowing in contention. Along with two companions (a secret and secretive special agent known only as Cody, and a Naval intelligence officer whose voluptuousness matched her intelligence) Hutch embarked on a cruise of the South China Sea to investigate a number of sunken ships that may have had the long lost fossils on board at the time they went down.

What follows is a game of deep adventure and more thrills than Hutch ever bargained for. He is fragged, shelled, shot at, and stranded on a jungle isle; he is pursued by radicals who are more concerned with his extinction than that of Peking man; he dives into the deep blue sea and penetrates far into the collapsing corridors of rotten, rusting hulls. And all the time he is pursued relentlessly by multinational adversaries who also want to solve the mystery of Peking man—and who are not beneath killing for the solution.

Hutch's scientific inquiry into the understanding of man's past quickly becomes a struggle for personal survival. But at the end of the action—if he lives to write about it—is the answer to an age old riddle: where did man come from and where is he going? Somewhere, deep underwater, the past is about to catch up with the present. And the truth portended is ominous.

Also by Gary Gentile

Fiction
Entropy
Lonely Conflict
The Lurking
Mind Set
Return to Mars
Silent Autumn
The Time Dragons Trilogy:
    A Time for Dragons
    Dragons Past
    No Future for Dragons

Nonfiction
Advanced Wreck Diving Guide
Andrea Doria: Dive to an Era
Track of the Gray Wolf
Ultimate Wreck-Diving Guide
USS San Diego: the Last Armored Cruiser
Wreck Diving Adventures
The Popular Dive Guide Series:
    Shipwrecks of New Jersey
    Shipwrecks of Delaware and Maryland
    Shipwrecks of Virginia
    Shipwrecks of North Carolina: from the Diamond Shoals North
    Shipwrecks of North Carolina: from Hatteras Inlet South

THE
PEKING PAPERS

a novel by

GARY GENTILE

GGP
1992
P.O. Box 57137
Philadelphia, PA 19111

GGP
P.O. Box 57137
Philadelphia, PA 19111

The dust jacket photographs were taken by the author. The casting of the Peking man skull is in the collection of the Academy of Natural Sciences in Philadelphia.

International Standard Book Number (ISBN) 0-9621453-6-X

First Edition 1992

Printed in Hong Kong

Contents

(The following is an extract from "The Peking Papers," by William Waldo Hutchison, III, Ph.D., first addressed to the International Conference on Anthropology and Archaeology, Paris. Limited edition published by the Superintendent of Documents, U.S. Government Printing Office, Washington, DC 20402. Out of print.)

"Of all the mysteries in the world, the most cryptic are related to the sea."

The *President Harrison*

1941

Chang Wung Su wiped his wrinkled brow as the Japanese soldiers left the train. He had been nervous ever since leaving Peking with the crates, but when Imperial occupation forces flagged down the steam locomotive and ransacked the boxcars, he was fearful they might scatter over the desert plains whatever goods they considered useless.

He was old, and tired—tired beyond his years. His long, white hair was falling out in patches, his skin was pockmarked and peeling, he could not keep food in his stomach, his eyes ached and begged to be closed. Yet he could not sleep, he could not rest for a moment—not until he made sure that the precious cargo under his care was delivered to the proper authorities in Chingwangtao, and loaded aboard the American troopship.

The steam whistle blew. Smoke poured out of the engine's stack, and a caterpillarlike lurch jolted the long line of rickety cars. Wind devils whipped across the siding, blowing Chang's silklike hair across his weathered face. He forced his bent, emaciated frame to move through the tangle of rubble and loose debris left by the reckless, uncaring soldiers. He stumbled at the chest-level opening, and leaned against the metal edge to catch his breath.

To the tune of banging and screeching, the train moved again: at first only inches; then, by feet. Chang could not be left behind. He reached up for a handhold, exerted the last of his energy reserves, and pulled himself aboard. He hung precariously at first, by the waist, with his face and chest lying on the straw-covered floor, and with his feet dragging over the dry-rotted railroad ties. He gulped in air like a fish out of water. Slowly, he wriggled and kicked until most of his weight was inside. He rested again. Finally, he rolled over on his back and lay still. One leg dangled over the edge, but that was unimportant.

All that mattered was that the crates be delivered to Camp Holcomb, the U.S. Marine base in Chingwangtao, before the Japanese made their invasion official. Already their military presence in the northern provinces was causing great strife, great suffering.

Chang shivered in the freezing air. Eventually, he crawled into a corner of the boxcar, and huddled against one of the wooden crates from the Cenozoic Research Laboratory. The Japanese had forced open the lid, rifled through the straw. But when they found nothing but scrap metal, rock samples, and bits of bone—nothing of any value to them—they moved on. Little did they know that the exhumed relics of ancient man were priceless.

The cold and the sickness kept him awake. He retied the belt and drew the woolen coat tighter about his middle. Still, the frigid air seeped through. His fingers were numb, his hands like ice. His body shook in the unheated compartment like a man with ague. He curled into a ball and waited out the long, bumpy ride. One interminable stop followed another. It took three days to travel one hundred forty miles. When the freight train at last rumbled to a halt, Chang was near death. Outside, the temperature was thirty below zero. He lingered on only because he must discharge his duties in this world before passing on into the next.

Warm hands touched his cheeks, his forehead. He opened his eyes. Through the film he saw a youthful, familiar face. "Chu Shih."

"You are very sick, Dr. Chang."

"It is of little consequence." He tapped the redwood boxes behind him. "This is what is important. The guards—"

"They laughed about the old Chinaman who stayed with his bones, while they sat around the kerosene stove in the day coach. They are anxious to leave our country."

"The Japanese—"

"Are many. They have been asking about the freight. But we are within the Camp, and they have no jurisdiction here. The Marines, at least, will not let the invaders inspect the boxcars."

"The ship—"

"All the Americans are packing. They await a passenger liner that has been chartered by their Navy. Even now it discharges its civilian cargo in Shanghai."

Chang coughed: a deep throated, rasping, painful cough. "We must make plans. We must—" He choked on a clot of phlegm.

Chu Shih cradled the old man's head in his lap. "We must get you to some place warm. You must stay with me, with my family. We will take care of you."

Almost without knowing it, Chang nodded. His eyelids slipped closer together. He was so tired. He wanted to sleep, but could not. He let himself be half carried through the frigid, cobbled streets, to the already crowded bungalow. He was grateful for the comfort.

He lived in a limbo world where shadows crept up the wall and the windows became dark and the glass brightened and cast again strong shadows. He saw a young woman. Over and over she forced food into his mouth. Many times he spit it back out. He had no control over his bowels. But at least he was warm.

"Dr. Chang? Dr. Chang? Are you awake?"

Of course I am awake. It was impossible for him to sleep until his duty was properly carried out and the relics were on their way to America.

"I have repacked the contents of the crates into Marine Corps footlockers, and stenciled them as the Peking Union Medical College would have done. The transport is due any day now."

"You have done well."

We cannot let the Imperialists have such a treasure. It is our heritage, and they would use it against us."

Chang blinked. It took every effort just to perform such a simple task. Still, he must not sleep.

Chu Shih was shaking him again, only suddenly his face was in shadow. He held a candle between them. In the flickering, yellow glow Chang could barely make out the other's grim features.

"Dr. Chang, wake up."

I have not been asleep, you fool.

"Dr. Chang. It is war. The Japanese have bombed the American Naval base at Pearl Harbor. They have taken over Camp Holcomb and imprisoned the Marine guard."

"The crates—"

"The American ship, the *President Harrison*, will not be docking here. It was pursued by the Imperial Fleet, and the brave captain chose, instead of capture, to run his ship aground. It lies beached off the Yangtze River."

"Then how—"

"I have made arrangements. Just as you left two mock crates at Peking, I have made decoys. They are well concealed in several places. Should they ever locate them, a few bones and a skull in each of the false footlockers will lead the Japanese astray."

Tears welled in Chang's eyes. His affairs had been taken over by competent hands. "There is something you must have." He fumbled inside his shirt—*where was his jacket?*—and brought out the bundle he had secreted around his body. There were photographs, and sheaves of paper filled with drawings and Chinese characters. "You must take this, too. And you must take care that it does not fall into the wrong hands."

Chu Shih nodded grimly. "I will see that it is done."

Chang managed a faint smile. He allowed his eyes to close. At last, he could sleep.

The *Viking*

The water was bitterly cold; it stung Hutch's forehead through the thin neoprene of the face seal like a block of ice placed against his skin. Most microorganisms did not like the temperature any more than he did, and the resultant lack of free-floating plankton left the ocean crystal clear.

As if it were laid out on a museum exhibit floor, the worm-eaten timbers of the Viking ship were only partially exposed. Sand filled the center of the sunken vessel to a depth of several feet. Rounded ballast rocks peeked out here and there, like varicolored eggs in a giant Easter basket. Around the edges, rotted frames stabbed upward.

From the middle of the wreck, Hutch could see what was left of the sternpost at one end and the truncated bowsprit at the other. He rechecked the knot of his descent line, and moved the cinderblock to which it was tied several feet away from the weathered, sandblasted strake. He tightened the straps on his ankle weights, and positioned them so they would keep his overbuoyant feet down below his head. He kicked slowly, stifflegged, and propelled himself along the nearly sterile bottom.

Large sea anemones reached out with long, waving, graceful tentacles. Six-inch bergalls swam in lazy circles. A small skate flapped its wings and buried itself under the white sand, so that only its eyes protruded. Hutch grabbed it by the tail, and watched it dart out from its cover, to settle down twenty feet away. It eyed him warily.

It took him but a moment to reach the bow of the eighty-foot-long Viking ship. He flexed his fingers inside his mitts: the digits were already becoming numb in the thirty-five degree water. He placed his pencil and white plastic sketch pad next to the ancient, worn figurehead. For the next several minutes he stretched the nylon tape in various traces over the artistic curvatures, and took measurements. He ignored the buzzing sound in his ears.

For fifteen minutes he kept his nose to his work, the silicone mask acting like horse blinders. Fish swam in and out of his field of vision, but he ignored them. He concentrated on the accuracy of his drawing.

The buzzing became a persistent hum, like a swarm of angry bees roaming the forest for a new nest. Hutch swung around, and looked up. His orange inflatable boat hung by a silver thread to the bobbing marker buoy, tethered to the bottom by one-hundred-twenty feet of quarter-inch sisal. He certainly did not expect any company in this tiny, out of the way cove, sequestered along the rocky Canadian coastline.

Possibly a fisherman, he thought, *checking his lobster pots*. Numerous clawed crustaceans hid in the shallows where the kelp grew thick.

The sound was definitely an engine, but the pitch was too high for the slow Cape Islanders and their chug-chug six bangers. This sounded more like a fast motorboat.

Even as the thought came, he saw the sleek fiberglas hull racing in from offshore. The black streak veered in a tight circle around the inflatable, seemingly standing up on end. If this was the marine police, it was a new tactic. Hutch put down his tools and started back to the anchor line. He hoped he had done a good job of cleaning up his campsite. It would not bode well to be caught with even the tiniest bit of lobster shell: incriminating evidence of poaching on strictly forbidden preserves.

The explosion hit him in the head like a two-by-four. He squinted at the burst of pain in his ears, as if someone had stabbed him with dual ice picks. Tears welled up in his eyes, and threatened to wash out his contacts. Although he could not tell from which direction the detonation had come, he instinctively looked up.

The speedboat leaped across its own wake just as another explosion occurred. Hutch saw the sudden foaming bubbles a microsecond before the concussion slammed into him, blinding him with pain. Since water was essentially noncompressible, any violent discharge carried the shock of expanding gases a long way.

Doesn't that idiot know that a cherry bomb could kill him?

Only the fact that he was so deep, and that the force of the explosion was directed upward, toward the surface, saved him. But it meant that as long as that moron was up there, Hutch could not go up his ascent line.

The speedboat headed straight out to sea, but, as if leaving a parting shot, the inflatable exploded into great, streaming tatters of rubberized canvas. The three-and-a-half horsepower outboard motor plummeted to the bottom, dragging the wooden transom with it. The buoy had also been holed. Slowly, the whole mess—inflatable fragments, tethered gas can, tool kit, oars in their locks, and the remains of the burst buoy—gyrated toward the center of the Viking shipwreck, slinking down as the quarter inch rope coiled itself neatly over a dislodged, oaken keelson.

A tiny black ball hit the surface with a splash. It descended only a few feet before blowing into a froth of air and water. Again the awful concussion hit him. Hutch swung up vertically, shaking his head, and started back peddling. He had to get away from there.

He yanked his gauge console in front of him. He had plenty of air, but he had exceeded the time limit for a nondecompression dive. He had only a ten minute penalty, of which four was ascent time. But with his mooring line gone, and someone up there trying to murder him, he had no choice but to head for shore underwater. It was only a couple hundred yards, but the added time at depth would increase his decompression time.

With the decision made, he started kicking—hard.

He pressed the inflator button on his chest. Air from his tanks passed from the regulator's first stage and through the low pressure hose into the suit. The hiss was accompained by the scrape of harness straps readjusting themselves as the rubber stretched and the suit expanded. The added buoyancy pulled him off the bottom, and his route became a vector of horizontal travel and vertical lift. The engine whine faded to the limit of audibility.

At eighty feet, Hutch rolled over onto his back and pushed in the exhaust valve, rolled back, started sinking, then added air in tiny bursts until his ascent was under control. The sandy bottom was still clearly visible below him. At sixty feet it became indistinct. Ahead, the rock jutted out to meet him.

He swam into the long, flat kelp fronds and grabbed onto a ledge for support. He realized he was overbreathing his regulator: he was working too hard in his dash to get away. He forced himself to calm down, to take deep breaths, to let out all the air in his lungs before gulping down another lungful. He pulled himself through the kelp forest into shallower water. At forty feet he paused to study his gauges: still plenty of air, decompression of fifteen minutes starting at twenty feet, water temperature of thirty-seven—he had passed through a slight thermocline. He started shivering. The drysuit zipper leaked where the hard rubber material was tearing away from the neoprene, and he could not make repairs unless he let it dry completely.

He crawled along a gully effulgent with marine life: the boulders were carpeted with green sea urchins, flowering sea anemones, starfish, and brightly colored nudibranchs. A flatfish beckoned to be stabbed with a knife, but Hutch had thoughts moving in directions other than dinner. The surge was restless, escalating him five feet one way, then back again, unceasingly. A school of silvery baitfish accepted the undulations without concern. Hutch felt a little queasy, although some of his anxiety was probably leftover adrenaline from his recent escapade with the mad bomber.

When the digital display on the decompression computer registered a safe ascent to ten feet, Hutch slipped further up the rock gorge until he reached the allowable ceiling. Because the crevice was narrower, he was able to lock himself into it with his back and feet braced against opposite walls. He watched the waves crashing overhead.

The minutes ticked by slowly. Hutch heard nothing but his own exhaust bubbles rattling past his ears. His head was still ringing, but his eardrums were intact despite the proximity of the fireworks. He had a slight headache that might just as well have come from stopped up sinuses. And he was *cold*. This far north, the Labrador current had no mixture with the Gulf Stream—it curved right down from the North Pole via the Arctic Sea. At the moment, its heat transfer ability felt nearly infinite.

Finally, Hutch was free to come to the surface without suffering the bends. He rose up through the thick kelp beds, poked his face out of the water, and glanced around for signs of human visitation. As the surge banged him against the jagged rocks, he gazed out to sea. The Atlantic Ocean was a shimmering, opalescent lake, quiet except for gentle rolling swells and an occasional white sea gull enjoying the roller coaster ride. Only against the shoreline did the waves make their presence known, as the water bunched up and poured up the barnacle-encrusted rock face.

He kicked his flippers in tune to an incoming wave, and rode the crest over a slippery, kelp-covered slice of granite. The water receded, leaving him high and dry, but sliding back down. He dug his numbed fingers into the dark green fronds and held on until the next wave caught up with him. He squirmed and slithered up the rock face, over the brink, and rolled down the other side ungracefully, like an awkward sea lion pup. He landed in a three-foot-deep puddle which rose and fell with the surge, but which was at least out of the onslaught of the ocean.

Hutch sat up and spit the regulator out of his mouth. He doffed his mask, ran the strap up his wrist, pushed back his hood, squeezed water out of his blonde, close-cropped beard, and studied the rugged, barren landscape along the edge of the Straight of Belle Isle. His brown, mud-spattered van was the only manmade object in sight. The lichen-covered bog swept back from the high tide mark to a forest of balsam fir and black spruce some two hundred yards away. A few ducks rested in a nearby pool. The only sound was the gentle lapping of water.

Hutch backstepped a couple feet until he could find some stability by resting one hand on a quartz intrusion. He bent down and ripped off his flippers. He had just gotten the second one loose when he heard the engine whine. Rounding the western cape was a jet black cigarette boat going at least fifty knots. It skipped along the surface carving a rooster tail that cut deep into the water. Hutch stood dumfounded as the sharp pointed bow closed in on him.

The speedboat veered off a collision course, but kept racing for the rocky shore. The lone occupant stood behind the steering wheel with calm resolution. Just before impact, he threw the transmission into reverse. The engine clanked and groaned in protest. The boat slowed. It was picked up by its own wake, carried over the barrier rocks, and set down high and dry when its own generated waves receded. A blue uniformed officer rolled over the gunwale and hit the ground running.

At Hutch.

He held a rifle at port arms.

Hutch slowly raised his hands, mask in one and fins in the other. "Are you out of your goddamned mind?"

Helicopter blades chopped the air, and an olive drab machine rose above the trees from behind a tall bluff a quarter mile down the coast. It tilted far to the side, chose a course, and leveled out with the tail riding high and all power applied.

The man spun around. Bandoliers swung around him like flags on a Maypole. He appeared to be rather heavily armed for the marine police.

Hutch lowered his arms a hair. With a hundred pounds of twin tanks on his back, he was tiring quickly. "Don't you think this is a bit of overkill? I know there are laws protecting historic wreck sites, but I didn't remove anything—"

He was cut off by a rat-tat-tat that reminded him of a backfiring Model-T. Beyond the man's head he saw red flashes emitting from the undercarriage of the helicopter.

"*Get down!*" Rifle tossed aside, the man charged forward and hit Hutch in a flying tackle that would have done justice to a full back.

Barely on balance to begin with, Hutch needed no urging to fall over backward. He had a wild sensation of popping sounds and red fireflies and buzzing insects. As his tanks hit the water, and a tidal wave cascaded outward, he had one crazy moment of clarity. He saw the normally submerged rock face covered with limpets suddenly exposed to the air. Then the water splashed into his face. He caught it on an inhale, and instantly started coughing and sputtering. He fought to climb up, but the tank harness held him down like a ton of bricks saddled to his back.

Then he felt air on his face—and saw a knife at this throat.

The red necked man grimaced down at him. "How do you get these straps—Never mind." One deft slash severed the shoulder harness, another cut away the waist strap. "Come on." He pulled Hutch up by the neck.

"The inflator hose—" Hutch gurgled, still spitting water. He grappled with the release mechanism, with hands that were still stiff from the cold. When it came free, the man yanked at him furiously. He got only to a sitting position when he was stopped. "The crotch strap."

Another slash of the incredibly sharp knife, and Hutch was free from his aluminum encumbrances. He also felt the frigid intrusion of salt water—the leg of his drysuit had been punctured by the steel point.

"Come on, chap. We don't have much time, eh. They're making another pass."

Hutch struggled to his knees. "Who are you? And what he hell do you think you're—"

The lean man picked up his rifle and used it as a pointer. "Can we talk over there behind those rocks, before the nice chaps in the chopper swing around?''

Hutch saw the helicopter veering out to sea in a tight circle that would soon bring it back. He opened his mouth to protest, made an instantaneous decision, closed his mouth, and nodded jerkily. The water was only up to his knees, but the footing was still slippery because of the kelp. Like a mud crab he scuttled up the rocks on all fours until he reached dry ground, then waddled for the protection of the boulders. His right leg was filled with water; it ballooned like an African tribesman with elephantiasis.

A firm hand gripped his arm and hurried him along. "Duck under there, eh." The man gave him a push toward the protection of a great, rounded boulder.

Hutch limped the last several feet on his own. He sat down gratefully just as the helicopter zoomed by at over a hundred miles per hour. The ruddy-faced man placed the rifle to his shoulder and melded the gunsight to his cheek. He let go an entire magazine on full automatic. With lightninglike speed he dropped out the clip and slammed in a new one. By that time the gunship was flying past them. He ran the gun barrel in an arc over his head, firing continuously.

A moment later a tremendous explosion sounded from the water's edge. Hutch felt the flash of heat as a great, roiling ball of smoke and fire gushed into the air. His face was spattered, and he felt wet. But when he licked his lips he found it was only salt spray.

The man sat down beside him, leaned his back against the rock. "Phosphorus grenade, eh." The speedboat was a mass of flames and melting fiberglas.

Hutch gulped, shaking his head slowly. "What the hell is going on? And who are those guys?"

The man slid another clip into the rifle and chambered a round. "Can you run in that thing?"

"Not with these ankle weights on, and a leg full of water. My clothes are in the va—."

The survival knife sliced through the plastic strap and gouged the heel. The water began to run out. A second later, and the other ankle weight lay on the ground beside the first.

"No time. We gotta run. And they may send ground troops, eh?"

"Mister, that's a thousand dollar suit you just cut to ribbons. Don't you goddamned Newfies have any—"

"How much is that neck of yours worth?"

Hutch could still hear the helicopter blades beating the air. He swallowed hard. "A lot more than yours."

The man grinned, showing a mouthful of white, sparkling teeth. "I hate to agree with you, chap, but you're closer to the truth than you know."

Hutch ran a jaundiced eye up and down the man's uniform. In the brief moment while the helicopter banked, he noticed that the shirt bore no badges or nametag, the collar sported no insignia of rank. There was enough to make him look like a policeman from a distance—until he threw on the combat harness rigged with pouches of ammunition and double rows of hand grenades.

Hutch winced. "Who are you?"

The man smiled again. "Commando Cody."

Hutch rolled his eyes. "Don't give me that crap—"

He held up a finger. This time the helicopter did not fly directly overhead, but veered over the bog. The man who called himself Commando Cody took careful aim, leading the plexiglas pilot's cage to account for its forward motion, and fired controlled bursts. Two black eggs dropped out of the crew cabin, fell toward the sitting truck.

One hit a muddy pothole and sank in with a plop. The other hit a rock outcropping, bounced, and rolled under the rear axle. They went off in rapid succession. The truck was lifted a foot, then engulfed in a fireball that completely hid the vehicle.

"*My van!*" Hutch started up.

Cody held him back with a one-armed jab. "Only property, eh."

Hutch's voice was throaty, and rasping. "Yeah, the only property I own."

"Can always buy more. Buy you can't get a new lease on life unless you pay the rent—or run out on the landlord."

Hutch's attention was riveted on the burning van. "Huhn?"

Cody watched the trees long after the helicopter disappeared over them. "I think I got a couple rounds in them, but they may have backups. Can we go now?" He did not wait for an answer, but took Hutch's arm and dragged him along.

They slurped through the bog and scampered over colorful, lichen covered rocks. They ducked into the shadow of the forest. Hutch stopped and took one last look at the scene behind them. The two conflagrations were still burning nicely. Twin streamers of black smoke billowed several hundred feet into the blue sky. "I don't understand—"

Cody pulled him deeper into the woodland. Soon, the crackling metal parts and bursting bubbles of fiberglas were part of the background noise. Somewhere off in the distance, a loon let out its lonesome call.

Hutch had a hard time trudging over the uneven terrain in rubber booties. "Cody—if that's really your name—what did you do to those guys in the chopper? Who are they? Who are *you*? And why are they after you?"

"In sequence: nothing, I don't know, me, and because they think I'm you."

"*Me*! What have I got to do with all this?" Hutch slapped at black flies on his face. "I'm minding my own goddamned business. No one but me knows that's really a Viking ship down there. And I wasn't sure until I surveyed the wreck. And even so, that's no cause to blow up my van and try to kill me. If you wanted to get me out of the water, dropping explosives was not the way to do it."

"That wasn't me. That was the chaps in the chopper." In the lead, Cody stepped over rotting logs and shoved thick vines out of the way. "They were looking for a rich kid out on his own. I doubt they bothered to take down your license plate number, although the New York tags are a dead giveaway—literally."

"Now wait a minute. Granted I was brought up in the Hamptons, and my folks have money, but since college I've made my own way in life— littorally. And I wasn't breaking any regulations just by diving—Cody, this is ridiculous. I don't have the faintest idea what this is all about. And who's side are you on, anyway? You're not the marine police."

"I'm on your side, Hutchison."

Hutch wiped spider webs from his hands. "So you know who I am?"

"I was sent to find you."

"By name? Or just someone who was diving what might possibly be the most historic shipwreck in North America?"

"William Waldo Hutchison the Third. And I don't give a damn about Viking warships."

"It's not a warship. It was a colonial trader, carrying settlers. I just proved that by the carved headpost. It was buried under the sand, protected from natural deterioration and hidden from the teredoes."

"Ship worms?"

"Wood boring mollusks, really. It was the ultimate piece of information. Land settlements have been found, but archaeological digs always produced artifacts made *after* landfall—never anything from the settler's point of origin. There's no telling what lies under the sand in the hull of this wreck. Plenty, I'm sure. And it'll prove definitely that Norsemen from Greenland had outposts here in the eleventh century—maybe earlier. The paper from this will rouse quite a few egotistical, self-centered heads— and earn my Ph.D in the bargain."

"I thought you didn't care about academic degrees."

"I don't. But if I can get it for nothing, and it can add authority when I say some—Hey, what the hell do you know about my likes and dislikes?"

The pearly whites came out again. "Oooooh, we've got quite a file on you, eh."

Hutch brushed the swarm of black flies congealing in front of his eyes. "All right. That's enough. Hold it. I'm not going any further."

Cody stopped and turned around. "What's the matter, chap?"

Hutch wiped an arm across his forehead, smearing the beads of sweat across his brow. "Cody, I'm walking through a hot forest at high noon in a rubber suit. I'm dying in this thing."

Cody whipped out his knife. "No problem."

"*Wait.*" Hutch stepped back a pace. "Let me do it my way. It's easier on the equipment."

He pulled the waterproof zipper up across the chest until it ran out at the shoulder. He tore the beaver tail from its Velcro fastener. With his fingers inserted around the neck seal, he held his breath, closed his eyes, and pulled up. He wiggled and wormed his face out of the rubber vice, took a deep breath when his head was free. He massaged his sore throat. "Whew, it's like being born again." Hutch wriggled his arms out, pulled the suit down to his waist, and tied the floppy arms in front of him.

"Strangest looking wetsuit I ever saw."

"It's not a wetsuit, it's a drysuit. Actually, after you've had it a month or so, it becomes a dampsuit."

"What've you got on under it?"

"Everything I could find. Two layers of long johns, a couple of sweaters, insulated socks. That water's *cold*."

Cody's hazel eyes sparkled. "You've got more guts than I have, chap. The only water you'll catch me under is a shower—a *warm* shower."

"It's safer than dodging bullets for a living—and grenades."

For the first time, Cody's mein became serious. "What about sharks?"

Hutch rolled his eyes. "Why does everyone think of sharks as soon as you mention diving. Do you think of bears and mountain lions in National Parks?"

"I—"

"No. You think of beauty, serenity, waterfalls, mountains, snow, and hot springs. And squirrels and rabbits and flowers and trees. You can get nipped by a kangaroo mouse as easily as you can get bit by a triggerfish. Nothing a little bandage medicine won't fix."

"I—"

"Forget it. Just tell me what the hell is going on. Archaeology isn't going to change the course of human history, or heal the sick, or help the poor. It's a purely cognitive science, with no redeeming social function other than putting a few interesting paperbacks on a corner bookstand. So why is this Viking ship so goddamned important?"

Cody tilted his head, his ever-present smile back on his lean face. "I hate to burst your bubble, but as far as the Vikings are concerned, no one I know really gives a damn. But *you*, on the other hand, are very important."

"Hey, I don't know any national secrets. I've never been involved in politics. I'm not a communist. I haven't robbed any banks or Brink's trucks. And I haven't started any revolutions—not yet, anyway. Although, after I publish my Viking papers it's likely to shuffle the hierarchy in the profession. So what is it?"

Cody nodded with his pronounced chin. "Are you rested up?"

Hutch sighed.

"Let's get moving." Cody started off through the forest, swinging the rifle casually by the extended sights. "I'll explain a few things on the way."

Hutch hiked up his woolen underwear and retied his sleeves like a cummerbund. "What's that Matty Mattel toy you have there?"

Cody swung up the black, plastic stocked rifle so Hutch could see it. "It's an M–16, the finest light-weight, high-power, long-range weapon ever made."

"You like it."

"My constant companion for two tours in Vietnam."

"Are you American?"

"Don't let the accent fool you, eh. It's part of my cover. I've been playing a Canadian cop, and I don't want to get out of character yet."

The brush was as thick as elephant grass and as sharp as barbed wire. The soft-soled booties that were part of the drysuit did not offer the best protection. Hutch kept stepping on sharp-pointed sticks and razor-edged rocks. "Okay, so you're not the Royal Canadian Mounted Police. What are you really? CIA?"

"I'm part of a quasi military force specializing in covert operations."

"Which says just about nothing." Hutch climbed awkwardly over logs and rotten tree trunks, hardly able to keep up with Cody's pace. "So how do I figure in on all this? And why are those guys trying to kill you because they think you're me? What did I do?"

"So far, nothing. It's what you *might* do that makes you such a worthwhile antagonist."

"You must be a politician, the way you can go on and on without actually saying anything. Get to the point."

"There must have been a leak. The only possible reason they can have for going after you is, they found out *we* were going after you. And they don't want any competition."

"That's clear as mud. Can you at least tell me who 'they' are?"

"No." Cody snapped off a brittle sapling and tossed it to the side. "Not because it's classified, but because I don't know. I was as shocked as you were when those chaps showed up and started lobbing grenades."

"Is that what was going off in the water?"

"Fragmentation, not phosphorus. They were dropping them from a hundred feet up, so they cooked off for two and a half seconds before hitting the water. $S = 1/2 \, gt^2$, eh?"

"Are you a physicist, too?"

"Ballistics expert. Demolition. Weapons. Infiltration. Undercover. Hand-to-hand combat."

"Quite a list of merit badges. Now tell me you're thrifty, brave, clean, and reverent."

"Don't go to church. Never did, never will."

"This is getting us exactly nowhere. Speaking of which—" Hutch stopped to wipe more sweat off his brow. If his long johns had not been wet before from salt water intrusion, they were soaked now from perspiration. "Granted you don't know where you're coming from, but— do you have any idea of where we're going?"

Cody pulled a map out from inside his blue shirt. "Checkpoint Lambda."

"Great. Do you know how to get there?"

Cody pursed his lips. "I think that falls under trustworthy."

"Goddamn. You *were* a Boy Scout." Hutch leaned against a peeling birch tree, swatted at the swarm of black flies coagulating before his eyeballs. "And what happens when we get there?"

Cody slipped his harness off so he could get to the fanny pack. He rummaged through it for a moment, then brought out a tiny plastic bottle and handed it to Hutch. "N, N-diethyl meta-toluamide. Effective insect repellent is *the* most essential tool for survival in the wilderness."

Hutch read the label. "Hundred proof. Good stuff. Mine's only seventy-five."

"Yours is zero."

Hutch squinted, thinking of his customized van. "Yeah." He squirted the clear liquid into his palms, rubbed his hands together, then washed his face, neck, even his hair. "Little buggers get everywhere."

Cody folded his lanky body on a convenient stump. He telescoped the aerial of a cigarette-pack-sized box, flipped open the cover, and held the device close to his lips. "Hellbent. Hellbent. This is Leather, Come in please. Over."

The squawking reply was instantaneous. "This is Hellbent. Go ahead Leather. Over."

"Hellbent, this is Leather. I'm landlocked and need pickup. Can you arrange? Over."

"Leather, this is Hellbent. Will do. Your choice. Over."

"Hellbent, this is Leather. Checkpoint Lambda. Time seventy-six hundred hours. Over."

"Leather, this is Hellbent. We read you as Checkpoint Lambda, time seventy-six hundred. Confirm. Over."

"Hellbent, this Leather. You got it. Out."

"Wait, Leather, this is Hellbent. Condition of quarry. Over."

"Terminated. Out."

"Out."

Cody folded the miniature transmitter and slipped it back into its pouch. He unfolded the map. After several seconds of study, he motioned Hutch closer. "Just in case we get separated, or something happens to me, this is where they'll be waiting for us." He indicated a headland that projected several hundred yards offshore. "It's quite a few hours walk in this terrain, so we'd better get started. We've only got until midnight."

"I thought you said—Hey, wait a minute, there isn't any seventy-six hundred hours."

"It's calculated from a pre-set, arbitrary time."

"Oh." Hutch raised his eyebrows. "You know, it'll be a lot faster if we just walk out on the rocks."

"Where we'll be sitting mallards for a search party without our best interests at heart."

Hutch's shoulders sagged. "I didn't think of that."

"That's all right. It's not your business. I wouldn't recognize a Viking warship, either."

"It's not a warship, it's a—Hey, what was that about 'quarry terminated'?"

Cody stood up and readjusted his web gear. "There's been a leak in our intelligence. That's the only way they could have found out about you. If they ever get a transcript of this broadcast, I want them to believe you're dead."

"What about you?"

"I'm not important. Not in this case. They won't come after me."

"I still don't understand. Who are *they*."

Cody looked grim. "We're not really sure. Oh, it's a foreign government, and we have our guesses. But we don't really know just yet. That chopper was Russian made: a modified, stripped down Hind. But it could have been bought by anyone on the open market."

"Eh?"

Cody squinted one eye.

"You're losing your accent, eh. You're slipping out of character."

Cody chuckled. "I like you. From the reports you seemed like some wise ass, highfalutin, independent rich kid. A jet setter with an interest in history. But you're all right. Real down to earth. Apple pie and—"

If Cody hadn't looked up through the branches at the puffy white cumulus, Hutch probably would not have noticed the eerie, droning sound that was dopplering in on them from the sky. "Hey, that sounds like—"

"*Incoming!*" Once again Cody knocked Hutch down, then covered him with his body.

The explosion was so near it sent shrapnel through the trees and cut loose leaves that fell on the pair like confetti at a tickertape parade. The second explosion was closer. Birch branches were scythed off like wheat. When Hutch opened his eyes, he thought he was at the bottom of a pile of pickup sticks. The third explosion straddled them, blowing great clods of earth and decomposing plantlife into a dirt-filled cloud that engulfed them both.

Cody pushed up through the debris, with sticks, mud, and leaves cascading off his back like snow in an avalanche. "Damn. They must have triangulated our position. That means they've got more than one base in the area."

Hutch spit out a mouthful of topsoil. "What the hell does that transmitter do, send out over the wire services?"

"Come on, we've got to *move*."

"Eh?"

Cody was in no mood for games. He yanked Hutch to his feet and dragged him along through the tangle of ruined forest. As soon as they reached relative clearing, he ran—and made sure Hutch was running with him. Hutch's drysuit had slipped down until he felt like a penguin dancing through the woods. The sleeves had come untied and there was no time to retie them. He grabbed handfuls of material at the hips, and did his best not to fall down when crashing through the underbrush.

They broke out into a clearing, part of which was an ancient, rutted trail that was more rocks and potholes than level ground.

"Hey, this is the logging road I drove in on."

Cody pushed Hutch out of the open and tucked him under a giant, overhanging rock that was covered with green reindeer moss. "How the hell did you ever get it in here? There's not enough ground clearance for a Sherman tank."

"I had a four-wheel drive conversion installed. It was jacked way up and could—"

"You're not the only one. Listen."

The road had more doglegs than a pet store. Anything farther than a hundred feet away was out of sight. While Cody fumbled with his fanny pack, Hutch cocked an ear. The whining was coming closer, and closer, and—He slapped at the mosquito settling into his ear. "What's that thing?"

Cody quickly unwound a set of wires from what looked like a curved waffle iron on spindly legs. He propped it up alongside the dirt road and covered it up with leaves and needles. He wrapped two stripped leads around the terminals of a small battery. A fine piano wire he ran across the trail, around a balsam fir, and back again, then tied it tightly to a fallen birch. Another stripped lead completed the circuit.

"Claymore with a trip wire. I don't know what they're driving, but it'll slow them down."

"Wait a minute. Suppose they're just civilians who heard the—"

"Believe me, you're the only human being in this neck of the woods who hasn't got a loaded gun."

"Hey, maybe they're just local hunters."

Cody pushed him steadily away from the trail. "Nothing's in season except you and me."

Hutch tripped over wild blueberry bushes. "Cody, you might kill someone."

"That's the idea. Give unto others before they give unto you. It's the way this business works."

"But—"

"This isn't academia, where the sharpest thrust is an inuendo to the dean, and the parry is an expletive. You stick to your specialty, I'll stick to mine."

They were only a hundred yards away when the explosion rattled the somber silence of the forest.

"Speaking of mines—"

Cody kept tugging Hutch along. "That's a booby trap, not a mine. And we barely got away from the backwash." He shook his head. "How can they be reacting so quickly? First a chopper, then a jeep. These people have some resources, and ain't afraid to use them. And their strike force is set up better than the average espionage network. Man, I don't know what we're dealing with. And that scares me."

Hutch pulled his arm away, but kept running along with his new found partner. "Cody, I don't like this cloak and dagger stuff, but—I'm dammed glad you happened along. I wouldn't have stood a chance."

"We're not out of the woods yet. Where they got us is—we're trying to stay clandestine, and they just don't give a damn. It's as if an international incident doesn't mean anything to them."

They fought uphill through foot-deep piles of springy sphagnum moss. Hutch was exhausted and out of breath at the top. Cody yanked him the last few feet. The trees and underbrush were so dense that visibility was limited to twenty or thirty feet. Cody slipped a lensatic compass out of the fanny pack and took a reading.

Hutch bent over at the waist, hands on hips, and fought to get his breath back. "What other sundries do you have in there?"

Cody smiled. He handed Hutch a canteen and a compressed food bar. "Have some pemmican."

Hutch gratefully accepted the water, and gurgled half of it down in one long, continuous gulp. "I'm not dressed for this." He sat down and peeled the aluminum foil off the densely packed solid. It tasted sweet and salty at the same time, satisfying more than one hunger. "Hey, this is pretty good."

"Keep your voice down. There may be survivors."

Hutch almost choked on the food. "You mean, you might have killed someone—for real?"

"That claymore wasn't loaded with paint pellets. You better get used to the fact that these guys are out to send you up to that big shipwreck in the sky. You can still write your paper in Valhalla, but you won't get a university degree out of it. Now let's *move*. Depending on how they were sitting, I might have done nothing more than given them a few flat tires."

Cody was up and moving. Hutch had no choice but to run to keep up with him.

"But, Cody. Why me?"

"Later. It's too complicated to explain right now. And I want to concentrate on saving your ass."

"But, am I in trouble? I mean, with the government."

Cody laughed. "Not with ours. Hell, right now you're worth more money than all the gold in Fort Knox."

Hutch ducked under some low-lying branches. His legs were awfully sore—running in a drysuit forced him to stretch the neoprene with every step. It was like working an exercise machine with rusty springs. "Everything I owned was in that van—my scuba gear, underwater camera equipment, camping supplies. Hell, even my clothes went up in ashes. I'm not just broke, I'm destitute.''

"But you still have life's experiences, and that's something that can't be taken away with you.''

"Doesn't that leave when I stop breathing?''

"As long as I know CPR and mouth-to-mouth, you'll breathe.''

Hutch grimaced. "Just knowing you might attempt it will keep me inhaling. So, what exactly are these life's experiences? And what are they going to do for me?''

"Get you out of hock for one thing. And help the—'' Cody stopped so suddenly that Hutch crashed into him. "Do you smell that?''

"I can't smell anything, damn it.'' Hutch cupped his nose. It was bleeding from where it had banged against Cody's back. "Hey, is that smoke?''

Cody glanced at the compass. "Inland. Sixty degrees. Let's go check it out. And for Odin's sake, be quiet.'' Five-foot-ten of leanness hunched into a raccoonlike ball, and slinked through the trees with the hush of an Apache. The rifle never left his hand.

Hutch tried to imitate him. His form was the same, but twigs kept crackling under his booties. For the hundredth time he pulled up his sagging drysuit.

There were no flames. The perpetual dampness of the boggy terrain had snuffed out any original fire. Neither was there movement. The helicopter lay on its side like a child's toy, fairly well intact except for the sheared off blades and gun platforms. The tail was bent at a ninety degree angle, the stabilizing rotor was missing. The splintered plexiglas bay window was no longer transparent—it was a dull, charcoal black.

Cody kicked in a side panel, letting out the odor of burnt insulation and incinerated flesh. He put a handkerchief over his nose and peered inside the cockpit. "Damn. Beyond recognition.''

Hutch coughed and gagged. "Is that all you can say for them?''

Cody backed away. "What do you want me to do? Sing a requiem? These blokes tried to kill me. And you, too.''

"They're dead. Have a little respect.''

"They're failures, otherwise we'd be dead and they'd be drinking champagne by now.'' Cody circled the smoking wreckage. He placed his free hand on several places along the hull. "Pretty cool.'' He turned and handed the M–16 to Hutch. "You know how to use this thing?''

"I fired a blunderbuss once during a college reenactment. That's a fat, flintlock musket with a—''

"Spare me the lecture.'' Cody indicated the selector switch and trigger. "The safety's off. Just aim and shoot at anything that moves.''

Hutch held the weapon delicately with both hands, away from his body as if the barrel were a rattlesnake preparing to bite. "I don't like guns.''

Cody climbed up the body of the helicopter. "It's not a gun. It's a rifle." He kicked in the cargo door, and a moment later dropped down inside the crew compartment.

Hutch heard him rumbling around inside. It was not until several minutes later, as Cody was climbing out, that he remembered to take a look at the forest for intruders.

Cody jumped lithely to the singed ground. "Two gunners, both dead. And not much meat left on them. All the ammo cooked off in the fire." He slapped his hands together, then wiped them on his trousers. "Black jump boots and olive drab fatigues. No labels, not even size tags. Everything was stripped down to complete anonymity. The only thing I could tell was they were using AK–47s."

Hutch gladly relieved himself of the rifle. "What's that?"

"Automat kalashnikov. Soviet assault rifle. More accurate than the M–16, but heavier and with larger bullets. You can buy them anywhere except Macy's. If I had more time, I might be able to find some identification. But it's getting dark and we've got a deadline to make. Let's go."

Hutch hiked up his sweat-filled rubber suit, and retied the flopping arms yet again. "Why do I have the feeling that you're always in a rush? I can read maps. We're practically there."

"It's the military ethic: hurry up and wait."

Beating through the bush was draining Hutch of his energy. "Cody, you have any more water?"

Cody handed him the canteen. "Finish it."

Hutch did. When he passed it back, he said, "You know, I haven't seen you drink anything? Or eat, either. What are you, solar powered?"

"I'll relax as soon as we get to our checkpoint."

When they did, Cody picked a spot of high land at the edge of the tree line, from where they could see for miles across the strait. The setting sun created reflective diamonds on the smooth surface of the sea. A wooden trawler, booms out, cruised parallel to the beach. Cody pulled a monocular from his neverending kit of goodies, and studied the work boat intently.

"Too small to be a launch ship. Back home I'd say that aerial was for a single sideband, Coast Guard reg." Cody pursed his lips and shook his head. "But not here. The local fisherman don't have the money for it." He passed the seven by thirty-five lens to Hutch. "Those rockets had to come from someplace close."

Hutch adjusted the diopter. "Hmmn. You can barely make out the coast of Labrador. But that—looks like an innocent fisherman to me."

"Everything is innocent to you." Cody bent down over a puddle infested with mosquito larvae, made a hole in the floating top scum with cupped hands, put his lips to the surface, and started sucking.

"Yuck." Hutch had to turn his head. "How can you drink that stuff?"

"I'm thirsty. You'll drink it, too, when you're thirsty. Besides, bioorganisms are a good sign the water's potable. Have another pemmican.''

Hutch took it, and munched.

Cody chewed his food rapidly, swallowed, and gulped down more pothole water. "Time for some shut eye." He leaned back onto the sloped sphagnum moss, rifle in his lap and one hand on the trigger guard, and closed his eyes.

Soon, Hutch wanted a drink. He held off when he looked at the puddle and saw the squirming, wormlike forms darting back and forth. But later, he found the real meaning—Cody's meaning—of thirst. He imitated the commando's tactics and sipped delicately at the forest fountain. The water was cool and tangy, probably from the lichen growing in the bottom. Actually, it was not too bad.

Then, he lay back and watched the sun set on a day in his life he was not likely to forget.

Hutch awoke with a touch on his arm.

"Come on, sleeping beauty. Your prince is here."

Hutch was tucked up in a ball, shivering. He rubbed the matter out of his eyes. "Damn, it sure gets cold when the sun goes down."

Cody crouched with the monocular glued to his eye. He scanned the northern horizon with long, slow sweeps, apparently ignorant of the temperature. "Look over there."

"Oh, *wow*. Fantastic, man." Great, green shimmering curtains, interspersed with splashes of pastel red, rose vertically from ten degrees above the sparkling water and arced halfway up the brilliant, starstudded sky. "Must be some heavy duty sunspot activity."

Cody snatched the lens away from his face. "What the *hell* are you talking about?"

Hutch sat up and nodded with his chin. "Aurora borealis. The Northern Lights. Let me see what it looks like through the monocular."

"Go back to dreamland. This isn't a vacation we're on, and we haven't got time to watch the scenery."

"It's there. Why not take advantage of it?"

"Because it misdirects your attention. Because while you're gazing at the stars, somebody's sneaking up to stick a knife in your back."

"Geez, what a way to go through life."

"Get used to it, because whether you like it or not—you're in it."

Hutch stabbed an extended digit into Cody's chest, between the tiered grenades. "Yeah, well, listen to me, mister. I didn't ask for this. I didn't ask to have bombs dropped on me. I didn't ask to be shot at. I didn't ask you to come out here and drag these goons along. I don't know what your game is and, frankly, I don't give a damn. The only reason I'm hanging in with you at all is because, for the moment, it's the only rational path to take. I've got no food, no clothes, no wheels—nothing but a couple of sets of smelly underwear and a religious drysuit made holy by a knife you covet like your pecker. You've got an insecurity problem as long as your gun barrel—''

"It's a rifle."

"—and you'd be lost in this world without your weapons. You want to kill and be killed, that's your choice. But don't drag me down with you. I'm a scientist, I'm a historian, I'm a pacifist, I'm—"

"I've read your file."

"—an environmentalist, and I'm damn sure *not* a secret agent double-oh-seven with delusions of grandeur. You've destroyed everything I own, and you've taken away everything I stand for. And the only thing I want from you is transportation back to civilization, so I can try to pick up the pieces of my life that have been shattered in these last twelve hours."

Cody's eyes were bright spots of white in the otherwise utter darkness. "Okay, I guess that's been building up, and you needed to get if off your chest. I guess, too, I've had it coming. I'm sorry if I haven't been more—sensitive—to your plight." Cody snickered, and stared out wistfully over the headland and crashing waves. "You know, when I'm home, with the family, I'm not under this kind of pressure. But on the job, things are different. Being alive is one of your pleasures. Staying alive is my necessity. And right now, big things are afoot, to which the minor inconveniences we've had to suffer are inconsequential."

"*Inconveniences? Inconsequential*? Man, if you're looking for a Nobel prize in understatement, you've got my vote."

"Do you know your teeth are chattering? And your words are slurred?"

"Goddamn it, I'm freezing to death. How can you stand it in that short sleeve shirt?"

Cody shrugged. "I don't enjoy it. I just endure it. Why don't you put that suit of yours back on?"

"Good idea." Hutch stood up to his knees, stretched the crushed neoprene, and forced his head through the neck seal. He smoothed out the soft rubber, then inserted his arms both at the same time, and poked them out the wrist seals. "I may as well close the zipper."

"All right, let's crawl down to those rocks and get ready to take a ride." Cody got down on all fours and crept with Navaho stealth over the reindeer moss. None of his equipment rattled or made a sound.

Hutch followed him. He caught up with the commando at the water's edge, behind a boulder. "Hey, you got any more of that pemmican?"

Cody handed him a processed food bar. "You can have all the emergency rations you want. I'm holding out for a nice, juicy steak."

"Grandeur's not your only delusion. Cody, what the hell are we waiting for?"

"Mother Goose."

"I knew I shouldn't have asked."

Cody tilted his head toward the sea. "Take a look out there. *No*. Not over the rock—around the side."

Hutch sneaked one eye to where he could see the water. At first he saw nothing unusual, just the gentle rolling swells and the shadow of the headland. Then, he thought one of the shadows moved, got closer. He kept watching it, and sure enough, it was coming toward him. Whatever it was, was black, and moved like a dark phantom. It did not resolve itself into anything recognizable until it actually grounded on the rocks lower down.

Hutch smiled. "All *right*. It's a raft." He pushed himself upright. "Like the shepherd said, let's get the flock out of here."

Cody grabbed him and yanked him back down. "What're you trying to do, give our position away?"

Hutch stared at him, stunned. "How—how else are they going to find us?"

"Just stay put, will you? And keep quiet." Cody detached two grenades from the front of his web harness, and pulled the pins out with his teeth. The metal clips disappeared into his mouth. He peered around the edge of the smooth boulder.

Hutch held his breath, straining his ears for every sound. Faintly, he heard a loud whisper.

"This is Mother Goose. Is any of her family out there?"

Cody called back, "This is the Ugly Duckling."

"Jack be nimble?"

"Pail of water."

"Cody, is that you?"

Cody eased up. "Who the hell were you expecting, the Easter Bunny?"

"Hell, we get any closer to the North Pole, I'd be looking for Santa Claus. This is Rich." The man's voice was getting closer.

Hutch pushed himself up, breathing again. "Man, you guys sure play it to the hilt, don't you."

Cody shoved him back hard. "Stay down, you fool." The commando stood up in full view, with his hands away from his sides. Hutch heard the man calling himself Rich stop directly in front of the rock. "I've got two grenades here, and the pins are in my teeth."

Hutch rubbed his shoulder, where it had been slammed against the ground, and looked up at Cody's silhouette. He saw starlight glint off the metal clips he was biting.

The other man smiled. "Thank god it's really you. We thought that rocket attack might have gotten you."

"Whoever it was had damn good surveillance."

"The captain'll debrief you on that. Let's get the hell out of here. We stick out like a sore thumb against all these stars. And the moon'll be rising in an hour."

Cody worked his mouth so the pins stuck out beyond his thin lips. He reinserted them into the handles of the grenades, and clipped them to his harness. "Okay, you can come out now."

Hutch rose slowly to his feet. Rich was dressed in flat black, with his face rouged right up the the brim of his black beret. He wore black gloves, and the polish on his boots was scruffed up so it did not reflect. If he had lain on the ground he would have looked like a ditch. "Man, you're like a fairy tale come true."

Rich's eyes widened. "Who's he?"

"Quarry."

A slow smile crept across Rich's Face. "So, you pulled it off again, you sly dog. *Okay*, let's go home."

Cody motioned for Hutch to follow the other commando. At the water's edge lay a black raft with three, similarly clad men holding paddles. It was crowded with six of them aboard. Rich pushed the raft away and jumped in, then took up the port bow position. The men in the other three quarters straddled the pontoons, and paddled in time with Rich's strokes.

No one spoke a word. Hutch sat in the middle of the raft, on the resilient rubber floor, facing Cody. The commando winked at him once, but otherwise, ever vigilant, kept a sharp lookout on their surroundings.

Hutch was still chilly, especially sitting on the floor with the cold water a fraction of an inch from his buttocks. He crossed his legs Indian fashion, and leaned back against the stern panel. He felt oddly aware. The sleep had done him a world of good, and now that rescue was really happening, and this whole crazy mess was nearing an end, he began to relax. The Northern Lights were fading, but the stars shone brilliantly; without heat inversions they were steady, untwinkling beacons. The Milky Way was a brightly lit arch across the middle of the sky.

The paddles dipped into the sea with such smoothness, with such precision, that the raft moved ahead as if on an escalator. Not once did Hutch hear a splash or dripping water. The ocean was as placid as a mill pond. The only sound was the faraway rustle of leaves keening on the wind. Farther offshore, even that faded to nothingness.

So quiescent was it that Hutch drifted into semiconsciousness, his mind dissociated from his body. Instead of looking up at the sky, he felt as if he were lying on his belly looking down into a sparkling, swirling pool of cosmic dust.

The sudden eruption of water snapped him back to reality.

"Incoming!"

The dull thud was immediately followed by a fine, evil-smelling spray that drenched every part of the raft. Before the last drop finished falling, the four paddlers and Commando Cody were lying flat on the bottom. Hutch watched, goggle-eyed, at the five grown men groveling like sardines between the fragile pontoons of the seven foot raft.

Cody leaped back, grabbed Hutch by the shoulders and yanked him violently to the yielding, rubber floor. *"Get down, you fool."* The commando crawled on top of him and pinned him down like a wrestler.

Hutch struggled, and found the lithe, lightweight man more than a match for his size. "Cut it out, Cody. It's only—"

"Stay down!" Cody clamped Hutch's head in a forearm vice. "The sidewalls are made of kevlar—bulletproof and damn near bomb proof."

Another eruption burst off the port bow, farther away, but the edges of salt water spray drifted across the raft. The air was filled with a slightly foul, deeply musky odor. The third waterspout was out of range.

"Goddamn it, let me up!" Hutch jabbed upward with an elbow that caught Cody in the ribcage. The commando grunted, groaned, and rolled over, clutching his side. Hutch pushed up from the pack of bodies. He stared out over the starlit ocean, and saw another spout a hundred feet away. "They're whales. They're only whales."

Slowly, the four paddlers resumed their seats. Hutch smiled broadly, but saw that none of the others took the situation with anything less than abject solemnity. Cody still lay on the floor.

"That's not chordite you smell. It's cetacean halitosis."

Several more whales surfaced, spuming great towers of water as they exhaled from their long submergence. The pod must have numbered scores, for they broached on every quarter at frequent intervals.

"Cody, you okay?" Rich bent down, and ran his hand along the commando's body. "Where'd all the blood come from?"

"Shrapnel," Cody squeaked.

Hutch's jaw dropped. "That's impossible. They're just migrating finbacks. Huge, but harmless—unless you're a microorganism of free floating plankton."

Cody rolled over on his back, and pulled back his bandoliers and shirt. Even in the dull starlight. Hutch could make out the fluid smeared over the man's abdomen. "From that strafing this afternoon. I'm okay."

"Hang in there, man." Rich ruffled Cody's military haircut. He took a handsized device out of his pocket, and studied the numbers on the liquid crystal display. "We're almost home."

Rich went back to paddling. Like automatons, the other three men resumed their quiet, steady pace.

"Cody, I'm sor—"

Cody wrapped a fist around Hutch's leg, and offered a friendly squeeze. "It's only a flesh wound. And don't worry about it. It wasn't your fault. Just caught me off guard, that's all."

Hutch saw the mouthful of teeth twisted into a smile, but did not believe it. He leaned back against the sternwall, cogitating. The world was no longer peaceful, no longer a playground. Something was happening that was beyond his control—an experience he did not relish; that was, in fact, foreign to him, and to his nature.

"Hold it up, men." Rich spoke quietly. The paddles dipped into the water, and stayed there. He referred to his electronic device. "Let her drift." His eyes never strayed from the flashing, changing numbers.

Another whale broached several hundred feet away, its gigantic, fifty-foot-long body carving through the water with grace and speed unthinkable in a creature of such size. It was followed by several others, all moving in the same direction. Occasionally, one would come up so far that in the reflected starlight Hutch could see the longitudinal grooves on the throat.

Rich pressed a button on the black box. He stared up at the sky, found the North Star, and tilted his head a little bit west. After sixty seconds of paddling, he relaxed. "Okay, ship your paddles. It's up to them, now."

They waited in utter silence. The raft floated on the calm Atlantic swells while every once in a while another giant finback rose to the surface for a breath of air. The water glistened with serenity. Out here, without the intrusion of man, Nature was in control. The water sparkled with the bioluminescence of dinoflagellates washed up against the kevlar hull.

The water began to boil.

Hutch gripped the sides of the raft as it started rocking. It was as if a volcano had erupted directly beneath them, spewing upward a column of water which reached the surface and bubbled outward on all sides. The men sat serenely on their pontoons, glancing about them with a look of unconcern, or disdain.

"Do something! It's coming up right underneath us." Hutch hung onto the rubberized sternwall as if his life depended on it. Visions of Captain Ahab clinging to the side of the great white whale danced through his brain like a movie montage on fast forward. Only this Moby Dick was real, and—

The black, hulking shape rose out of the water only fifty feet off the bow. In tubfulls, the aquamarine ocean cascaded off the rounded, rising snout. Hutch knew that the Jonah legends were impossible, for the whale's baleen was a boney strainer that prevented large objects from being swallowed by the monstrous, cetacean maw. But a hundred tons of living blubber rolling over the tiny raft would not leave much to be found.

The titanic specimen towered above them. The raft was picked up on the rising surge and carried toward the blackness. Hutch dug his fingertips into the material with the strength of desperation.

Cody sat up and winked at Hutch. He was grinning broadly.

The *Awa Maru*

1945

(The following is an extract from "The Peking Papers.")

"More treasure has been lost through shipwrecks than exists today in the hands of man. More time and effort will be spent recovering it than was ever expended in losing it."

Special Agent Hidake Watanabe marched stiffly up the tilted gangplank, while overhead a crane hauled aboard the cargo net with three olive drab cases. His sharp eyes watched not only the lading procedure, but scanned the dock handlers as well. To Watanabe, anyone who touched the dirty crates, with their remarkable contents, was suspect.

He saluted smartly as he placed his hightly polished boots on deck. "Captain Yoshita Hamamura."

The elderly captain returned the salute with less precision. "I have been expecting you, Watanabe. I have been instructed to put myself and my ship at your command."

The ship was a madhouse of noise and activity. Nearly two thousand officers and high ranking political personnel bustled loudly along the crowded decks. They were leaving Singapore before the inevitable collapse of Japan stranded them there with their enemies.

"I require very little of you or your ship. Only that you do not interfere."

The cargo boom swung inward, and the crane operator eased the steel cables so the net dropped gently onto the wooden deck. Stevedores in tan uniforms and peaked caps rushed forward as soon as the weight was off. They loosened the shackles, released the lifting lines, and let the net drop off the wooden cases. Hurriedly, they picked up the heavy crates, two men to each, and moved them aside so the cargo net was free. The net was reshackled, and the loading of other materials continued.

"What is it about three old crates that gives them such value?" Captain Hamamura wanted to know. "Do they contain the Emperor's jewels?"

"Your curiosity is unbecoming to an officer." With his hands clasped firmly behind his back, Watanabe clicked his heels on the deck as he approached the three cases. They were still covered with dirt and clumps of mud. There had been no time to clean them. "You should know that security measures preclude my discussing anything of such a delicate nature."

Captain Hamamura strolled after the special agent, staying always one step behind. "Ah, but I am not a military officer. I am a ship's master. My oath is to the sea, my service is to my ship. It is my business to know everything that goes on aboard my vessel. And there is already much about this voyage of which I disapprove."

Watanabe did not turn around, but looked down instead at the lockers in his charge. "These must be placed where I can guard them at all times. I must not leave my post. I think—your sitting room will do nicely."

Hamamura stepped closer, where he could be heard without shouting, and where he could look straight into Watanabe's dark eyes. "You presume too much."

Watanabe swung about, his face a sheet of cold steel. "I presume nothing. I have the authority I need, but I will use force if necessary." One hand slid out from behind his back; long fingers wrapped around the pistol at his waist. "I want these moved. Now!"

The captain stared back, unblinking. He let five seconds pass; ten. Then he nodded. He motioned for a squad of soldiers to take the cases, and led them to the bridge deck. Watanabe followed behind, closely, ever watchful.

The bearers struggled with the heavy crates, and called for additional help in getting them up the steep ladders. They grunted and groaned, shouted and cursed. Banged shins and scraped arms did not incur any sympathy from Watanabe. He stood by resolutely, his bland face a mask. When finally the crates were positioned inside, against a bulkhead where he could observe them from a comfortable spot on the clean, quilted side bench, he nodded.

Watanabe stood just within the room and scrutinized each man as he left. "Please remain, Captain Hamamura." He closed the door. With a practiced eye he studied the fastenings, the jamb, the sill, the latch. "I want a hasp installed inside. A strong one. And I want the largest lock you have. All the keys will be in my possession. It that understood?"

The captain returned his gaze without acknowledgment. The crates not only had their own hasps and locks, but each was bound in stainless steel cable which was pinched together in compression fittings. "Your precautions are paranoid, Watanabe. Perhaps you should engage a private yacht to carry your ill gotten trove to the Home Land."

"You criticize!" Watanabe was not emotionless, and his face flushed with anger.

"The Americans have been gracious enough to give us safe conduct because this is supposed to be a hospital ship. Did you see the big white cross painted on her sides? But are we carrying relief supplies for prisoners of war, as we agreed? No. We stoke our holds instead with gold, silver, and other precious metals; diamonds and jewelry; antiques and artifacts plundered from occupied territories. The Red Cross boxes are filled with gold bars, instead of medical supplies. And we carry not a single patient. Not one. And now, I must harbor a Kempeitai officer in my own quarters. Yes, I criticize. And you, with all your techniques of interrogation and torture, can do nothing about it. This is *my* ship. The secret police have no jurisdiction here."

Watanabe's features gradually relaxed, and he allowed a half smirk to creep over his face. "Well stated, Captain. You are a man of courage, to be so outspoken."

"On the contrary, I am a man weary of war, and frustrated by the deceit under which we must fight. I want it all to end, so that I may return to my peacetime duties of transporting passengers." Captain Hamamura placed a well manicured hand on one of the crates. Under the layer of dirt the letters 'PUMC' were faintly legible. The crates were individually designated 'A', 'B,' and 'C.' "I am responsible for this ship, yet I have been forced to carry contraband. If we are caught by the Americans, it is I who will be held accountable. These new arrangements are against my nature."

Watanabe's smile broadened. "Your hand rests on that which is not new, but which is perhaps the oldest recorded knowledge of mankind's entire history."

The captain's mein remained solemn. "You speak in riddles."

"No. I speak of truth. Ultimate truth. Have you ever heard of—Peking man?"

"What is he, another of your infernal agents?"

"He is not a man, nor a code name. He is a tribe, the root stock of humanity, our revered ancestor."

"*Shogun?*"

Watanabe enjoyed the captain's ignorance. "Much older than that. Prehistoric, you might say. Within these boxes are the remains, and the possessions, of a people who walked the Earth hundreds of thousands of years ago, at a time when the land of the rising sun was an uninhabited jungle island. From them we have much to learn—about our past, about our evolution, about our own beginnings."

Captain Hamamura pinched his brow, and wrinkles formed on his aged forehead. "It surprises me that the Kempeitai are interested in such intellectual pursuits."

"We are interested in anything which may be of military, political, or scientific value."

"I see. And how many people lost their lives for these relics?"

Watanabe laughed right out loud. "You imply that subjects must have died during my investigation. However, such was not the case. The Chinese did their best to conceal the Peking man collection by creating a false trail. They left behind the Upper Cave fossils: the bones of a race of man only ten or twenty thousand years old. Interesting, but not earth shaking. I was not so easily deceived. During further inquiry I was able to persuade certain individuals with families to divulge information that led to a cemetary outside Peking, where the other two crates were buried under a fraudulant tombstone. Under the gunsights of an entire Company the crates were exhumed. We have been on the road ever since: by handcart, by wagon, by truck, by rail."

Captain Hamamura raised one brow. "It is three thousand miles by land from Peking to Singapore. Why did you not just load them on a submarine headed for home?"

"Our own I-boats are out on suicide missions, and American submarines prowl our waters with virtual impunity. The Yellow Sea is theirs. I cannot allow three and a half years work to wind up on the bottom of the ocean. But the *Awa Maru* has a special mission, and the Americans themselves will ensure that its cargo reaches the shores of Japan."

"You are a devious man, Watanabe. I admire your tenacity, if not your methods. All right, I shall see to your demands. A shipwright will be here shortly to attend your needs."

Watanabe bowed graciously. "Thank you, Captain Hamamura. I apologize for appropriating your salon. I must also respectfully request that no visitors of any rank be allowed entrance here. I will lock myself in, I will sleep here, and I will take all my meals here."

"I understand. I will have bedding sent up directly."

Captain Hamamura was good for his word. Everything was carried out to Watanabe's satisfaction, and that night, for the first time in weeks, he slept soundly, locked inside the captain's sitting room. The only key to the lock was in his pocket; the others he had thrown overboard.

He relaxed his vigil, and during the daylight hours read from the captain's personal library. He sprawled out in his private suite, snickering inwardly at the men, women, and children who must be jammed in common quarters in the heat below decks. He rested in the knowledge that his quest was at an end, that his voyage was nearly over.

He ate sparingly, in order not to lose the firmness he enjoyed. He drank nothing but water. And every once in a while, to make sure of their reality, he walked over and *touched* the three crates. Then he smiled at his triumph. The Emperor would be proud of him.

The dull thud roused him from a light slumber: he was sitting up on the bench, with a magazine on the table in front of him. He thought perhaps the heavy cargo stored below had shifted. He rose and went to the door: the lock was secure. He lifted the curtain off the glass port. The lifeboat immediately outside the room partially obscured his view of the calm South China Sea—or had they already entered the Formosa Strait? The ship was well lighted, as she was supposed to be according to recognition instructions, but the searchlight beams bounced back off a thick, white fog.

The next thud was not so dull. It was accompanied by the screech of rending metal, and a splash of water that rose higher than the main deck and sprayed across the portlight only inches from Watanabe's eyes. He backed away from the glass, his heart thumping loudly. Two more explosions tore into the *Awa Maru's* steel hull. The vessel lurched suddenly to starboard, and Watanabe was thrown off his feet.

He slid across the deck and crashed against the locked door. He crumpled into a ball on the smooth linoleum, and hunkered under the books and magazines, cups and saucers and dinner plates, and other loose debris, that skittered over the angled deck and smashed on top of him. In less than a minute the ship had sustained a terrible shock, and Watanabe's composure had suffered the same fate.

The ship creaked and groaned. Outside, soldiers and civilians shouted as they raced in a panic along the slanting decks. In the next minute the vessel listed ever further, and Watanabe knew that it could never recover, that even now the sea must be pouring into compartments below the waterline.

His hand went to the pocket of his clean and newly pressed uniform. He brought out the key—if he did not use it immediately, his life was forfeit. A scraping sound behind him diverted his attention. He turned just in time to see the heavy wooden crates sliding across the tilted deck. The corner of the first hit him a terrible blow on the head, blinding him for a moment with stars of pain. The others pinioned his arms to his sides, crushed his legs against the bulkhead.

The key was gone, his fingers were limp. He could not move under the weight of the crates. His throat was choked with blood. As if from far away, he heard anxious shouts, and an imperious knocking on the sitting room door. He recognized Captain Hamamura's voice, but was unable to reply.

He was alone.

The list was nearly verticle. He heard the waves lapping at the superstructure. A glass port burst in, and water shot up and across the room as if from a torn hydrant. The sea bubbled around the door frame.

Knowing that death was inevitable, he chose to meet it his own way, the way of his honored ancestors: *seppuku*. He squirmed so that he could reach the short sword at his side. His left hand, practically limp with shock, pulled it out of the jeweled scabbard.

A cold spray of water hit him in the face. He coughed. He struggled to get up above the rising tide. His legs and lower body were underwater. He inhaled more of the sea, and the involuntary gag reflex sent him into spasms. Then his face was submerged. He was choking on a mixture of salt water and diesel fuel. The sword slipped from his grasp.

Watanabe did not die the death of a true samurai.

The *Charles Lockwood*

"Excuse me. How do I get to the infirmary?"

The rating pointed aft. "Along this corridor and through the hatch. Down the ladder to the next deck, then forward. There's a sign."

Hutch smiled. "Thanks." He followed the directions, although the ladder was more like a grand staircase, and the sign was glowing neon the size of a movie marquis. He tapped on the bulkhead and leaned in. "Anyone home?"

"I was just getting up." Cody swung his feet off the bunk and tightened the bathrobe. Hutch caught a glimpse of swaddling and bandages around the commando's midriff. "I've got to get some decent clothes, or I'll look like a patient."

"Here, let me help you." Hutch reached out to steady him, but Cody waved him off. "Still a little woozy from the drugs?"

"Hell, no. I wouldn't let them give me any."

"But, I thought you had to have quite a few stitches, and—"

"A few, not quite. And I don't need pentathol for twenty minutes on the board. Hell, today these doctors'll shoot you up to clip a hangnail."

Hutch stammered awkwardly. "Uh, listen, I'm sorry—about the elbow, you know. I didn't know—"

"Forget it." Cody slipped his feet into hospital slippers. "What about you? You okay?"

Hutch breathed deeply. The conditioned air was sweet scented and pure. "Couldn't feel better. I've had a shower, a couple cups of hot coffee, a fresh change of clothes—they even had my size—" He shook his shirtfront as proof. "And free rein of this tub. Well, okay, so I can't see the reactor room, the missile silos, the propulsion gear, the mechanical spaces, the communications console, or the navigational controls. But I'm allowed anywhere in the crew's quarters. Come to think of it, I'm pretty limited. But the place is so big I got lost three times just getting from my room to here."

"It's *our* room, and if you stick close I'll see you don't get lost again. You might get into trouble.

"I almost did. Because of the uniform, a technician mistook me for an officer. He started showing me how the access trunk unseals so they can work on the missiles. Then he saw I didn't have any commissioning shingles and he called security on me. Did you know they can flood those silos at a thousand feet, and pump them dry again?"

"Terrific. Just so you don't get arrested and keelhauled, you'd better follow me."

"Cody, I'm getting awfully tired following you around. You have a habit of leading me to places I don't want to go."

"Did you forget I got you out of some situations you didn't want to be in? Besides, the fun has just begun." Wearing shower shoes, he padded into the corridor with Hutch in tow. "But first, I've got a date with a big, juicy sirloin steak."

"Cody, it's three o'clock in the morning."

"Doesn't mean a thing on a submarine. The mess hall's always open, and the cook'll always make you anything you want. You hungry?"

"Is the bear Catholic? Does the Pope live in the woods? I could eat the leather off my shoes. Well, with a little salt and pepper."

"How about a pemmican bar?"

"Don't make me puke."

"You loved them before."

"I used to like canned tuna and freeze dried beef stew, when it was the only thing available. But I haven't had any real food in weeks. You don't know what it's like camping out in the woods."

Cody scowled at him.

"Well, okay, maybe you do. Damn it, why the hell didn't you tell me we were coming out here to meet a nuclear submarine? I was waiting for some seaplane, or helicopter, or patrol boat, or something."

"I told you what you needed to know."

"Yeah, but that's going to change. I'm tired of your half truths and clandestine personality. I want to know what the hell's going on."

Cody cackled like the Wicked Witch of the West. "All in good time, my dear. All in good time." He pushed open the door to their room, threw off his bathrobe, and stood stark naked for several seconds before noticing someone sitting in the chair. "What the hell are you doing here?"

Hutch stumbled over the sill when he saw the Navy lieutenant in dress blues. The normally shapeless uniform could not possibly hide the expanse of her chest, or the constriction of her waist, or the contour of her hips.

"Hunting for our wayward quarry. I figured you'd bring him right to me." It was not just her smile that made her beautiful, but her mellifluous voice. She spoke with perfect enunciation, and with a faint British twang. Even in regulation short hair, she was a showpiece.

Cody turned his back on her, kicked off his footwear, and pulled on a pair of camouflage fatigue pants. "Damn it, I'm a married man. And being caught in the altogether with a luscious woman is not in my book."

"Don't worry, I didn't see a thing. It must have been cold out there."

Cody buttoned his trousers and reached for a white t-shirt. He looked directly at Hutch, and jerked a thumb at the radiant officer. "You may as well get used to her now, because you're going to be spending a lot of time with her. Lieutenant Veronica Wakefield, William Hutchison."

She held out her hand. "Mr. Hutchison."

Her skin was cool and soft, and sent tingles up his arm. "Uh, pleased to—uh—it's good to—uh, call me Hutch. Everybody does."

"Except your mother, who calls you Will."

Hutch jerked back. "Uh, that's right. How did you—"

"You can call me anything but late for dinner." Cody sat down on the bunk and slipped on olive drab socks and combat boots. He neatly bloused his cuffs. "Let's go get some chow." He grabbed a shirt and swung it over his arms as he stepped out the door.

Hutch backed out of the way, glancing from Cody to Lieutenant Wakefield. He shrugged. "Uh, are you coming?"

"Not yet. But I'm breathing hard." She winked in a way that nearly made Hutch pass out. She had dark, fawnlike eyes that were fathomless pools. "And call me Ronnie. Everyone does. Except Cody. He never calls anyone anything."

She took off after the striding commando, and Hutch tagged along like a playful puppy.

"I heard that," Cody said, over his shoulder.

"Your psych file has all your character faults documented in meticulous detail."

Cody tucked in his shirt. "Watch her, or she'll be analyzing your every movement."

Hutch hurried to keep up. "The only faults I have are geological."

Ronnie swung her head, smiling. "And ego."

"There's nothing wrong with a little self confidence. Hey, Cody, where's the fire?"

"His stomach is—"

Cody interrupted. "Are you eating with us, or is this just a social call? You've already debriefed me."

"I'm supposed to make our friend here at home, and give him an initial briefing. Knowing your penchant for taciturnity, I assume he knows nothing more than Descartes about this mission. But as long as we're here, I wouldn't mind a little snack."

Cody executed a sharp left turn and entered the chow hall. It was designed like a restaurant, with four person booths along the bulkheads, and long, open tables in the middle. At the far end a lone cook dressed in white and wearing a billowing baker's hat lounged behind a cafeteria counter.

"Pick a seat." Cody kept walking.

The cook smiled at him as he approached. "The thickest steak we've got, baked Idaho potatoes with lots of gravy, and a pile of vegetables that would choke a horse."

Cody held up his fingers. "Times three."

"It's on the grill.'

Cody sat down in the booth alongside Hutch, who had positioned himself opposite Ronnie. "I didn't go into any details other than—"

Hutch exploded. "Details! You didn't tell me a goddamned thing. You drop on me out of nowhere, you drag me from one fire zone to another, you blow up half the island, kill I don't know how many people, and laugh like crazy when an atomic submarine surfaces right underneath us."

Cody said laconically, "Everything went pretty much according to plan." He moved his elbows back as the cook arrived with three heaping salads and a steaming loaf of French bread. "Thanks."

"Sure thing, Mr. Cody. You folks want yours medium rare, too?"

Hutch dived into his salad. "Well done, for me."

Ronnie said, "I don't think I can eat all this—"

"Make hers medium rare. What she can't finish, I'll take." Cody ripped off a chunk of bread and padded it thickly with butter. "Let me ask you something. In science, do you publish theories just because you happened to dream them up, or do you wait until adequate proof exists for a substantial foundation?"

Hutch swallowed a mouthful of spinach leaves and cucumbers. "I would—"

"Keep your mouth shut until you either finished chewing or had something to say. You would, in effect, be holding back on your fellow scientists. But only because it was necessary at the time to keep your own council. It's the same in my business: I don't want to tip my hand, especially when a premature intelligence leak may have international repercussions. If I glutted you with information, and you got captured, they could torture it out of you. What you don't know, as the old saying goes, won't hurt us."

"In other words, I'm just a pawn. And it doesn't matter if I get taken, as long as I don't leave the king unprotected."

"We're all pawns to a certain extent, and expendable when the time comes. And we all have ideals we'd sell our souls for. Yours may be different than mine, or they may be more or less valuable." Cody had no trouble talking with his mouth full of food. "Look at yourself, and your career. You've walked out on jobs, turned down well paying positions, worked for nothing, and wouldn't accept a chair unless certain criteria were met. You've got your own set of standards which are much more complicated than mine.''

Hutch slowly put down his fork. "How do you know so much—"

The cook arrived with a tray and placed the meal on the table. "Let me know if you want more." He winked at Ronnie as he sauntered off.

"You may be a cook in the Navy but you're a chef to me." Cody sniffed the charcoaled vapors. "Hey, I'm buying the drinks. What'll you have?"

Hutch said, "What's on the menu?"

"You name it, this place has it. Iced tea, soft drinks, any kind of juice, only three kinds of wine, chilled or warm—"

"How about a diet Pepsi?"

Cody snickered. "Watching your figure, eh?"

"I'll watch his figure, you just get the drinks. Coffee for me." Ronnie winked at Hutch. "And to answer your question, the reason we know so much is because we've investigated you. Thoroughly."

Hutch carved into his steak. "Is that good or bad?"

"It's not a moral judgment at all. Checking into your past was not nearly as difficult as locating you. You're not quite as secretive as Cody, but almost as peripatetic. Don't you ever call home?"

"I'm a big boy now."

"I can imagine. Anyway, your mother would like to hear from you. We made discreet inquiries with friends, acquaintances, working associates, lovers—"

"And what did you find out?"

"That you're a hell of a lay." Cody slipped into the booth and placed drinks in front of them. "You nearly gave us the slip because of your poor spelling. In one of your letters you said you were going to St. John, and we had half the subsurface fleet heading for the Virgin Islands before we discovered you were actually going to Newfoundland. What a difference an 'apostrophe s' can make. Then we—"

"Wait a minute! I know who I wrote that letter to, and there was a lot of personal stuff in it. How did you—how much did you—"

Ronnie reached across the table and placed her hand on Hutch's. "Believe me. Everything will be held in the strictest confidence. Cody and I, and a few others in higher echelons, are the only ones with access to your file."

Hutch's face flushed with anger. "Just who the hell do you people think you are? You can't go breaking into a person's life, checking up on his past, digging out dirt—"

Cody did not stop chugging down his potatoes, but said with an even voice, "What are you afraid of? What kind of criminal activities are you hiding?"

"I'm not hiding a damned thing. But I resent it when the government pries into my private affairs, when it decides to take over my life, when it sticks its nose into business where it has no right to be." He slammed down his fork. "I think you people are despicable."

Cody reached for Ronnie plate. "Are you finished with this?"

"Take it."

Cody dumped her steak onto his plate, and cut it up. "I think you're getting riled over nothing. First of all, you have to understand that this is a national security measure, and that gives us quite a bit of constitutional latitude, should we choose to exercise it. However, in your case—You explain it to him. You're the counterintelligence expert."

Ronnie lowered her head and raised her eyebrows, but Hutch refused to meet her gaze. He stared out into space.

"Hutch, we did not break any confidences, we did not lie to anyone we interviewed. We conducted a perfectly normal background investigation, the same as we would do in any case requiring a top secret security clearance."

"Top secret!"

Ronnie did not smile; now she was all business. "An examination like this usually takes months, sometimes years. Yours was conducted in *weeks*. And you passed with flying colors."

"I'm thrilled."

"Hutch, I'm sorry. I know it seems inappropriate to interrogate your ex-girlfriends, but it was necessary. As much to protect you, as to study your psychological profile. And believe me, someone with your record of honesty has nothing to worry about. You are a superior citizen with strong personal convictions, fair dealings, and little or no ill will toward anyone— or, at least, you're not outspoken about any bad feelings you may harbor. And that shows a fair degree of maturity."

"I've had Psych 101, so forget the stroking."

Cody pointed his fork at Hutch's steak. "Are you going to eat any more of that?"

"Where do you put all that food?" Hutch shoved the plate aside.

"My mother used to say I had a hollow leg. I'll take those potatoes, too."

Hutch scowled, but already his anger was dissipating. "This guy'll eat anything that doesn't move."

"Even if it's slow," Ronnie added. "Anyway, I drew up your personal profile so I think I understand you pretty well. And even if you choose not to accept this mission, which I doubt, we had an obligation to protect you."

"What is all this protection crap? If you people hadn't come looking for me, none of this would ever have started."

Ronnie shook her head. "No, they would have come after you in any case; not just because of your credentials, but because of the potential impediment you could pose."

"That's it. Right now, right here, I want the mystery to stop." Hutch held out his hands like a state trooper holding back three lanes of traffic on a crowded interstate. "First of all, who the hell are 'they'?"

Cody paused to gulp down some iced tea. "That's hard to tell. The computerized image intensification equipment in that chopper was manufactured in the States. Those rockets were pretty damn near on target—could have been guided by satnav, and that would mean Russians. But we're more inclined to think either Chinese Nationalists or the People's Republic of China."

"Why didn't you tell me," Hutch said. "A close examination of the skulls can differentiate between Mongoloids and Caucasoids."

"Wouldn't have made any difference. They'd hire local mercenaries to cover their tracks. No, what's more important is how they were tipped off. Isn't that right?"

Ronnie looked up sharply, then nodded when she saw Cody's eyes were on her. "Yes, the problem with any intelligence network is that there are always leaks. We can counter this in many ways: by limiting the number of people involved, by keeping constant checks on them, by laying traps such as giving out wrong, misleading, or traceable information. It's a never-ending process of spy and counterspy. It's also frustrating because you never know who you can trust, and disappointing when a trust is misgiven."

"It sounds like something I don't want to be involved in," Hutch said.

"But it does have its positive sides." Cody engulfed the last bite of meat, and slid out of the booth. "What say we retire to the briefing room?"

The cook called out from behind his counter, "Hey, don't you want some fresh baked cherry pie, with vanilla ice cream?"

Cody slapped his belly. "I don't want to get fat." He flashed one of his ever present smiles. To Hutch and Ronnie: "Shall we?"

They left the messhall and wound through corridors now flushed with naval personnel changing shifts. Men and women in dress uniforms or working fatigues scurried about, some fresh and ready for work, others tired after a duty watch.

"So what do you think I'll get out of all this?" Hutch wanted to know.

"Adventure."

"Dodging bullets, rockets, and grenades is not my idea of adventure. That's insanity."

"Granted there's an element of risk. But it's in your nature to accept that. Even enjoy it, according to your file."

"Did my file also happen to mention that I don't approve of war?"

"Yes, in the same breath it said you were opposed to being invaded. You are strong in your beliefs, but fortunately a realist."

"You've got an answer for everything, don't you?"

Ronnie jumped in with a response. "I've analyzed you as well as I could without ever having met you. My evaluation is greatly in your favor. Even more so now that I've seen you—and touched you."

Hutch shrugged. Ronnie was beginning to look good again. "How do you know you've touched me?"

She tilted her head. "Well, I can hope, can't I?"

Cody dodged a pair of officers and ducked into a spacious room. No one saluted, but there were smiles all around independent of rank. It was a fraternization which dispelled Hutch's notion of shipboard discipline: the Captain Blighs of the world were dead, and the Fletcher Christians no longer necessary.

"Quite a set up." Hutch glanced around at the computer consoles, banks of monitors, and silent printers. "How come this place isn't clacking with programmers and data entry personnel?"

Ronnie locked the glass door behind them. "This shift is using the starboard backup, so we'll have it to ourselves until zero eight hundred." She unlocked a file cabinet built like a bank vault, and took out a Manila folder. She paced along the bulkhead reading from the white printed sheets. "Hutchison, William Waldo. Father, William Waldo. Mother, Emily. No brothers or sisters." She looked up. "I've got your whole family tree, living and dead. Hmmn, blonde hair, blue eyes, six foot two, one hundred seventy pounds, good physical shape—"

"Does it say that?"

Ronnie winked. "A personal judgment call. Forty-two chest, thirty-four waist, thirty-six inseam—"

"You know all my vital statistics, don't you?"

"Not *all*. But maybe I'll find out the rest later." She ruffled through the pages. "I've got your school record from first grade report cards to field reports from the University of Pennsylvania, plus notes from your teachers and professors. Mrs. Higgins, your ninth grade adviser, said you were independent but resourceful. In college—hmmn, started out in geology—"

"Mineralogy was my downfall. I could sometimes tell apatite from hunger, but I usually took everything for granite."

"Majored in anthropology and archaeology—"

"I wanted to cover all manholes."

"Off beat sense of humor—"

Hutch blinked in surprise. "Who said that?"

"I did. Master's thesis on the Peking man. But, upon graduation, took off for the Mediterranean to study a Byzantine shipwreck at Yassi Ada, off the coast of Turkey."

"Just an introduction into underwater archaeology. Nothing new."

"Spent a year and a half before going to Tanzania, where you worked with the Leakys excavating Australopithecus—did I pronounce that right— fossils from the Olduvai Gorge. Two years, your longest employment."

"There was nothing more I could learn there."

"Back to shipwrecks, this time to Cyprus: a Greek merchant ship off Kyrenia, sunk circa 300 B.C. Then off on your own for a while, trucking around Truk, in Micronesia—"

"I wanted to study the progression of a ship's collapse, something that hasn't been done yet to a sufficient degree."

"—from where you visited nearby Java for another land dig: ancient hominid remains known as Java man."

"Pithecanthropus erectus, lately reclassified as an extinct species of Homo erectus. The closest I could get to my main objective, Sinanthropus pekinensis."

"Peking man, on which your dissertation was based. Some more side trips to various shipwreck locations around the world. Back to New York for a spell in the Natural History Museum. Twenty months, this time, where you studied women for a change instead of man."

"Can we skip that part?"

"You left despite the offer of a large increase in salary and a nomination to the Board of Directors."

"The work was dull: cataloguing fossil finds and bone fragments, and listening to a bunch of crotchety old men yak about their urinary problems. But it did give me the opportunity to do more studies on the Peking man castings."

"You headed south, in search of shipwrecks. Stopped off at the Yorktown Project, where a scuttled vessel of Cornwallis' fleet was being excavated from inside a cofferdam."

"They were milking that job for all it was worth. They had research grants extending for seven years, and they wanted to make damned sure they used up every penny of it."

"In Florida you did some survey work on one of the Spanish plate fleets, the *Nuestra Senora de*—"

"Treasure diving just wasn't my bag. I've never been lured by the glint of gold. Knowledge is its own reward."

Cody broke into the private repartee. "And adventure in pursuit of that knowledge makes it that much more satisfying." He pulled a chair out from under a table, turned it around, and sat on it with his arms crossed over the plastic back. "And do you have to rebut everything she says?"

"I'm not afraid to make social commentary, or hear redress. If I have something to say, I say it, and damn those who don't like it."

Cody made a showing of hands. "I like you, but you wear thin on me."

"Just remember that I didn't pick you; you picked me."

"I'm trying to forget." He nodded to Ronnie. "Can we skip the rest of 'This is your life' and get to the issues at stake?"

Ronnie held out the folder. "Hutch, in all fairness, you can go through this at your leisure. Make any comments, corrections, or additions you want."

"How about deletions?"

"It's all on computer, so it won't help. As I said, it *is* held in the strictest confidence."

"Nothing like having your life pass before your eyes—and a couple hundred others'."

"I know. You're not a belonger. You like your privacy. You're a low-key individual, undemanding in personal relationships, highly competitive in professional relationships, lackadaisical about family relationships. You form fast bonds with friends and lovers, you—"

"Please! Cut the free psychiatric treatment. I know who I am, what I want, and where I'm going. I'm secure, and I don't need you to tell me."

Ronnie smiled. "Well, if I can be of any help—"

"Not right now. Let's stop talking about me and my motivations, and talk about what the *hell* is going on. Have I been drafted, or what?"

Cody grinned. "The age limit is one score and six, so you're half a dozen years too old. No, we don't need to force you into anything, because you're going to volunteer. In fact, you may even beg."

Hutch wrinkled his brow. "And how do you propose to make me do that?"

Ronnie folded her arms under her breasts, and hiked them up an inch. "We've got reliable intelligence on the whereabouts of the lost Peking man remains. And we want you to recover them for us."

Hutch froze, as if someone had just dropped a grenade into his bathtub. His gaze shifted from Ronnie to Cody and back to Ronnie. He pulled out a chair and collapsed into it like a strand of overcooked spaghetti. He stared sightlessly, lost in thought.

"You bastards. You knew you had me all along."

Cody's grin grew even broader. "Offered the proper stimulus, I was sure you'd want to cooperate."

"But, those fossils have been lost since before the war. And Janus made an incredibly thorough search for them in the seventies. How did they suddenly surface?"

"Wait a minute," Ronnie said. "No one said they've surfaced. According to our best intelligence, they're still *under* the surface. But we have limited the possibilities to a handful of locations."

Hutch nodded in immediate understanding. "The major theory about their loss was that they went down with a ship during transport. Which one, and where is it?"

"Whoa, wait a minute, you're going too fast." Cody spread his hands, and tucked the chair further into his crotch. "This is a complicated story, as you are well aware—and you know only the published version. You have no idea how much we forced Janus to leave out of his account."

"Do you mean to tell me the government was behind his entire scheme?"

"Not one government, but several. There were also several governments against it. Still are. So much against it they'll stop at nothing but total war, and maybe not even that. There are tremendous political forces at work here, considering the nature of the fossils."

"Hold on," Hutch said. "Now *you're* going too fast. Granted, Peking man is of significant anthropological importance because of the strong possibility that he might prove to be the missing link between Homo habilis and Homo erectus, and—"

Ronnie waved for a halt. "Hutch, you'll have to use simpler terms. I don't understand the difference—"

"Sorry. Between a manlike ape and an apelike man. The evolutionary path that eventually led to intelligence and Homo sapiens: modern man. But that information is not contained in the original bones. The teeth found by Haberer on Dragon Bone Hill in 1899 wouldn't prove a thing, except the existance of something more. And casts were made of everything Andersson and Black later unearthed. I've studied them in detail—did either of you read my dissertation?"

Ronnie shrugged. "I muddled through it."

Cody switched off his grin. "It took me an hour just to translate the title, and I still didn't know what it meant."

"All right, then let me simplify it. First of all, understand that a thesis is written with one major objective in mind: to convince a panel of reviewers that you know what you're talking about, so they'll grant your degree. The excuse is that you're supposed to do something original, some advancement in the cause of science. But all you really want to do is pass the damned test and get your letters. Why do you think they call it a B.S. degree? So, in order to impress the committee, you pad your writing with as much obfuscation and as many multisyllabic words as you can. Maybe they won't know what you're talking about, so they'll have to agree with your conclusions just so they don't look like a Ramapithecus.

"The jist of my argument was this: the one hundred seventy-five specimens from Choukoutien do not offer sufficient evidence to postulate the linkage. Peking man did have fire, and he appears to be the first ancient hominid to use it. But that was evidenced by archaeological provenience—I'm sorry, by studying the placement of the bones, and their condition. Where they lie in the sedementary strata is what determines age. The bones by themselves, out of context, can give information only about the individuals from which they came, not about their specific relationship to the evolutionary tree.

"This isn't to say there's nothing to be learned by examining the bones, especially the four partial skulls. Weidenreich did an exhaustive descriptive analysis, but in light of modern technology we could learn more about cranial force lines, chemical makeup, tissue structure, and so on. This is the only real value those lost remains hold today."

"What about radiocarbon dating?" Cody inquired. "That wasn't developed until after the war."

Hutch shook his head vigorously. "Carbon 14 can only be detected back to about 25,000 years. Peking man lived around 500,000 years ago. Not that I'm trying to put a damper on your plans. Believe me, I'd love to get my hands on the original specimens. But in all honesty, I doubt if the results would be worth the effort. What would really be the cat's meow would be to reopen the digs.''

Cody pointed an index finger at Ronnie. She nodded. ''Hutch, we have proof that local authorities kept up the excavations after Weidenreich left the site in 1937. They found a lot more, including one perfectly intact skull.''

''My god, that's incredible. I had no idea—No one did. They—Why did they keep it a secret? And where are the specimens now. Janus didn't see them when he visited the Peking Man Museum in 1972. Or did he? You said you—''

''No, he didn't see them, although he was looking for them.'' Cody ran a hand through his dark, close cropped hair. ''He was told of their existence before he ever started out. Seeking the lost *known* fossils was his cover story, but what he was really looking for were clues to the *unknown* specimens. You see, back then, with the war coming on, everyone including the Chinese thought the U.S. would be a safer place to store the Peking collection. With the Japanese pounding on the Great Wall, and on the lookout for national treasures, they would have absconded with the collection as soon as they crossed the border. So, the bones were packed in trunks for shipment. Then came the day of infamy, and the ship never arrived. The marine detachment at Chinwangtao was captured by invading Japanese, and held as P O Ws for the entire war. Some even survived. The fossils disappeared. But get this: not only did the original two trunks vanish, but so did several others that had been brought in at the last minute. They were all together for a while. Then—gone.''

Ronnie said, ''You understand that this story includes more than the official version released by Janus. And it embraces background material of which he was unaware.''

''Meaning, you kept him as much in the dark as you're keeping me,'' Hutch stated flatly.

''Meaning that he had no need to know,'' Cody responded. ''Great militant forces are at work here and—hell, you saw that. Janus, at least, was a wealthy, self-made, international business entrepreneur who was beyond approach and who owed no favors. He couldn't be bought. *But*, he could have slipped up. He could have misspoken. And we couldn't chance that. But decades of private investigation had proved fruitless. So, we decided on the public approach: advertising for information. It worked—partially. It brought some people and a lot of intrigue out of the woodwork. It gave us the leads we needed. Now we're so close I can taste it. We know where the fossils are. But they're in sensitive waters, and the political situation is—touchy.''

Ronnie leaned back against the filing cabinet. ''During the Japanese occupation of China, the Kempietai—the Japanese secret police—conducted their own investigations into the search for the Peking collection.

There has been no official declaration that it was found. But, there's a possibility that they shipped them out on a hospital ship granted immunity, but which was later torpedoed and sunk by the USS *Queenfish*. The *Awa Maru* was off course, and was not recognized because of fog. The Soviets might also have absconded with the crates during evacuation after the war, on a Russian freighter bound from Shanghai to Yalta. Then, when the Chinese Nationalist government fled the communist regime in 1949, they took with them to Taiwan some four thousand crates of cultural treasures: antiquities, artwork, documents, and religious relics. The Peking collection might have been part of the shipment, yet curators of the National Palace Museum will not admit to possession of the fossils.

Hutch scowled. "And they just might have been left in China, unrecognized, and scattered over the ground as fertilizer. Okay, so you've got all these possibilities, all these potential locations. What, pray tell, does any of this have to do with me?"

Cody was again grinning like a Cheshire cat. "Besides the obvious? That you can positively identify the bones, either the originals whose casts you've studied, or later finds which you can authenticate through professional analysis?"

Hutch glared at him.

"We need you to handle the diving operations."

"Oh, come on. You've got the entire U.S. Navy diving unit at your disposal, with enough salvage vessels and support personnel to raise the Imperial Fleet."

"That would be rather obvious, wouldn't it?" Cody slowly shook his head. "No, this mission must be carried out in complete secrecy. We don't exactly have multinational support. The political issues at stake are explosive. We need to rely on stealth: to sneak into foreign waters, make the snatch, and leave unnoticed."

Hutch held out his hands, and shrugged. "So, interject an Underwater Demolition Team on a small scale."

"You just don't understand the problems. The water's too deep for UDT: they're not trained for anything other than shallow water diving. SEALs are just as bad. Sure, they'll crawl two miles up a sewer pipe to lay a satchel charge, or slink through a submerged rice paddy and slit some gook's throat, but put them deeper than thirty feet and they get delirium tremens. Besides which, they wouldn't know a Peking man fossil from a chicken bone.

"We can't use regular Navy divers because they'll only go down with umbilicals that tether them to the surface like babies. Hell, you can put a monkey in one of those deep water rigs; all he's got to know is how to breathe. Besides, those rubes'll only dive if they have total surface support to make up for their training deficiencies. You think because they're military, they're tough., But the system is designed so it attracts only men who are safety conscious to the nth degree; and their diving technique is nineteenth century, bogged down with so many precautions it takes an Act of Congress to get them in the water. Whenever the Navy has a job requiring real expertise, they hire commercial divers from the private sector to cover for them.'' Cody guffawed. ''It turns out to be cheaper, too, because a commercial diver will get the job done with a minimum of fuss; Navy divers won't start a project without an anchored salvage vessel, a boatful of backup equipment, half a squadron of personnel, a doctor, recompression chambers, air support, contingency plans—everything but someone to hold their hands. Hell, by the time they get around to doing any work, they're collecting Social Security.

''You, on the other hand, aren't afraid to get your feet wet. You dive deep, you dive alone, and you have a way of minimizing risks by utilizing up-to-date methods of scuba with the latest technological advances in equipment. You are truly self contained. I don't want to hold a convention out there in the middle of the ocean. For security reasons as well, the fewer people who know what we're doing, the better.''

Ronnie stepped forward, placed her lily white palms down on the table, and leaned over so her fragrant breath caressed Hutch's face. ''You're looking at the whole team right here. The three of us.''

Hutch almost swooned at the scent of her perfume—or was it her skin?

''Naturally, there'll be compensation,'' Cody intruded. ''In addition to a more than adequate salary, you'll be reimbursed for your van and all the possessions that went up in smoke. Uncle Sam'll even consider a bonus if you—''

''Forget the hard sell,'' Hutch interrupted. ''You bought me a long time ago.'' He tried to make his glance at Ronnie casual. ''If I had any hesitations they were completely dispelled—''

There came a tapping at the door. The man standing outside was resplendant in dress uniform, and the gold braid sanctioned him as a high ranking officer. Ronnie reclaimed Hutch's personnel file, locked it up in the filing cabinet, then let in the smiling gentleman.

''Captain Cosgrove. Nice of you to stop by.''

The captain nodded pleasantly, his chipmonk cheeks bulging with each nod. ''Lieutenant Wakefield. Cody. My executive officer had the conn when our guest arrived, and since I'm coming on duty I thought I'd pipe him aboard, so to speak. Mr. Hutchison, welcome to the *Charles Lockwood*.''

Hutch stood up and took the outstretched hand. ''Pleased to meet you. This is a hell of a boat you have here. I'm impressed.''

''I'm quite proud of her myself. Have you had a tour of her facilities?''

''Not yet.''

''We're completely self sufficient, with the latest in long range fuel capacity. Our oxygen extraction equipment utilizes the hydrolysis of sea water. Our carbon dioxide scrubbers can be used alternately so one can be cleaned while the other is in use. About the only thing we can't produce are food and toilet paper.'' Captain Cosgrove laughed at the inside joke. ''I'll see to it that you are escorted around some of the more confidential areas. We've got a science lab with everything from microscopes to Gieger counters, and complete chemical facilities. I'm quite proud of it. Or perhaps you might like to work out in the gym. We've got a racketball court, and basketball, too.''

"Are you serious?''

"Absolutely, although the ceilings are not regulation height. How are your accomodations?''

"Not what I expected in a submarine. And the corridors are so *wide*. Even during rush hour there's plenty of room.''

Captain Cosgrove smiled quixotically. "We've come a long way since the World War Two models. Excuse me, but, Cody, what is the message situation?''

"I've still got a clamp on all transmissions. You know we were attacked on shore?'' When the captain nodded, Cody went on. "I want complete coding and record keeping. Everything goes through me. As soon as we're done here, I'll start working on approvals. Until then, maintain radio silence.''

"I understand. How about Lieutenant Wakefield's situation reports?''

"They can go, but nothing else.''

"Okay.'' Captain Cosgrove checked his watch. "I'll be in the control room if you need me. Mr. Hutchison, feel free to call on me any time.''

"Thanks, captain. But I'm going to get catch a few zees as soon as we finish the Peking debrie—''

"Whoops, Mr. Hutchison. Whatever you're discussing is classified information.''

Hutch shut his mouth, casting aspertive looks at Cody and Ronnie. "But, you're the captain. I thought—''

"I don't have a need to know. Cody is the senior officer in charge, and this vessel is at his disposal. I just supply transportation and logistical support. Remember that. Don't tell me anything.''

"Uh, well—sure thing.''

The captain nodded. Ronnie locked the door behind him.

"Sorry. I hope I didn't blow it.''

"No harm done,'' Cody said, smiling. "But don't let it happen again. The next person might not be so discreet.''

"So, where were we?''

"We're just about done. I think you have a fair understanding of the political sensitivity of the situation.''

"I understand that the Japanese wanted to take the remains out of China during the occupation. But they're a bit more refined today than they were during the war. Peaceful, even. The Nationalist Chinese would like to have them so they can thumb their noses at the People's Republic, who want them so they can do the same. Russia wants everything, not necessarily with good reason. The posture of the U.S., at least according to Janus, was to locate the collection so it could be returned to its rightful owners,

although it was never established who that would be. And I want them
because I think they may hold the secret to man's evolutionary history. But
there's one thing I know for goddamned sure: the Peking man fossils are
not worth the time, effort, cost, and danger of international upheaval that's
being spent on this pursuit. In the final result, they're still just a box of
bones. It's not a killing matter.''

Hutch faked a toothless smile and tilted his head at Cody. "So what
is this *really* all about?'' He looked up at Ronnie. "Come on. What gives?''

Cody sighed. "Show him.''

She nodded, and reopened the vault. She took out a leather case and
placed it on the table in front of Hutch.

"You were holding out on me, weren't you?''

"No, this time I was going to tell you—''

"When? Next week? Next year?''

"No, it has to be now, because we can't let these documents exist. In
case they fell into the wrong hands, or were seen by the wrong eyes.''

"But you were testing me, weren't you? You were going to hold out
on me just because that's your nature. You don't come clean just because
someone hands you a bar of soap. You wait until it gets rubbed in your
face.''

Cody smiled, but it was not his usual broad grin. "I'm just trying to
handle this in chronological sequence. Nothing personal.''

Ronnie unlocked the attache case with one key, then spun it around so
it faced Cody. He unlocked it with another key. Ronnie punched out a
combination, a buzzer sounded, and the snaps popped open. She laid back
the lid. Hutch gazed at the shiny steel lining, at the devices inside which
must have been fire bombs. Ronnie took out a black and white, eight by ten
photograph, and handed it to Hutch.

The print was new, and still smelled of chemicals. But the subject was
yellowed with age. "This is a copy of the original,'' Ronnie said.

Hutch turned it this way and that until he caught it in a nonreflective
light. It was a close up of a skull, held in a pair of cracked, leathery hands
with dirty nails.

"The intact skull, found several feet deeper than the Andersson
specimens.''

"A little older.'' Hutch ran a practiced eye along the cranial sutures,
the graceful supraorbitals, the low, flattened forehead, the projecting
canines. "You don't expect me to make a positive identification without
comparing this to measurements of the castings?''

Cody shook his head. "Just background, to show you what we've
got.'' He held out his hand. "Have you seen enough of this one?'' When
Hutch nodded, Cody took the picture away from him. He left his seat and
stood in front of a machine. A flick of a button switched it on. He fed the
glossy print into the shredder, then shook the bag into which the confetti
fell. "Next.''

Ronnie handed him another. This one showed an overview of the excavation from a height of about five feet. Depicted was the cave floor where it had been swept evenly to show several bits and pieces of bone still embedded in the concretion. Off to one side something glistened, or reflected back from the light of the flashbulb.

Wordlessly, Hutch handed the photo to Cody. The commando shredded it. Ronnie took out another picture and placed it on the table.

In the extreme closeup, a whiskbroom had just revealed a tiny swath of—"What is that? Cloth? Material? Some kind of fiber? It doesn't look like animal skin."

Cody shredded the picture, and Ronnie took out another.

It was shot under a microscope. The parallel crosshatched lines overlaid a surface which was smooth even under magnification. "Was this in the matrix, or is it an intrusion? It looks artificial."

Cody took the picture and fed it into the shredder. "That was taken with an electron microscope, one hundred thousand power."

"But, there's no definition, no relief, no holes. With that kind of magnification . . . "

The next picture showed the excavation proceeding. More bone was exposed, a few teeth, odds and ends of metallic shards, and a long, dome shaped, grayish mass not quite cleared of the final layer of dirt.

"These can't be tools." There was a tremor in Hutch's voice. "It's impossible. And this thing—some kind of mineral vein."

The picture went into the shredder. The next one made Hutch's eyes pop out. The grayish mass was revealed as a cylindrical object with a dull patina which appeared somehow out of focus. Yet the hand that was next to it showed up perfectly right down to the swirls in the wrinkled skin.

"Is this a joke? Or did someone bury an old oxygen flask by accident, at the Low Cave site?"

Ronnie's voice was clear, and calm. "It's real, Hutch. Whatever it is, it was already there at the time Peking man inhabited the cave."

"Are you—" Hutch tried to keep his jaw together so he could formulate the words. "Are you trying to tell me that—this was embedded in the earth?"

Cody was deadly serious. "What we're trying to tell you is that—it is not *of* the Earth."

The *Gremyashchi*

1946

(The following is an extract from "The Peking Papers.")

"The underwater world is a vast, unexplored territory we are only now beginning to discover. Who knows what secrets it contains, what knowledge there is to be learned, what riddles remain to be solved? Only those who seek, will find."

Comrade Yuri Petrov stared through the scratched glass of the port at the distant, jagged coastline. Where before it had been a flat beach covered with palm trees, now it was a monolithic cliff face: a gray granite wall topped by lush jungle greenery. The idyllic backdrop had given way to a wild, prehistoric landscape.

"Have you ever been to Borneo?"

Petrov turned slowly, beads of perspiration dripping down from dark hair and thick, bushy eyebrows. "This is as close as I care to be, comrade."

The woman laughed, with sparkling eyes as well as with parted lips. "Then you have heard about it. A strange land inhabited by wild animals and backward people." She thrust out her hand. "Really, though, there are no indigenous carnivores. I am Catarina Kardova."

Petrov grasped her hand weakly, not wishing to inflict damage on digits so delicate. "Yuri Petrov." He was captivated by the beauty and the openness of her face. After a pause, "Is it true, there are no dangerous meat eating animals on the island?"

Catarina continued to smile, showing white, even teeth. "No, it is not true." When Petrov's eyes narrowed, she explained, "It is your choice of words which makes the statement false. Elephant and rhinoceros can be dangerous if one happens to fall underfoot, or startles a horned brute. And mosquitoes are a veritable plague, although they survive on blood. But there are no large mammals, such as lions and tigers, which prey on man—other than man himself, of course."

Petrov allowed his guard to ease. "You know much about the equatorial environment."

"I lived in Brunei for five years before the war, under British rule. During the Japanese occupation I returned to Moscow for a—a government position. Now, with the Dutch returning to Borneo, and the Brookes to Sarawak ... " She shrugged her slender shoulders. "My assignments carry me elsewhere. And You?"

"In civilian life, a policeman. In the army, a tank commander. For four years I saw the war from the turret of an American made Grant. My discharge came through while I was still in Shanghai. Now, after a long absence, I return home."

"And the crates?"

Petrov jerked back, unable to contain his shock. His brows touched when he pinched his eyes. "What crates?"

Catarina laughed. "The crates you spend most of your time in your stateroom protecting."

"Are you KGB?"

Catarina's laugh was loud and voluble, but as they were the only two people in the freighter's tiny dining room, she was unrestrained. "No, comrade, I am a teacher—a language teacher. But the mysterious boxes were the talk of the town before we left. You are either a poor smuggler or an innocent dupe. I doubt either."

"And what was the talk?"

"Fossils, of course. Very old fossils. Surely you heard the rumors yourself."

Petrov nodded slowly, without smiling. "Not only did I hear them, I started them."

"Indeed." Her face never stopped smiling, her eyes never ceased dancing. "That is curious. And why did you want to attract attention to yourself and your stolen cargo?"

"Is it considered stealing to take something out of the ground? Does the farmer steal tomatoes from the earth?"

"The farmer puts in before he takes out. Besides, he owns the soil in which he sows."

"Unless it is owned by the state."

"Government was created to protect man, not to own him or his land."

"On a Soviet vessel, one who is thus outspoken treads on shaky ground."

"I tread only on that which is mine. If you think otherwise, you are trespassing."

"In the world of the future, everything will be owned by the state."

Catarina's smile dissolved into a distorted frown. "*I* will never be owned."

"You speak with bourgeois affectation."

"I speak what is on my mind. If it offends you, the offense is yours."

Petrov tilted his head curtly. "You are indeed an individualist."

"And you are a nonentity—an insignificant member of the masses, like a single, unthinking cell within the human body. Perhaps I was wrong in seeking you out. But as the only other passenger on this stinking, dirty, roach infested ship, and the only intellectual among a crew of oilers and stokers, your conversation is welcome, if not particularly enlightening."

"Your skin is fair, and your face beautiful; but underneath I suspect you are a very ugly person. Or, perhaps, just misunderstood."

"I understand myself as well as I understand my deposed ancestors. The Bolsheviks took everything from my family—everything except our dignity."

Petrov was silent for a long time. He gazed into Catarina's frantic, fiery eyes. "I see."

"I doubt it. You cannot comprehend, because you do not have the basis for comparison."

"I'm sorry. I guess you are right. I have never had money, influence, or position of authority, so of course I cannot miss it."

"But now, you have power."

Petrov squinted. "I don't follow you."

Catarina pursed her lips, and some of her whimsy returned. "I know about the crates, about the need for a cover story."

"I assure you—"

"Yes, yes, yes. I know they contain the Peking man fossils. But they also hold something else, something far more interesting—and far more powerful."

"Rumors abound—"

"Truth, Petrov. I know the truth." Her voice was harsh and crisp. Inherited aristocracy was veiled by the venomous twitching of her lips. "I am not aboard this rat's nest by accident. I, too, learned of Peking man's terrible secret. I was on the trail myself, but your organization was too quick for me. And too stupid. You don't even know what you have."

Petrov nodded slowly. There was no fooling this woman. "What I have, I don't understand. What you want, I cannot comprehend."

The gun appeared in Catarina's hand as if by magic. It could not have been concealed inside her flimsy dress, so it must have been in her small handbag. Petrov recognized it as a Tokarev automatic pistol; he had carried one on his hip for five years.

"I want power."

"You would kill me for a box of bones?"

"The bones you may keep. I want the other."

The barrel pointed steadily, unwaveringly, at his chest. "It is for the people, comrade."

"I'm tired of hearing about the travails of the people. I want something for myself. And whatever it is—whatever is so important—must have great value."

Petrov had faced larger guns than this, and in more dire straits. He was unruffled by the threats of this madwoman. "The value is not in the object itself, but in understanding its function."

"I care nothing for knowledge except what it can buy me. I will gladly ransom it back—for a price."

"You are indeed an ugly person."

"Why? Because I look out after myself?"

Petrov shook his head. "Because you would rob from others for personal gain."

Catarina laughed haughtily. "As you stole from the Chinese."

"But they have not the technology to make use of it. We can learn from it. We can make good of it."

"And will you share that good with the world, or hold it for your precious state?"

"That is not for me to decide. I am only—"

"A fool. A damned fool. And soon—a dead fool. You see, you care nothing about *the* people, only about *your* people."

Petrov never took his eyes from hers. "You can't get away with it. You can't—"

"They're all down in the after steerage, working on the mechanism. When I push your body into the water, you disappear, no one knows where. When the ship refuels in Singapore, I offload the cargo. Then, I sell it to the highest bidder. You see, the people still get it in the end. I am merely adding a tax."

"Your capitalistic ideals—"

"The philosophical discussion is over. Now, I suggest, you think about yourself. Out there—" Catarina gestured with her eyes. The gun never moved. "Is the most inhospitible hinterland in the world. But fresh water is available, and food is plentiful. It is several weeks by foot to civilization, and that is all the time I need. So—" She tilted the gun sideways. "Will you have lead, or water?"

Petrov turned slowly, and peered out the port. "You give me poor choice: a quick death, or a slow one."

"I give you a chance. Whether you take it or not is up to you."

"I cannot swim."

"You may have a life ring. Now move."

"What about—"

"*Now!*"

Petrov sighed. He stepped through the doorway to the promenade deck. Leaning over the rail, he looked down into the clear, blue water swirling along the rusted, steel hull. "We are moving, They must have fixed—"

"Jump, or you are a dead man."

Even as he looked, the water took on a darker color. The *Gremyashchi* shivered, and an awful rending sound echoed up from the bowels of the double bottom. Petrov was thrown forward with one hand still on the rail. His body was spun around and slammed into a lifeboat davit, knocking the breath out of his lungs. He gasped. His whole right side seemed to be numb.

When he again was able to take note of his surroundings, he saw Catarina lying in a daze on the worn deck. Blood trickled from her temple and stained her dark tresses. Quickly he regained his balance, stepped over her, and crushed the hand that held the deadly pistol. The woman screamed in pain. Petrov bent back her fingers and relieved her of the gun. He jammed it under his belt.

Petrov had seen enough of death, enough destruction. "Come on, comrade. I believe we are sinking."

The freighter was still on an even keel, but it was lower in the water The bridge watch scrambled down the offshore ladder and worked the releases on the starboard lifeboat. Aft, the working party and engine and boiler room crews ran the stern lifeboats down their falls. There was not much time. Air hissed out of the hatches and ventilators as water poured in through gashes torn in the hull plates by the sharp pointed rock.

Petrov yanked a fireaxe from its niche, and chopped the lashings of the solid core emergency raft. The rectangular float slid off its angled retainer, to crash on its edge in the foaming sea. It flopped over with a splash.

"Jump, comrade, or we are doomed."

Catarina was hardly conscious. She shook her head, and made ineffectual motions with her hands. Petrov picked up the delicate woman who had been about to shoot him, cradled her in his arms like a baby in swaddling clothes, and tossed her overboard. Her screams stopped when she hit the water. Petrov hesitated. He saw no lifebelts. He stooped and pulled off his heavy shoes, and jumped into the South China Sea.

He came up next to the raft and immediately clambered aboard. He had not been lying about his lack of swimming ability. "Over here, Catarina." He pulled out a paddle, straddled the hard pontoon, and dug the flat blade into the water. The raft kept trying to pivot, and it was only with great effort that he reached the struggling woman before she went down. When he at last pulled her aboard she was choking on salt water. He laid her in the rope mesh center, wallowing in the water, but with her head held up on the end pontoon.

Petrov knew about suction, and worked hard to get away from the sinking vessel. But he had paddled only a few yards when the aging freighter gave a loud burp that lifted off part of her upper decks. One funnel fell over when its guy wires were pulled from their turnbuckles. Otherwise, the ship settled perfectly level, sailing on her final cruise.

Unexpectedly, there was no suction. With a sigh almost of relief, the tired tramp freighter disappeared quietly. The water came together with a slap above her upperworks. There was a gurgling and bubbling that went on for a long time. Only the masthead light marked the grave of the *Gremyashchi*.

Now Petrov could see the starboard lifeboat pulling out to sea. The two aft boats were headed north, along the desolate coast. Petrov aimed the raft toward land. He paddled first on one side, then on the other. As he did, he carefully noted ranges and markings on shore. It was important that he be able to relocate the sunken freighter and its small but valuable cargo. The first storm would knock down the slender mast.

The sun was bright, the heat unbearable. For relief, Petrov splashed water on his face and clothes. He squinted hard in the eternal brightness. The beach was getting closer. Catarina lay comatose, and barely alive. The graceful contours of her body were sharply outlined in the plaid dress. She had lost a shoe.

It was hours before the raft reached the outer breakers. The waves crashed straight against the shore, each time bringing the raft a little closer. The cliffs were sheer, but a long stretch of sand jutted out from the base. Petrov was trying to figure how to land among the jagged, barnacle-covered boulders that littered the low tide mark, when the raft suddenly fetched up. An awful tearing sound was accompanied by the ripping of the foam core. In a moment the raft was in two pieces, held together only by the rotted material of the mesh.

"Catarina!"

He hooked his large hands under her shoulders. Red fingers of blood raked her back from where her unconscious body had dragged along the sharpened rock projections. The raft was pounded back and forth in the surf. Waves crashed over Petrov's head as he struggled to free Catarina. The mesh parted, and the raft separated. The half with them in it was carried toward the beach in the churning waves.

Petrov slung one arm over the hard fibre side, and held onto Catarina with the other. He kicked his feet in desparation. A swell submerged his head, and he swallowed a mouthful of salty water. Then his grip was torn away from the raft. He went down. When he bobbed up a moment later he was coughing and gagging, and the raft was out of reach. He had a fleeting glimpse of Catarina lying limply over the tattered pontoon.

He splashed the water with his hands, fighting to keep his head above the roiling waves. He went down again. He could hold his breath only for a second before he was forced to inhale. He sucked a stream of warm water into his throat. Miraculously, his head bobbed to the surface. He struck out with flailing hands as he spat out half the ocean. But he could not hold himself up. Down he went again.

His feet touched something, were dragged along, touched once more. Petrov extended his legs, straightened his feet. His toes dragged along the sand. The waves crashed against him with the fury of a storm. His head came up. He gasped for air. His body was spun and twisted in the surf, his legs dragged out in the undertow. He went under, fought his way back to daylight, was pulled down and tumbled around like a leaf in a gale. Then he was on his hands and knees, crawling.

The waves pounded at him, rolled over him. But he clawed his way up the beach, ever higher, his fingers digging into the sand. He coughed, and coughed some more. He spat out more water. Finally, he collapsed. Water washed around his lower body, but his mouth was able to suck in the air he so desperately needed.

Catarina and the raft came to rest a dozen yards away. She lay face down in the upper reaches of the waves, and the water gurgled about her head. But Petrov was too weak to move. He was exhausted, and could not do any more for her.

He heard shouting: not words he recognized, but a deep throated war cry. He lifted his head, saw two dark men descend upon Catarina's still form. They dragged her up high, rolled her over, felt along her body, under her dress.

"Here! Here! Leave her alone."

He had to stop to catch his breath. He watched helplessly as one bronzed native stripped the material from her body, revealing her pale nakedness. Another grappled with her hand, and soon peeled off her ring.

He pulled the gun from his belt. "You animals!"

Then he was being manhandled by the two scantily clad aborigines. Rough hands ran over his back, along his legs. He wriggled weakly, but could not break free. He was thrown about like a baby. They forced him over on his back and pinioned his arms. Hands went into his pockets, into his trousers. He was relieved of all his possessions, including the blued steel pistol.

Completely drained of energy, Petrov lay back on the sand. He watched the tall native play with the gun, rotating it, staring at it from all angles. He looked down the bore, fingered the cocking mechanism, flicked the safety switch back and forth. With the barrel pointed toward him, he stuck his thumb under the trigger guard.

The other native, the smaller one, reached out and yanked at the gun. The deafening roar was accompanied by a blast of flame. A bloody hole appeared on the man's painted chest while, in slow motion, he toppled over backward. He twitched once or twice, then lay still.

There followed a moment of stunned silence. Petrov twisted around onto his side, managed to push himself up onto one arm. "You must be careful. You don't understand its power." He crawled toward the fallen robber.

But his companion was faster. Deftly, he disentangled the pistol from the dead man's hand. He held it out in front of him, gazing upon it in awe. More shouts arose from the nearby bush. A horde of screaming natives, spears tipped forward, charged out of the jungle. The one with the gun looked up, looked back at the gun, touched the hair trigger. His eyes grew larger. He pointed it at the vanguard of the attackers. He wrapped his middle finger around the unfamiliar mechanism.

The gun exploded. The lead man dropped like a stone, his face a mass of blood and froth. The rest of the mob fell back.

For a moment, there was stunned silence. Then, the native with the gun smiled. He looked upon the pistol as if it were a gift of the gods. He waved it in the air.

"Be careful with that thing, you fool."

The native shouted. He waved the pistol, and the others retreated. He waved it again, shouting, and several approached warily. His grin ran from ear to ear. He indicated the white woman, and the others slunk to do his bidding. He swung the weapon downward.

"Turn it away. You'll use it all up, and then it will be useless to you."

The last thing Petrov saw, in this world, was the muzzle flash.

The *Awa Maru*

The East China Sea shone with a radiant, cobalt blue that was clear as air and warm as a sauna. A few feet above Hutch's head the waves rippled incessantly in a short chop that was growing with the increasing wind. But underwater, topside weather made no difference. This was a three dimensional medium of current and surge, but without the dragging influence of gravity.

He made a perfunctory stop at ten feet to check his gauges: tanks were filled to thirty-three hundred p.s.i., his decompression computer was actuated, his depth gauge, backup watch, and compass were all functioning. He took one last look up at the sleek hull of the *G. Willie Makit*, then let some air out of his buoyancy compensator and dropped slowly down the anchor line. As the pressure increased, he cleared his ears by pressing a finger against the lower edge of his face mask, and blowing slightly.

He rolled his shoulders so the tepid surface water filled in the voids between the wetsuit and his skin. He hit a thermocline at fifty feet, but the temperature differential was only a few degrees. The line slid faster through the circle of his enclosed fingers as his descent increased in speed. Pressure squeezed the rubber suit close to his body, and forced the neoprene bubbles to contract: the deeper he went, the thinner the wetsuit became. But loss of thermal protection in these waters was insignificant.

At a depth of one hundred feet he felt himself falling too rapidly. The anchor line was no longer perpendicular to the bottom, but trending off at an angle. Now he pressed the button that would allow air from his tanks into the BC, compensating for the compression of depth. He held in the button until he was equalized, neither dropping nor rising. He inverted his body and pulled himself head down toward the murky depths below.

For a while he was in limbo: he could see neither the surface nor the bottom. Microplankton floated past like a thin, brownish mist. Because visibility simply faded away with distance, the sea appeared infinite in all directions.

At one hundred fifty feet, Hutch became aware of a dim silhouette taking form to his right. The shape coalesced out of the azure background into a brown, rusted wall of steel. A cloud of fish hovered over wreckage he could not yet identify. Hull plates were bent and twisted, and strewn about like fallen leaves in autumn. Beams and angle iron lay in a jumbled heap like a pile of gargantuan pickup sticks. Very little of the ship's original integrity was unbroken.

Hutch settled on the bottom. A playful cloud of silt, the result of iron oxides and decomposing organics, puffed up around him. His head buzzed. He forced himself to breathe slowly and deeply, but could not shake off the side effect of nitrogen narcosis. It did not prevent him from functioning, but it dampened his powers of observation—he felt like a horse wearing blinders, peering into a fog. He had to concentrate with extra effort on what he was doing.

The first thing he did was to recheck his gauges. The digital depth readout was two-oh-four; he still had three thousand p.s.i. in his double tanks; and he was already four minutes into his dive. The grapnel was snagged loosely on a piece of rotted rope. To make sure it would not pull out, and so the boat did not drift away during his dive, he reset it so the curved tines caught under an I-beam.

Taking a look at his surroundings, he looked right through the schools of rainbow hued tropicals that swam in the tens of thousands over the coral covered wreckage. Tall sponges and long gorgonians waved placidly in the mild surge, lending motion that was tranquil and utterly silent. The sound of his exhaust bubbles was blocked out of his mind.

Hutch added enough air to his BC to make himself neutrally buoyant, then kicked gently toward a thick, round shaft of iron. He ducked under a jagged sheet of metal. His cotton glove made no impression on the veneer of marine encrustation. It was solid and immovable. Yet, there were patches of bare metal exposed as if the surface had been scraped clean.

The buzzing continued to haunt him. He kicked upward, and got above the main pile of wreckage. Looking left, he could see where the horizontal pillar terminated just beyond an A-frame. This was definitely the propellor shaft, so he was at the stern of the wreck. Once oriented, he spun and took off in the opposite direction, maintaining his elevation from the bottom not just so he could slow down the nitrogen dissolving in his tissues, but so he could have an overview of the sunken vessel.

The *Awa Maru* was laid out like a great, flenced whale, with beams for ribs. It rose up forty feet from the bottom on one side, then curved down to the clean white sand on the other. The skeleton was crushed flat in some areas, dragged out in others as if worried by some gigantic sea creature that consumed iron. Very little was recognizable as a ship: it could just as well have been an underwater scrap yard.

The prop shaft was swallowed up by a huge iron block that was the triple expansion steam engine. So thick and effulgent were the corals, anemones, and barnacles, that it could very well have been a naturally jutting rock on which indigenous marine organisms had attached themselves. Forward of the engine was a jumble of fifteen foot diameter cylinders, the ship's boilers, strewn haphazardly and no longer aligned with the axis of the wreck. The open condenser tubes offered homes to myriads of fish which backed their hindquarters into the protection of the copper tunnels, and stuck out only their ugly faces.

The navigation bridge was just beyond, but away from the hull and spread out in the sand. Too quickly, Hutch's time was up. At twelve minutes into the dive, he stopped. Still hovering above the wreck, he held his compass up to his nose. The great iron mass would deflect the needle off its true course, but the reading at least would be accurate within the quadrant. For his purposes, that was all he needed to know.

He dropped into the wreckage, facing aft, and started working his way back to the anchor line. Now he studied close up the detail of the remaining framework. Much of the superstructure was flattened and buried in the sand. The thinner metal was not built to withstand the rigors of the pounding sea, so it rusted through more rapidly. Fragments of badly deteriorated bulkheads littered the sand in an immense debris field which spread out from the intact hull structure. Brass portholes were practically impervious to the corrosive action of the sea, and lay about denoting where once had been staterooms.

A piece of glass attracted Hutch's attention. He dug it out of the sand, and saw it was a bottle with Oriental writing. But it was not from the war: screw caps were much more recent, so it was probably trash thrown overboard from one of the Chinese salvage vessels. He let it go.

He turned on his underwater light and flashed it under the overlapping iron leaves. The local denizens retreated from the bright intrusion. Hutch saw nothing of note other than a conch lying next to a huge egg mass, which she had probably been laying for several days. He wished he had his camera along. But this was just an exploratory dive.

At seventeen minutes he was getting anxious. His decompression requirement was more than thirty minutes, and he did not want to overstay his bottom time by failing to locate the anchor line. At over two hundred feet, nitrogen dissolved in the tissues at a rapid rate.

He kicked up clear of the wreckage, a couple body lengths above the sand. When he looked up he saw the half inch nylon line stretching over his head toward the milky white surface. He breathed a sigh of relief. While his eyes followed the sagging loop, he kicked in the direction of the grapnel. He reached it with a thousand p.s.i. still in his tanks. It took but a moment to pull it free, loop the chain under the tines, and let it go. Then he started his slow ascent, at thirty feet per minute. Gradually, the buzzing of narcosis left his head.

It took nearly five minutes to reach his first decompression stop, at sixty feet. One minute later, his safe ceiling rose to fifty feet, and he moved slowly hand over hand up the white anchor line. He settled down for a long, boring hang: his computer called for another forty minutes of decompression. With practiced ease he slowed down his breathing rate, first to four breaths per minute, then to three. He dragged air through the regulator for eight seconds, then exhaled for twelve. The bubbles escaped through the exhaust ports and rose in twin columns on opposite sides of his mask.

Two minutes later, he moved up to forty feet; three minutes after that, he ascended to thirty. The water was warm, his weight was neutral. He closed his eyes. His only touch with reality was the anchor line in his hand. His mind drifted in a world of sensory deprivation, where time and space were intellectual concepts.

The rope jerked hard. Hutch opened his eyes, and looked up. He saw a vision he thought he would never see this side of Valhalla. A Valkyrie, one of Odin's handmaidens, was flying overhead, waiting to escort him victorious through the battlefields. His soul skipped a beat.

Ronnie wore a mask and fins and a *very* brief bikini. She let go the anchor line, and waved. With his free hand, Hutch waved back. She bent sharply at the waist, let her feet rise high in the air, and dived straight down. She met Hutch at twenty feet, and spun around to resume a vertical position. She hovered practically forever, smiling at him. Finally, she reached out and touched his regulator delicately with one finger. He took it out of his mouth and passed it over. Ronnie put the mouthpiece in her mouth, blew it clear, and took one deep breath, then passed it back to Hutch. She swam around in a lazy circle, gradually rising. A steady stream of bubbles escaped her pink lips as she exhaled the compressed air on her way to the surface.

Like a playful porpoise, she gamboled about for the next half hour, helping Hutch wile away the time. He had a difficult time remembering to practice his slow breathing control. When he finally broke the surface, after forty-five minutes, he had lost it completely. He kicked back to the stern of the fifty-foot sailboat. Ronnie climbed up the ladder before him. Cody leaned over the gunwale and took his light off his wrist. Hutch stuck his long rubber fins through the rungs and climbed aboard.

"So what do you think? How's it look?"

Hutch leaned back so his tanks rested on the transom, and took off his mask. "It's a junk yard. The Chinese must have blown it to smithereens."

"But did you see any bones?"

"Cody, I spent twenty minutes looking over a five hundred foot long ship. At that depth I only had time to pass over half of it."

"How about—"

Ronnie pushed the commando aside and started pulling Hutch's tank straps through the D-rings. "Give him a break, Cody. Let him at least get his breath back."

"I won't be able to do that unless you put some clothes on."

"Don't you like my outfit?"

"I think you'd look better in a one piece bathing suit." Ronnie jumped back, momentarily crestfallen. Hutch added slyly, "But I'm not sure which piece."

Cody scowled. He turned and walked across the swaying deck to the cabin entrance. "I can see it's going to be a long trip."

Hutch shrugged out of the tank harness, and placed the air cylinders carefully on the teak decking. "So, let's enjoy it while we can, for tomorrow we dive."

Cody groaned. "Of all the cards I had to draw for this mission, it had to be a joker."

"And don't forget the Queen of Hearts." Hutch winked at Ronnie. He unclipped his beavertail, bent over double, and pulled the wetsuit jacket over his head. A moment later he had the bottoms off, as well. He wore only a pair of swimming trunks; his long, lean form was bronzed by many days sailing across the East China Sea. "Besides, I'm having the time of my life. We're out here on a long sea voyage, visiting exotic ports, diving historic shipwrecks, and there's half of good company. What more could a man ask for?"

"Right now I could ask for some help getting the hell out of here. We spotted a couple of suspicious looking boats on the horizon while you were down."

"Do you think they saw us?"

"I could read them on our radar, so I guess they could read us on theirs. If it's a surveillance ship they can interpolate our position from theirs, and they'll know we're over the *Awa Maru*. Did you free the grapnel?"

"Sure. I foul hooked it."

Cody pointed about one hundred twenty degrees to port. "We're still next to the buoy, so we haven't moved."

Hutch climbed past Cody and ran up to the bow. "There's not much current, and the hook's probably lying in the wreckage. But it's not snagged. I'll pull it up."

Ronnie ducked into the cabin. "I'll get the engine going." A moment later the auxiliary inboard diesel chugged to life.

"Run up on it and give me a little slack," Hutch called out.

Cody walked up to the bow in his crepe soled shoes, looking like a regular yachtsman in his black, bell bottom trousers, striped polo shirt, and peaked cap. "Take up the strain and I'll get a couple of turns around the windlass. So what can you tell me?"

Hutch grunted as he leaned over the bowsprit rail, the anchor line gripped in one veined hand. He jigged it up and down. "She's lying on her starboard side more than ninety degrees. Looks like she rolled over when she sank. That means the bridge wreckage'll be off in the sand, maybe a hundred feet away from the main hull. Those passenger ships are pretty high above the water line. Oof, here it comes."

He quickly hauled in some thirty feet of rope, to get the grapnel off the bottom. Cody wrapped it around the chrome plated drum, stepped on the rubber coated deck button, and kept out the slack while the windlass pulled in the rope.

"It lies northeast southwest. We were anchored right in the fantail, so next time we'll want to drop the hook more to the northeast."

When the anchor chain clattered up over the roller, Cody made a double wrap on the line and snugged it tight. He waved to Ronnie through the forward glass. "Okay, let's move it." He worked his way aft and yelled into the cabin. "Haul around so I can pick up the buoy."

"Why don't you leave it so we don't have to search for the wreck again?"

"Because I don't want to leave any signs that we've been here. This is a covert operation, remember?"

Ronnie turned sharply to port, and brought the boat right up alongside the white plastic jug bobbing in the swells. Cody reached out with a long-handled gaff and hooked the line under the float. He pulled it in and handed it to Hutch, who wound up the string while Cody hauled up the weight.

"We'll go about a mile, than raise the sails and make like a tourist."

Ronnie nodded, swung the helm, and headed south. "Aye aye, captain."

Hutch padded barefoot into the cabin, yanked a fluffy red towel off the table, and vigorously rubbed down his head and body. "Anyway, I got up as far as the boilers, just shy of the bridge. I had to turn around at that point, but it was strange, almost as if there was nothing out there. Next time, we'll fall back about three hundred feet—about six microseconds on the loran."

"How much surface interval do you need?"

"At least three hours, but six would be better."

Cody finished stowing the buoy and entered the cabin. "It'll be dark by then. I'd like to get this survey over with as soon as we can. If the goods are gone, let's skedaddle."

"I'm not going in before three hours. That's the minimum for a safe repetitive dive."

"I thought that computer of yours gave you more time than the Tables."

"The Navy Decompression Tables are outdated by anyone's standards. That's why only the Navy uses them any more. The factor that limits bottom time and dictates surface interval is not the Tables, or a computer, but the human body. The computer doesn't give me anything; it just calculates my time and depth profile with more precision. I could make another dive right now, but I'd have to hang till I was a prune. With the equipment we have and under these conditions, it wouldn't be wise. So why push it?"

Ronnie stepped back from the helm. "Cody, take the wheel while I dry off."

Cody moved into position, checked their bearing, and altered course a point.

Hutch held out a dry towel. "Need some help?"

Dark eyes flashed with a light all their own. "No, but I'll take it anyway. You can do my back."

"I'd rather do the front."

"Maybe later." Ronnie ran her fingers through her hair and combed it back over her head.

"Would you two please cut out the inuendoes and just go ahead and do it?" Cody grimaced, glaring at them alternately. "After a week on this boat you're driving me crazy."

Hutch laughed. "It's just a game. Nothing to worry about."

"I don't play games," Ronnie said. "I play for keeps."

"I don't care if you play for tiddlywinks, just as long as you remember we've got a job to do. And that takes precedence over everything. I want both of you to have your minds on your work, not occupied with sexual fantasies."

"Oh, Cody, you're such an old fogey. Don't tell me you don't have fantasies about your wife."

"Of course I do—but I keep them to myself. I don't wave them about in the open like a toreador waving a red flag in front of a bull."

"And I suppose you never did? I've seen your file, Cody. You've sown enough wild oats to apply to the Department of Agriculture for commodity stabilization. Why, if I had ten cents for every one of your affairs I could put the March of Dimes out of business. You've laid more shag then a carpet vendor. Once you get a—"

"That's enough!" Cody's face, tan as it was from a week in the sun, turned a darker shade of red. "I'll take the outside helm." He tramped out the cabin door and slammed it behind him.

"Whew, you really know how to get his goat. That's the first time I've ever seen his lion tamed."

"You're mixing your metaphors."

"No, I was describing the Chimera, which is what I think we're chasing."

"Yet you're still willing to go along with this search."

"There's hundred percent chance that if we don't look, we won't find anything."

"I'm glad to see you have a sense of humor. You need it in this business. And if you rub my back any more, I won't have any skin left."

Hutch stopped with a jolt. "Sorry. I guess I got carried away."

"So am I." Ronnie took back her towel and dried off her hands. "How about something to eat? I mean, like a sandwich. I made lunch while you were down."

"I'm famished."

"Have a seat." Ronnie took a tray of prepared meats and cheeses out of the refrigerator, and placed it on the table. The sailboat was luxuriously appointed, with a main cabin that looked more like a Miami condo kitchenette than a cramped crew galley with a hotplate. "We're all out of rolls, so I defrosted a loaf of sliced bread."

Hutch helped by grabbing the condiments and drinks. He laid a towel on the table so the glass jars would not slide as the boat rolled gently from side to side. Just as he sat down the background noise of the engine cut out.

"Thank god for that." The sudden silence left a dull ringing in Hutch's ears. He heard the small electric motor that raised the mainsail, and saw the white sheet unfurl over the after deck. "I hate noise with a passion."

Ronnie sat down opposite him. "Is that why you like diving so much? Because of the silence."

Hutch grabbed some bread and spread on the garnishes. "No, that's incidental. If I were to analyze it, I'd say it satisfies me on many levels. When I was a kid I liked exploring. We had a pretty good scout troop, and did a lot of traveling. But even around home I would go out in the woods, camp out, study nature, collect things like bird nests and bee hives and any rocks or minerals that struck my fancy—which was almost all of them. I also had an ant farm, raised pitcher plants, and kept pet snakes. And I dug up fossils, and carted them to the library to identify them so I could make up name tags. I think my mother was glad when I moved out just to get rid of my collections. But I give her credit, she put up with me all those years.

"Anyway, when I got old enough to drive, I discovered the bays on the Long Island Sound. I started snorkeling. Right away I found I couldn't stay down long enough to satisfy my curiosity. So, I took a diving course at the local YMCA. As soon as I hit the water, despite visibility that was like day old coffee, I found a shipwreck. It was only an abandoned wooden barge, but it was a new world to me. I brought up some iron nails and was tickled do death. Then I started dreaming about salvaging rare antiquities."

"College gave me the opportunity to study the importance of history, and how much of man's past has yet to be learned. So, I set out to learn all I could—first through anthropology. But underwater archaeology was still an attraction. Still is. I can study and learn history, I can find things to collect, and I can, as Cody so aptly noted, experience the thrill of adventure while doing it." Hutch snickered. "Looking for ancient, prehuman fossils on shipwrecks is the best of all worlds."

Ronnie put her sandwich down, and smiled. "You know, I'd like to go down with you sometime. Not here. This is too deep for me. But maybe later."

"Ronnie, I don't think I have time to teach you. And I wouldn't want you to get hurt just because—"

"I already know how to dive."

"You do?"

"Sure, my father taught me. I've been diving ever since I was a little girl. I've been all over the world, and all under it. Dad was a Navy man. We were always picking up and transferring to some distant corner of the Earth—and not always civilized places. Mother passed on when I was young. But Dad and I kept up our wanderings. When he retired, I joined up. The Navy tradition in our family goes back through quite a few wars. The Great Barrier Reef was exotic, but my favorite place was the Red Sea."

"Wow, that's terrific. I thought you took to the water too casually. And after I gave you that air from the regulator, I was afraid you'd hold your breath and embolize. But I couldn't call you back. You know, with all the gear we've got we could start our own dive school. Maybe if we can take a day off—"

"Not likely, with the slave driver out there." Ronnie tilted her head in Cody's direction. "He's worse than my father when it comes to dedication to duty."

"Come on. Be fair. He couldn't have been that bad. It sounds as if he spent a lot of time with you."

"Oh, he did. I just meant he was driven to perfection: in his life, in his job, and in his daughter. But he was good to me, and full of love."

Hutch shook his head. "I have trouble understanding that. My father was completely different. He thought kids were like weeds: you plant them in the garden, water them once in a while, and they grow. We were always at odds because he wanted me to follow his footsteps in the business world. His whole rationale for living was to transfer money from other people's pockets to his own. He couldn't understand—"

The cabin door burst open, and Cody stuck his head inside. "Get out here. We're being scanned."

Ronnie dropped the remains of her sandwich. She jumped up and was out the door before Hutch completed his next chew. He was still swallowing when he joined them on the after deck.

Cody handed the binoculars to Ronnie. "It's a gunboat coming right toward us. And it's got funny characters on the bow."

Still wearing her bikini, Ronnie did not look much like a Naval officer. "Yes, they're sailors."

"I mean the funny characters *painted* on the bow."

She steadied the glasses. By bending her legs and moving up and down against the waves, she managed to hold the oncoming boat in focus. "It's Chinese."

Cody was beyond exasperation. "I know that. Is it Red or White?"

Hutch squinted his eyes against the sun. "Can you tell that?"

"*I* can't," Cody admitted. "But she's a linguist. Knows more languages than God."

"They're Nationalists."

"Is that good or bad?" Hutch asked.

Cody caught the slowly swinging helm, and veered two points. "Depends on whether they shoot at us."

"Are they allowed to do that?"

"People with guns can do anything they damn well please to people without guns. What do you think the arms race is all about?"

"But this is international water. They can't claim jurisdiction."

"Tell that to the government. Didn't our own Congress enact legislation to lay claim to the *Titanic*. And that was a *British* ship. When you have power, you don't need to worry about right and wrong. Just remember our cover story—we're rich tourists sailing around the world, and writing a book about historic shipwrecks."

"Do you think they'll buy it?"

"You've got to write it first." To Ronnie, "You'd better get out of that bikini. We don't want to attract any undue attention."

"If she does, they'll inspect us for sure."

Cody scowled. "just go cover up."

Ronnie ducked into the cabin, snatched a green bathrobe, and hurried back outside.

Hutch humphed. "That's like trying to disguise the Grand Tetons with grass. Cody, I thought we recognized Taiwan."

"I only recognize it when it's in sight. Officially, our government does recognize Taiwan as the seat of the Chinese Nationalist goverment, and they have an embassy in Washington. *Un*officially, we recognize the People's Republic of China because they exist and because they present a powerful influence in the world through sheer mass of humanity. We deal with them through their embassy in Ottawa. In actuality, we try not to get caught in the middle by playing up to both, and by playing down our relationship to each with the other. The real problem is—they don't recognize each other."

"I swear, I'll never understand international relations."

Ronnie overlapped the folds of the robe and snugged the belt. "That's an oxymoron."

"A what?"

"An oxymoron. That's when you put two contradictory words together and end up with an absurd phrase. Like 'jumbo shrimp.'"

"Or 'honest politician,'" Cody added.

Hutch nodded slowly. "I see. Or 'military intelligence.'"

"You catch on fast, but don't push your luck." Ronnie picked up the binoculars and took another look at the gunboat.

Hutch could see it clearly enough to make out a large gun barrel on the bow, and shrapnel shields on the upper works that protected smaller guns. "Shouldn't we try to talk with them on the radio? You know, like 'breaker breaker one nine, good buddy. What's your ten-four?'"

Cody cast an aspersive glance at Hutch. "If we had you as an ambassador they'd be lobbing shells at us by now. What we do is we sit tight like typical tourists, show a mild interest, and wave like mad when they swing by."

As they got close, Hutch started waving. The gunboat was passing them forward, but suddenly it changed course and aimed for their bow. Hutch dropped his hand like it was made of lead. "It's not my fault, I was just—"

"They're just testing us." Cody, who had one hand on the wheel, spun hard aport. "They want to show us who's boss."

"It's a pecking order drill," Ronnie explained. "They do it all the time."

"The big question is not what they'll do, but whether they're out here by accident or design."

Hutch braced himself on the chrome plated railing. "Don't they normally patrol half way across the Strait, to keep tabs on the Red Chinese? Who are patrolling to keep tabs on the Taiwanese?"

"Yes, especially this close to Taipei. But I've learned to always be suspicious of coincidence."

"I thought you were suspicious of everything."

The sailboat heeled over as it tacked away from the gunboat. "And everyone."

"What happens if they board us and find all these guns and explosives?"

"We lose the power of speech. What do you see?"

Ronnie still had the binoculars glued to her eyes. "I see someone looking back at me. And about twenty AK–47s pointed in our direction. That's in addition to the fifty calibers and the antiaircraft guns. Nothing to worry about. It's a show of force."

Hutch found himself sweating despite the cooling breeze. "They've got *me* fooled."

"Okay, they're veering off." Cody pressed the button that activated the sail motors, and let down a little more sheet. "We'll keep right on going south. You can forget about diving any more today."

Hutch's eyes never left the departing gunboat. He could see that all the guns were still aimed directly at *him*. "I'm too wrung out, after that. I'm just glad they took us for tourists."

Ronnie put down the glasses, and glanced up and down Hutch's body. "One look at you and they knew we were clean."

Rivers of perspiration ran from under Hutch's arms all the way to his swimming trunks. "I need a shower."

Below decks, the *G. Willie Makit* was sumptuously furnished with four bunks, a commodious dressing room, plenty of cabinets and closet space, a shower, and a separate head. Hutch stood under the hot water and lay on a thick lather of soap. He washed the sea salt from his hair and beard, and the odor from his body. He stepped out wearing a large towel, and feeling completely refreshed.

"Need your back dried?"

Hutch swallowed hard, and tried to turn his thoughts in directions that would be more productive. "I think Cody's right. For my sanity, at least, we've got to cut out the double-ententres and concentrate on the job at hand."

"It's no fun that way." Ronnie perched on the edge of her bunk, smiling slyly. "Hutch, I just don't figure you. You face death from all kinds of things in the water, yet you wilt at the sight of a boat load of sailors."

"You want to know the only thing I'm afraid of in this world? It's my fellow man. Underwater, I'm in control—of me, of the environment, of everything that's happening except the way-out possibility of equipment malfunction. And for that I have backups. I'm completely free down there. But throw in the human factor and things become dangerous. This world wasn't a jungle before man entered the scene—it was a paradise. It was man who turned it into a jungle."

"But, what about sharks, and wild animals?"

Hutch sat down on his own bunk, rolling his eyes. "Why does *every*body think of sharks. You've been watching too much 'Sea Hunt.' The biggest peril is not from a lower lifeform which responds according to a genetically implanted set of commands, but from the unpredictable nature of man. You know whether or not an animal is dangerous, but when you're dealing with people, those you trust the most may be the very ones to betray you."

Ronnie lowered her head. Her features clouded over in deep thought. "I guess—I guess there's something to what you say. But, Hutch, without trust, you have nothing."

Hutch pulled his log book out of the mesh catchall next to his bunk, and entered dive times and depths. "Hey, I didn't mean to get down on you. It's just—Ronnie, I'm not use to this James Bond stuff, and I don't like it. I'm in pursuit of something of great anthropological significance, and this political intrigue is so many moose patties."

With a paperback book in hand, Ronnie leaned back on her pillow and switched on the nightlight. "Hutch, you're so innocent. So—ingenuous. No, I mean that in a complimentary way. It's gratifying to see that kind of—simplicity, for a change. I was brought up in the world of espionage. I was the only person my father would confide in. I even knew military secrets that Admirals didn't know. Well, I can't go into that."

"I can see our backgrounds are completely different. You grew up in a world of charade and chicanery." Hutch closed his book and pushed it aside. "You're full of knowledge you can't talk about." Hutch shrugged, and smirked enigmatically. "And I'm full of knowledge nobody cares about."

"But our attitudes are similar: ultimately, we're both seeking truth in our own ways—scientific truths as opposed to political truths."

"'Political truths' is another one of those 'morons'" Hutch opened a looseleaf binder and placed it across his lap. With a dark pencil he began to sketch the wreck of the *Awa Maru* while it was still fresh in his memory. The light angling in through the small port was sufficient for the task. "The problem with politicians is that they're people."

"Your scientific truth may not be much better. After all, truth is a matter of perspective."

"No, truth is a matter information. It changes not by will, but by the accumulation of further data. It evolves all by itself, and there's nothing we can do about it."

They both lapsed into silence. Ronnie turned the pages of her book with systematic regularity. Hutch built up a picture of the wreck as the details of his dive came to mind. He had no idea how much of it was important; or, indeed, if any of it was important. But his was a mold borne of scientific exactitude, and difficult to break out of. Knowledge did not always assume importance until the multifarious parts had been pieced into the framework of the whole. And often, the resulting product was not only unforseeable, but, in light of preconception, unacceptible.

*   *   *

When Hutch opened his eyes, the porthole was a dark circle of twinkling stars, like a sequin-covered mud pie. The boat creaked and groaned as the wooden hull worked itself in the ocean swells, and a loose piece of tackle tapped rhythmically against the cabin roof. The only other sound was the soft slap of water against the hull.

He dug his fists into his eyes and rubbed away the film that had coagulated on his contacts. When he rolled over, he found a sheet had been tucked around his body. The towel was a clump between his legs.

"Have a nice nap?" Ronnie's voice cooed out of the darkness from across the aisle, soft and melodic.

"I must have fallen asleep." He pushed himself up to a sitting position. Enough moonlight filtered through the screens for him to make out shapes in the gloom. "Thanks for the cover."

"How do you know it wasn't Cody who tucked you in?"

"I didn't have any nightmares."

"What *did* you have?"

"Just what you'd expect in the middle of the ocean: a wet dream."

"Would you like me to dry it for you?"

"Only if you use your body as a towel."

Hutch saw shadows move. Ronnie threw aside her own sheet and placed her feet on the deck. Without standing up fully, she swiveled around and placed her well formed derriere on Hutch's bunk. Her hand landed on his chest, and worked its way up to his throat, caressing.

"Cody was right. Our verbal shenanigans have got to find an outlet."

Hutch stiffened at her touch. "And what do you mean by that?"

Oh, just that you and I have the same thing on our minds, and as long as we're going to be together for a while, we may as well take advantage of the situation. I'm attracted to you, Hutch." Her fingernails scraped along the nape of his neck, sending tingles along his entire body. "It's frustrating being so close to you, and not being able to do anything about it. I propose we change that."

Hutch gulped, but the lump in his throat did not go away. "You don't beat around the bush, do you?"

White teeth glistened in the moonlight. "I'm leaving that for you."

"Yes, well, I sure must admit you have a way of coming right to the point."

"It's been a long time. But I can be demure without being bashful."

"I'm not sure I understand the difference. But since you're the language expert, I'll have to take your word for it."

Her hands were cool as they ran down his naked chest, tickled his abdomen. "I'm also adept at reading body language. Oh, my—it doesn't take much to translate *this*."

Hutch shuddered as she switched to braille. "Uh, Ronnie, don't you think we should talk about this first?"

"We've been talking about it for weeks."

"That isn't what I mean. After all, there are certain precautions we should—"

"Hutch, I'm more sophisticated than you give me credit for. I've kept up my medication."

"Ronnie, I'm talking about Cody."

She laughed softly, but with a ringing in her vocal chords that was not diminished by the damper of audibility. "It's okay. He understands."

"I'm not sure he does. But even so, he may walk in here and catch us in an—embarrassing situation."

Ronnie lay flat across his chest. Her bare breasts, nipples erect, dragged across his skin like twin plowshares. She kissed his lips, his cheek, his neck. "No, he won't."

Involuntarily, he placed his hands on her back, and massaged her delicate shoulders. "But you don't *know* that."

She slid her legs around so their bodies lay together lengthwise. "Yes, I do. I asked him to stay out."

Hutch ran his hands through her hair as she moved her mouth across his chest, kissing and biting. "But, what did you tell him?"

Now she was practically on top of him. "I told him we were going to make love."

"You what?"

She kissed him full on the lips, lingering, her tongue darting. "It's okay, Hutch. He understands."

"But, he *knows*—"

"He's not stupid. We couldn't very well hide if from him." She pulled him down by the shoulders, until he lay flat in the bunk. Then she rolled over on top of him. "Hutch, the first time's going to be fast. I can't control myself. Let's not hold back, and just get it over with. We'll take the next one slow and easy."

Hutch had no chance—or desire—to protest. Ronnie slid down over him and contracted her muscles with gripping tension. She seesawed her hips only twice, and he barely had time to arch against her, before he was out of control. He had only one moment of passion before it was over, although he kept up the motions until Ronnie, teeth gritted and gasping gutterally, eased up on him. The perspiration they developed between them in that scant number of seconds was hydrodynamic.

A long time later, he remembered to breathe. A *long* time later, his heart was still pounding.

Ronnie finally broke the lingering silence. "My mother always told me to be good. Was I?"

"You are a consummate undercover agent, and a mistress of many talents. Although sometimes your expertise frightens me."

"Why, Hutch, are you afraid of your fellow woman, too?"

"I am when she's a powerful personality who knows all about me, and when I don't know *any*thing about her."

"Would you feel safer if I told you that my background investigations on you were strictly factual? That there's nothing in your file that would guide me in predicting your emotional responses? Inside, you're pretty much of a mystery to me."

"It's nice to know I have some protection against your charms." Hutch continued to run his hands along her supple back. Her body was nicely contoured at the waist, and her buttocks were just round enough to be shapely without being ponderous. "And you are *very* much of a mystery to me."

"Why so? Because I'm a woman in a stereotypically male occupation?"

"No, because you don't seem to fit the guerrilla warfare image. Yet, you're out here with a guy who thrives on murder and mayhem."

"You should have more faith in him. He's a complicated individual, with none of the baser instincts of the average warrior. He's not a crusader, and he's not a cold-blooded killer. He's a highly patriotic and extremely reliable operative, as much of a craftsman in his trade as you are in yours. His motivations are strictly humanitarian. He's a true ethicist. But he *is* a survivor, and he'll do whatever is necessary to accomplish his mission and stay alive—in that order."

"Don't tell me he has a hollow tooth full of quick acting poison."

"Now *you've* been watching too much television. I'm just saying that he has a one-track mind. When he's on a mission, that mission is—his mission. And he goes at it with almost religious zeal. He's like a machine. And he won't stop until he finds—this thing, whatever it is we're looking for. To him, that's the most important thing in the world right now."

Hutch rubbed Ronnie's back mechanically. He stared up into the blackness of the overhead as if it were the center of the Universe. "*That* I can understand. If all these stories are true, and Peking man actually did find some evidence of a—visitation—it could shake the foundations of anthropology—of our entire concept of our place in the scheme of things. The implications are profound, to say the least."

He stopped rubbing, and froze into a position with his hands clasped behind her lower back. He drew her close, as if for comfort. "Ronnie, I'm scared by what we may uncover. If this—artifact—really exists—it may—tell us things we don't want to know. The secrets it may hold—transcend imagination."

Ronnie kissed him lightly on the neck, where her head was buried. She whispered into his ear, "Then you can begin to understand how it caused two antagonistic nations to set aside their differences in order to work together toward its rediscovery."

"What do you mean?"

"I mean, what do you think forced President Nixon to override two decades of broken diplomatic relations in order to establish a new relationship with a country with which we were technically at odds?"

"Ronnie, I've been so wrapped up my studies that I'm not always up to date on current events."

"Get your nose out of the books, Hutch. That's not current any more. You did know that the President went to China in 1972, didn't you."

"Well, yes—"

"And you knew that he met with Premier Chou En-lai and Chairman Mao Tse-tung?"

"I wasn't sure of the names—"

"And that they chose to meet, of all places, in Peking?"

Hutch was silent for a moment. "Now, *that's* interesting."

"No coincidence, either. Hutch, it was the People's Republic of China that opened negotiations for that meeting. The Chinese knew about the lost Peking man fossils, and of their importance in the course of human events. But *they* didn't have them, and they wanted *us* to help locate them."

"Because they thought the remains had been shipped to the States?"

"Or that they went down on the *Awa Maru*, in which case they needed positioning information from the log of the *Queenfish* to help them locate the wreck. When Nixon stated that his visit to Red China was 'the week that changed the world,' he wasn't talking about arms limitations or improved relations or the eventual establishment of embassies—he was talking about the importance of the artifacts that were excavated along with the Peking man fossils."

"You mean, this has been going on for all these years—"

"Yes, although not always at full scale. As bits and pieces of information surfaced, the search would become more intense, then wane and die off."

"Ronnie, I—I just don't understand. What do *you* expect to learn from these remains—these artifacts?"

She shrugged. "Whatever its secrets are, we're better off knowing them, and having the information to use, or not to use, as we see fit. Counterintelligence is somewhat like science. You pursue a branch of study, not knowing exactly where it may lead, but just because it seems interesting. After you make a discovery, you determine whether or not it has any value. Right now, we're just seeking. Later on, we'll try to justify the search."

*   *   *

When Hutch woke up again, he was curled up against Ronnie like a mated spoon, and he held one of her pendulous breasts in his hand. His kidneys ached something fierce. Very slowly, he disentangled himself from her body, slipped out from under the sheet, and climbed over her to get out of the bunk.

The second time had indeed been long and unhurried and, with the assurance that there would be no sophomoric withdrawal, more at ease. He had allowed himself to enjoy it, instead of merely completing the act in order to have it done before she changed her mind. Ronnie was not like that.

By the time he reached the head, he had another erection, and it was impossible to urinate. Sighing fatalistically, he scooped the towel off the deck and wrapped it around his middle. Cody was not in his bunk, nor was he topside in the galley. Hutch slipped outside into the cool night air. Now that the moon had set, the stars shone down with all their brilliance.

"Cody," Hutch whispered.

"Back here." The commando was lying down on the afterdeck aft of the helm.

Hutch padded across the damp teak. "Hey, have you been steering all this time?"

"We've been at anchor since nightfall—or haven't you noticed?"

"Uh, well, actually—"

"Never mind. I stepped down below decks and it was like a sweat house. The air's a lot more breathable up here. Besides, I can keep an eye on passing navigational lights."

The *G. Willie Makit* was completely blacked out, a condition illegal as well as unfavorable, since they could be run down in the dark.

The wind whipped through Hutch's hair. "Looks like we're in for some bad weather. Do you think this'll die down?"

"It's getting worse." Cody sat up, and wrapped the sheet around him a little tighter. "And the forecast isn't too good. I'd say we're in for a bit of a blow."

"Can we dive tomorrow?"

That's up to you. We're not too far from the wreck, but you're the diver."

Hutch humphed. "If you can anchor it, I can dive it."

"Yeah, well, we'll wait till daybreak before scudding back up north. If we try to run at night and we're spotted by that Chinese gunboat, they'll know we're up to something."

"If they saw the amount of electronic equipment and all these watertight cases they'd know it, too."

"We can refuse a boarding party. And I doubt seriously if they want to start an international incident by shooting at us. After all, they're supposed to be our allies."

Hutch was cooling off rapidly; the evaporative process left his body dry and comfortable. He stared upward, disoriented by the appearance of unfamiliar, southern constellations. "Listen, Cody, I'm sorry you got kicked out of your bunk. I didn't know—"

"Forget it. I told you I prefer it out here in the open. Always did. I just love sleeping out under the starlit, purple canopy. It's one of the few times I feel really at peace. Of course, when it comes to feeling a piece, you're a lot closer than I am."

"I'm embarrassed enough, I don't need your criticism."

"My, we're touchy;" Cody laughed cattily. "You ought to be feeling pretty high, right now. How'd it go?"

"Cody, I don't think it would be—gentlemanly—to talk about it."

"Sorry. I wasn't trying to be licentious. What I meant was, how do you feel about it. About her?"

Hutch blew out a large lungful of air, then inhaled deeply. "That's a good question. I don't think I've had much time to think about it."

"Then let me give you a word of advice: she's quite a femme fatale. Not that there's anything wrong with a healthy sexual appetite, as long as you know the source of the hunger. It sure relieves the tension. But she's pretty active. I don't want to say she sells common stock, but she's damn near incorporated. And she's checked more people into Heartbreak Hotel than Elvis Presley."

"She speaks more highly of you."

"That wasn't intended as an insult, just an observation. I've known her a lot longer than you have."

"In the Biblical sense?"

Cody laughed again, warmly. "No, we don't have that kind of relationship. We're partners, and that's all. Besides, I'm a happily married man, with three wonderful kids. I don't fool around."

"You don't strike me as a family man."

"You don't know all there is to know about me. You don't have the need to know."

"I know I can trust you."

"You *think* you can trust me. In this business, you learn not to have too much faith—in anything. You're only asking for disillusion. Being an agent means that everything is done with a purpose, and, on the baser side, for a dollar. There's no such thing as a free agent. We're all paid to perform."

"Not a very nice attitude."

"Don't get me wrong. There's a lot more to life than money: prestige, power, even, believe it or not, principle. You can be paid in many ways. I'm just cautioning you to keep your eyes open."

"Meaning . . . "

"Meaning, that you can screw around all you want. There's nothing wrong with it. You certainly don't have to worry about losing your virginity. But just understand what you're getting into. This is not a simple neighborhood gal you're playing around with; not even a college sophisticate. She's a temptress, and make no bones about it." Cody was not smiling, and his voice carried with it a timbre of solemnity. "My advice is: put your penis anywhere you want, But hang onto your heart or you're likely to undergo some surgery."

"I don't think you're being fair—"

"For the first time, I'm being completely honest with you. This is something you need to know. For the sake of this mission, I can't afford to have you fall apart because of an unrequited love affair. I'm just telling you to make sure you know the difference between the feeling in your groin and the feeling in your chest."

"Do you care about me, or the mission?"

"In this case, both. But the mission comes first."

Hutch nodded slowly. "It seems as if I've heard that before."

*   *   *

When Hutch got up the morning was late, the sun was high, and the sea was a churning maelstrom of whitecaps. Ronnie was no longer in the bunk with him. With a queasy feeling in the pit of his stomach he rolled out of bed, located a pair of shorts, and managed to get his feet into them. The sailboat was heeled over at an awkward angle that made the port bunks useless. The bow rose and fell like a broken rocking horse, and the boat crashed into the waves with bone jarring violence.

Groaning, he struggled up the steps into the galley. "I feel awful."

"A touch of *mal de mer*, dear?"

Hutch peered at Ronnie through half-opened eyes. "Seasickness in any other language feels the same." He clutched his stomach, bulged his cheeks like a stuffed chipmunk, and made a dash for the door. He made it to the teak gunwale in time to keep the decks clean, but a wave came up and splashed across him, and the wind swept the salt spray and his dinner back into his face. He lay for a long time hunched over the rail like a Raggedy Ann doll. He let the cool water wash him down.

"It must have been something you ate," Cody shouted into the freshening breeze, from his place at the helm.

Hutch turned his head and grimaced at the grinning maniac.

Cody stood with one foot on the deck, one braced against the starboard rail, and both hands held tightly onto the wheel. The sails were only partially reefed. He seemed like some mad sea captain, with his eyes glistening, and salt water pouring off his yellow sou'wester and matching oilskins.

Hutch crawled along the madly tilting deck and into the cabin. Ronnie tossed a large towel with a perfect arch: the terrycloth wrapped itself around his head. Hutch sat in the angle of the deck and lower cabinet, and dried off.

Ronnie checked the lashings on the aluminum waterproof cases stacked up against the port bulkhead. "The worst of it is over."

"Tell that to my stomach."

"I guess you don't want breakfast—or lunch. Cody has been collecting flying fish that flew in over the gunwale, so I could make some fresh sushi, Or, we have some canned octopus we picked up in—"

Hutch held up his hands. "Spare me the detailed bill of fare. How about some dramamine and a box of crackers?"

Ronnie lurched across the rolling deck without spilling a drop from the tall glass of water. "You look a little green around the gills."

"Thanks." He swallowed the pills, then started munching the crackers. "So what's the situation? Are we almost in port?"

Ronnie sat down beside him. "No. Cody's heading back for the wreck. He says this is the perfect time to make a clandestine dive because the weather will prevent surveillance craft from putting out to sea."

"Did he happen to mention that the weather might also sink us next to the *Awa Maru*?"

"This is an extremely seaworthy craft. I've been out on smaller boats and in worse conditions. We're not in any danger of sinking, unless we run into a typhoon."

"You make me feel so much better. If you don't need any help handling the lines, I'll just scrawl back into my bunk and pray for a quick death."

"Would you like me to join you?"

"I don't think I'd be much good to you."

Ronnie pulled on a slicker. "I'm disappointed. I thought you had more seaman in you than that. Maybe you'll feel better after a nap." She winked as she stood up, grabbed a handhold, and worked her way outside.

Hutch got up on wobbly legs and returned to his bunk. He dozed fitfully for a seeming eternity. More than once he had to dash for the head. After each bout he felt weaker. He forced more crackers down his throat, hoping to settle his stomach, and drank a little water to ward off dehydration. And still the boat pitched and yawed and slammed over the short, choppy swells.

Sleep was impossible. As he lay on the sheet the bow suddenly dropped away from under him, leaving him momentarily suspended in the air. He braced as his body started to fall, only to meet the bunk on the way up the next wave. He crashed down hard, then waited for it to happen again. Ad infinitum, ad nauseum, ad vomitus.

Somewhere in a dream resounded shouts of "Buoy! Buoy!" And after that he heard the rattle of chain links slipping over the roller. The sickening sidewise motion eventually eased off, but the fore and aft pounding continued.

"You look like death warmed over."

Hutch rolled over and squinted through pain-filled eyes. "Please, take one of those guns and shoot me."

Ronnie tsk-tsked and shook her head. "I can't do that. I need you."

"Again?"

"Once you crack the dam you can't expect to hold back the water."

"Please, I'm in no mood for aphorisms."

"Then how about a simple truism: the sooner you get in, the sooner we can move on."

"Back to Okinawa?"

Ronnie shook her head.

"Would it be revealing too much of the future to ask where?"

"The Philippines, for provisions, then on to Borneo and the *Gremyashchi*."

Hutch leaped suddenly out of his bunk, fumbled with the latch of the head, and barely got his mouth over the bowl before he started retching. He was still groveling on his knees, with his hands wrapped tightly around the seat, when Cody climbed into the cabin.

"Is he still riding the china chalice? Hey, hot stuff, we're anchored. Are you ready to go down?"

Hutch spit the last particles out of his mouth. "I hate boats."

"What? I thought you liked the idea of a long ocean voyage to exotic lands."

"I've changed my mind since then—and my stomach. If I never, ever again in my life, see another boat, it'll be too soon. They're just necessary evils required to get to the wreck sites. How far do we have to go?"

"All the way to the other side of the South China Sea: about fifteen hundred miles. Nautical miles, of course. We'll make landfall in Manila Bay in about a week if the wind keeps up."

Hutch slithered across the deck and back to his bunk. He sat on the edge next to Ronnie who smoothed his hair back over his forehead. "Then what?"

Cody removed his sou'wester and shook off the water. "By that time we'll have quite a few targets to check out. I've got a couple of boats disguised as fishing trawlers but crammed with side-scanning sonar gear dragging towfish all over the west coast of Borneo. Rumor has it that the Russians were smuggling the Peking man remains out of Shanghai in 1946.

The *Gremyashchi* was a tramp steamer en route to Yalta when her steering gear broke down. She drifted for a couple days while her men made repairs. Unfortunately, as they warped on a new course within sight of the mainland, the ship scraped over an uncharted rock and tore the bottom out of her. She went down in twenty minutes.

"No one went down with the ship, but some forty sailors, including several women, got off on rafts and lifeboats. The lucky ones floated out to sea, and a few survived the thirst and equatorial heat until they were picked up by a passing British frigate about ten days later. They said the tips of the masts were still sticking out of the water the last they saw the ship. Probably means we're looking at a depth of about a hundred to a hundred and twenty feet."

Hutch drank deeply from the bottle of electrolyte that Ronnie handed him. "And what happened to the unlucky ones?"

"Oh, they made it ashore—and were never heard from again. Probably killed by headhunters: the wild men of Borneo, you know."

"Here, eat something. It'll fill your stomach." Ronnie pressed a sandwich into Hutch's hand. "And you *do* need your strength."

He grimaced, but took a small bite. "Thanks for dribbling out the info."

Cody grabbed the sandwich and took a large bite, then handed it back. "Can you get dressed now so we can get this road on the show?"

"I don't know if you've noticed, but I'm not feeling too—"

"I don't care. I told you, you can do anything you want, as long as you don't curtail the efficiency of this mission. Now, we got Japanese processing ships in the vicinity, and enough trawlers to walk on from here to Taipei without getting your feet wet. Everybody and his grandmother must know we're out here, and before the Japs start screaming that we're disturbing a war memorial, I want to get this check-up over with."

"Cody, if the Chinese did pull a fast one, and found what you're looking for on the *Awa Maru* without sharing the secret, what do you expect me to find down there?"

"I just want to know how extensive their salvage operation was. A cursory examination, just so we have the information. We can't trust the Reds, and you know it."

"But if they worked this wreck for two months with saturation divers—"

"Just do it, and tell me what you see."

"But, I'm not going to be able to find anything they overlooked—"

"*All right!*" Cody screamed. He threw his sou'wester down hard on the deck. "All right. There's a reason."

After a long, embarrassing silence, Hutch took another bite of the ham and cheese. "And what is it?"

Cody sighed, and rolled his eyes with exasperation. "You know there's an intelligence leak. You know somebody's out to scuttle this operation.

Okay, so we know the Chinese already did a thorough job on the *Awa Maru*. And through our intelligence network we know they didn't find a damn thing—unless we're being fed wrong information. Maybe they've got the artifact so far under wraps it'd take a mole to dig it up. I don't know. What we do know is that they're onto us.''

"Who are 'they'?''

"The enemy. Everybody who isn't us. Do you want this explanation, or don't you?''

Hutch shrugged, and ate some more of the sandwich. It was beginning to taste good.

"They expect us to look here because none of the other wrecks have been identified. So this is where we start. But this phase of the mission is a decoy. We know we're under observation. So, we set up a crack surveillance team to watch whoever comes out to spy on us. We need to get the rats out of the woodwork before we can get on with the real search.''

"Watchers for the watchers.''

Cody displayed open palms. "It's all part of the business.''

"And a dirty business, at that.'' Hutch finished the sandwich and swished down the breadcrumbs with more electrolyte. "Why not just hang in here for an hour or two, as long as it would take to make the dive?''

"Because it's like teeing off at golf, or bowling a ball, or continuing to lead the duck after you've fired: it's part of the motion. Just do it.''

Hutch sighed heavily. "All right, let's get it over with.''

In the upper cabin he climbed into his wetsuit, then worked his way out to the pitching, holystoned deck. He rigged his regulators on a set of doubles, and slung the tanks onto the transom. Ronnie held them upright while he slipped into the nylon harness and cinched down the D-rings.

"Careful.'' Ronnie grabbed him as he nearly slid across the boat when a nasty roller swept broadside under the hull.

Cody tied a half-inch line to the bow and dragged it back along the starboard side. "There's a bit of a current, so you can pull yourself up forward on the geriatric line.''

"Thanks.'' Hutch performed a last minute check on his gauges, sucked off each regulator, donned his mask and fins, and nodded. "If I'm not back in an hour, send down a rescue party.''

"You're on your own, pal. You'll never get *me* underwater.''

Hutch rolled over the side with the rope gripped tightly. He pulled himself along until he reached the anchor line, then transferred and started his descent. It was a relief to get below the surface, where the storm did not reach, and where the water did not undulate. He slid quickly down to the bottom. The visibility was even better than before, and he saw the wreck a long time before he reached the broken hull plates. This time the grapnel was hooked on the intact bow, around the winch and hawse pipes.

By the time Hutch checked his air pressure and tested his regulators, he was four minutes into the dive, most of it descent time. Then he noticed that the grapnel lay free on the bottom, and that only the anchor chain lying over the windlass drum was holding the boat in place. He pressed his hand up against the steel links while he looked around for someplace to snag the curved tines, but a surface surge yanked the boat upward and stretched the anchor line taut, and snapped it off its precarious perch.

The surface current dragged the boat away, and with it the grapnel. The steel tines caught on Hutch's pressure hose, whipped him around upside down, and dragged him off the wreck and across the sand. His mask was dislodged, letting water under the face seal and into his eyes. He closed his lids to save his contacts.

With one hand he gripped the chain and pulled, releasing the tension on the grapnel. With the other he grabbed the tines and deftly unsnagged it from his hose. Lying on his side, he opened his uppermost eye and saw that the wreck was still in sight, some fifty feet away. He held tightly onto the grapnel. He could easily have aborted the dive, and returned to the safety of the boat. But he desperately wanted to complete his task and leave the wreck for good.

His decision made, he tossed away the grapnel. He drew his knees under him and got upright so he could blow the water out of his mask. When he was able to see clearly, the grapnel was gouging furrows through the sand as the boat dragged down current. Not even breathing hard, Hutch kicked out for the wreck.

The bow section, coming to a point, was structurally the most stable portion of a ship. It lay on its side with the deck machinery still firmly attached. Hutch looked into the chain locker. His dive light illuminated the interior. Thousands of densely packed, silvery fish about two inches long filled the cavernous room. As he swung his light around, the baitfish skittered out of its path with such speed that he appeared to be cutting through the school with a laser beam, as if the fish had been disintegrated. Jokingly, he carved a Z for Zorro through the mass; it remained for several seconds before the tiny fish slowly filled in the blank spaces.

The bow was broken off about seventy-five feet aft of the point. From there on the wreck was pretty much as Hutch had seen it coming forward from the stern: the hull was a tangle of wreckage that had the appearance of having been dynamited. The debris field was nonexistent.

Before extending his explorations any further, Hutch removed his emergency decompression reel from the back of his tanks, found a suitable place to tie off, and attached a liftbag to the end. The only thing he wanted to lift was the line, so he could use it to ascend to his decompression stops. The orange bag, too, would act as a marker buoy so those on the *G. Willie Makit* would know where he was.

A long puff of air from his regulator started the liftbag upward, unreeling the line off his carefully wrapped reel with ever increasing speed as the air in the bag expanded from the lessening pressure. When it finally stopped, he slashed off the sisal with his knife, and tied the end to a convenient beam. With ten minutes to spare, he continued on his dive.

He came across a pile of brass shell casings, definite contraband on a hospital ship, but nothing much more. Without realizing he had gone so far, he reached the first boiler. That meant he had passed right over the bridge wreckage without noticing it. He turned around and bent his fins into the current.

Trending away from the hull, Hutch circled the area that should have been a debris field from the bridge. What he saw instead was pure white sand in a deep depression that went down to a depth of almost two hundred twenty feet. Here and there a stray piece of metal protruded from the pit, and he found the broken stub of a human femur. Other than that, there was nothing.

He was nineteen minutes into the dive by the time he returned to his tied off line. He began his ascent, continuing to look down at the excavation. Not much of the *Awa Maru* still existed in the form of a ship. And, in a few more years, in the destructive chemical action of the sea, it would flatten out to little more than a pile of oxidized iron. Man's artifices did not long outlive their loss.

Hutch stopped at sixty feet for a minute, then went up to fifty. The current was still strong, and it had pulled the liftbag some ten feet below the surface. But with a physiological ceiling over his head, he could do nothing about it. Twenty minutes later, when he reached the ten foot level, he took his regulator out of his mouth, pushed in the purge, and put more air into the bag.

This close to the surface, the swells reached down with sickening fingers. Hutch felt his stomach turning, and his seasickness returning. He closed his eyes and tried to relax. He swallowed hard. But it was no use. Eventually, the undulating motion got to him, and he felt the upheaval coming. There was nothing to do but hang onto the line, hold the regulator in his mouth, and vomit through the mouthpiece.

His body doubled over with the effort. The particles passed through the valve and out the exhaust ports, surrounding his head with a yellow cloud of partially digested ham, cheese, and bread. Tiny fish darted in and out of the cornucopia, snatching up tasty morsels. Tears formed in Hutch's eyes. The minutes ticked by slowly.

By the time his decompression was over, he had recovered from the stomach wrenching onslaught. He usually felt better after throwing up. He held onto the top of the bobbing liftbag, trying to see the boat in the six foot seas. He had only a brief moment of vision from the crest before falling into the trough. He was torn away from the bag by the pounding seas. He ducked his head back into the water, and kicked hard until he regained his handhold on the short leader. Then, he waited until he was pushed up onto a crest; quickly he scanned the horizon in the direction he was facing.

He did this over and over, but could not find the boat. With its tall sails it should be easy to spot. When he determined that it was not close by, he concentrated his gaze down current. Still, he cold see nothing but an endless ocean and a field of white caps blown off by the wind.

His stomach tightened into a knot. He was alone.

For five minutes he spun around crazily at every wave crest, but there was nothing to see. Certainly, the sailboat had drifted off when the grapnel pulled loose. But that was an hour ago, and Cody should have discovered it immediately, and come back to hover around waiting for him to come up.

Hutch's mind filled with presumptions of the worst kind. Was the battery dead? Did the starter malfunction? Was the engine out of order? Had the sails ripped free, or broken the masts? Had the boat capsized in a sudden squall? Or, had the sailboat been blown out of the water by one of their many adversaries?

A half hour later, Hutch was no closer to an answer. In order to conserve the precious bit of air left in his tanks, he reached for the snorkel attached to his mask strap and swung the mouthpiece into his mouth. He inflated his BC so he was riding high.

He was weakening rapidly. There was no possibility of swimming to shore: the tiny Chinese island of Niu-Shan Tao was fifteen or twenty miles away, and it was twice that to the larger Hai-T'an Tao. There was no likelihood at all of surviving long enough to make landfall. His only hope was to maintain station on the wreck site, and wait. And pray.

When his arms could no longer take the strain, he cut a ten foot piece of line from his reel, tied it with great effort in the bouncing seas to the liftbag clip, and attached it to his tank harness. Then, he lay face down with his mask in the water, and inhaled through the snorkel. He had to blow hard before every breath, because the waves rolled over his head and filled up the plastic tube.

He tried to quell his anxiety, but every five minutes Hutch rolled up to a vertical position, swung around facing down current, and peered futilely for sails on the horizon. His stomach heaved a few times, but nothing came up except stinging bile.

The sun was low, and half hidden behind a ring of dark clouds. Hutch made up his mind that at nightfall he would drop his tanks and weightbelt. He *might* be able to survive the night—although, for what purpose, he did not know.

The seas were short and choppy, and large whitecaps broke all around him. One huge whitecap bore down upon him. He sucked in a quick breath and waited for the water to cascade over his snorkel. But the wave stayed there, tall and unwavering, without breaking. Finally, he had to breathe. He gasped for air, wondering why the wall of water did not descend.

Then he heard the shout. He focused his eyes, and saw the billowing white sail luffing in the wind. His heart rejoiced. He waved first, then patted the top of his head: the diver's hand signal that he was okay. A moment later the boat pulled up abeam, and Ronnie flipped the aluminum ladder over the side. Hutch cut himself free, and severed the down line as well.

Cody let go the boom so the sail went with the wind. As the boat lost headway, Hutch grabbed onto the stanchion and got his knees on the lower rung. Ronnie pulled him up by the double tank valve. He was never so grateful to swing his long legs over the rail. Wobbly from exhaustion and the after effects of adrenaline, he collapsed to the deck in a heap.

Ronnie pulled the liftbag aboard. "Hutch, I was worried sick about you."

"*You* were sick? I've been puking my guts out for the past hour. Where the hell have you been?"

Cody quickly pulled the straps through the D-rings and released Hutch from his gear. "Sorry about the delay, but the grapnel must have snagged the buoy line. I kept seeing the float off to port, so I thought we were still on the wreck. We were looking for your bubbles for a long time before I noticed the loran numbers were way off. Are you okay?"

"I am now. But I was sure scared as hell. I thought I was going to have to spend the night."

"I wouldn't leave you—not without the information."

Hutch scowled good naturedly. "Thanks." He was so happy to be aboard he could have kissed Cody, and was willing to tolerate every obnoxious remark the commando could make.

"Get him something to drink. So, what did you find out?"

"That Chinese salvage team did a hell of a job. After all these years, there's still a huge hole in the sand where the bridge used to be. I don't know whether they got any gold, but they removed every scrap of material that could have resembled Peking man or his artifacts. If there was anything there to find, they found it."

Cody shrugged. "They recovered over a hundred and fifty bodies—or body parts—which they turned over to the Japs. I guess all the bones they got weren't Oriental."

Ronnie appeared with a bottle of vegetable juice. "I'm just glad you're okay."

Hutch gratefully accepted the bottle, and did not mind the red liquid pouring out of the too large opening and down his cheeks and neck. He gasped, then drank some more. "This has been a hell of a day. But that's one experience you can't get watching boob tube."

The *Ting-Yuen*

1949

(The following is an extract from "The Peking papers.")

"Mankind has been plying the seven seas for thousands of years, littering the bottom with ships and cargoes that depict his maritime past in painstaking detail. Indeed, his entire history is written on the ocean floor: a vast book waiting only to be opened, and read."

The captain peered throught the black, leather gripped binocular, while his lips curled in disdain. "They are gaining on us."

The Chinaman nodded grimly. "Tell your men to follow my instructions."

Slowly, the binoculars left the grim face. Dark, piercing eyes stabbed out of flesh that was drawn tight as stretched leather. "There will be loss of life."

"It is a burden I must bear."

"Quite the contrary. It is a burden *they* must bear. You have the right to do as you please with your own life. You do *not* have the right to forfeit the lives of others."

Sunken cheeks and pale skin displayed no sign of emotion. "A military commander performs such a duty all the time. There is never a question of right or wrong, only one of necessity."

"And is it a necessity that you scuttle my vessel?"

The dark-haired head did not move, the eyes did not blink. But there was a faint intake of breath. "Yes."

"And your precious art treasures?"

The Chinaman did not nod. He stared out the bridge window at the oncoming destroyer. "They must go, too."

"You must sink this ship, drown those men, sacrifice your collection of antiquities—all to mask the existence of one lead-lined box? What are you transporting that can have such import?"

"It is better that you do not know."

"Is it uranium? Or an atomic bomb? Is that what you are smuggling?"

The Chinaman directed his gaze at the captain. "I think you had better attend to your duties, Captain. You understood the possibilities before we left port. We cannot allow the communists to have this cargo, and that is all you need to know. Better that it be consigned to the sea than it fall into the wrong hands. Now, would you please give the order?"

The captain stared into the deep, reflective pools of the Chinaman's eyes, but they did not soften. They were adamantine, formed by tremendous pressure. "If I can show them my papers, they might be dissuaded from boarding."

"We cannot afford to take that chance. Please give the order."

The captain waited a full minute before turning to his bridge watch and initiating the defense plan. Within seconds, a trained gun crew readied the gunboat's main armament, a three inch bow gun, while marines manned machine guns along the rails. Below decks, sailors opened the seacocks in the engine room. The ship was preparing for its last battle.

The speedy destroyer steamed up quickly from the stern. Black smoke disgorged from her funnels. A puff of smoke from her bow was followed by the whining of a warning shot which passed lengthwise over the *Ting-Yuen*, very high. The shell exploded harmlessly in the sea several hundred yards away.

The helmsman swung the wheel to port. As the gunboat tacked, the gun crew swiveled the deck gun until its barrel sighted right alongside the port bridgewing. The explosion of powder sent a shell whistling toward the destroyer. It fell far short, sending up a spray of water which for a moment obscured the communist warship. The captain ordered the ship hard astarboard, and full speed ahead.

The destroyer must not have been expecting return fire, for its guns were silent for a long time. The *Ting-Yuen* fired off another round on the starboard tack before the destroyer responded. Again the shot passed well overhead, while the destroyer nearly reached the position of the falling gunboat shot. The spume of water rose off to the side, spraying the decks.

The destroyer charged ahead. Twin puffs attested to the firing of both bow guns. This time the shots fell short, exploding aft of the quickly maneuvering gunboat. The *Ting-Yuen* swung to port just as two more blasts left the destroyer. The singing shells straddled the gunboat. Hot shrapnel pounded the steel hull, and chunks of metal the size of orange peels tore through the superstructure of the bridge.

· The Chinaman fell back with the implosion of glass. The wind whooshed through the holed bulkheads. The bridge was a shambles of splintered wood, torn cables, and broken tiles still raining down from the overhead. The helmsman was a bloody pulp nearly decapitated. The captain squirmed on the deck like an epileptic, reaching for his back where steel shards had sliced away his jacket and shirt and most of his skin. The Chinaman scrabbled to his side, held his head in his hands.

Bubbles frothed on the captain's lips. The eyes fluttered open for a moment. His throat gurgled as he spoke haltingly. "This—is—what—you—wanted?"

The Chinaman swallowed hard. "No. I would have had it otherwise. But this is the way it must be."

The captain's mouth moved. He struggled for air, coughed, and spit out a clot of mucus and blood. He inhaled again, but the eyelids slowly closed, and his body went limp. Reverently, the Chinaman placed the captain's head on the debris of the deck. The moment of silence was broken by the screams outside. The gun crew scampered for the protected side as the *Ting-Yuen* lost speed and the destroyer pulled up to starboard.

When the Chinaman looked out the doorless bridge, he saw the destroyer's rails lined with marines. They were returning the gunfire from the gunboat, and very quickly put down all resistance by sheer fire power. The screams of the injured wafted across the after deck like howling banshees. A boarding party got ready its boat on the destroyer's upper deck.

The *Ting-Yuen* was settling, but not fast enough. If the People's Republic marines acted with speed and surety, they could close the seacocks before the gunboat could sink. The big guns no longer discharged. Only the occasional crackling of small arms shattered the calm air. The destroyer's broad side loomed over the bridgewing of the gunboat. The boat was swung out, and sailors prepared to leap over the sides right down onto the *Ting-Yuen's* deck.

The Chinaman saw only one chance to sink his ship. He ran back inside, grabbed the spokes of the helm, and spun it hard astarboard, directly into the path of the oncoming destroyer. The unexpected maneuver caught the destroyer off guard. The tall, knifelike bow rammed into the gunboat broadside, abaft the bridge. Its speed and momentum carried it through the outer hull with a long, rasping crunch of shrieking steel.

The *Ting-Yuen* heeled over under the impact. The Chinaman was thrown from his stance. He skidded along the steeply sloping deck along with the helmsman's body and piles of cascading debris. The whole conglomeration slid out the port bridgewing, which had been blown off where the pelorus had stood. The ocean was strewn with flotsam and screaming sailors. The Chinaman crashed into the sea.

The destroyer continued to push the *Ting-Yuen* sideways, like a bulldozer shoving a downed tree. The Chinaman was sucked under the careening hull. His body crashed first into the bilge keel, then was raked along the main keel. Because of the port list he missed the starboard bilge keel. Miraculously, he bobbed up to the surface on the other side of the hull. He was immediately run down by the destroyer's starboard side, but it was only a glancing blow on the head. Disoriented from his underwater passage, numb from concussion, he lay half dead in the water while the destroyer still thundered ahead. His body dragged the entire length of the long warship, pummeling him into insensibility.

Just when he thought the worst of it was over, he was caught in the wash of the madly whirling propellers. He was sucked under the fantail. He had a fleeting image of being buffeted by solid walls of water, then his body was spun violently in the maelstrom of the bronze blades like a baby in the surf. He was slammed against the massive rudder. Sharp barnacles sliced his skin with the ease of a cheese grater.

Then he was spit out behind the ship. He floated up to the surface along with the mascerated bodies and churned up flotsam from the gunboat. The surface of the sea was stained with blood, littered with debris. He grabbed onto a timber, the rounded after cargo boom, and pulled his pain racked body onto it like a turtle in the sun.

Weakened though he was, lying with the waves washing over his face, he watched the demise of the *Ting-Yuen*. He had gone unseen because all the ship's personnel lined the destroyer's port rail, or were crowded onto the warship's bow. The two vessels separated as the destroyer finally brought its forward motion to a halt. The gunboat rolled back upright, but as water gushed in through the mangled opening in the hull, it kept right on going the other way.

Now the destroyer backed off as it reversed engines propelled it away. The *Ting-Yuen* heeled to about forty-five degrees. As water poured over the longitudinal bulkhead and flooded the opposite side, it gradually returned to a vertical position. But when it did, its decks were awash. With water gurgling from skylights and hatches, it slowly slipped beneath the calm surface of the Yellow Sea.

Eventually, the destroyer took off on a new course.

The ocean was littered with wood, hatch covers, life rings, and bodies held up by orange kapok vests. The Chinaman floated aimlessly, delirious and seriously injured, and closer to death than to life. But he cared not what happened to him, as long as his terrible secret was safe from the warlike annals of mankind.

Salt burned his wounds like acid. The sun beat down unmercifully. He licked dry, chapped lips. His tongue was swollen, and clotted his throat like a wad of cotton. Yet, despite his suffering, life seemed inconsequential. He had done all he could. Failure was not his, but that of his fellow man.

As he had once promised to another who had commanded him on his deathbed, he had discharged his duty. Now, at least, he could die in peace—but not without regret.

The *Gremyashchi*

"What is it? What have you got?"

Hutch handed the line to Ronnie, then took the regulator out of his mouth. "It's a bell. It's the ship's bell."

"Oh, Hutch. That's wonderful."

Cody took the line from her and pulled the liftbag to the side of the boat. "Hell's bells. This ain't any goddamn souvenir hunt."

Hutch clambered up the ladder, and tossed his mask into his gear bag. "Cody, don't you know they put names on bells? What better way to identify the wreck."

"Does it look like the *Gremyashchi*?"

"As nearly as I could tell from photographs, yes. The damned thing is sitting perfectly upright, like it was in dry dock. The wheelhouse is gone, but the other decks are intact." He shrugged out of his tanks and fins. "I counted the bow portholes just in case."

"All right, let's get it aboard."

Ronnie snubbed the safety line on a cleat. "How heavy is it?"

"I used a two hundred fifty pound bag, but it was only a third full when it left the bottom."

"Hell, that's nothing." Cody grabbed the top of the liftbag and hauled it straight up. But as soon as the bell cleared the surface, its weight was no longer supported by the water. He almost dropped it.

Ronnie said, "Careful not to scratch the paint."

"Let me get a hand on it." Hutch took a handful of plastic material, and together they manhandled the bronze, thickly encrusted object onto the deck. Huge fan corals completely masked the shape.

"My god, does everything look like that underwater?"

"Sure. What did you think, it looks like the picture? After you've been diving a while, you learn to recognize things. I had to chop coral for ten minutes just to be sure this thing *was* a bell. The marine growth around here is fantastic, full of color and—"

"Spare me the graphic description and guided tour. Just give me your hammer."

Hutch slipped the three pound sledge out of the loop on his weight belt, and handed it to the commando. Then he dropped the belt as well. Cody pounded on the bell, smashing coral and barnacles without abandon.

"Cody, you'll nick it," Ronnie said.

"So what?" He pounded even harder, completely oblivious of the worms and miniature starfish moving sluggishly through the grosser encrustation. In a short while his face, arms, and striped yachtsman's shirt were speckled with black chunks of mud and pieces of shell. "I just want to see the goddamn name."

"Well, now, not every bell had the name on it ..." Hutch started.

Three quarters of the surface was cleaned, and still no name was visible. Cody never slackened the pace. The veins in his forearms stuck out like writhing snakes as he wielded the hammer. His hands were filthy black.

"There's a letter," Ronnie shouted.

Cody slacked off for a moment. "Yeah, but, I don't recognize it."

"That's because it's Cyrillic."

"Uh-oh," Hutch uttered. "Ronnie, is Russian part of your repertoir?"

"Are you kidding," Cody laughed. "She can read, write, and speak the lingo better than Dostoyevsky."

"It's an 'I'. Chip over here where the word should begin."

Cody hammered away. Chunks of coral broke away with each blow, revealing the smooth, silvered surface beneath the encrustation.

"That's it. It's a 'G.'"

Cody slammed steel to bronze. "All *right*. Way to go."

"That's an 'R.' That's an 'O.'"

"O'? Are you sure?" Hutch said. "There's no 'O' in *Gremyashchi*."

"And that's an 'M.'"

"There's only room for one more letter."

"'K.'" The single word was arched across the bell. "G–R–O–M–K–I. Gromki. The *Gromki*?"

Hutch uttered the geologist's epithet. "Schist. You mean I found the wrong Russian freighter?"

Cody's grin was a broad white swath across his face. "I wish I could lie to you, but I can't keep it in. *Gromki* was the original name of the *Gremyashchi*. This is the right wreck, all right. You hit pay dirt."

"All *right*." Hutch screamed, and did a jig on the teak deck. "Two weeks, ten wrecks, and more rock piles than I care to remember. I was beginning to think this thing didn't exist."

"This calls for a celebration." Ronnie stepped into the cabin. "I'll get the champagne." She came out with an unopened bottle and three crystal glasses. She popped and poured, and touched her glass to each of the others. "*Nostrovia.*"

They all drank heartily.

It was too late in the day to make another dive, so they relaxed and had dinner, cooked by Cody, on the afterdeck. The fish of the day was blue spotted argus, a type of grouper. He had caught it on rod and reel while Hutch had been checking out a depth sounder target that morning. Unfortunately, bottom recorders could not distinguish between steel and rock. But the fishing had been excellent.

Afterwards, Cody rummaged through the many waterproof storage cases in the forward compartment, and brought one out while they were sipping brandy. "I want you to take this down with you tomorrow."

The sun was setting behind low-lying clouds, sending varicolored beams across the western sky. The ocean was so quiet, so peaceful. The sailboat rode softly on the gentle swells.

Hutch studied the clear plastic case and the instrument inside. "It looks like a—a Geiger counter."

"Give the boy a star. I had this case specially made for it. It's got no control handles, so it has to be turned on before you clamp down the lid. Just keep an eye on the dial."

"Are we looking for radiation?"

Cody shrugged. "You never know." He took out the instrument and a shielded test piece. The counter clicked noisily whenever the radium tab passed in front of the induction tube.

"You're right, *I* never know. But *you* usually do. What is it this time? What do you know that you aren't telling me?"

"I know that we're dealing with an unknown quantity." Cody greased the rubber o-ring, replaced the unit, and sealed it tight. He checked all around to make sure the o-ring was seated properly. "We don't know what this thing is, and we don't know where it came from."

"But what makes you think it's radioactive?"

"I didn't say it was. I said it might be. And if it is, I want to know about it before you get cooked."

"Cody, you're deeper than a coelacanth. I'll take it, but we're going to have to make some modifications on it."

"Why?"

"With all that air space, the thing'll float like a cork. We'll have to add some lead weights to it to make it neutrally buoyant. Then, I'm going to have to strap a light to it. The case is too cumbersome to hold in one hand, and I need to carry a light so I can go inside."

"Can I go with you?" Ronnie sat up in the lounge chair. "How deep is it?"

"One-forty to the sand, but the main deck's at one-ten. I was going to ask you anyway. When I go into the corridors to check out the rooms, I'd like to have a backup.''

"She made that dive to one-fifty last week," Cody said. "So she won't have any trouble. I'll be glad to stay topside.''

"I was sure you would." Hutch finished the last of his brandy. "Whew, I don't think I need another one of these. I'm bushed as it is.''

"If we want to get an early start in the morning, we should get to bed soon." Ronnie drained her own glass. "You think?''

Cody huffed. "I think if you two want to get to sleep by midnight, you'd better get started now." He dabbed some insect repellent behind his ears. "You can leave me out here in the weather.''

Ronnie laughed. "You love it out here, and you know it.''

"All right, but try to be quiet.''

"Beast. Hutch?''

Hutch kept his eyes averted from Cody as he followed Ronnie into the cabin. "That guy is incorrigible. And a lot of other things, too. Hey, I'm all for a quick shower. Want to join me?''

"I'll scrub your back if you'll scrub mine.''

*   *   *

When Hutch woke up during the night, Cody was in his bunk but Ronnie was not in hers. The temperature was too hot for sleeping together, so Ronnie and Hutch usually slept separately after making love. He found her in the galley, typing on a lap-top computer situated on the table. The only light came from the miniature screen and a couple of red power switches.

"Burning the midnight oil?''

Ronnie practically jumped out of her seat. "Oh! You startled me." She powered down the computer, flipped some other switches, and packed up the storage case with its other electronic components.

Hutch pushed aside some loose wires and antenna leads, and sat down opposite her. "Are *you* hiding things from me, too?''

She smiled. "Hardly. The heat was keeping me awake, so I figured I may as well get these reports out of the way. And because of the humidity, I like to keep these watertight cases closed whenever I'm not using the equipment. Water is hell on the electronic circuits, and we're a long way from a repair shop.''

Hutch nodded. "I couldn't sleep either. I kept tossing and turning, but not from the heat. Ronnie, I'm—excited—about what we may find. But I'm also a little worried about Cody's sudden concern for radiation.''

"Oh, it's not so sudden. We've had the Geiger counters on board ever since we left Okinawa. We just never had any use for them until now.''

"And no reason to tell me I might be swimming into a gallery full of shooting electrons.''

"Hutch, don't take everything so personally.''

"But you're not telling me the whole story."

"It's not my job. Just like intelligence work is not yours."

"I would think after all these weeks—after what you and I have been through—and what we mean to each other—that you'd at least have the courtesy to—"

"Hutch, please, don't make something out of this that isn't there."

"And what's that supposed to—"

"Hutch, listen to me. We're dealing with a concept that is literally out of this world. We have no idea what this thing is, or what it can do. It might—"

"What do you mean, what it can do? Do you expect it to get up and walk away. It's a half a million years old, at least."

Ronnie wagged her head. "Listen to me, will you? It's an alien artifact. It came from outer space. And out there, without the protective envelope of atmosphere, hard radiation is incredibly intense: from the sun, from the stars, from who knows what else. At the very least, it's been bombarded by cosmic rays."

"Well, I never really thought—"

"But I'll tell you more. This artifact—"

"Wait a minute. You keep saying 'this artifact,' as if there's only one. I thought there was a whole collection?"

"Yes, but one is of particular importance, because it might be intact—a complete unit. The cylinder you saw in the pictures is not in pieces like the rest of the objects. It's not just discarded junk—or, at least, we don't think it is."

"Hmmn, I never considered—"

"And remember where this thing came from. Any visitation to this planet had to have been made by beings not just from another planet within our solar system, but from another part of the Galaxy. Hutch, whatever these artifacts are, they came from a civilization as far advanced from us as we are from—the amoeba. Well, perhaps the dinosaur. We don't know. But whoever brought them here, carried them across the cosmos. What we're looking for are—parts of a starship."

Hutch leaned back against his seat. He stared out the windows and looked up at the Milky Way. Each pinpoint of light was a celestial body, the possible abode of some super civilization that had been traversing the Universe when man was—not yet man.

"So if it crashed, and it ran on some kind of atomic drive—"

Ronnie reached out and placed a comforting hand on his. "Then it could be the most important find in the history of man."

* * *

The sun had barely cleared the lush, jungle treetops when Hutch started putting his gear together. He donned a shorty suit that left his arms and legs exposed: all that was necessary in the warm, equatorial water.

"Now, remember, there's a pretty good surge down there, so be careful you don't get banged up."

Cody winced. "Can you leave that stuff for night time?"

"Why is your mind always in the gutter?" Ronnie slipped a rubber vest over her red bikini. She slipped a large, lethal-looking knife into the sheath on her calf. "Hutch, what kind of shark was that you saw yesterday?"

"It was all by itself, so it must have been a Lone Shark. But you'll have more trouble with the Sergeant Majors. They're as thick as flies, and they nip at everything: hair, skin, loose strings on your trunks, and the cuffs of your gloves."

"Are they the ones with the dark vertical stripes?"

"Yes. The ones with epaulets on the lateral fins are Lieutenant Colonels."

Cody helped Ronnie strap on her tanks. "You just be careful when you go inside this wreck. I don't want it collapsing on you."

Hutch threw his tanks over his shoulders and let them slip down his back. "Cody, the probability of that happening is a million to one. That wreck's been down there for decades, and we'll only be inside for half an hour. Use one of your formulas to figure it out. If any bulkheads were ready to go, they'd have done it during the last big storm—not when we're diving."

"Just don't get rammy. You have too much self confidence for my tastes."

Hutch connected his BC. "It's all an act. I'm scared anytime I'm underwater—especially on *this* mission. Fear is what keeps me from being too bold, and getting into situations I can't get out of."

Ronnie stood up, ready to go. "Besides. This time he's got a buddy."

"Sure. That way, in case of a shark attack, there's a fifty-fifty chance it'll go after her instead of me."

Ronnie showed teeth in an exaggerated grin. "You make me feel so wanted."

"Just remember, float and finger creep when we go inside so you don't kick up too much silt." Hutch shoved the regulator into his mouth, and, with one hand pressing his mask to his face, put one knee on the gunwale, and rolled over so his tanks hit the water first. The momentum carried him deep, but the air in his BC brought him right back up. He reached up, and Cody handed him the encased Geiger counter. Hutch slipped the lanyard over his wrist. The contraption was awkward, but approximately weightless. His only problem with it would be dynamic drag.

Ronnie sat on the rail and did a back roll into the water. She splashed in beside him, twisted, and bobbed back up. She shook her head, and fixed the seal of the silicone mask against her high cheek bones. She gave the okay sign. Together, they kicked for the anchor line and began their descent.

The grapnel was wrapped around the port midship lifeboat davit. The wooden boat had long since deteriorated, and the iron falls were cemented to the stanchions by calcium extrusions. With visibility in excess of seventy-five feet, more than half the tramp freighter could be seen at once. As the only object on a purely sand bottom, the wreck was an oasis in an otherwise sterile desert: a micro-environment that started from the minutest plankton feeders and ran all the way up the food chain to the larger predators. Tropical fish of all sizes and colors, most of them unidentifiable to Hutch, swam by the thousands in, on, and around the steel habitat. What had once been man's now belonged to the denizens of the deep.

Hutch settled down on the rusting deck and checked the grapnel set: he had hooked the tines back around the chain, and it did not look like it would come out on its own. The surge pushed him several feet away, then brought him back. Instead of fighting it, he went with the flow. He gave the okay sign, circled thumb and forefinger, to Ronnie. She checked her gauges and returned the sign, nodding. He stood on his fin tips and adjusted his buoyancy. He signaled for her to follow him, then turned and kicked gently toward an open doorway.

The doors had long since fallen off, but the bulkheads inside still stood, although they were pitted and rusted through. The fantastic array of coral growth lessened somewhat because of the lack of sunlight, but as long as the current flow was strong, the filter feeders grew thick. Large sea anemones stretched out their fragile tentacles, but retreated quickly when Hutch brushed up against them.

He turned into the first doorway. The room was bright with ambient light, and green circles lined the outer bulkhead where the ports yawned glassless or open. Where the portholes were closed, the marine growth was so thick that no light came through. Hutch switched on his dive light, playing its powerful beam around the encrusted interior. Two cylindrical posts in the middle of the room attested to where tables had once been, their wood long since eaten by various forms of shipworms.

Ronnie's light vaulted over Hutch's shoulder. Its beam illuminated multicolored bulkheads, and reflected off schools of tropicals that swam freely throughout the sunken hulk. She moved ahead, and they explored the room side by side.

The fish near the portholes could be seen moving back and forth as the surge was funneled through the openings in a venturi effect. Hutch kicked by too close and was instantly caught in the outsweep. He felt himself being pulled sideways across the deck. When he put out his hand to ward off the bulkhead, his arm was sucked right through the port, and his body was pinned up against coral-encrusted steel. His mask was pushed askew, letting in a dribble of water. He pushed frantically, but he was powerless in the strong ocean force. Several agonizing seconds later, the surge reversed, and Hutch was propelled across the room and spun around in the whirlpool. He fetched up against the opposite bulkhead, momentarily disoriented.

He blew the water out of his mask. Ronnie floated in front of him, her eyes pinched. She gave him the okay sign. Hutch nodded. Despite the sharpened shells he had been pressed against, the material of his BC had not been punctured. Gradually, he became aware of a feeling of discomfort along his forearm. When he looked, he saw a scratch that extended from wrist to elbow: not deep, but bleeding. He had been ripped open by the tip of a barnacle that lived on the inner rim of the porthole: the perfect location for a filter feeder.

Ronnie waved Hutch on, then kicked for an alcove at the end of the room. She pointed her light down. The deck was littered with china plates, bowls, and cups, all of plain white design. Hutch nodded. He knew where they were. They turned and retreated across the room.

The door they had entered was no longer visible. As careful as they had been in working across the room, every kick of their fins had churned up clouds of silt that spun around in cyclonic circles and filled the room with particles which not only blocked light and obscured visibility, but which scattered light beams back in their faces: like headlights on a foggy night.

Worse than that, and unavoidable, were exhaust bubbles bursting against the overhead and sweeping along the under surface seeking a way up, like waves in reverse. These ripples of air dislodged precariously hanging rust, metal chips, and accumulated organic debris so that it rained down like orange flakes of snow.

Because the room was so open, and because ambient light was so bright, they had little trouble following a straight course and ducking out into the corridor. Hutch checked his gauges, then motioned Ronnie to follow him deeper into the wreck.

The short passage opened into the central, longitudinal corridor that extended aft for ten feet and out a door, and forward all the way under the midship wheelhouse. Hutch turned around to motion to Ronny—and could not find her. He swung around in a complete circle. There had not been time for her to go back outside, and the two corridors were as yet not mucked up by a diver's progress.

Something tapped him on the back of the head. He rolled over on his back, and saw Ronnie floating above him just below the overhead. She was doing her best not to kick up bottom sediment. Hutch laughed at himself. He pointed down the corridor. She gave him the okay sign, and off they went.

Hutch entered the first room on his right, aiming the box with the attached light. He heard no telltale clicks. The debris on the deck was a foot thick, and was covered with a layer of black mud. The porthole was closed, making the room dark as a coal bin, but the dive light illuminated the cubicle with the intensity of an aircraft landing light. The single entrance created a cul-de-sac in which rusting and decomposing ship parts accumulated without any possibility of being swept away by the current.

Ronnie knelt in the doorway while Hutch poked around inside. In this first, cursory examination of the *Gremyashchi*, they merely wanted to scope out the condition of the wreck before conducting a more intensive search program. Hutch saw the neck of a whiskey bottle protruding from the muck. When he plucked it out, a great gob of ooze swirled up with it. He quickly realized his mistake, dropped the bottle, and swung his light around the rest of the room before the rain of overhead debris descended upon him.

Ronnie checked out the room opposite, while Hutch stood in the doorway as safety. She hovered several feet above the silt layer, playing her light around the room, into the corners, and up at the overhead. A cage light hung from an exposed beam; the glass globe was still intact. Again, the lack of current flow severely limited the amount of marine organisms which could survive here.

For twenty minutes they surveyed the rooms. The paneling had long since fallen off the bulkheads, and all signs of furniture were gone. Occasionally, Hutch saw a table leg or chair frame angling out of a protective layer of mud. Wires, cables, and conduits were constant entanglements, but in most cases the carrying trays had long since collapsed. The radio room was completely free because cracks and rust holes in the deck had allowed the silt to filter through, exposing a junk pile of condensers and vacuum tubes.

The corridor terminated at a transverse bulkhead with a porthole in the middle. A railing curved around an opening in the deck that housed a metal staircase going below. Hutch shone his beam down into the dark maw, where no outside light penetrated. He signaled for Ronny to stand safety. She nodded. He aligned himself vertically and lowered himself into the hole. His tanks scraped, and his BC got hung up, but by wriggling and letting out air, he managed to drop through the opening into the lower level. His outstretched arm hung up when the ungainly Geiger counter case snagged, but Ronnie freed it for him. What had once been sectioned off into several cabins was now one giant room—all the partitions had collapsed, leaving a tangled heap of sharp metal projections, fallen ceiling tiles, a spider's web of electrical wiring, and canted plumbing pipes. A porcelain, footed bathtub was sequestered in the forward corner, adjacent to a sink broken in two and a toilet whose bowl was completely filled with mud.

There was no color or contrast in this sealed off compartment: everything was a uniform reddish brown, the result of admixture with iron oxides. Further along the port bulkhead lay a bedspring, half its length exposed above the silt and debris level. Above it was a dogged-down porthole, glass intact, with the outside so overgrown that no light penetrated.

The glint of brass attracted Hutch's attention. He kept his bright beam on the object while he picked his way across the room on his fingertips, barely pushing upward so as to keep down the silt. He used his fins not at all. He saw the Ballantine sign sticking out of a jumble of metal detritus. He grabbed one of the three circles and pulled out the curious device. It was not until he saw the colored filters and lens attachments that he recognized the sextant.

He gently placed it back on the muck. Any other time he would have taken it as a souvenir, but the importance of the quest put relic collecting in the back seat. He reached a corner and veered along the bulkhead. He saw odds and ends of personal belongings sticking out of the mud, but did not pick up anything that would further obscure visibility.

He moved along the transverse bulkhead all the way across the ship. Then he hit another corner, and turned right once more. He worked his way aft along the starboard bulkhead. A metal ledge jutted out, the leading corner held up by a bent support. The other leg was gone, causing the ledge to angle down diagonally.

A slab of wood showed partially out of the silt. The edges were full of holes, and the front had a spongelike texture where teredoes had eaten their way inside. The tongue and groove lines were clearly visible because no marine growth covered the surface. This was a dead room, where only a few fish frequented, and where only mud crabs lived.

Hutch eased the board slowly out of the muck. A speck of color caught his eye: a red arch painted on the laquered veneer that had managed to survive decomposition because of its muddy interment. He pulled it out more, until he could see a circle with one end flattened. From there on the mud clung like black icing. He set the Geiger counter case on the canted metal ledge so the lashed light beam cut across in front of him. He wiped off the layer of ooze.

The flattened circle became the letter 'P'. Silt swirled around Hutch's mask, and for a moment he was blinded. He moved a few feet away, out of the cloud, and wiped off the rest of the wooden panel. The thick ooze dropped off, but he was forced to move again in order to find a clear spot in the quickly darkening chamber. His heart skipped a beat when he finally spelled out the word: PUMC.

He placed the board on the ledge, leaning across the top of the Geiger counter case. His backup light was clipped to his weight belt, along with a mesh bag. He opened the brass snap hook by feel. He slipped the light lanyard over his wrist so it would not float off, turned on the beam, then opened the metal hoop and shoved the piece of wood into the bag.

He lay horizontal, with his light close to the mud, looking for other bits of evidence. Slowly, he fanned the clouds of silt away, clearing the water while at the same time removing a layer of mud from where the wooden slat had resided. Even with his face only a foot away from the work area, he had difficulty seeing.

He picked up a rounded object caked with mud. It was the size of a cantelope split in half, with grooves of some kind along one edge. In order to see at all, Hutch had to rise up out of the silt almost to the overhead. There, he shook the thing until the smooth orange surface appeared. It was an inflexible, oblate ball with mud jammed into the open end.

As the silt cleared, the eye sockets and nasal openings glared luridly in the stark white beam. Some of the teeth remained in the upper jaw. What he held in his gloved hand was a human skull.

Or a prehuman skull.

Hutch stared at it for a long time, hardly believing what he was seeing. He turned it all around, dug out the mud filling the inner cavity. The supraorbitals bulged more than in modern man. The cranium was long and narrow with exaggerated sunken temporals snapped off at the mastoid process. He tried to define all the parts, knowing that he should just shove the skull in his bag and make cranial measurements later when he had the proper equipment. It was several minutes before he could force his attention back to the situation at hand. He carefully placed the bony remains in the bottom of the bag, and hung the hoop on the projecting metal ledge so it stayed open.

He lay back down in the muck, with his light held next to his mask. He swept his hand back and forth over the bottom, watching for other items to appear. His patience was rewarded by other bits of bone, and what he thought was a tooth.

Hutch had a vague awareness of clanging, or of the pinging heard in a submarine movie. He ignored it, and continued his digging. There was nothing for a long time: just mud, and blackness. He found more wood, other bits and pieces of metal, a brass hinge, a chunk of rock.

The shiny, chromed cylinder seemed out of place. It showed not a speck of rust. Quickly, Hutch dug all around it until it lay completely exposed. It was a foot long, rounded at both ends, and perfectly smooth. Light reflected off it with mirrorlike brilliance. Hutch did not want to put it in the bag, because it might crush the more delicate bones. But he had to take it with him. He decided to just pick it up and carry it loosely under his arm. But, when he went to lift it, it would not budge.

The cylinder did not roll, did not swivel, did not move at all. Hutch took out his knife, and tapped it. The sound was dull, and solid. Somehow, another tapping sound echoed his own. He tapped it again. A few seconds later there came the other tapping. Then he realized that Ronnie was signaling to him by banging her tank with her knife.

Hurriedly, he pulled his gauge panel out in front of him and held the light right on top of it. A chill ran up his spine when he interpreted the instruments: he was forty-five minutes into a planned forty minute dive, his decompression penalty was climbing rapidly, and his air gauge read less than a thousand pounds of air. It was time to leave.

But he could not go without this curious metallic object.

He tried to slide his knife underneath it, to determine what was holding it in place. The knife went into the mud, and stopped suddenly. He dug all around until he had it completely excavated. The silt was so thick that he had to inspect the shiny object by inches. Still, he could see no point of attachment. With the light in one hand and the knife in the other, he worked around the curved perimeter. If it was frozen by encrustation, his chopping should loosen it. Finally, he stuck the knife in so it stayed, pinched somehow, and slammed it with the palm of his hand. It went in a little more, and remained stuck. He pulled up on the handle, using the knife as a pry bar. The cylinder moved incrementally before the blade snapped off an inch back from the tip.

He could not afford to wait any longer. By feel, he shoved the stub back into the sheath. Visibility was absolutely zero. He worked his fingers along the bulkhead until he felt the slender metal leg, then traced a path up to the ledge and along the side to the mesh bag. Hugging the bagful of goodies, he continued in braille to the transverse bulkhead, then felt his way back the way he had come.

He heard Ronnie tapping. Instead of taking out his knife to tap a response, he kept moving. He would be by her side in a moment. He reached the other bulkhead, turned, kept moving. The visibility improved to a foot, but that was all. The entire room was now a coal bin of black mud, descending rust, and swirling silt. When he blundered into the bathtub he knew he was almost home.

Hutch churned past the shattered sink and upright toilet. He held the light out in front of him so he would not bang his face mask on the metal steps. He crawled along the base of the transverse bulkhead, expecting at any second to bump into the bottom stanchion. It seemed like a long way—inordinately long.

When his light again saw metal, it appeared in the black cloud to be more solid than he remembered. He knelt, and ran his gloves along the flat iron surface. It felt like another bulkhead, one that was not there before.

Had he passed the stairs, or not gone far enough?

He seemed to be in another corner. He explored a little further, turning at right angles once more. Visibility grew worse as he passed over more thick mud. Then he felt something, looked up, saw a light, breathed a sigh of relief. He had gone completely around the room and wound up back at the ledge on which he had placed the Geiger counter case. Thank god, or Cody would be very unhappy at his forgetting it. He slipped the lanyard over his wrist.

Carefully, he retraced his path to the forward bulkhead, turned right, and inspected every inch of blackness as he crawled along the rusting upright. When white porcelain again appeared out of the gloom, he knew he had once more passed the stairs.

Hutch heard Ronnie's insistent tapping, but could not determine where she was. He pressed the BC inflator button. The added hiss of air made him buoyant enough to rise to the overhead. Since most of the silt was setting to the bottom, it was slightly clearer at the top of the room.

He worked back across the ship, knowing that he *had* to pass the stairwell. Again he missed it. Hovering in the upper corner, Hutch pushed the bulky Geiger counter case out of the way, pulled his gauges in front of his face, aimed his light on the plastic faces. He was down to two hundred pounds.

He forced himself to inhale slowly, and deeply; to savor every breath. He was within feet of the exit, but he could see only inches. In this black fog his only hold on reality was his physical contact with the bulkhead. He could not let go of it, for then he would be lost in the microcosm of the room. He kept reviewing his mental image of his path, looking for faults. He could find none. The stairs should be there.

But they simply were not.

He went back and forth, over and over. He had to keep trying to figure his way out of this maze. He could not imagine where he had made his mistake. His breathing became labored. On the next inhalation, the air flow lessened. Without bothering to look at his gauges, Hutch spat out the regulator and shoved in the backup slung around his neck. The small pony bottle nestled behind the double tanks had an additional twenty cubic feet of air—about five minutes worth at this depth and under these conditions. It was time to start skip breathing. He just hoped he did not pass out from carbon dioxide build-up. He hated the thought of dying with air still in his tanks. Actually, he hated the thought of dying. But worse than death, was the fear and panic that preceeded it; the moments of anguish, fighting the inevitable. With great difficulty, he fought off the terror that had gripped him, and forced himself to concentrate.

Very diligently, he went completely around the room. He located the bathtub, found the ledge and after a long sweep ended up back at the bathtub. There were no stairs or other obstructions in the room. He had only one other option—turn off his light, lie still, and wait for the silt to settle.

He switched off the light attached to the Geiger counter case, but the other he held against his chest: bulb filaments had a nasty habit of breaking during the expansion and contraction process of going on and off. He stood upright with his tanks against one bulkhead. He took a deep breath, held it as long as he could, exhaled slowly, and stared into the blackness beyond his mask. He looked for the telltale green glow that should depict the staircase opening.

His heart would not stop racing: it was totally out of his control. But he had fought down the initial panic. Only cool, level-headed thinking would get him out of this one. And a lot of luck. And a good dive buddy.

Hutch saw an infinitessimal white glow in front of him. His eyes were so full of stars from the Stygian blackness that at first he took it to be just another ghost pattern being played on his brain. When it went away, he knew it was. But a moment later it returned, brighter, almost as if it really existed. He held his breath, watching with all his might that faint, pinpoint of light, as if he could will it into existance.

It passed his way again, like the dim flash of a lighthouse beacon seen through a foggy night. Hutch did not know what it was, but he took what felt like the biggest step in his life: he pushed off the bulkhead and glided into the great infinity of the unknown.

He swung his light around and pointed it toward the glow. The sweeping beam immediately swerved in his direction, and stayed there. A moment later, he saw Ronnie's face, upside down. She was halfway down the staircase, head first, holding onto a piece of railing. She backed out of the way.

Hutch shoved the Geiger counter box up above him. Several agonizing seconds passed while Ronnie struggled to remove the lanyard from his wrist. Then he hugged the iron rungs and slithered up through the opening. His tanks caught on something, a projecting piece of metal perhaps, and stopped him cold. Ronnie's hand pushed down on his head, forcing him back into the room. He went down a foot, felt her adjust his tanks, then rose slowly. He made it up into the brightness of the upper deck.

As soon as he was clear, Ronnie charged along the corridor with the speed and grace of a propoise. It was all Hutch could do to keep up. She executed a sharp left turn. Then they were out the door and going up the anchor line. Hutch's instinct was to race for the surface, and it was only with great will power that he forced himself to maintain the proper rate of ascent. More cases of the bends were brought on by rising too quickly, than by leaving the water without adequate staged decompression.

They stopped at forty feet. For the first time since leaving the wreck, Ronnie took the time to make hand signals. Hutch glanced at his gauges: his main tanks were empty, his pony bottle on the verge, and the decompression requirement nearly an hour. There was no way he was going to make it.

Ronnie showed him her air gauges. Because of the weight of Hutch's rig, she was using two separate tanks without a pony bottle, each tank having its own regulator and acting as a backup for the other. One tank had eight hundred pounds, the other three hundred. She handed him the regulator leading from the fuller of the two, and, held close together by the length of the hose, they settled down to sweat out the long hang on the anchor line.

Hutch's eyes were glued to his decompression computer, except for once a minute when he checked Ronnie's air gauge. She seemed so calm, so placid, as if nothing were wrong. She even carried the Geiger counter case without concern. She kept asking him if he was okay. All he could do was nod. He was screaming to tell her what he had found, what was—

Oh, my god, did he still have it? He looked down at his weight belt, saw nothing. He felt around his waist. The belt had come loose at depth when the neoprene of his shorty suit compressed. The buckle had slid around behind him. He worked feverishly to realign it. Then he saw the mesh bag still hanging from the clip. He could not see any of the bones, but the board was still in it. Dear lord, if he ever got out of this predicament alive, he swore never to let it happen again—at least, until the next time.

The regulator bogged down on him. He took a look at the gauge, saw the needle resting on the peg. He spat out the mouthpiece and reclaimed his pony bottle regulator. He sucked out the last remaining breaths: an extra minute, even a few more seconds, might prevent decompression sickness. Ronnie checked both gauges. She nodded as she showed him the one she had been breathing off. There was a hairline between it and the peg. And there was still fifteen minutes of decompression to go.

Suddenly she was not there. Hutch looked all around, and down the anchor line. If she had passed out and fallen—

She was above him, rising to the surface. Rather than share some of his remaining air, she was sacrificing herself to the bends. Tears welled up in his eyes. He wanted to follow her, to drag her down, to give back some of the air he had stolen. Already she was on the ladder. Now he could accomplish nothing more than getting them both bent. His feelings were in such turmoil that his own safety hardly mattered. He could not bear it if she died, or was paralyzed for the rest of her life. Without a recompression chamber, the only way of reversing the effect was—

—to get back in the water. And there she was, coming back down wearing a single tank, and holding another under her arms. She met him at ten feet. Hutch would have kissed her had he not needed the air so badly. He took the other regulator, then relieved her of the tank. She had saved the day.

Fifteen minutes later, Ronnie pointed thumbs up and rose to the surface. Hutch disentangled himself from the anchor line. He waited half a minute, then went up the final few feet. He swam back on the surface, breathing through his snorkel. Ronnie was still standing on the ladder when the single tank slipped off her back and sank slowly through the clear water. Hutch let air out of his BC, but realized there was no way he was going to make himself negative fast enough to catch it.

When his head came out of the water, and he could hear, Cody was cursing a blue streak. As Hutch put a foot on the bottom rung he was yanked up by the commando.

"Get rid of those tanks! Quick!"

Cody pulled the single out of Hutch's arms and let it drop. Already he was fumbling with the upper D-rings of his harness.

"Hey, what're you do—"

"Get rid of them. They're coming 'round again, and I don't want them to see any diving gear."

"Cody, what's going—Wait! The weight belt is over the crotch strap."

"Dump it!"

"I can't. It's got—" When the upper straps let go, the tanks pivoted off his back. They were still held on by the waist straps. Hutch sank back in the water, pulled the quick release, and slipped the crotch strap out from under the weight belt. Aluminum tanks were buoyant when empty, but the weight of the regulators and emergency decompression reel slowly pulled them under. "Cody—"

The commando dragged him over the gunwale and plopped him onto the deck like a sack of potatoes. He stripped off the fins and mask, and tossed them in the corner. "We may still have a chance if they think we're just tourists."

"Who? What are you talking about?"

"Them." He pointed up into the air. A silver speck streaked silently across the azure sky.

Hutch struggled up on his elbows. "It's only an airplane."

"It's no goddamn commercial airliner. It's an F4 Phantom: attack bomber, fighter, and recon jet. Besides twenty millimeter cannons, it can fire, drop, and launch anything ever made."

When Hutch heard the engine exhaust from a point way behind the plane, he realized how fast it was going. "Isn't that an American—"

"Here it comes. Hurry with those cases."

Ronnie raced out of the cabin with two plastic watertight boxes. "Cody, what about—"

He threw the binoculars up to his eyes. "Grab everything you can. And get the life raft in the water." He put down the glasses and stared fiercely at Hutch. "*Do it!*"

Hutch realized that Cody meant him. He climbed to his feet and, mesh bag dragging behind him, ran past the cabin and up to the bow deck. He pulled the tiedowns off the plastic cannister, rolled it free, and unsealed the pod. The life raft was packed as tightly as a sausage in its skin. Hutch pulled and yanked. When it came free he fell backward on his rump with a painful thud.

The jet nosed down, screeching like an artillery shell. Still sitting, Hutch watched its approach. It leveled out about five hundred feet above the water, broadside to the *G. Willie Makit*. Two shapes detached themselves from the belly. They tumbled end over end like poorly thrown footballs. Afterburners lit up the jet's tail as it streaked ahead of the falling drums. At better than five hundred miles per hour it was only a blur to Hutch as it screamed overhead and veered left toward the coastline.

"*Incoming!*" Cody screamed.

The drums had more foreward momentum than gravitational speed. They vectored over the sailboat barely skimming the mast tops and contacted the water several hundred feet beyond. Twin spouts of fire burst from the surface of the sea, boiled upward and onward like erupting volcanoes, and burgeoned into huge, churning streamers hundreds of feet long: all in the blink of an eye.

"Get that raft in the water. *Now!*"

Hutch rolled out the material on the top of the cabin. "I can't find the inflator." He rummaged through the folds of orange material until he located a carbon dioxide flask. It was connected to a flattened pontoon by a brass valve with a handle and a pull cord. "I got it—"

Cody ripped the emergency release out of Hutch's hand just as he was yanking out the retaining pin. "I didn't say inflate it, I said get it in the water." He dragged the raft to the rail and rolled it over the side. "We don't need any targets they can see. Throw over anything that'll float—I want to create a debris fields."

Hutch was still sitting down. His head quivered nervously. "I don't under—"

"Do it!"

Cody raced back to the after deck. He tossed overboard all the cases Ronnie had already brought up from the forward compartment. He passed her in the galley. "Everything loose goes over." He came running out with blankets, sheets, pillows, and mattresses.

Hutch pulled the life rings out of their holders and heaved them overboard, along with the two coils of rope and the Emergency Position Indicating Radio Beacon. He thanked the U.S. Coast Guard for making EPIRBs required equipment on all U.S. registered ocean-going vessels. As soon as the external contacts were shorted with water, the sealed device would give off an internationally recognized signal in the megahertz frequency.

"Here they come! And they've got our range this time." Cody climbed up on the rail, pulling Ronnie by the hand. They jumped into the water among the widening circle of jetsam. "Come on!"

Hutch saw the silver streak coming in for another pass. He gathered up the mesh bag still clipped to his weight belt, put it outside the rail, stepped on the gunwale, snagged the bag on the rail, and fell gracelessly overboard. When he started sinking, he put the oral inflator into his mouth and started puffing.

Cody swam up to him. "Don't blow that thing up. They'll see it."

"It's the weight belt."

"Drop it!" Cody reached for Hutch's waist and grappled for the quick release buckle.

"*Don't!* It's got the bones in it."

"What bones?"

"The ones I found. A Peking skull." A wave washed over Hutch's face. He caught it on an inhale, came up gurgling. "And a piece of wood—"

Cody grabbed him around the neck and held him up. "What the hell are you talking about?"

"Ronnie! Where's Ronnie?"

"I'm here." She swam easily toward them and halted in front of Hutch. "I'm right here."

The whining grew louder. The jet finished its curve and made its approach on the sailboat at a height on less than a hundred feet.

"Get in here, close to the hull. It's our only chance." Cody let Hutch go as he peered around the tip of the bow. "They're gonna get us with this one. The bastards."

Ronnie clung to Hutch with both arms. "Honey, are you all right?"

"I will be if I don't get Kentucky fried by the next napalm chef. Who the hell *are* these people?"

Already the flames from the previous strike were going out. The jellied gasoline continued to burn on the surface, but there was no fuel for the fire. Two tracks of black smudge wafted downwind in a diminishing cloud.

Hutch peeked around the sailboat's stem. Two more drums dropped from the plane's undercarriage. "Holy Christ." They hit the water about fifty feet off the starboard side. Forward motion carried both lines of erupting flames right across the *G. Willie Makit*: one over the transom and one over the midship cabin. Spears of napalm shot over the hull a mere twenty feet away from where the three of them treaded water.

"Hold your breath," Cody yelled.

The sudden heat was intense, like the blast of red hot coals from an open furnace door. Hutch had trouble rolling over because of the air-filled BC on his chest. His face was seered before he could bury it in the water. The back of his head felt like an ironing board on Monday morning. The air crackled as the oxygen was gobbled up by the fire.

Hutch popped up like a surfacing loon. He shook the water out of his eyes. Two trails of billowing flames cascaded off the boat. The staysail was a mass of blazing material, while the reefed mainsail was a tall funeral pyre with a crossstree that burned like a crucifixion in effigy. He instinctively kicked away from the conflagration.

"Over here. Toward the smoke." Cody doggy paddled away from the boat, parallel to the fire track. "Don't let them see you."

Ronnie swam with long, agile strokes toward a mattress. Hutch, lying on his back and looking over his shoulder, scooped water with his hands.

Half the boat was a boiling holocaust. Red lances climbed a hundred feet into the air; shreds of sail and splinters of wood spat off to the sides. Decking exploded upward as the auxiliary engine fuel tank was touched off, the flaming shards of teak filled the air like a Roman candle out of control.

Ronnie ducked under the mattress and stayed hidden until most of the heavier particles descended. Hutch watched the destruction of the expensive sailboat with almost detached fascination. Most of the sky was oblitered from his point of view by black smoke.

Cody treaded water alongside him. "Can't you get rid of that thing? You stick out like a candle in a coal bin."

Hutch put in another lungful of air. "I don't know how to swim."

"Whaddaya mean. You're a diver, for chrisesake."

"Why do you think I have all that fancy gear?"

Cody sputtered. He submerged his body and held a pillow close to his face. "Never mind. Just throw one of those blankets over you, so you won't be so visible from the air. If they think there were any survivors, they're likely to strafe us."

Hutch did not need to be told twice. "One thing I don't need is lead poisoning." He caught up with a drenched sheet and draped it over his body up to his chin. "What about the life raft."

"When they're gone, we'll go after it."

"Cody, I have the feeling somebody's out to get us."

"If you've got paranoia, it's catching."

Ronnie swam toward them one handed, pulling the mattress. "It must be contagious, because I've got it, too. Cody, how do they keep finding us?"

"You should know that better than I do." He stared up at the thick clouds of smoke streaming off the sailboat and passing over them. Ronnie opened her mouth to speak when Cody added, "You're the intelligence part of this team. I'm a grunt."

Hutch placed his arm around Ronnie's shoulders, hugged her tight. He could neither see nor hear the jet. "And I'm the ignorant part. Now, who the hell *was* that?"

All three clung to the mattress, under the dark, smoky camouflage. The napalm trails were burning out, but the sailboat was still supplying huge volumes of black smudge. Ten feet of clean air reached up to the heated interface. The *G. Willie Makit* was consumed practically down to the waterline. The hull crackled, burped, and exploded with gunlike detonations.

Tears streamed down Ronnie's face. "She's going."

The stern settled slowly, and the sailboat listed slightly to starboard, away from them. The leaded keelboard kept it from capsizing. As the flames reached the munitions locker forward, the top of the bow blew off in a titanic explosion. Flaming brands rushed outward in a wild, broiling, pyrotechnic finale. The mainmast collapsed seething into the sea. Steam hissed volubly as the searing hull slipped majestically beneath the waves. Nothing but smoke was left to mark the grave.

"Gee, Willie didn't make it." Cody squinted into the sun with his hand held over his eyes. "But if that jet doesn't spot us, we've got a good chance of reaching shore."

"Is it all right to get the raft, now?" Hutch looked around but did not see it anywhere. "Or are we going to swim?"

"I'll get it." Ronnie let go the mattress and carved through the swells with effortless, even strokes.

"Swims like a fish, that woman," Cody said.

"Or a mermaid." Hutch crawled up onto the soggy mattress and managed to get halfway out of the water. "So, why are we being bombed by our own planes?"

"Anybody with a Visa card can buy an F4. They've been sold to quite a few third world countries." Cody climbed up on the other side of the mattress. They lay head to head. "I wouldn't doubt if the napalm was ours, too."

"Well, if it makes you feel any better, I got the EPIRB off."

"I know. I saw it melting."

"You mean—"

"It got off a signal for ten seconds at most. It might be enough to locate us, but I don't know. There aren't a whole lot of tracking stations in this part of the world, so, unless a satellite was conveniently overhead ..."

"Oh, great. So here we are off the coast of Borneo, and no one knows where we are. Just great. You and your goddamned secrets."

"Hey, if you men are finished sunbathing, you can swim over this way and help a lady ashore." Ronnie sat in the fully inflated raft with a paddle across her lap and her hands on her slender hips. "I'm not going to do *all* the work."

Hutch rolled off the mattress and backstroked toward the raft. "You know, I think I'm getting used to being left out in the ocean."

Cody did his swimming dog imitation. He rolled aboard expertly, then held out a hand to Hutch. The four person survival raft was crowded for two, and an orgy for three. Ronnie took the rudder position, and let Hutch and Cody straddle the side pontoons. Once the two men got synchronized, they dipped their paddles with timed regularity. With her open palm Ronnie beat the rhythm on the flexible floor. They picked up anything still afloat.

Hutch grabbed a plastic box by the handle and pulled it aboard. "It was good thinking having all our equipment in these watertight cases."

"Terrific," Cody groaned. "Except that this one is filled with low voltage transformers, power converters, and control boards. Not exactly hot items for trading with the natives."

"Didn't any of the radios get off?"

Ronnie shielded her eyes from the bright sun. "I know I threw two of them overboard, at least. But the current was taking everything into the flames."

"Do you know smoke signals?"

"I think I missed that class."

Hutch shrugged. "Well, at least our friends from the Anti Maim society are gone. Cody, I know how much you like to keep things to yourself, but—is there a chance we'll be reported overdue?"

"About as much chance as getting a refund on your taxes. This is a radio silenced covert operation."

"Are there any nuclear submarines up your sleeve?"

"I had a call sign for help, to be used for pick up upon successful completion of mission, or in case of dire emergency."

"This does classify as 'dire', doesn't it?"

"Yes, but the transmitter went down with the boat. We're on our own."

"Ronnie, didn't you have a radio out last night, when you were doing your reports."

"It was in the same case as the lap-top. But that one has to be connected to a power supply."

"Oh. I thought I heard you talking before I came up. I must have been dreaming."

"No, I sometimes vocalize my reports while I'm typing. Anyway, it went up in flames. Cody, the beach looks pretty rough along here. Why don't we head north, toward those cliffs. I think I see a clear spot."

"Yes, it looks like a stream, or a small river, flowing down those rocks. I think we can pull right up into the jungle."

The swells grew to monstrous proportions as they got close to shore, but where the fresh water stream flowed outward there were no offshore boulders blocking the way. They paddled alongside a sand spit and fought a mild current into a placid lagoon a couple hundred yards across, with a waterfall cascading down nearly vertical rocks into the opposite side. The beaches along the edge of the pool were flat and sandy. The lush jungle began about twenty feet back, and looked like an impenetrable green wall.

Hutch glanced around at the unbroken hinterland. "I guess I don't have to tell you that, although Borneo has fairly extensive coastal communities, they exist only around the great river deltas. Everything in between is primeval swamp and rugged mountain ranges."

Cody said, "Save the geography lesson and jump ashore with the painter."

Hutch stepped into the warm water. His wetsuit booties sank in the soft sand. He took the rope and waded ashore. "Oh, god, it feels so good to stand on something that doesn't move." He tied the line to an exposed mangrove root. "I've got to get out of these clothes. I'm dying." He quickly stripped off the weight belt, BC, and shorty suit. His body was bathed in sweat. "It must be a hundred degrees in here. There's no wind."

Ronnie glanced at her underwater wristwatch. "Ninety-three Fahrenheit, but the humidity is probably close to a hundred percent. We're getting close to the monsoon season."

"I don't need a weather report." Cody dragged the life raft high up the beach. He looped the painter and knotted it short. "Now what's this about bones. What did you find down there?"

Hutch picked up the mesh bag, unclipped it from the weight belt, dipped it in the water to clean off the sand, and, kneeling, laid it across the spread-out shorty suit. He pulled out the long board. "See the initials? It part of a crate from the Peking Union Medical College."

"You son of a bitch, you've been holding out on me."

"I finally got the chance. My turn had to come sooner or later."

Ronnie twisted the board all around. "Honey, why didn't you tell me?"

"Well, for one thing I had other things on my mind—like breathing. And besides, I haven't learned how to talk underwater. I almost died when I found this thing—literally." He dipped into the bag and felt through the folds of mesh. "These are phalanges. This is a metacarpal. This looks like a rib segment, this line being the costochondral junction. And this looks like the acromial end of a clavicle. See this bulge? That's the conoid tubercle. Hmmn, this is definitely a molar, but I can't tell—"

"Hutch, what's that big thing in there?"

Carefully, he brought out the prize. "I don't have the material to do a comparative study, but I'm sure its the skull of Sinanthropus pekinensis. And Cody, the cylinder was there, too, just like in the picture. Only I couldn't move it. It must have been—welded to the deck by encrustation."

Ronnie bent over and threw her arms around Hutch's shoulders. She gave him a resounding kiss on the cheek. "Oh, Honey, that's wonderful."

Cody's grin nearly split his face in two. "Goddamn it, after all we went through, you came through with the goods."

"You don't know the half of it. I got disoriented in a room—"

"Damn it, this is important. We've *got* to get a message out. We have to let them know."

"No, problem. You can use my Calling Card."

"This is no time to be funny."

"Cody, this whole situation is ridiculous. We're nowhere near civilization. You're on the world's third largest island, with more land than the original thirteen Colonies. It's got only three thousand miles of roads, hardly any of it paved, and none of it near here. Inland is sparsely inhabited rain forest. The population is centered around the dozen or so rivers that cut through the jungle, and most of the people live in the coastal deltas. This—" He made a sweeping gesture at the gushing waterfall. "—is not what I call a major river. It's hundreds of miles to the nearest settlement. And we don't even have roller skates."

"We'll find a way to get out a message."

"How? A manuscript in a bottle? Everything we owned went down in flames."

"Hutch, please don't be a defeatist." Ronnie placed a warm hand on his shoulder. "People have been shipwrecked before, and survived."

"And *that's* the point I'm trying to make. The only thing on Cody's mind is completing his mission. But I've got a different purpose in life: I want to die of old age. I think it's high time we rearrange our priorities and put aside the mission. Let's get out of this situation alive, then let's find out who the hell is trying to put out our headlights."

"We've got to get out a message."

"Cody, I know this is against your principles, but this time we're going to have to stoop to saving our lives to get that message out."

"We'll do it somehow."

"Great. Just great. Well, you just flag down the next stage coach. I'm going over here to Federal Express. They always deliver." Hutch trudged off along the beach, kicking up sand.

"Hutch. Wait." Ronnie ran after him. "It won't do any good to argue among ourselves."

"I'm not arguing, I'm doing something. Talking to him is like talking to a machine—worse, because you can't unplug *him*. But right now, I'm going over there to that gorgeous looking waterfall and take a long, cold shower. Want to join me?''

Ronnie downturned lips transformed into a smile. "I'll rub your back if you'll rub mine.''

"Sold. I'll race you.''

He took off at a run, with Ronnie close on his heels. They followed the curvature of the lagoon to where it met the rock wall that was the edge of a broad, intricate cascade. A cool, fine spray splashed off boulders smoothed by millenia of waterborne sediment. They splashed through puddles and gurgling streams. They had to climb up thirty feet of cataracts to reach the lowest part of the falls. Hutch opened his mouth, and walked into the downpour sucking in fresh, aerated water.

Ronnie let a side trickle douse her hair. She held her hands upright, stepped into the main stream, and shreeched like a hoot owl when the cold water inundated her body. Hutch laughed, his body tingling from the temperature change. Standing alternately on each foot, he yanked off his booties and tossed them onto a dry slab. He let two converging runnels pound the top of his head.

"This is fantastic!''

Ronnie laughed and shrieked as she pulled the rubber vest over her head. She got stuck bent over with her arms and head caught in the material. "Hutch, help me.''

"Glad to.'' He reached past the rubber, ran his fingers over her back and under the bikini strap, and deftly unsnapped it. He whipped it off before she had a chance to move. "Voila!''

Ronnie screamed. She stood upright with her breasts bubbling free and her arms overhead, still in the folds of the vest. "You beast.'' She wriggled out of the rubber suit, and slapped at Hutch with it. "Cody can see us.''

"So what? He knows.''

"But this is different.''

"Yes, it *is* different.To paraphrase a cliche, the bra is in the other hand. Oh, you must be cold. Your indicators are on.''

"You are insufferable.''

"If I said you had a nice body, would you hold it against me?''

"Hug me, you beast.''

"Gladly.''

As they kissed in the spray of the waterfall, Hutch felt as free of encumbrances as he had ever felt in his life. The problems of the past no longer existed, and the future was of no consequence. He held onto Ronnie, held onto the moment, and dared not let go for having to face the present. It seemed that with her in his arms, nothing else mattered. He hoped it would always be that way.

Hutch returned her bathing suit top. "Hey, let's go play umbrella. I'll keep the shade off you for a while, then you can keep it off me.''

"Sounds like fun."

Eventually, they strolled back along the beach, hand in hand.

Cody had his long pants rolled up to below the knees. He was wading in the shallows, dangling a length of string in the water.

"What're you doing, Cody?"

The commando held up one hand for silence. He stood stock still, gazing intently on something under the rippling surface. He moved his arm slowly behind him, until the string lay next to his leg. With catlike reflexes his other hand darted into the water. He grabbed a large, speckled crab by the body and yanked it out of its environment. The claws were wrapped around his hand, fiercely pinching his forearm. Cody jerked up his leg at the same time he swung down with his arm. He smashed the crab on his kneecap. With a loud *crack* the shell shattered and the crustacean split in half.

Cody sloshed out of the lagoon, grinning. "Just bait. We're not going to eat it. There are lots of fish out there. I've seen them."

"How did you lure that crab out of the sand?" Ronnie said.

Cody pulled up his trouser leg to expose a lean, muscular thigh. A chunk of flesh was missing from the meaty part a few inches above the knee. He threw the crab on the sand as he knelt down by the open watertight case. "The string was used to tie the bubble plastic around the electronic components. I used a few windings from the transformer as a leader, and fashioned some hooks out of these diode ends. We're having sushi tonight."

Hutch nodded. "Why not a fish bake?"

"No fire. I don't want to give our position away."

"Yes, I guess you're right. We wouldn't want to be rescued, or anything like that. Is there anything we can do to help?"

"Find a camp where we can bed down for the night." Cody used his ever present survival knife to carve chunks of crab meat out of the shell. He baited his hook. When he stood up with his fishing line and shoved the raft into the lagoon, he reminded Hutch of Huckleberry Finn pushing off down the mighty Mississippi.

"Just be careful of—Oh, never mind."

Ronnie pointed to the other side of the waterfall. "I saw some rock ledges over that way. We might be able to clear out an overhang, and pad it with vegetation."

Cody paddled off into deeper water. "Okay, I'll meet you over there."

"Want us to take the case with us?" Hutch shouted.

"Go ahead."

Hutch repacked the mesh bag with the board, fossils, and shorty suit, and clamped down the lid on the watertight case. "You know, I don't think I understand him all the time, but if there's anyone I'd rather be stranded with on a desert isle—that is, as far as survival goes—" He gave her a peck on the temple. "I'd want it to be him."

Ronnie led the way back to the falls. "He's a survivor. And he thinks of things we never would. That's why he's got such absolute control over his operations. He's not a team person. He works as a loner. Prefers it really. He likes a low profile and uses it to his advantage."

They skipped across the lower cataracts getting only their feet wet. The ledges were shallow, dipped outward at an uncomfortable angle, and offered no protection from the weather. But at least they were off the ground and away from the myriads of insects that inhabited the jungle. A fine spray of mist from the waterfall nurtured a thick bed of moss by the water's edge. Hutch found the background noise of cascading water a pleasant melody. Mosquitoes and flies buzzed annoyingly, and other six legged denizens chirruped and stridulated like the soundtrack of a Tarzan movie.

"You know, when I first heard you tapping down there, I wasn't even paying attention. Once I picked up that board my mind went into overdrive. It was like wearing horse blinders."

Ronnie pulled creepers off the ledge and tossed them in a pile. "But I heard your response."

"No, I was just tapping on the cylinder." Hutch stripped broad leaves off an evergreen. He placed them in overlapping layers on the ledge. "At that point I didn't know I was lost. I was so excited at finding the fossils, nothing else mattered."

"But when you answered with such—deliberation—I thought you were all right. I was using dots and dashes to get your attention. I guess you don't know Morse."

"Never met the man. And the only code I know is the genetic. You know, we were way past our time—and low on air. When I couldn't find those stairs I wasn't sure you were still waiting for me."

"Honey, I'd never leave you in a situation like that."

Hutch pursed his lips, nodding. "Yes, I—Those stairs. I didn't notice when I went in, but they came down in the middle of the room. So as I kept going around the bulkheads I never bumped into it. Let me tell you, I was scared there at the end. You can't imagine the feeling of relief when I saw your light."

"It was so black when I looked down that opening. I figured the only thing I could do was drop down with my light and sweep it around in circles. I could hardly see it myself."

Hutch placed his hands on her shoulders, looked down into her clear, brown eyes. "Thanks. Thanks for being there."

"I could never leave you, Hutch. I—I love you."

Hutch continued staring for several seconds, his heart fluttering. Then he pulled her close and squeezed her tight. He closed his eyes, lost in a dreamland where everything he wanted came true, where whatever he wanted was his. He did not want to let go of her. Ever.

"Ronnie, I think I love you, too."

They kissed, slowly and delicately at first, then passionately, desperately. Hutch felt much more than the stirring in his loins; he trembled with the upwelling of emotion that was throbbing in his breast. The sexual satisfaction of the previous weeks was only a glimmer of light compared to the solar prominence that now blinded him.

A sharp scream of terror burst from the direction of the lagoon.

Hutch and Ronnie broke apart. Cody paddled toward them furiously. He slammed the paddle in the water first on one side, then on the other. Spray kicked up behind in twin rooster tails, and the raft carved water like a speedboat.

"What the hell—" Hutch started.

Ronnie pulled the knife out of her calf sheath and raced for the beach. "Cody, what is it?"

Hutch reached the sand spit right behind her. He pulled out his own knife, even though the tip was broken off. He cupped one hand along the side of his mouth, and shouted. "You're gaining on him."

Ronnie ran knee deep into the water. She held her arm out for the approaching raft, and grabbed the bow line as soon as it came within reach. She turned and ran with it at the same time Cody leaped out, and together they hauled it up the beach.

Hutch sheathed his useless knife. With a quick snap he broke off a rotted branch. As the reptilian head came within striking distance, he swung down and smashed the beast right between the eyes. It sank, turned, and, lashing its tail from side to side, swam submerbed toward the middle of the lagoon.

Cody stood at the tree line, breathing hard.

"By the way, be careful of the saltwater crocodiles."

Cody was livid, his face a bright crimson that was not all tan from sailing across the South China Sea. "You bastard. You knew about them."

Hutch shrugged. "I knew they existed. Actually, they're not nearly as dangerous as the poisonous snakes. I just didn't think you had the 'need to know'." He flashed a mouthful of teeth.

Cody slammed his paddle on the ground. "Goddamn it, I could have been killed. That dinosaur was twenty-five feet long."

"Cody, you're right. And these babies are maneaters, too. I was going to mention it, but I thought you'd accuse me of being an alarmist. I didn't think they'd come into a cut-off place like this. There's not enough food to support a beast of that size. They usually stay offshore."

"Well, goddamn it, from now on you tell me everything and let me make the decisions."

"Hey, maybe we can do a little horse trading. You know—tit for tat."

"You get that from her, not from me. As long as I'm in charge of this mission—"

Hutch was bent over, laughing, "Cody, that's a croc. What do you say we discuss it at our bivouac site, before that guy comes back and tries to make you imitate Captain Hook."

Cody's expression changed as if someone had thrown a mask over his face. He stabbed a finger at Hutch, and grinned in his usual manner. "Okay, you got me that time, but this is serious—"

"Cody, honestly, I didn't plan it. I just didn't think, that's all."

Ronnie joined in the laughter. "Cody, I wish I had a picture of your face. I've never seen you so—I don't know. You're a gem."

"Twenty-four carats," Hutch added.

"Okay. Okay. I got the point. Now, if anyone is hungry, I *might* be talked into sharing the catch of the day." He took a stringer of snappers out of the raft. "Any takers?"

"Couldn't we start just a *little* fire?"

Cody looked up at the sky. "Okay. But not till after dark."

During the remaining daylight hours, Ronnie and Hutch gathered driftwood. They dug a pit in the sand, surrounded it with rocks, and laid in a stack of thin branches which Hutch reduced to kindling by shaving with his half knife. Cody returned from his solo explorations just at dusk, as the low-lying clouds took on rainbow hues and the heat of the day began dissipating.

"Cody, I hope you're a better Boy Scout than I am, because I can't start a fire without matches."

"I picked up a couple of hard rocks. I think I can get a spark off the steel transformer block."

Ronnie fluffed up the tinder in the bottom of the pit. "I've filleted the fish. And I'm starved, so you can go to it any time."

It took five minutes for Cody to get a spark that would catch. Once he had an ember, he blew on it until it crackled into a miniature flame. Very slowly he added bark peelings and wood shavings. Hutch had constructed a pyramid of sticks. When Cody nodded, he placed it carefully on the growing fire. Soon they had a sizeable blaze going.

Hutch stabbed a chunk of fish on a sharpened stick. "After this morning, I never thought I'd want to *make* a fire."

"Yes, it has been a hell of a day. Where'd you put the artifacts?"

Hutch pointed with his chin. "I'm keeping everything damp, especially the wood. It'll shrink up if it dries out without being treated. A fifty percent solution of four thousand molecular weight polyethylene glycol would be perfect. Barring that, swamp water will have to do."

While the fish cooked, Cody pulled out the mesh bag and inspected the contents. "It's too awkward to transport like this. I don't want to carry anything other than the plastic case."

"The board's too long to fit."

"I have a solution for that." Cody snapped the board across his thigh. It broke in two nearly equal pieces.

Hutch yelled, "What the hell did you do that for? I wanted to preserve it."

"This isn't a laboratory experiment. The board means nothing. We don't even need it. All we need is the information on it. Even the skull doesn't mean anything to me, other than proof of authenticity.''

"But you never know what you can learn—"

"We can learn later. For right now I'm more concerned with hauling this stuff a couple hundred miles along the beach. With this dense jungle behind us—Just tell me about the cylinder. What did you notice about it?''

Hutch scowled. He was silent for several minutes while he nibbled around the scorched edges of his fillet. "Like I said, it was stuck. And it was shiny, and perfectly smooth, like a vacuum flask that had been left there the day before."

"Did it have any openings?"

"None that I could see. Visibility was pretty bad, just a matter of inches, at best. It was solid, and—"

"How could you tell."

"Well, it gave off a dull sound when I tapped it. Not a ping, like you would expect from a hollow—"

"How about radiation? Did the Geiger register at all."

Hutch thought for a moment. "You know, I didn't really check. It was so silted up in there, when I started finding fossils, I put the case down and used my wrist light."

Ronnie stirred the fire, and shoved her spitted fish into the blue flames. "I couldn't believe you brought that box out with you, in the condition you were in."

Hutch humphed. "Yes, and you dragged it out of the wreck and hung onto it for almost an hour. Then we lose the damned thing any—"

Cody interrupted. "So you didn't notice any clicking."

Hutch shook his head. "No, after that I was pretty shaken up. I didn't notice much of anything. I just couldn't believe those fossils—"

"Honey, I was wondering. I thought bone decalcified in the water, that after a few years you don't find the bodies of shipwrecked sailors."

"That's only partially true. Fish eat the flesh, microbial action takes care of any tidbits leftover, and bones become friable. That is, the organic material consisting of collogen and fats decompose by hydrolysis. The sixty percent of bone that's made up of calcium compounds becomes porous, like a solidified sponge, and it'll last fairly long if it gets covered in mud and is protected from the acidic pH of sea water.

"But fossils, remember, are not bone. They are petrifactions in which all the original material has been replaced by minerals, usually silica, although there are dozens of others: carbonates, phosphates, pyrites, even the brilliant red jasper. On the gem hardness scale the quartz compounds rate a seven, so they can be cut and polished and made into jewelry. That's why you see petrified wood—"

Cody interrupted. "I was asking about the cylinder. The bones, or fossils, are of secondary importance—maybe no importance."

Hutch shoved more fish into the fire. "You know, Cody, I have trouble accepting this entire scenario. I mean, let's face it—beings from another planet, from another star, visiting Earth half a million years ago ... "

"It could explain a great deal," Ronnie said.

"That's what scares me. Not the aliens themselves, but the influence they might have exerted over prehistoric man. There're a lot of theories that explain the survival of our progenitors. Most of them, however, are theorized in reverse. That is, they use as proofs the habits of modern man, and dwell excessively on the exhibition of aggressive tendencies."

Ronnie handed a spit to the commando. "Cody, you haven't eaten a thing, yet."

He took the smoking morsel, and sniffed it approvingly. "I had some clams along the beach, when I was scouting."

"I've seen the way you can eat, though. Honey, I've read that man's aggressiveness may not be related at all to inherent hostility. It could be a pathological condition brought on by overcrowding. After all, most so-called primitive societies display very little aggression, except where territorial encroachment causes social or economic discomfort."

"The hungry-cats-in-a-bag theory. It explains why country folk are so down-to-earth and go out of their way to be neighborly, and city dwellers'll bite your head off for standing too close in a theater line. If you've ever driven through New York City, you know what it means. Wow, this fish is hot." Hutch blew on the white meat to cool it off. "That has nothing to do with instinct, or inherited response to stimuli. Man is no longer a puppet of Nature. Once he began regulating his environment—by wearing clothes, by building shelters—his physical evolution ended. According to Hutchison's Theory, since man dominates his living conditions, his genetic past ceases to be a factor in his further development. Now man is in control of his own destiny.

"The only evolution we will experience from here on is cultural. And that's guided not by the blind chance of intertwining chromosomes, but by the choice of intellect. Prehistoric man can be likened to a child, acting according to the precepts of his upbringing. But when that child grows up, and attains a sense of responsibility, he does what he *wants*. If he conducts himself in a mature manner, he's become a true adult. At this stage in our existence, man doesn't have to be aggressive—he *chooses* to be aggressive. I think it's a very poor choice.

"But back then, during the time of Peking man, he didn't have the vision of hindsight. He didn't know where he was going. Yet, that primeval creature achieved something that no other apelike forebear was able to manage: he survived. For some reason all the other lines of primitive man died out. I like to think it's because we were tougher, or smarter; that we brought ourselves up by our own bootstraps. Not just a chance ecological niche we happened to fill.

"That's why I shudder when I contemplate alien influences. It's antagonistic not only to the way I think, but to the way I feel." Hutch picked up the Peking man skull, and ran his hands over the cranial bulges.

"What did this creature see? And what did he do about it? Or worse, what did it do to him?"

*   *   *

"Get up! Get up! Get up!"

Hutch made a slit in one eye. Squinting, he pulled his arm tighter around Ronnie's middle. "Huhn."

Ronnie pulled free, rolled off the narrow ledge, and sat up. "Cody, what is it?"

Hutch lay with his head on his arm. "Another crocodile?"

The commando ran along the lagoon's sandy beach as if a thirty foot specimen were nipping at his heels. "Somebody's coming."

"Oh, darn. Just when I was beginning to enjoy being shipwrecked on a secluded isle with a placid lagoon and a gorgeous—"

Cody ripped open the raft's pontoons with a few jabs of his knife. It deflated with a hiss. "I'll cover our tracks. You start climbing that cliff."

"Huhn?" Hutch leaned up on one elbow. "How're we going to get rescued if—"

"No time for games, Honey." Ronnie pulled on her wetsuit booties. She took the mesh bag, now emptied of its goodies, and shoved it way back through the shrubbery where it did not show. "Let's get moving."

Still half asleep, Hutch worked his feet into his own booties. "I don't understand—"

Ronnie slipped her rubber vest over her head. "Put on your shorty suit, too. These are the only clothes we've got."

Hutch nodded, and did as he was told. Cody dragged the slashed up raft into the bushes. He disappeared into the dense foliage for a few moments. When he came out he brought a hacked off branch with him. He swept the beach with long, sideways strokes, to obliterate all footprints.

Ronnie grabbed the plastic watertight case. Cody had made a tump line and carrying straps out of plaited vine. She slipped the makeshift harness over her shoulders, tied the improvised belt around her waist, and strapped her knife sheath to her leg. "Don't forget your knife."

Hutch followed her example. In a moment, she was off, and he had to run along the lower cascade to catch up with her. "What're we running away for? What's—"

"Because Cody said so."

They scrambled up the lower outcrops, slipping and sliding on the treacherous, moss-covered rocks. Where it was dry, the pleated rubber soles gave them good traction. Most of the cliff proper was wet and slimy, but along the edge of the waterfall Ronnie picked out a path. She searched out handholds with long, bronzed fingers that pulled and tested each ledge surely but quickly. She climbed with the agility of a mountain goat.

"Come on, Hutch."

Hutch stared up at the towering vertical wall. "I *study* rocks, I don't climb them."

Cody raced up behind him. He had the two paddles slung over his back and tucked into his belt. "Call it hands on experience. Just put your nose to the grindstone, and move it."

Hutch climbed up behind Ronnie slowly. "Actually, I think this is igneous Precambrian—"

"I said move it!"

If Cody's imperious tone was not enough to make Hutch move, the paddle blade jabbing him in the butt was. "Don't get so close. I'm moving." He tried hard to keep his gluteus at maximus. Whenever he slowed down, the flattened aluminum end gouged into his legs, or worse.

From a height of fifty feet, Hutch glanced down at the serene setting. The blue water of the lagoon was the perfect setting for a holiday spa: sunny, shaded, secluded, and soundproof.

"We're running out of bare rock up here." Ronnie stood so close to the tumbling water that it sprayed out over her body in a thin sheet. "We'll have to move into the vegetation. Honey, don't use roots or branches for handholds, only bedrock. And if you start to slip, yell 'falling' and grab my ankle. I'll hold on."

Hutch could no longer bear to look down. He kept his body flattened to the rock face. He had to peel off his leg each time he wanted to move. The soft bootie soles were not meant for climbing. His arches ached painfully whenever he stood on a ledge not wide enough for his entire foot.

"Whoops!"

Cody stopped his backward lean with a well placed hand. "If you *do* feel yourself going, try to jump outward so you don't take me with you."

"Thanks."

Ronnie angled away from the water and crawled into a mass of vines. "Hey, we can duck inside this stuff. We'll be out of sight."

"Do it." Cody took Hutch's rear, and shoved. "If you'll stand upright instead of clinging like a limpet, it'll be easier."

"I can't. I'm afraid I'll fall." Hutch gulped. His foot slipped, and his whole body slid sideways. He clutched at whatever was under his hands. His fingertips scraped across bare rock until he gathered up an armful of vines that were tearing free from their precarious purchases. "Hellllp."

A hand clamped down on his wrist like the jaws of a moray. "Come on. There's a place up here where you can rest." Ronnie held on until he regained his balance.

Hutch chanced to look down, saw the sheer cliff face, the tumbling stream of water, the lagoon that was now no larger than a puddle. It all started to spin about in a large circle. "I think I'm going to be sick."

"Not on me, you're not." Cody climbed up from under him, pressed his body against Hutch's. He worked both of them up through the vines until they reached the hollowed out depression from which Ronnie was pulling. "Man, you're sweating like a stuck pig."

"Must be the suit."

Cody pulled down the front zipper for him. "All right, we'll hide in here for a min—Here they are. Be still."

Ronnie brushed Hutch's hair back. "Are you all right, Honey?"

"No. I've got a bad case of sewing machine legs."

Two lines of khaki-clothed soldiers marched into the lagoon along opposite sides of the inlet. They wore jungle boots and soft felt hats, and carried wooden stocked rifles.

"AKs."

"Cody, who are they?"

"I didn't get close enough to read their dogtags, but they sure as hell didn't come here for a picnic."

Hutch watched the men walking along the water's edge. "Has it occurred to you that someone isn't being as covert about this operation as we are?"

"Yes. I can't figure out how they've been able to trace us wherever we go. It doesn't make sense. I just hope they don't see any footprints in the— Uh-oh."

The lead soldier on the right bank stopped, and halted the line behind him with a raised arm. He bent slightly at the waist. He stared into the water for several seconds. Suddenly, the calm surface of the lagoon was broken with a large splash. A greenish leviathan streaked out of the water with amazing celerity.

The soldier took a step back with one foot, while the crocodile hissed, snapped, and turned away with the other. The man was still standing on his one remaining leg as the beast plunged back into the lagoon with a mouthful of calf meat. The soldier swayed, put out his other leg as a brace, and fell down when he shifted his weight where there was nothing left to stand on.

Three rifles opened up at once, on full automatic. Bullets from both sides of the lagoon skimmed along the surface, splashing and ricochetting off into the jungle. As one, both squads backed away from the water's edge. One soldier knelt by the man screaming and writhing on the beach. He removed the man's belt and used it as a tourniquet on his stump.

"Oh, god." Ronnie swallowed loud enough to be heard. Her grip sent shooting pains through Hutch's shoulder. "That poor man."

"Yeah, well, that poor man was sent out here to blow our brains out."

"Why? I don't understand." Hutch said. "What do they want from us?"

"Our lives."

"But that doesn't make sense. We haven't done anything."

"Welcome to the world. Just because *you're* rational doesn't mean the other guy is."

"But, we have courts to settle disputes. We have—a legal system."

"In court, that guy doesn't have a leg to stand on. But that's not going to prevent some radical group that opposes our point of view from doing what they damn well please. It takes two to tangle."

Someone thought of dropping grenades in the water. Half a dozen water spouts rose high in the air and rained down like a tropical storm. Schools of gaily colored fish floated belly up to the surface.

"That croc is halfway out to sea by now."

The wounded man was helped to his foot by two companions. They hobbled back along the beach while the rest of the soldiers fanned out and examined the bushes. An officer raised a pair of binoculars to his eyes. From the constricture of the sea entrance he scanned the terrain, the cascades, the waterfall, the cliff face. At one point Hutch thought the man was looking directly at him, but the glasses passed on. The officer walked around the lagoon until he caught up with the soldiers bunched up at the campsite.

Ronnie said, "Did you disperse our bedding?"

"Yes."

The squad from the far side of the lagoon crossed over the lower cascades. Some of the soldiers inspected the ground while others observed the surrounding jungle. When they converged, the officer held a conversation with the platoon sergeant and squad leaders.

"Okay, our cover's blown. Let's get out of here."

"You don't know that," Hutch protested.

"I *do* know it. I can tell by their gestures. They're trying to put on an act of nonchalance, but they've found something: a footprint, a piece of thread, something we dropped. Maybe they dug up the fire pit. I don't know. But they suspect something. I'll take the lead."

Cody removed the paddles from his back because they kept catching in the vines and bushes. He carried them both lashed together in one hand. He crept along the cliff face away from the falls, until he found a fault line angling up. Ronnie and Hutch followed close behind.

A gunshot rang out, and a bullet spanged off the rocks too close for comfort.

"They've seen the bushes move," Cody yelled.

A wild fusillade sent lead spattering through the underbrush and zinging off the cliff face like an opera finale. Hutch heard an all-to-human scream of pair from above. A moment later a body crashed through the bushes next to him. A raucous cacophany filled the treetops at the ridge line as a troop of gibbons swung by their hands through the upper canopy. Hutch stared at the one singled out for death. Its long, muscular arms twitched feebly for a few seconds. Then it lay still.

"Come on! Get up here."

Cody knifed through the jungle like a wraith. Ronnie waited for Hutch to catch up. She showed him the way. Gunshots still rang out from the lagoon, but the trio had crested the hill and were out of the line of fire. Cody crouched in a closet-sized clearing.

Hutch wiped sweat off his forehead. "I guess this is going to change our plans about beachcombing."

Cody cut some thin vine from the bole of a huge tree. He lashed his knife to a paddle handle, testing it several times by stabbing the bark and pulling it back out. "The only thing we want to do now is get lost, and stay lost. They'll never find us in here."

Hutch slapped at something biting his neck. "Did anyone bring a compass?"

"Just the one in the sky."

Ronnie looked up. With a hundred-fifty feet of broad-leaved foliage between them and the clear blue, it was dark as a pocket. "I don't like those storm clouds rolling in."

"I don't like these bugs crawling down my neck."

Cody tossed Hutch a bottle of repellent.

"Where'd you get this?"

"I always keep it in my pocket because of the gnats on the boat. You, of course, slept inside with the door closed."

Hutch rolled his eyes. He squirted the liquid onto his palm, and rubbed it vigorously over his exposed flesh. He handed the bottle to Ronnie.

"All right, here's what we'll do. We cut back this way and regain the creek, then stick to the water while we pick up elevation."

Hutch said, "They don't have dogs to sniff us out."

"No, the reason is it's the only way to make any time through this mess. Rivers are highways. This creek may only be a footpath, but it'll get us through. Hey, is there anything we should look out for? I don't want any surprises."

Hutch shrugged. "Snakes'll be our worst problem. Stay away from all of them. Leeches, but they can't really hurt you. If we get into open country there might be some small rhinos. And wildcats, but they'll run before we ever see them."

"No piranhas?"

"That's the Amazon. Borneo's got orangutans that're strong enough to crush a man, but they're pretty shy. Believe it or not, the biggest danger comes from the smallest predators: virus, bacteria, and protozoans. You can get dysentery from the water, malaria from mosquitoes, and fatal infection from minor cuts and scrapes, even insect bites."

"Just like 'Nam. Okay, keep it tight. If we get separated in this jungle—well, keep close behind me."

"My hand's in your pocket."

Ronnie sighed. "And to think I gave up a desk job."

They beat through the bush for several minutes, through nearly impassable thickets. The understory was a biologist's delight: hundreds of varieties of fern which grew in great profusion, creepers as large as small trees, and thousands of smaller plants as yet to be categorized. Feet sank into the springy litter that was in places knee deep. And *everything* was wet.

Ronnie gave a sudden yelp. She drew her hand back and wiped it furiously on the moss-covered ground. "Yuck. What *is* that?"

Hutch bent close to the fat, cigarlike object. "Looks like a slug. They won't hurt you. These are closely related to the nudibranchs we saw on that wooden wreck last week. Remember the one with the copra—"

"Hey, professor, can you cut the natural history lesson and keep the voices down? I'd rather not megaphone our presence."

They splashed into the creek, a welcome relief after the brutal climbing, bending, crawling, and face slapping of the snarled shrubbery and sharp-pointed sticks and lower branches. Water babbled over a smooth course that was a tunnel through the jungle denseness.

Hutch sat in the cool stream and washed the sweat and grime from his face, neck, and arms, and let the current pour through his open shorty suit. His legs were dotted with bloody pinpricks: stab wounds from sharp leaves and broken twigs. "Cody, do you have any idea where we're going?"

"No, just what we're getting away from."

Ronnie loosened the tump line and shrugged off the plastic case. She poured handfuls of water over her short hair and let it drip down her body. "If we keep going up, eventually we'll get out of the rain forest and into open grassland. The going will be easier. We can find food, and we can reach a river which will lead us to civilization."

"Or savages who'd like to have us for breakfast."

"No, she's right," Hutch said. "Most of the native population is concentrated along the river deltas. It's a largely agricultural community that grows rice, corn, sweet potatoes, beans. The real savagery is behind us—those foreigners with guns. The natives had a bad time with the Japanese during the occupation, and don't tolerate armed invasion."

"I hate to break up this tete-a-tete, but, am I the only one starving?" Ronnie washed down the rest of her body. "I could eat a horse."

"The Equus is not autochthonous to Borneo. Eohippus crossed the land bridge to Asia, but—"

"Professor!"

"All right. I'm sorry. You're the Admirable Crichton, you get us something to eat."

An hour later, he did.

"Honey, what *is* that thing?"

The beast that writhed in its death throes under the point of Cody's makeshift spear looked like a large armadillo with a long, pointed snout and a thick tail. Its entire body was covered with overlapping scales, giving it the look of a giant pine cone with legs.

Hutch prodded it with his own, unarmed paddle. "It's a pangolin. A scaly anteater. They're usually nocturnal, but—"

Ronnie was aghast. "With scales?"

"Well, they're actually fused hairs—"

"Can we eat it?" Cody kicked the still jerking body. "That's all I want to know."

"Careful! It doesn't have any teeth, but those claws can rip you apart." Hutch shivered when he thought of the animal as a food item.

"You won't find them on any menu, but—they're mammals, so I guess it's edible."

"Then let's get a fire going. I don't want to get poisoned by gamy, worm-filled meat. With this mist rolling in, they'll never see our smoke."

Ronnie laid the plastic case in the middle of the grassy clearing. "I don't care what it tastes like, as long as it's meat."

They were halfway through their meal when tiny droplets started falling from the trees. Hutch looked up without missing a bite. "It probably started raining an hour ago. It just took this long to find a way to the ground."

Cody chomped merrily on a blackened rib. "It was like that in the 'Nam, in the highlands. You'd be walking through the jungle in a downpour, completely soaked—but you'd still be hot. At least it kept the bugs down. Then you'd break out into the LZ and find out it stopped raining two days ago. It just keeps dripping through the leaves of that triple canopy."

"You love this stuff, don't you?"

Cody turned the bone around in front of his eyes. "It's not bad, but it could use a little salt."

"No, I mean this." Hutch swept his arm around his head. "The jungle. The fighting. The suffering."

Cody reached for another piece of meat. "I like adventure."

"Is that why you volunteered for Vietnam?"

"I didn't volunteer for the first tour, only the second. It kinda got in my blood."

"What? Shooting and killing?"

"Naw, nobody likes killing. At least, no sane person. No, what I meant was the excitement. You can't understand. You don't know what it's like. When you're out there on patrol, all your skills are put to the test. It's you against the jungle, you against Charlie. It has nothing to do with— machismo. It's not a manly thing, not in the sexual sense. It's personal. Man against Nature, and against his own nature. The ego against the Universe.

"And when a firefight is over, when you've run your hands over your body and found it's still in one piece, and you're still breathing—you realize you've lived through it. And you're so happy—so happy to be alive. It's like being born again, but on a higher plane."

Cody stopped chewing. He stared into the glowing embers, his eyes glazed and reflecting the fire like twin pools of lava. "Later, you forget the fear. You forget the pain, the trauma. You look back on it, and all you remember is the absolute divinity of the moment when you were *that* close to death—and survived." The bone hung listlessly in his fingers. His eyebrows pinched in deep concentration. "The adrenaline release is like a drug. It gets you high, and you become addicted to it. The blasé, civilized world seems tame by comparison. So, you either seek out more adventure for your next fix, or you stifle it and it smolders inside you like a dampened fire waiting to burst into flames with a puff of air. And the worst part is, no matter how hard you try, you can never quite recapture that first moment, that first flush of excitement. But you try, in your dreams, to relive it. Man, you sure as hell try."

Cody ran out of words, but the jungle was never silent. The trees were filled with brightly plumaged birds that chirped incessantly. Monkeys chattered like a group of housewives at a yard sale. Exotic insects buzzed, hummed, clicked, crackled, crowed, twanged, and rattled in overlapping concatenations.

"Cody, did you ever feel—I don't know—let down? About the war. The way it was fought. About the way it turned out."

"I felt abandoned. Orphaned. But it never hurt my fighting spirit. I know there's been a lot of talk, and controversy, about withdrawing support for the war effort, but that didn't involve me. I was a soldier, and I did my part. It was the politicians who lost the war, not the men in the bush."

"But you were the one who lost in the end."

"No, it was the Vietnamese who lost. But that wasn't my doing. I was more of a—well, say a carpenter, building the framework of a house, putting up the walls, hanging the doors and nailing on trim. If the house fell down because the foundation collapsed, blame the block setter. I still put up a damn fine home."

"And we don't even know yet if the house isn't still holding together." Ronnie wiped greasy fingers on a large, waterfilled leaf, as if it were a chemical-soaked napkin. "We haven't advanced far enough in time to enable us to see the Vietnam war in perspective. American involvement was neither cultivation nor culmination, but only one phase in the course of human events. The struggle is still going on.

"A single episode cannot be viewed out of context. You need to observe continuity. When you are too close to the event, you cannot discern the effect of interaction any more than you can perceive a pattern from a single thread. But back away from the material, watch how the other threads are interwoven, build up a picture of colors and contrast, and gradually the true form begins to take shape. You may have to get very far away from it all before that happens. And then, just when you think you can see it all—you back up further and see a still larger pattern of which the smaller was just a part. There is no real end to the process. Only history can determine the outcome. But just when we think that human history offers the proper hindsight, along comes planetary history—or galactic history. We are all in our insignificant ways parts of a pattern whose design we can never conceive, or comprehend if shown."

Hutch nodded slowly. "No wonder people turn to religion. The world of make believe is a lot easier to accept than the uncertain knowledge of reality."

"Right now, the only certainty is that we're gonna get wet." Cody tossed the gnawed bone into the fire. His shirt was in tatters from scraping through the brush, his pants legs full of holes. He rolled down his sleeves. "But, I guess that's why they call this the rain forest."

They kicked out the fire. Upstream, cascades carved a broad swath through the vegetation. Travel was easy on the open rocks except where sheer walls stretched higher than a person could reach. Then it required careful negotiation along the edges, or building a human pyramid to scale rock walls.

Hutch complained at every maneuver. "This is supposed to be an Underwater Strike Force, not a mountain climbing expedition."

Ronnie's hair was soaked, and matted to her head. "Wow, this rain is really coming down."

Hutch had to squint in the downpour to see where he was going. Wind drove the tiny, pinlike droplets into his eyes with painful force. "If it ever starts going up, we're in trouble."

Ronnie rubbed her arms vigorously. "This is the first time in weeks I've been cold."

"Maybe cold, but never frigid." Hutch pulled the zipper tighter to his neck. Flocks of goose bumps covered his exposed arms and legs. He had to shout to make himself heard against the torrent of water pounding his head and running by his feet. "Cody, I should warn you. This type of hard rock bottom prevents percolation. These are prime conditions for flash flooding."

Cody shouted back. "There's a clearing up ahead."

Hutch continued wading through the swiftly running stream, using his paddle as a cane where necessary and making a pretense of stroking otherwise. "Good idea."

They gathered under the spreading leaves of a huge oak, on the edge of a vast plane dotted with trees of the oak and chestnut groups. The rain whipped across the grassland in sheets. The ground was soggy, but not as harsh as the rain forests of the lower elevations.

Hutch put his arms around Ronnie, as much for comfort as for warmth. "There's not much chance of finding shelter, but walking will be a hell of a lot easier."

Cody said, "We can build something if we have to. You want me to take that for a while?"

Ronnie shifted the case, and repositioned the vines around her body. "It's not heavy. And with the rubber padding it doesn't dig into my shoulders. But I'm not used to the tump line. My neck is sore, and I think I've got a permanent furrow in my forehead."

"You're doing fine." Cody cupped both hands over his eyes, to keep out the water while he scanned the valley beneath them. "Let's wait here until the rain slackens. Then we'll strike out over that way."

"The monsoons usually last a couple months," Hutch said.

"But this is just the beginning. It's like you: it only comes in spurts. It'll be over in an hour."

It was over in an hour.

They strolled over the sloping flatland in a fine drizzle, but soon even that ceased. When the later afternoon sun came out it began to warm them up. The rain water on Hutch's skin soon evaporated, to be replaced almost immediately by beads of sweat.

"Isn't there any way to stay dry around here?" Ronnie complained.

Hutch shook his head. "It was just like this in Java, when I was working on the excavations. You either die from heat and thirst, or you drown. There's no comfortable middle ground. That's probably why there have been so many migrations. There's evidence that Java man visited Borneo, although he didn't last long."

"I can't imagine why," Cody said.

"That was back in the Pleistocene epoch. Since then, a succession of Hominidae have invaded the island. None of them, judging by the paucity of fossil evidence, appear to have made a big impact. They were all Australoid in appearance. Then, maybe fifteen thousand years ago, we begin to see the influx of Mongoloid people from mainland Asia. There's some intermingling of groups, leading to a homogenous native population that still exists in the back country. About ten thousand years ago migrations became fairly common, mostly by nonagricultural food gatherers. This forced a lot of people inland. Today, instead of distinct ethnic groups, you've got such a melting pot of people that you can find examples of every phenotype among the forest nomads."

Ronnie took over without a pause. "There's a large Chinese influence in the language, with overtones of Malaysian and Polynesian among the coastal settlements. Midland, due to the prerogatives of terrain, there's a wide separation between population groups, even between domestic units. This social isolation has resulted in a plethora of dialects and permutations that—"

"Man, is this how you two talk when you're down in that cabin together? Give me the rain and the gnats any day."

"What do you talk about when you're with your wife?"

"We talk about the kids. One's going out on her first date, the other put chewing gum on his teacher's seat, the other's losing a molar and how much are we supposed to leave under the pillow from the Tooth Fairy. You know, typical, mundane parent talk. When we put our heads together, we kiss. We don't get caught up in screwball pseudointellectual jargon. We've got enough prob—"

Cody turned suddenly and knocked Ronnie and Hutch to the ground. "*Get down!*" he hissed.

Hutch struggled to get his head out of the knee deep grass, but Cody pinned him to the ground. "What is it? A rhinoceros?"

"Worse. Half-naked savages."

Ronnie rolled free but continued to lie flat. "In these duds, they may think the same of us."

Hutch said, "What do you expect them to wear in this heat? Tuxedos?"

"Cut the vaudeville act." Cody's wiry arm released its hold on Hutch's. "Just sneak a peek and tell me what you think."

Hutch pushed up to hands and knees, peered over the swaying, still damp blades. He saw a line of native women wearing white blouses and short skirts, and carrying woven baskets on their heads. They were too far away to see their features, but from their black, waist length ponytails he took them to be Oriental.

"Hello," he shouted, standing up before Cody could grab him. He waved both hands above his head. "Over here."

"*You fool. Get down.*"

"It's okay, Cody. They're not the enemy. They live here."

The parade stopped. The women chatted quietly to themselves as Hutch approached. "Hi, there." He smiled as broadly as he could. "How are you today?"

Keeping up the singsong flow of words, they exchanged looks among themselves.

"We were shipwrecked." Hutch made dipping motions with the paddle. "We landed on the beach and climbed up the great falls. We're looking for a town, or a village." With thumb and pinky extended, he put his left hand up to his ear. "With a telephone. Can you help us?"

They were not at all afraid. They talked incessantly among themselves. Hutch understood not a word of it. From behind, he heard Ronnie's voice spout strange, unintelligible words. The women's eyes lighted up and their language became more voluble.

"Can you understand them?"

Ronnie cocked her head. "Not all of it. But there are enough Chinese idioms so that I can pick out a few phrases, if not the proper syntax." She switched back to the foreign tongue, accompanied by gestures. Several of the women responded with verve, gesticulating and pointing. "We're in luck. They're from a nearby hamlet. I can't make out the distance, but since they're carrying sugarcane and mellon from the fields, it can't be too far. *Cody.*"

The commando was nowhere to be seen. Ronnie called again. The grass moved, and Cody stood up with the tip of his paddle spear foremost. He scanned the grassland all around them before coming closer.

"What the *hell's* the idea? How could you be sure these weren't cannibals?"

Hutch laughed out loud. "Cody, there haven't been anthropophagi on Borneo for millenia, perhaps never."

"Yeah? And what about the crew of the *Gremyashchi*? What makes you think they didn't end up in a pot?"

"I admit they were probably killed, maybe even by people of this very tribe, since they live close to the coast where the survivors came ashore. But there might have been extenuating circumstances. These people were rather gun shy after the Japanese occupation. If the crew members brandished weapons—uh, Cody, could you put down that spear. I think you're making the women nervous."

Cody stopped in front of Hutch. He jabbed the knife point into the ground. "Well, you could have told me."

Hutch put on a serious mein. "I would have, if I thought you had a 'need to know'."

Ronnie smiled quixotically. "Anyway, these women have agreed to take us to see their village chief. They say that if anyone can help us, he can. He is very old, very wise, and very powerful. I suggest we go along with them."

Cody stabbed a finger at Hutch, millimeters away from his nose. "Okay, mister wise guy. But you're carrying this joke a little too far."

Hutch broke into a conservative smile. "You know, I'm beginning to enjoy the USF."

*   *   *

The village was constructed almost entirely of bamboo. Every thatched roof hut rested on four-foot stilts that kept the floors off the rain-sodden ground. A maze of bamboo walkways connected every building, lending a look of solidarity. Tall palms were strategically placed to offer shade. Inland, mountain peaks rose high above the jungle, so the community appeared to be nestled in its own, secluded valley.

Ronnie wiped her muddy booties on the bottom poles of the ramp. "From what I gather, the local chief is highly respected. His influence extends to many neighboring villages."

"That's uncommon for this region. Their social organization is largely bilaterally cognatic, with equal emphasis on patrilineal and matrilineal connections but limited to the domestic unit." Hutch leaned toward Cody and lowered his voice. "That means kinship ties through mom and pop with no extended family."

Cody scowled. "You're so condescending, it hurts."

"They also have a system of beliefs in the supernatural, and appeasement through ritual, that borders on the complexity of Catholicism."

"I'm thrilled."

"Cody, you'll like these folks. They're monogamous, have detailed property laws, and a high regard for order and authority. They're perfect capitalists."

As they climbed up onto the walkway, the bamboo creaked and groaned with their weight. The babbling women led the procession past several huts bursting with curious children and elderly, matronly females. They all wore simple tunics and shorts of universal black: no-frills clothing.

Ronnie was introduced to a tousle-haired young man who nodded and grinned profusely. He made sweeping gestures and spoke slowly with exaggerated enunciation that Ronnie could follow.

"He says the chief, whose name is Buching, is very old and very ill, and does not receive visitors except on special occasions. But he will announce us, if we will accompany him to his home."

"That's as close to a written invitation we're likely to get." Cody stepped forward with his universal smile. "Lead on, my man."

With his head bobbing like a dashboard puppy, he became their guide. The women smiled at them as they passed, then went about their tasks. The man led them through the village maze, over the rickety platforms and through concourses crowded with goggle-eyed natives.

"Epicanthic folds demonstrate a strong Mongoloid background, with—"

"How many credits is this course worth?"

"I was just making observations—"

"Try doing it without moving your lips. All I care about is that they're friendly, and won't give us away to the guys with the guns." To Ronnie, "Can you sling enough of their lingo to make them understand that we're just passing through. If they'll just give us directions to the nearest signs of civilization, we'd be very—"

"That would offend them because they consider themselves very civilized."

"You know what I mean. Technological civilization. Paved roads. Phone booths. Hot dog stands. Double parking."

Hutch noticed the cleanliness of the bamboo pathways, while underneath, pigs wallowed in the ooze and vegetation. "In social graces, these people have it all over us. They may be poor by our standards, but they're rich when it comes to dealing with their fellow man."

"I just don't want my head dealt on a platter. Make them understand—"

They encountered a large group of senescent, gray-haired men, huddling on their haunches in the shade of an overhanging eave. They looked up silently as their young guide talked with them and made gestures toward the oddly dressed trio. Then he ducked into the hut.

"These are the village elders, part of Buching's retinue." Standing in the sun, Ronnie peered in through the open door. "Buching is inside."

Hutch stood by Ronnie side. The hut had windows, but they were covered with plaited vines that served as curtains. The large single room was dark, but he could discern a figure lying on the central mattress. The young man bent over him, whispered into his ear. The old man stirred, rolled over on his side, facing the doorway. With the creaking slowness of decline, he allowed himself to be helped to a sitting position. The young man pulled him up to his feet. With extreme care, like a nurse helping a weakened patient, the young man wrapped an arm around a wizened shoulder, and half carried the oldster to the shaft to sunlight that permeated the opening.

The primogenitor leaned against the sill. He was ancient and stooped, with skin like cracked parchment. A few bristles of strawlike hair clung precariously to a dome-shaped scalp. Thin arms were like strands of spaghetti, thickly ribboned with blue, bulging veins. He wore nothing but a pair of off-white shorts. He stared wild-eyed at Ronnie.

Cody tightened his grip on his paddle, but kept the knife tip pointed down. "What's that gibberish? What's he saying?"

"It sounds like—I don't know. A literal translation would be—badge of office?"

The younger man left for a moment, then reappeared with a multicolored, feathered belt of woven cloth. He wrapped it about Buching's waist, and tied it in the back. Then he handed him an antique, rusted gun.

Cody brought his paddle up to present arms. "What the hell—"

"*Cody.*" Ronnie pushed him back and glared at him. "Let me handle this."

"That's a Tokarev automatic pistol. What the hell's he doing with a Russian handgun?"

"It's a symbol, not a weapon. Just let him be."

Cody gradually lowered the paddle, but his arms bulged with the tension he kept on the handle.

Hutch smirked. "And look at the rust. That thing would blow up in his face if he tried to shoot it."

Buching slipped the gun under his belt. It took three tries before he fixed it so it did not fall into his shorts. With the help of the guide, he stepped out into the sun and walked directly, if sluggishly, toward Ronnie. Rheumy eyes ran up and down her body, and lingered long on her face. The ancient head twitched with his babbling.

"What's he saying?" Cody said imperiously.

Ronnie cocked her head. "Something about a white woman—being rare."

"Uh, oh. I can see it coming." Hutch took a deep breath. "Shades of King Kong. He wants to trade six of his wives for you."

"*Shut up!* What's he saying now?"

Saliva drooled from the corners of the chief's mouth. He spoke haltingly, feebly, with no animation. He leaned heavily against the younger man.

"He's not very coherent. He has trouble forming his words. I think—"

"What was that? What did he say?"

"It sounded like—"

"Ask him to repeat it."

Ronnie leaned close as the old man uttered barely audible sounds. She swallowed, and turned. Her eyes were wide, almost fearful. "He said—he said—*Gremyashchi.*"

*   *   *

"Hey, this stuff is pretty good." Hutch dug the wooden spoon into the bowl of mixed tomatoes and squash. "Cody, you know what your problem is? You're too suspicious."

The commando shoveled in his own vegetables as if he were stoking a coal furnace. "Part of the business. If you start trusting people, you get hurt. And I don't mean just a broken heart. I mean a broken body. After a while you learn to take offensive action all the time. It's easier to back down when you make a mistake than to climb out of your grave with all that dirt on your head."

"Cody, take my anthropological word for it. These are not warlike people. They're primitive, yes. But they're also full of primitive innocence. And they're not nearly as backward as you think. The seaports have concrete cities. They have oil refineries, hospitals, police, and a thriving export industry. On a different scale, this village is the equivalent of an American rural community—inhabited with friendly people without the pressures of city crowding."

"I hear you, I just don't take it for granted like you do. To me, people who are closer to savagery have less self awareness, less feeling, and less comprehension of the consequences of death."

"If you're trying to tell me a Borneo mother doesn't love her child as much as a suburban housewife, you're full of crap. Love isn't predicated upon technological advancement. It's not even a cultural commodity. It's human nature, pure and simple. Scientifically speaking, love is an emotional rendition of an instinctive mammalian process, emotion being the equivalent of parental protection in human terms. People are people, Cody, despite venue and without prejudice of educational benefits. You have a warped view of—"

Cody scooped more food into his bowl. He leaned back against the bamboo wall of their private hut. "I'm just being cautious. And if you want a word of advice, you should be a little less naive about your fellow man—and woman."

"And what's that supposed to mean?"

"Just that—nothing is ever what it seems. Beauty may be skin deep, but there're an awful lot of thin-skinned people in the world. You want to stay on top of the human quagmire, you gotta learn that. And you have to learn to accept it when your preconceived notions turn out to be full of misconceptions. Then, at least, when you get smacked in the face with reality, you don't wilt like a poisoned flower. You just draw in the petals and wait for the next sunrise."

"Cody, that's quite a poetic sentiment, coming from you."

"I have my moments." He dug his fist into a gourd full of peanuts, and crunched them a handful at a time. "In this business, everything is never as it seems; and what seems, is never as it is."

"I think that statement's redundant."

Cody kept on chewing. "Redundant, but not adament."

Hutch raised his eyebrows. "And that's a contradiction."

Cody shrugged. "That's life in the big ville."

Footfalls sounded on the walkway outside, and a moment later Ronnie entered the single room enclosure.

Hutch jumped to his feet, and took her in his arms. "How'd it go?"

She separated from Hutch, wriggled out of the vine straps, dropped the plastic case onto the slatted floor, and slunk down on crossed legs. "Okay, I guess."

"What do you mean, you guess?" Cody said firmly. "Are they going to help us out, or what?"

Ronnie nodded weakly. "He didn't give me any trouble, really. It's just—well, he's senile, and doesn't always make sense. He loses his train of thought."

"Then why the hell is he the village chief?"

"For many years he led his people well, and united many villages with great prosperity. He holds a venerated position. Because of his sagacity the people have great respect for him."

Hutch squatted by her side. "I wish I could have been there to help you. I understand how these people—"

"I know, Honey. But he wanted only me."

Cody said, "Why? Don't tell me that old lecher—"

"It's nothing like that. I couldn't get it all. He kept fading out on me. Something about the survivors from the *Gremyashchi*."

"What survivors? They're weren't any. These bastards slaughtered them all."

"That's not strictly true, although they probably mistook them for Japanese invaders. Anyway, I did a little bartering with him. Made him some gifts—"

"What did you use for trade?"

Ronnie did not appear to notice the innuendo. "A box full of low voltage transformers, power converters, and control boards. They make nice ornaments." She shoved the case over to Hutch. "I kept the fossils and the wood."

"All *right*. You are a dream boat." Hutch knelt close, and hugged and kissed her. "So he'll help us get out of here?"

"Yes. His grandson, Balaka, the young man who took us to him, will escort us. It's a very complicated route, with no road signs. Because of the impassible mountains we have to go inland to a pass, then across some deep gorges. He'll take us as far as the river, where we can get transportation to the coast."

"Honey, you are a charmer. Here, have something to eat." Hutch handed her the serving bowl. "Home grown vegies, and the stuff is *good*."

Ronnie shook her head. "I'm too exhausted to eat right now. This whole—everything is just catching up with me."

Cody grinned. "Suffering from deja vu?"

She looked up suddenly, her eyes pinched. "What do you mean by that?"

"Well, I just thought this situation might bring back thoughts of your—father."

Her shoulders slumped. "Yes. Perhaps so. I don't know. I'm just—"

"Wait a minute," Hutch protested. "What's this about your old man?"

After several moments of silence, Cody said, "He was lost at sea."

Hutch was horrified. "But, I thought he was dead."

Ronnie looked up sharply. "That's the official version. Neither he nor his boat were ever found."

"It was in the Caribbean," Cody supplied smugly. "He might have gotten caught in a storm, or captured by druggies and fitted out with concrete shoes. If he stopped on a deserted island that was a transfer point—"

"Cody, what the hell has gotten into you?" Hutch glared at the commando with fiery eyes. "Have some sensitivity."

"It's okay, Honey. It was more than a year ago. I'm over it by now." Ronnie drew close to Hutch. She slipped her arms around his middle, and squeezed. "Almost."

"I don't care. He's got no right—"

"Hush, Honey. Hush." She lay back and pulled him down. "I'm so tired. Would you just—lie down with me? Just hold me."

Cody stood up and padded to the doorway. "That's my cue to go. But I'll be back after dark. So whatever you're going to do, have it done by then."

Hutch lay down with his arm over Ronnie's shoulder. She melted against him and closed her eyes.

"Cody, you bastard, sometimes I think you're completely without feeling."

"Sometimes I wish I were."

*   *   *

For three days they tramped along the jungle paths. For three nights they slept in hammocks to the tune of feral animal growls and insect sounds. They subsisted on corn and sweet potatoes, and pineapples whenever they could find them.

The muddy trail rose and fell with steep irregularity. In the course of a day they climbed bare mountain ridges and descended into lush, secluded valleys. Balaka introduced them to the people of the many villages they went through. Some consisted of no more than half a dozen huts along the path, some were sprawling, elevated aeries that thrived with children and livestock. Once they had to run from a charging water buffalo.

They stopped at a small creek that flowed through a field of tall grass. Hutch scratched under this native garb. "Do these things *come* with lice, or are they added later?"

Ronnie plopped her worn, rubber booties in the water. "Vermin for these people are a way of life."

Hutch splashed water in his face. "So are snakes. I never knew there were so many different kinds, and came in so many different colors. Hey, Cody, don't you ever relax?"

Cody stood guard while the others knelt by a large pool. His vigil was constant: he never took his eyes off the surrounding jungle. "Can't afford to. Not in a war zone."

"What do you think? You're in Vietnam?"

"Naw, this is easy compared to the 'Nam. No mines, no booby traps, no bouncing betties, no snipers, no mamasans concealing guns under their *ao dais*, no papasans leaking troop movements to the VC or the NVA, no kids carrying bombs or grenades. But these damn people'll grin you to death."

Hutch sat wearily on his haunches. He poured cool, soothing water on the back of his neck, and let it dribble down over his chest and back. "Well, this is the hardest trek I've ever taken. But I know what you mean. If I have to smile and bow and shake hands with one more village chief, I'm going to run for President."

Balaka came back from where he had disappeared into the jungle on the opposite side of the clearing. He rattled off in his native tongue, and gestured for them to come.

"What's he saying?" Cody wanted to know.

Ronnie said, "He says there's a village up ahead where we can rest."

"Here we go again." Hutch groaned as he straightened out his aching body. Wearily, he followed the bouncing native.

Ronnie was right behind him. "It's very close."

Only two minutes passed before they broke into a clearing. Before them sprawled a huge village, with a center thoroughfare thronged with people wearing simple attire. Along the sides of the market place wares were for sale: everything from pots and pans to tables full of fruit and vegetables. Women and children carried folding umbrellas to ward off the sun. Men carried poles across their shoulders, with their goods balanced in reed baskets fore and aft.

From the rear of their four-person safari, Cody said, "I can hear the river. And I can smell the cool air."

Hutch stopped in front of the first building, of block and stucco. Parked in front of it were a rack of motor bikes. Overhead, wires ran from the peak of one bungalow to the peak of another. He stared at the ancient red and white object standing on the porch.

"It's a goddamned Coke machine. We're saved."

Ronnie rambled alongside. She leaned against him, and lay her head against his shoulder. "Honey, we don't have any change."

The *Dudley Morton*

The twenty-inch computer screen filled with data at a touch of the keypad. Hutch ran his fingers over the console, wiped the screen, refilled it with corroboratory figures. He left the columns of numbers in place while he keyed the adjacent monitor for a sequential readout. He made notes with good old-fashioned paper and pencil, where it was available for easy reference.

"How's it coming, professor?" Cody was resplendent in his newly pressed camouflage fatigues and spit-shined boots. His beret was cocked at a rakish angle. "Find anything worthwhile, yet?"

Hutch rubbed his eyes, then scratched his blonde beard. "I think I'm suffering from boat lag. I've spent so much time in the water, I'm beginning to feel like a porpoise."

"Want to go back to humping the Borneo boonies?"

"No, I just want to get some rest. But I've got some things that don't corroborate. And with this mainframe, and all the lab equipment—"

"I told you these subs had everything you could possibly want. With the technicians doing all the work, why don't you go snooze out for a while?"

Hutch smirked. "Because my scientific curiosity has got the better of me. I've always had to do my own lab work, and I was never too good at it. It took me forever. I'm a field man. But this way, with round the clock assistants taking measurements, performing tests, and keypunching the data, I can concentrate on analysis as the computer collates and continuously updates the records. They do the input, I review the results. It's too good to pass up. I love it."

"You're a natural born administrator." Cody put on his perpetual grin. "You should consider doing more of this kind of work."

"That sounds like a veiled compliment. I didn't know you cared."

Cody slapped him on the shoulder. "I always get mushy at the end of a mission. Once we pick this baby up, I'm home for leave and some R and R with the missis."

"Till the next mission."

Cody shrugged. "Till the next mission."

Ronnie bumped open the door with her hips and entered the computer roon bearing a tray full of sandwich quarters and a pot of steaming coffee. "Anybody hungry?"

Hutch spun his chair around. "Starved, but you looked more appetizing in a bikini."

She put the tray down on the table, and smoothed out her skirt. With black shoes, silk stockings, white blouse, and dress blue jacket complete with silver lieutenant's bars on the lapels, she appeared all to prim. "I'm still a Naval officer, and when I'm on duty I have to dress the part. Cody, there's plenty of food, so dig in."

"You don't have to ask me twice."

"I didn't think so." Ronnie put a sandwich on a paper plate and handed it to Hutch. "So, what have you found out so far?"

"That this boat has some expensive hardware, and the most well-equipped laboratory on both sides of the Rockies. Everything from an electron microscope to a Wilson cloud chamber. And the personnel to operate it all. Oh, cream and sugar, please."

"I know."

"About the only thing missing is a pack of graduate students. Thanks." Hutch took the mug Ronnie handed to him, and sipped the hot brew between bites. "The data storage and retrieval is superb. Cody, will I be allowed to keep any of this information after the mission is over?"

"I insist on it. Part of our cover story, to account for your lost time in the real world, is your work on the rediscovery of the fossil remains. I expect you to write a paper on your finds, and present it publicly. You get all the credit. Naturally, certain intelligence of a classified nature must be omitted. You understand, of course."

"Of course."

Cody engulfed a second sandwich. "That way, the dissemination of scientific results will double as an explanation of our activities. For safe keeping, the fossils will be displayed in a yet-to-be-selected museum. You understand the policital sensitivity?"

"Sure. Although, placing the fossils in a museum doesn't necessarily mean they're safe. I think *you* should understand that museums are notorious for losing things and failing to preserve them properly. Didn't you hear about the Egyptian mummy that was found in the Natural History Museum? It was in all the papers."

Ronnie perched delicately on the edge of the table. She nibbled on a sandwich. "I remember. It had been packed away for fifty years, and nobody knew it was even there until a maintenance man cleaned out the basement. He found an unmarked crate, and when he opened it up, there it was."

Hutch nodded, swallowing. "Then there was the Mesozoic crocodilian collection destroyed in the Academy of Natural Sciences. It was catalogued and stored in a wooden cabinet. Nobody looked at it for years. Then, one day, a student opened the top drawer—and the shelf was gone. He opened the next one, and it was the same. Finally, at the bottom of the cabinet, he found a pile of dust and a few surviving remnants. The fossils had been improperly preserved. Over the years, the chemical solution reacted with the air to form an acid, which dissolved everything, including the specimen cards. Whoops, got some more data coming in."

Several parallel printers clattered at once. Sheets of fanfold spit out through the tractor feeds and laid in neat piles behind the machines. Hutch scanned the figures, equations, and word-processed information.

The door opened again, and a tall, gray haired, primly uniformed man entered. The gold braid on the brim made his hat top heavy. "Cody, I'd like a word with you."

"Speak."

Dark, deepset eyes took in the other occupants. "This is private."

Cody indicated Hutch and Ronnie with the hand without the sandwich. "We're a team."

"But he's a civilian."

Hutch tore the papers along the serated edge. He held out his other hand. "Hutch Hutchison, Captain. And I must say, this is a hell of a boat you have here. They sure don't make them like they used to."

Shoulders went straight back, bushy eyebrows knitted. "For your information, mister, I happen to be a commander, not a captain. And a nuclear submarine is a ship, not a boat."

"Yes, well, of course. I didn't mean—"

Ronnie stood at attention as she addressed the affronted officer. "You'll have to forgive him, Commander Petrie. Hutch is—Mr. Hutchison is unfamiliar with military parlance and order of rank."

Cody grabbed a cup of coffee, and spoke with nonchalance. "Yeah, anybody in charge of a vessel is called captain, but it's not a designation of rank. Even a lieutenant can be a captain. Rank is just a pay scale."

"Cody, I don't like your impertinance," said Commander Petrie. "On my ship, I give the orders, and you *will* follow the chain of command. All transmissions must be authorized by me and coded by my staff. I cannot allow private codings and secret messages. From now on, you and Lieutenant Wakefield *will* clear everything through me first. And, all civilians *will* be restricted to non-military zones."

"Sure, that's okay by me, just as long as this old tub takes me where I want to go."

"And that brings up my next bone of contention. I don't think you appreciate the national defense plan under which this submarine operates. The *Dudley Morton* is *not* your personal conveyance. As a deterrent to nuclear warfare I have a strictly confidential random patrol route to maintain. My orders specifically disallow this vessel to be put at risk by incursion into waters made dangerous by enemy presence, shoals, shipping routes, or other obstructions. Your proposal to approach a rugged coastline full of submerged rocks lies outside the purview of those instructions. Then, to ask me to remain in shallow water while you conduct a surface salvage operation is totally out of the question. I refuse to cooperate.''

One printer raised a din as the platen rolled out several sheets of twenty weight bond. Hutch leaned over the desk and read the printed output.

Cody's grin vanished, and in its place came a face that was grim and all business. ''Commander, I don't like to pull rank on you, but you give me little choice. If you will check Special Order 123, you'll find that your authority is superceded by mine. So, you keep heading this ship toward Borneo unless I stipulate otherwise.''

''Cody, I protest this abject disabuse of—''

''Protest all you want. You and your submarine are tools of the United States government, to be utilized as seen fit by your superiors. I'm sure you're very comfortable with the present arrangements: galloping through the ocean like a wild seahorse. However, at the present time, your vessel is needed to perform a useful function. When you check SO 123, you'll find that your *random* patrol can be altered from its course of fancy to suit the more iminent national security needs of the country.''

Commander Petrie was speechless. His lips quivered, and his hands balled into fists. His face turned a bright red.

''Honey, what is it?''

Hutch looked up from the readouts. His mouth was agape. He stared at Ronnie almost without seeing her. ''The—the—chemical analyses are coming through—''

Cody was by his side in a moment. He ripped the sheets out of Hutch's hand. ''Is there a problem?''

''I don't—I don't know. It doesn't make sense.''

Cody winced at the page full of numbers and chemical symbols. ''What doesn't make sense. Speak up, man.''

''Radioactive decay rates. I never would have thought to look for—'' Hutch shook his head. He sat at the computer console and punched the keypad. The three large monitors sprang to life with numbers and annotations. ''I asked them to check the stenciled board for cellular shrinkage, and they ran a whole gamut of tests. They found strontium—''

''Hold it. That's enough.'' Cody turned to the submarine captain. ''Commander, this is priveleged scuttlebutt. I'm gonna have to ask you to step outside for a moment.''

Petrie was fuming. ''Cody, this is an outrage. I've got top secret classifi—''

The commando took him gently by the arm and directed him toward the door. "I'm sure you do, but this is a covert operation that is not within your need to know." He pushed him into the corridor. "Now you wait here until further orders. I'll get back to you." He closed the door and turned to Hutch. "Is there a problem?"

"Well, I—"

"*Is there a problem?*"

Hutch rolled his eyes, seeking solace from Ronnie. "I don't know. I'm thinking."

"Honey, what about the strontium."

"Well, it's—there shouldn't be any." Hutch reexamined the readout, but the figures had not changed. "Not in 1946. That was before the atomic bomb tests on Bikini." He raised his eyebrows at Cody. "Wasn't it?"

"That was during the fifties. But what's that got to do with anything?"

"Because up till then, strontium 90 didn't exist on earth. With a half-life of twenty-eight years—"

"What are you getting at?"

Hutch held his hands in front of his chest as if he were praying. "All right, let me explain. Strontium 90 is a radioactive isotope formed during uranium fission. The main bad guy in radiation fallout. Geologically speaking, its half-life is extremely short. Any that was formed during the creation of the Universe, or during second generation stellar evolution, is long since gone.

"But, after they started exploding atomic bombs, radioactive byproducts contaiminated the atmosphere. Most of them have half-lives of less than a day and don't constitute an environmental hazard. But in human terms, strontium 90 lasts a long time. Gradually, rain washes it down into the soil. Plants absorb it, and from there it works its way up the food chain and into the human body where, because of its chemical similarity to calcium, it concentrates in the bones. Beta particle emission poses serious health—"

Cody threw his hands up into the air. "What the hell does this have to do with us?"

"Aside from bone cancer and leukemia? Well, in this case—I don't know. It's an anomalous finding that just—doesn't make sense."

Ronnie placed a warm hand on his. "Hutch, are you saying that this wood, this piece of crate, is radioactive with an isotope—"

"No, you don't understand. The board isn't radioactive in the way you think of radioactivity. Strontium 90 is a low level emitter. You don't pick it up on a Geiger counter."

"I still don't get the point," Cody said.

"Hutch, does water act as a shielding against radia—"

"No, no, no. You still don't understand. Boards do not absorb strontium 90; wood does."

Cody slapped his hands on his thighs. "Have you gone off the deep end? Boards are *made* out of wood."

"Whoa, hold on a sec." Hutch held out his palms like a traffic cop at a busy intersection with a malfunctioning signal. "All right, I know I'm not explaining this very well. I didn't emphasize that strontium 90 is only absorbed by *living* tissue. Once a tree is cut down, it doesn't take in any more—of anything. Osmosis and cellular activity ceases. It's dead. Whatever's already in it, whether its strontium 90 or cesium 137 or carbon 14, that's it. It's not going to get any more. That's how radiocarbon dating works: you determine how much unstable carbon 14 is left in your test piece, how much hasn't decayed into carbon 12.

"All right, so what I'm saying is that prior to 1945, *no* plant or animal had *any* strontium 90 in its system. But *after* the extensive test blasts of the fifties and sixties, *every* plant and animal living at the time showed traces of strontium 90. And that's the paradox. I'm—I'm totally disoriented by nonsensical data. We've found a piece of wood that just can't exist."

"Oh, my god." Ronnie stared up at the acoustical ceiling tiles. Her head nodded slowly, almost imperceptibly. "It's a plant."

"Brilliant deduction, Sherlock." Cody threw up his hands in disgust. "Of course wood is a plant. It sure as hell isn't animal or mineral. Meanwhile, I've got an irate captain out in the—"

"No! Cody, don't you see. Hutch has empirical data that *does* make sense, if you take certain political factors into account."

"Now, wait a minute," Hutch said. "Politicians emit a lot of high energy nonsense, but none of it's radioactive."

"No, it's a red herring."

"Herring don't even live in this part of the world. It's a northern fish that filters plankton through gill-rakers—"

"It's a hoax! The whole thing is a hoax!"

The room was quiet enough to hear a microchip switching.

Hutch looked at Ronnie through eyes the size of quarters. His mouth was half open.

She returned his gaze with equal intensity. "Yes, don't you see? It all makes a crazy kind of sense when you consider the various elements involved."

Cody blinked, and shook his head. "I thought strontium 90 was the only—"

"There are political factions of different persuasion complicating the situation. We've been working on the assumption that there are those who want the Peking fossils found, and those who want it lost."

"Why would anyone want to lose—" Hutch started.

"Suppose the faction that wants it lost is one step ahead of us. Suppose they already located the *Gremyashchi*, perhaps years ago, ascertained that nothing was there, but realized that competitors would probably explore the same route. So, they salted the wreck with a decoy that would mislead us into thinking we found all there was to find." She held out her hands, palm up. "End of search. We terminate the mission, and never know the difference."

Cody squeezed his freshly shaven chin. "You know, you might have something there. It does kind of hang together."

"I'm still in the dark," Hutch protested. "All right, I follow that bit about certain countries wanting the remains, and the artifacts, for themselves. I understand the political ramifications. But what's this about someone wanting them lost. How do they gain anything by that?"

Cody sighed deeply. He looked at Hutch, then at Ronnie. "I was hoping we wouldn't have to tell him."

Ronnie nodded. "But he has knowledge which is useless without a broader comprehension."

"Maybe, but how can we be sure—"

"Hey. Yo." Hutch waved his hands over his head. "You two are beginning to sound like my parents. I already know about Santa Claus and the Easter Bunny. Just tell me who wants the artifacts lost. Now."

Ronnie raised her eyebrows at Cody. "We haven't been able to identify any one particular nation because there is a cooperative effort—"

"Just give me the short version."

Ronnie humphed. "It's a conglomerate of countries whose economic stability relies heavily on the export of oil."

"OPEC?"

"In an acronym, yes."

"And, is that who's been out to get us?"

"We think so. Although we have no proof of direct involve—"

"Holy Christ. You mean we've been fighting off the biggest bunch of cornflakes since Special K? The only outfit with more nuts than Planters? A herd of wild asses more Trigger happy than Roy Rogers?"

"Do you have something against the Organization of Petroleum Exporting Countries?"

"I stood in line for gasoline. I've listened to their fatuous insults. I've seen them blow up ships and assassinate innocent bystanders. Hell, we've got a pack of lunatics on our tail." Hutch shook his head. "This mission gets more arabesque as it goes along."

"You can understand our concern for secrecy, then?"

"Yes. No! I still don't see what they have against a box of fossils and a few antediluvian artifacts. What's it to them?"

Cody supplied the answer. "Power."

"Come on. They have no political influence in the Orient, and nothing to gain by destroying Chinese relics."

"I didn't mean strategic power, I meant the sale of oil for conversion to electricity and the operation of automobiles."

After a long pause, Hutch said, "Do I have to prompt you?"

"It's a difficult concept to grasp."

"I went to kindergarten. Try me."

"All right. But understand that we have no scientific authority for this. It's mostly supposition based on third party evidence and hearsay testimony."

"This isn't a court of law."

Cody took a deep breath. "We believe that the artifact—*the* artifact—is part of an interstellar propulsion unit—the *main* part: the power module. And, there's good reason to suspect it may still be functioning."

Hutch chewed that over for several moments while he made lunch out of his lower lip. Slowly, his eyes widened.

Ronnie added. "Naturally, this could prove to be highly detrimental to the GNP of certain countries whose major income relies on the production of—"

"Energy!"

"It would topple their economy and drive them back into poverty—"

"*Hot damn!*"

"—so their only recourse is to destroy the—unit—or whatever it is—in order to insure the longevity of their opulence."

Hutch grimaced, and nodded quickly. "Now I see. If the consortium can prevent us from finding this—energy source, by whatever means, they can keep on sticking it to us with higher oil prices."

"And what better method of conspiracy than to practice a little sleight of hand to keep us off the right track."

"Typical bureaucratic legerdemain. I thought the U.S. government had a monopoly on that."

"So they planted a few false clues, knowing we would eventually find the right wreck. And we dug up a skull that was put there to mislead us. They never thought of making the crate out of aged wood. And they never thought we'd have a minor genius who would—"

"Wait a minute. Wait a minute. Wait a minute." Hutch held up his hands again. "All right. I agree with everything you said except the 'minor'. But there's one little chink in your scenario of skullduggery. According to the measurements of the partial skull we found, and the disk data on the casts at the Natural History Museum, this skull is one of the original four. *However*, the other three pieces don't conform to any of the one hundred seventy-five fossil fragments from the original collection, so they must have been found later. Something is rotten in the state of Peking."

Cody paced across the room like a caged tiger. "This is more complicated than I thought. We've got a skull that's genuine, some bones that don't conform, a piece of wood that's a forgery, and an artifact that—" He pounced back and stood nose to nose with Hutch. "The artifact. Did it—have a sheen, or a radiance?"

Hutch thought for a moment. "Well, it was very shiny, with a luster like polished metal, and—"

"No, I mean, did it have an aura all its own. When you took your light off it, did it—glow?"

"Not that I can—"

"And you never saw any Gieger activity?"

"No, but I didn't have it aimed—"

Cody waved his hands for silence. "And you're sure about the wood? It couldn't have been a slat from the original crate?"

"No way. But we can check the chemicals in the paint. It may be a formula that was unavailable back in—"

"Never mind. I'll take your word for it." He turned to Ronnie. "Your theory's got more holes than a screen door, but there's a definite conspiracy going on. Maybe some cabal we don't even know about."

Ronnie nodded. "The cylinder is an obvious cynosure meant to dupe us."

"We're going to get to the bottom of this." Cody spun around and flashed across the room with the speed of a short circuit. He ripped open the door. Commander Petrie, his face an unveiled picture of anger, opened his mouth. Cody cut him short. "Okay, Commander, we're not going to Borneo. Turn this tub around and head for Taiwan. I'm going on a date."

The *Pegasus*

"The culprit was never found, but someone matched the cranium of a man with the jawbone and teeth of an orangutan, and buried them at the site of an ongoing gravel pit. Workers dug them up, and turned them over to the authorities. It was examined by prominent people in the field of anthropology and paleontology. They determined they were the fossil remains of a previously unknown specimen: a dawnman that could prove to be the missing link. It wasn't till decades later that Piltdown man was exposed as a hoax. The British were quite humiliated."

Ronnie brushed a hair off the white ruffles of her low cut dress. "I'm astonished that fraud would take place in the scientific world. I expect it in politics, by definition, but a *scientist*?"

"*And* inventors. Very creative people. And often more interested in fame than actual accomplishment. Some people are all imagery. They don't care about who they really are, only about how others preceive them. They live their whole lives as fakes, and often are never found out till they make a mistake, and people start putting the pieces together." Hutch leaned on his elbows as he sipped his coffee. He pulled back the sleeve of his sport coat and scratched his wrist. "I remember in college, there was a kid who wanted to be a photographer. He was no good at it, so he took another guy's slides and showed them as his own. When he got caught, he denied everything vehemently, even though he had the stolen slides in his hand. He said it must be a mistake. Turned out it wasn't the only theft he had committed. He had to rent a garage to store all his stolen goods. He never admitted to any of it. And because he couldn't face the kind of person he really was, in his mind, he *became* the fantasy he had built up around himself. He could no longer distinguish reality from his dream world. I never forgot that. I guess, because I couldn't understand it. I just can't accept deceipt, or deviousness, in people. And believe me, if you think you run into it all the time in counterintelligence, try getting into archaeology. Some underwater investigations have more subversion than submersion, because everybody wants to get the credit. If I had a piece of eight or a silver reale for every—"

Cody pulled back his chair and sat down. He tightened his necktie with one hand while waving to the waiter with the other. "More coffee, please." He leaned across the table and lowered his voice conspiratorially. "If you're not going to finish that veal, I'll take it off your hands. I hate to see it wasted."

Ronnie snickered, and shoved the plate across the linen tablecloth. "That's just an excuse, and you know it."

Hutch said, "So, how'd it go?"

Cody pursed his lips and shook his head. "Not as bad as I thought. The boy fell off his bike and broke an arm, and the youngest has chicken pox. I was sure we had her innoculated against that."

Hutch was confused. "What?"

"The kids had shots for everything except rabies."

"Cody, just who were you talking to on the phone just now?"

"My wife, of course. You think the President relays top secret messages through AT&T?"

"But, what about our meeting? You know, with the agent."

"Oh. That. Sure, he'll be there. Says he's got a boat all lined up for us. We can leave tomorrow. Whew, I can't wait to get out of these fancy duds. I must say, though, my dear, you look charming in that outfit."

"Thank you." Ronnie took the cloth napkin off her lap and delicately touched it to her lips. "I feel charming, too." She smiled at Hutch. "Is that a fantasy, do you think?"

"If it is, we're both dreaming it."

The waiter returned with a pot of coffee, and poured the black brew into Cody's cup. The others refused a refill. The waiter nodded curtly, his tails standing out straight. The tuxedo was starched stiff as a board.

Hutch glanced around at the overdressed patrons, the bustling busboys, the scurrying waiters, the brocaded curtains, the silk trim, the marble columns and statues, the Oriental murals, the two-thousand-piece crystal chandelier. "I don't think I've ever been in such a fancy restaurant. I've never seen such sheer ostentation."

Ronnie said, "Taipei is the seat of the Republic of China, and the government intends to show off the results of capitalism."

"What I like best is eating on an expense account."

Cody glanced at his watch and gulped down the rest of his coffee, still steaming. "Let's go upstairs and wait for developments."

They walked out of the restaurant, past the ballroom, and into the house-sized lobby. The Grand Hotel was aptly named, sporting red velvet wallpaper, gilt-edged wainscoting, and deep pile carpeting. The circular, marble staircase was wider than the exit ramp from an interstate highway. The elevator cars glittered with burnished copper and spun brass.

"Would you like to come into my suite, sweet?" Hutch put his hand on the mirrorlike finish of the door handle, and twisted it.

Ronnie smiled mischievously. "Would you like to come in mine?"

"Don't think you two are going to slip off for another wrestling match." Cody followed them into the luxuriously furnished apartment, and locked the door behind him. He balked when he saw the sheets and blankets on the floor, and clothes spread haphazardly all over the room. He slipped a .38 automatic out of his shoulder holster. "The place has been ransacked."

Hutch and Ronnie exchanged guilty looks.

Ronnie put her hands on her hips, pinching the dress so it accentuated her waspish waist. "No, we were just in a hurry—to get undressed."

Hutch picked up the pillows and tossed them on the mattress. The silk cover undulated. "They gave us a goddamned water bed, and there was no way I was going to spend another minute on the waves. I want something solid beneath my feet—or under my back."

"So that's how you two do it." Cody holstered his gun. "Doesn't surprise me in the least." A knock came at the door. In a loud voice: "Who is it?"

"Room service."

Cody flicked the lock. The door burst open and slammed against the wall. A round, gray object the size of an orange sailed into the room, bounced off the headboard, and rolled into the quilted comforter.

"*Grenade!*"

Hutch froze. His mind accelerated through a sequence of probable events, but he was unable to act. He stood like an onyx statue, and just as pale, holding a sheet draped over his arm. He stared at the immobile, seemingly innocuous globe of steel.

"*Get down!*"

As he collapsed to the floor, his brain caught up with the backlog of events that he was only now interpreting. He saw Cody charge out of the room, heard Ronnie's frenzied command, felt the floor slam against his hands and chest, heard the retort from three distinct gunshots, cringed as a thunderous roar wracked the hotel suite. Hot, jagged pellets clattered against the walls and furniture, shattered mirrors and porcelain lamp bases, and fell to the floor like hail. Hutch jerked away from a piece of metal that landed on the back of his hand. The water bed exploded. The tide went out. The several hundred gallons of water that had protected him from shrapnel cascaded through the shredded plastic lining and flooded the fine carpet. Hutch was caught in the undertow, and soaked—but he was unable to move.

Ronnie grabbed him by the shoulders with both hands. "Come on, let's go."

At first, he could not get up. His sphincter had his body tied up in knots. Everything was pitch black until he realized that his eyes were tightly shut. When he opened them, he saw only motion without form: like a movie viewed through a foggy window.

Ronnie dragged him to his feet. "Honey, let's get out of here." She pulled a heavy duty .45 out of her sequin covered handbag. "*Now!*"

In the corridor he saw a man lying face down on the floor. One arm was twisted at an awkward angle, as if he were trying to get a stinging bee off his back. His bellboy's uniform was stained with red.

Cody spun around, gun smoking. "Are you all right?"

"I'm fine, but he's in shock."

"Hell, I thought he'd be used to grenades by now. All right, let's get out of here."

Already the hallway was gorged with awe-struck, inquisitive guests, most of whom kept their distance and stared from the safety of their doorways. Ronnie tugged Hutch along toward the main staircase.

"Too exposed," Cody said imperiously. "The fire tower."

They ducked into the concrete well. Cement steps led up and down, and an iron railing acted as a barrier against the central shaft. Cody led the descent.

Hutch pulled out of Ronnie's grasp. "Expense account or not, I think next time we ought to leave a tip."

Cody groaned. "I liked you better when you were in shock."

"So, what do we do now?" Ronnie wanted to know.

"We'll stay on the move. Let's grab a taxi and see the sights until appointment time. Then we'll head for the docks."

They burst out the door at ground level. Downtown Taipei was a froth of activity: bumper to bumper traffic, shoulder to shoulder shoppers, tourists, and tramps. Neon lights glowed with Las Vegas intensity, flashing like bolts of multicolored lightning. Signs shouted their wares in Chinese calligraphy.

Cody held onto Ronnie's hand, who held noto Hutch, and ran block through the crowded sidewalk. The Grand Hotel always had cabs waiting outside the lobby. He yanked open the door of the battered yellow car in the front of the column. All three piled in the back seat.

"Meander north, cabbie. Toward Chilung."

Ronnie still held onto Hutch's hand. "Are you all right, Honey?"

"Hell, no. I'm soaking wet."

"At least you're not hurt," Cody said.

"I don't know. My pride took quite a battering back there. Ronnie, doesn't *any*thing scare you?"

"There's a difference between experiencing fear, and showing it. It's part of basic training."

Hutch leaned forward and wrung out his tie on the floor. "Well, I'm just glad we won't be around when maid service arrives. And Cody, show a little concern, or at least some interest. Somebody tried to kill us just now.''

Cody put an index finger to his lips, and pointed toward the cabbie's head.

Hutch rolled his eyes. He squeezed water out of his shirt as he stared out the window at Japaneses influenced architecture and occidental facades. Ronnie helped him out of his jacket. Soon they left the dense city environment and the constant stop, crawl, and stop. The taxi hummed along smoothly through an outdoor shopping district that exhibited no activity at night, then passed by processing plants and textile factories that were kept alive by night workers. In a little while the dark, dismal Tanshui River flowed into view.

"This is close enough." Cody stuffed a wad of bills over the seat as the cabbie pulled over to the side of the road. "Keep the change, and buy something for the kids."

They got out at a darkened intersection that was several blocks from the commercial dock area, and strolled along the waterfront. Floodlights illuminated the continual process of freighters being unloaded. A few idlers roamed the sidewalks, and several cars full of teenagers cruised the streets; some parked in less lighted alleys.

Ronnie kept her purse clutched to her breast. "Cody, it's obvious that our cover's blown. Do you think it's safe to wander about in the open like this?"

"No. I think it's exceptionally dangerous."

Hutch stopped short. "Then what the hell are we doing here?"

Cody glanced at his wristwatch. "We've got a midnight tryst to keep. Besides, the danger's worse where we just came from. So, things must be looking up."

"I wish I had your outlook on life." Hutch donned his still wet jacket. "So, who is this guy we're supposed to meet?"

"I don't know. I've never met him. He's known only as the Chinaman."

"On an island with fifteen million Chinese, that's not a very descriptive nomenclature."

"He's been undercover since the war. Only surfaced recently. No one knows his real identity because he contacted our agent through an intermediary. She handled the initial negotiations."

Ronnie's high heels clicked on the wooden walkway. "He came to us through the Chinese embassy in Washington. Somehow—and he wouldn't say how—he knew about the intensifying search for the Peking man remains. Right away, I knew him to be a powerful man, because that information was highly classified. He's very cagey. He didn't come right out and say he knew about it, but the coincidence was too great to ignore. Anyway, I corresponded with him through the ambassador, trying to find out what he knew. He admitted to nothing other than he thought he could help in the search, but that the time was not propitious for his participation. What he meant by that, I don't know. We left it that he would get in touch when he felt safer about making contact.''

"Then, this guy actually knows something—maybe where the fossils are hidden?''

Ronnie shrugged. "Not necessarily. He was only one lead out of hundreds we've covered over the years. I just chalked him up as another con man out to claim the reward that Janus made in 1972. The offer was never withdrawn, so technically it's still outstanding.

"Then, while we were traipsing across the Kalamantan jungle, he reopened contact. We received the intelligence aboard the *Dudley Morton*. Surprisingly, he knew about our venture off the coast of Borneo. That lent real authority to the efficiency of his connections.''

"This guy sounds like a master spy.''

"No. I think he's someone who once had military affiliations, and who chose to go underground—probably because the Communists had something against him. Assassination runs rampant in this part of the world, so it's possible that his true identity might have an attraction for lead. The information he imparts tonight will hopefully redefine our quest in a more positive direction.''

"That won't be hard to do. We haven't gotten anywhere yet.''

"Quite the contrary. If we hadn't tracked down the false leads first, we might never have reached a negotiable medium with the Chinaman. He's a very cautious man. I gather he suspects a rather intricate web of conspiracy surrounds the Peking fossils, and he wants to make sure he doesn't get stuck to the wrong strand. If he doesn't show up, I don't know where we turn next. We might—we might have to dissolve this partnership for the time being, until—''

"Before you go and start getting maudlin, let's angle over toward that warehouse.'' Cody's gun glinted in the overhead incandescents. "I don't like the population movement. It seems to be converging on us.''

"Uh, oh.'' Hutch swallowed as he saw the seemingly aimless wandering coalesce into a recognizable pattern. "I don't like this. I hate crowds.''

"Just act casual. I want to get a wall behind my back. Let's head toward those packing crates.'' Cody stepped off the curb and angled across the street. Chinese stevedores, dressed crudely in shorts and pajama tops, started to take notice of the trio. "I think they're on to us.''

"I'm no nonchalant LaMont,'' Hutch said, in a scratchy voice. "They can probably tell I'm quaking like an aspen.''

"Honey, hold onto this in case we see some action.'' Ronnie slipped him a palm sized revolver.

"This wasn't exactly what I had in mind for tonight.'' The steel felt cold in his hand. "What am I supposed to do with this thing.''

Cody ducked into a closet-sized space between some roof-high machinery crates. "Just do what comes natural."

"I guess fainting's out of the question."

"Cody. Over there." Ronnie indicated a group of scruffy looking men coming their way. "Each one's got a crowbar."

"I didn't even know that bird's imbibed. Listen, do you think if we fire into the air, they'll leave us alone."

"Maybe." The .38 pointed out from the edge of the packing crate. "But if I blow someone's head off it's likely to have a more positive effect."

"Cody, you just can't just shoot someone without provocation."

"Watch me." The gun picked out a target. "I'm provoked."

All slanted eyes turned their way. A wiry arm went back, a three-foot length of iron soared through the air. Cody fired. The man was flung back; his body rolled against the opposite curb. The crooked prybar smashed into the wood over Hutch's head, splintering slats, and glanced off his shoulder.

"Is that sufficient provocation?"

Cody and Ronnie picked their targets, and fired. Hutch dropped down to one knee, aimed at the steel bulkhead of the freighter across the street, closed his eyes, and frantically pulled the trigger.

Some of the stevedores launched their weapons, others charged with ugly looking knives the size of machetes.

"Shoot, damn it!"

"I am, but nothing's happening."

Three bodies hit the dirt in the middle of the road. One twitched, the others were motionless. The rest scattered like seeds in a storm.

"They're not professional," Ronnie said coolly. "They weren't expecting us to be armed."

"Yes. Local hire." Cody snatched the gun from Hutch's hand. "Goddamn it, you forgot the safety. Here."

Hutch examined the tiny lever on the side of the breech. He looked up at Cody, then at Ronnie. "How was I supposed to know? I'm a goddamned archaeologist."

Ronnie ignored him. "Cody, are you covering? I want to reload."

"Go ahead."

Hutch peered around the edge of a crate. He fingered the trigger nervously. "Who the hell are *these* guys? They're wearing suits."

"You go out and ask them. I'll cover for you."

Hutch looked up sharply. "What the hell, are you cra—"

Cody grinned broadly. "Yes, but that's besides the point. I have a feeling we're outnumbered. The only thing to do in a situation like this—is take as many with you as you can. But leave one bullet just in case."

The injured man moaned. He rolled over in the street and crawled away, leaving a trail of blood. A dozen Orientals in tailored evening clothes moved into the cone of light. When the wounded man reached a pile of drums on the dock, a man holding an automatic rifle stepped on his back and pinned him in place.

"They've got firepower on us," Cody said laconically.

Ronnie slung the handbag over her shoulder so it hung behind her. She kept the pistol directed outward. "Something's not right here. Two of them are out in the open."

"Wait till they get in range. Maybe they want us to waste our ammo."

Hutch was still crouched between the two of them. "You think we can talk our way out of this?"

"It depends on who we're dealing with."

The smooth whine of an engine dopplered up the street. An ivory white Cadillac limousine, so long it looked like it needed training wheels in the middle of the chassis, pulled up silently in front of them. The magnesium wheels straddled two of the bodies; the vehicle stopped with its chrome plated fender touching the other.

"Won't—won't this noise attract the police?"

"Yes, but this action'll be over by then."

A door on the opposite side of the limousine opened. The man who stepped out stood only a head taller than the roof of the car. Sallow features were limned in the yellow, incandescent street light. Hair like snow swept back over a short forehead, and was plastered to his skull like a cap. He walked past the driver's compartment and stopped when he reached the slope of the windshield. He wore a black bow tie, white ruffled shirt, and a tuxedo jacket.

"Hold up your guns where I can see them." The words were spoken slowly, and with perfect enunciation: an eloquence born of heraldry. His voice was not loud, yet it carried unmistakable caveat. "I can easily have you overcome."

Cody eyes roved from side to side, but his gun leveled at the center button of the white shirt. He whispered out of the side of his mouth. "He's right. They can kill us if they want, or we can die trying to escape."

Ronnie nodded slowly. "*He'll* never make it, but I don't think it's worth the trade. Something fishy is going on. I think we should see what he wants."

"Agreed." Cody glanced down at Hutch. "Stand up tall, and don't make any suspicious movements. Just follow my lead."

"I sure hope you know what the hell you're doing."

"So do I."

Cody stepped out in the open, his gun pointing skyward. Ronnie was by his side. Hutch uncreaked his bones, stood to his fullest height, and looked over the heads of his companions at the man who was now in charge of the situation. As soon as they left the protection of the crates, half a dozen men slipped in from the sides. Cody, Ronnie, and Hutch were grabbed, and relieved of their weapons.

Ronnie wrestled with an oxlike gunman. "You don't have to prove your cavemanliness to me—I'll accept the fact that you're a Neanderthal."

"The Neanderthal is European, found in the Neander Valley of Germany, near Dusseldorf. What you—"

"*Shut up!*" Cody's face could have stared down Medusa.

The tuxedoed spokesman rounded the hood, and stepped over the body of the stevedore. He took the captured .38 from his henchman. He stopped in front of the trio, staring intently at each one in turn. Finally, his piercing gaze rested on Cody, held firmly by two stone-faced individuals.

Bowing slightly, he said with precision, "Dr. Livingston, I presume."

Cody stared back with equal intensity at dark eyes which not once wavered. His head tilted back ever so slightly. "Yes."

A wan smile touched thin, Chinese lips. "Mr. Watson, come here."

"I want you."

The smile grew broader. "I was hoping you would." He presented the pistol to Cody. "Forgive me the histrionics. As you can see, there are, shall we say, undesirable elements in pursuit. I wish to protect my life, as well as my identity. I am the one you know as the Chinaman."

"I'm Cody. This is Lieutenant Wakefield. And Mr. Hutchison, our anthropologist."

The other guns were returned. Hutch gave his back to Ronnie.

"I am happy to find you well." He made a sweeping gesture with his arm. "If you will escort me to my car."

The gunmen fanned out and accompanied them until they were safely ensconced behind steel doors and bullet proof glass. The Cadillac started out with a barely noticeable sway. Two cars preceeded them, two followed. The foursome took corner seats facing a round cocktail table in the luxurious living room.

"Whew, this is quite a car you've got here." Hutch ran a hand over the leather upholstery. "Is it real?"

"Scandanavian calfskin. Being in the import business has its advantages."

The Chinaman removed his tuxedo jacket, then unbuttoned his shirt. "Please, make yourselves comfortable. But do fasten your seatbelts because we *are* in motion." Under the white shirt was another. He pulled off the outer shirt, and dropped it with a clunk to the carpeted floor.

Cody picked it up and inspected it. "Kevlar."

The Chinaman put his jacket back on. "I was not sure what to expect, but I have learned that it does not pay to take chances. Do you agree?"

"You got that right."

The Chinaman exhibited a thin smile that was as ever present as Cody's. "Would anyone care for an aperitif?"

"None for me, thank you."

"I've had my quota."

Hutch stared goggle eyed at the interior of the limousine. The lighting was indirect. The front wall was a music and video center built around a two foot diagonal screen. The side curtains were made of brocaded silk. The bar was in the back, between the two rear bucket seats. "I could use some hot tea."

"Come, come, come. You are going to give secret agents a bad name." He poured himself a glass of sherry. After he put the bottle away, he switched on the electric hotplate. "You have a reputation to maintain. Or should I say, a movie image?"

"I don't live up to anything, except life." Cody pointed to the teapot. "Is there enough in there for two."

The Chinaman smiled. "Of course. Lieutenant?"

"It's past my bedtime, so I guess some caffeine wouldn't hurt."

As the percolator started dripping, the Chinaman set out delicate, exquisitely patterned china teacups and saucers. "Now that the preliminaries have been taken care of, let us get down to business. First, you must understand that I want no reward for my efforts. Money is of little consequence to me, in my position, and has no leverage. The Peking man remains have been a lifelong passion with me. I have waited patiently for many years for the culmination of this—dream. I am a patient man. Nor does my patience wear thin. However, mitigating circumstances have forced my hand. Man's future as well as his history are locked secrets, and I have the key to the mystery of both. But there are factions which would rather see that key destroyed, factions which are more primitive than the fossils we seek.

"As your future investigations will undoubtedly show, the name under which I conduct my business in Kung-sun Fei. It is not the name with which I was born, but I have used it for so long that I sometimes forget my ancestral patronymic, or the childhood appellation under which I was raised. I was called after my famous ancient progenitor Shih Huang Ti, the Emperor of China from 246 to 210 BC, and the builder of the Great Wall. I have a justifiable pride in my lineage. Family means a great deal to me, for it helped shape the person I am today. You, perhaps, will be more familiar with my original praenomen, Chu Shih."

Hutch fumbled with the cup he had been inspecting, and nearly dropped it. "You mean, the *real* Chu Shih?"

"Is there an impostor?"

"No, but—I thought you—I mean, Chu Shih—drowned in 1949."

"A cover story which has served me well these many years, and which has protected me and my loved ones from much possible abuse."

Ronnie said, "So you survived the wreck of the *Ting-Yuen*."

The Chinaman sipped from his crystal goblet. He summed up his entire, terrible ordeal with a single syllable. "Yes." He might have been run over by a feather rather than a destroyer.

Cody leaned forward on his elbows. "Then you're not just an intermediary. You know where it is."

Chu Shih smiled. "That is approximately true. Why don't you let me go about this my own way? Tea?'' He poured the hot liquid into the three cups. He took a silver sugar bowl from a shelf and placed it in the middle of the table.

"I have always been somewhat of a dilettante, with a passion for the arts. I suspect that is because I have no artistic talent of my own. Circumstances of birth, therefore, have forced me to become a patron. My name was widely circulated as a purchaser of rare books, historical documents, and works of art. I paid well, and supported my own private museum.

"Before the Japanese occupation, a man came to me with a startling story. A man named Dr. Chang Wung Shu. He had continued working the digs at Choukoutien after the Americans withdrew. It was he and his assistants who unearthed in a lower bed the older Peking man fossils and the attendant artifacts. Unfortunately, in that pre-atomic era, no one knew about the wasting disease of which he eventually expired—in my arms, I should add. Because of my position in government, he entrusted to me several crates of materials that included the artifact about which this commotion is concerned. I arranged transport out of the country, but events moved quickly and we all became trapped within our borders. Word of *the* artifact spread, through rumor, through word of mouth, through unofficial channels. In order to prevent unsavory and hostile governments from obtaining the artifact, I broke up the collection, carefully recrated everything, and buried boxes in various locations for later retrieval.

"Over the years, there has been great pressure from various nationalities to recover the artifact in question. In each case, I allowed agents of the host countries to think they had the actual object in their possession. My purpose was to allay suspicion about the true nature of the artifact until I could be sure that its power would not be abused.

"The world was involved in great political unheaval. I trusted no one. The Americans were flaunting their power with atomic bomb tests, the Russians were right behind, the People's Republic cared only for their own people, and my own country had neither the security nor the technology to make use of—the artifact. I kept it hidden.

"During the Revolution, however, I was forced along with Chiang Kai-shek and other Nationalists to flee my homestead. Publicly owned relics that had been removed from the Peking Palace Museum before the war had been stored in Shanghai, Nanking, and Chungking. I was in charge of removing as many of these national treasures from the mainland to the National History Museum, here in Taipei. At the same time, I also arranged for transportation of my own personal collection.

"I used several ships to carry the precious cargoes, so that I would not have, as you Americans say, all my eggs in one basket. All arrived safely, except for the gunboat on which I myself accompanied the most valuable trove of all. Please understand that my entire accumulation of historic relics and art treasures was aboard the vessel—and it all could have been saved.

It was I who gave the order to open fire against an obviously stronger adversary.

"The communist warship might have wanted only to check my papers. As everything was in order, they might have allowed me to proceed. But I could not take that chance. Rather than allow the artifact to fall into undesirable hands, I chose to scuttle the ship along with everything else on board. I needed return fire to mask the intentional sinking, so that it would not draw attention to my purpose.

"Unfortunately, there was great loss of life. Those who did not die by gunfire perished in the water. I alone escaped. When I was eventually picked up, naked, and without identification, I supplied my rescuers with the name of one of the crewmen. That day, in effect, the real Chu Shih passed away."

The rear panel above the hotplate folded down, and a tray of stuffed mushrooms was pushed out from the rear kitchen compartment.

"Ah, refreshments. Please, help yourself."

"Thanks." Cody did not need a second invitation. He tossed a steaming morsel into his mouth. Still chewing, he said. "So what you're saying is, the artifact went down with the ship."

"Precisely."

"And you know where the wreck is?"

"I can find it."

Cody took another mushroom. "And why, after all these years, should you suddenly decide to divulge this information?"

"Once I feared its power would be misused. I still harbor that fear. Yet, I have been forced to reconsider my position. Since the artifact appears to be in great danger of being lost to mankind forever, due to the intervention of third world powers, I have concluded that it is better in the wrong hands, than in no hands."

"Chu, why did you—"

"Please, Lieutenant. Lest you begin a habit which might possibly be overheard, call me Kung."

"I'm sorry. I've studied the historical references so thoroughly, and for so long, I feel as if I know you. It's almost as if—"

"I understand. Your question?"

"Why us?" Ronnie dabbled with her teacup, stirring the spoon absently even though she had added no sugar. "Why did you come to us, instead of your own government?"

"Or why don't you just do it yourself," Cody added. "You've got the means."

Kung smiled broadly. "Ah, you undoubtedly know that the Chinese never do anything without a reason." He poured himself a cup of tea, and tasted it ever so slightly. "To answer the latter question first, it is true that I have resources. I have a boat, I have divers, I have the equipment. What I do not have is government support. The hostility between the Chinese republics is not to be taken lightly; peace rests always on a knife edge. To involve my own country in this scheme would be exceedingly dangerous to the balance of conciliation.

"To answer the former, there is an old Chinese proverb: 'We do not mind who holds the cow, so long as we can milk it.' I think the United States is the most likely country to share with the rest of the world whatever it is we find. I think also it is the most capable of providing relief should events get out of hand. We have staunch adversaries whose intelligence network has shown an uncanny prescience."

"Yeah, we found out the hard way—more than once."

"That is precisely why I allowed the plan to unfold the way it has. As soon as the communists began their search for the *Awa Maru*, I knew it was time for positive action. Through old government contacts I kept myself apprised of the status of their salvage operation. I learned that they used deep water dredges to excavate the bridge area, where the fossil crates had been stored during her ill-fated passage. They recovered a curious cylinder of stainless steel which, because it was made of poor grade material, showed an excessive amount of rust. They were not fooled. Even a child knows that thirty years of submersion should not significantly harm an object which has rested in the earth without change for hundreds of thousands of years. But better materials were unavailable to me in war-torn China. Therefore, I had another cylinder forged out of platinum, with traces of osmium and iridium added as hardeners, and planted it on the *Gremyashchi* in place of the bogus original."

"So *you're* the one who salted the wreck," Hutch exploded. "And that explains why I couldn't move something that looked like a thermos liner."

"The weight of the ingot is well over a hundred pounds." Kung let a smile touch his lips. "Imagine my shock when I learned of your brilliant detective work."

Hutch rolled his head from side to side. He stared down at this half empty cup. "Well, it was partly luck that I—"

"Wait a minute," Cody interrupted. "How did you know where the *Gremyashchi* went down?"

"I did not, at first. I had only copies of the Kardova letters. At that point—"

"That's classified information!"

He had a persistent habit of simplistic summation. "Yes."

Kung continued. "From there, I went on an extended deep-sea fishing expedition on my specially designed boat, the *Pegasus*. While I trolled with rod and reel, my electronics experts scanned for sonar targets. In addition to effecting the exchange, I hooked and landed a black marlin which was larger than the record holder caught by your western writer Zane Grey. It was quite a profitable venture."

"Hah! But a bit of a waste. After going through all that trouble, you ruin your efforts by *giving* us the location of the *real* artifact."

"I haven't given it to you yet."

Cody's jaw dropped, and for once he was speechless.

Kung poured himself another cupful of tea. "But it is my intention to do so. And you are wrong: my expedience has proven its worth. Even now, our competitors are salvaging a Russian freighter off the coast of Borneo. You see, their intelligence is quite thorough, and they, too, have knowledge of your discovery. They do not yet, however, know of its counterfeit. Perhaps they will believe that the only value the cylinder has is in its bullion. That is what I hope."

Kung opened the door and stepped outside. So smooth did the vehicle run, that Hutch had not even realized the car had stopped moving. The three exchanged looks, and piled out of the lush interior. Under the yellow glow of sodium vapor lamps a flood of workmen hauled supplies aboard a sleek, forty-eight foot sportfisherman with a large single teak and aluminum fighting chair occupying the rear deck.

"Meanwhile, we embark on the final leg of our journey: a journey which began half a million years ago; and a journey of which the next few days will be not the culmination which you seek, but only another step."

*   *   *

"You seem awfully sullen this morning."

Hutch looked up from the black and white prints he was studying. "Yes, well . . ."

"And you're not just lost in thought. Honey, what is it?"

Hutch shrugged. He leaned sideways in the cubicle seat and stared through the spray-covered window. Whitecaps broke over churning seas, and flying fish leaped from foaming crests to glide across the troughs. "I was hoping to get a good night's sleep on solid land. Bouncing along the East China Sea at thirty knots is not my idea of a restful cruise."

Ronnie sat down opposite him. The morocco seat cover rippled as she slid across the bench. "Are Kung's pictures any help?"

Hutch bit his lower lip. "You know, they're positively fascinating. They were taken much later than the photos in your file, and they show a lot more bones—and the artifact after it was uncovered. But what I really want is to get my hands on this skull—" He flipped the glossy around so Ronnie could see it. "It's older than the other Peking man remains, and the anatomy is slightly different. It appears to have smaller cranial capacity, the occipital region is not as pronounced, and the frontal area definitely slopes more than—"

Wind and engine noise burst into the room as Kung opened the outside door and stepped in. In the silence of its closing, he said, "Ah, I see you have found the file folder I left out for you. Very good, Mr. Hutchison. And what have you learned so far?"

"Well, I'm beginning to see things in a different light. There's an overall pattern of evolution which is beginning to take focus. It'll take some more work, of course, and some more study, but—I sure wish I'd had these photos when I did my thesis."

"Ah, yes. You brought up some interesting points in the ape to man linkage. Do you think this added information may lead you to more positive conclusions?''

Hutch squinted one eye at the short Chinaman. "Have—have you read my paper?''

"But, of course. I told you that Peking man has been my lifelong interest. I have read everything about him.''

"But—my thesis has never been published.''

Kung laughed out loud. He stood calmly, hands by his side, despite the vibration and slight rocking of the boat. He wore a simple, shapeless pajama top over plain black shorts, and sandals. "I know, Mr. Hutchison. But I have, shall we say, connections.'' He raised his eyebrows at the last word.

Ronnie flapped her t-shirt and pulled it down from her pearly throat. "Kung, can you tell us yet where we're going?''

"To a small, rocky, uninhabited island off the coast of South Korea. It is many miles from the mainland, but claimed by them as their territory. It is patrolled somewhat irregularly.''

"Oh, that's just great." Hutch dropped the picture on the pile of others. "All we need is to drag another country into this mess, and we'll be starting World War Three.''

"Yes, you can understand the need for secrecy. That is why I would allow no messages or telephone calls last night. We are having a—plumbing problem. I have found one faulty joint, and, although it has been repaired, I am afraid of weakened pipes.''

Hutch waved his hands for time out. "Whoa, wait a minute. Are you saying what I think you're saying?''

"The leak has been soldered.''

"You mean you killed someone?''

Kung bowed slightly, but did not wipe off his smile. "That is the usual demise of agents caught double dealing.''

Ronnie looked up with a startled expression. "Did—did you break him first? Did you find out how . . . ''

"Most unfortunately, he was not conducive to surrender, and my people were too slow for capture. We are, however, tracing certain evidence he left behind.''

Ronnie glanced at Hutch. "That's—that's too bad. So you don't know his sources? You know, we've been dogged ever since we started this mission.''

Cody entered the plush cabin from the quarters below decks. He leaned against the music center, careful not to touch any of the fine tuning dials. To Hutch: "He's what we call an omnispy: a free lance selling information to anyone and everyone willing to pay for it. High return on investment, but very risky.''

"You know, you people treat death so callously.''

"That's life.'' Cody took a bite out of a thick, multilayered sandwich.

"Kung, that little cook you've got down there is hell of a guy. He sure knows how to make a Dagwood." To Hutch, "You see that picture of Chang?"

Hutch grappled with Cody's somber eyes for a moment, scowled, then rummaged through the pile of prints until he found the right one. The picture was taken at night, without flash or strobe. Dr. Chang smiled at the camera. He stood next to a makeshift hoist whose wooden crossmembers still wore a coat of bark. The cylindrical artifact was cradled in a rope mesh. It glowed of its own, so that its surface was smooth and undefined. Out of one end came a needle of light that illuminated sharply one side of Chang's body. Reflected light from the pencil beam filled the air with eerie halftones.

Hutch pointed to the rope falls. "Why the block and tackle?"

"The artifact is quite heavy, Mr. Hutchison. In the neighborhood of four hundred pounds."

"But, nothing in the world is dense enough to have that much weight in a cylinder that size."

"Yes, that is correct. Remember, however, that the artifact is not *from* this world. It is an exceedingly odd construct. A compass is useless within a fifty foot range. Correlating measurements I took at the time with what I now know about physics and the structure of the Universe, I strongly suspect that the cylinder is a magnetic container for a core of pure neutronium."

Hutch's jaw dropped. "Wow."

"You can appreciate, then, the significance of the artifact in terms of control. It implies a technology so advanced that it can manipulate particles of nature which to us are merely theoretical."

"Can this thing—go off?"

"Do you mean, like a bomb?" Kung smiled, but did not otherwise move. "No, it has been stable for half a million years. I doubt that anything we can do to it will affect that stability. I performed some preliminary experiments on it during the time it was in my possession. I was not able to cut it, nick it, or mar it in any way, even with an oxyacetylene torch. It was completely impervious to any kind of acid or chemical available in a laboratory. I even tried to shoot a bullet through it. The slug ricochetted harmlessly without leaving trace of its passage. The only danger I can ascertain is from contamination."

Hutch raised his eyebrows. "You mean, it's radioactive?"

Kung frowned, and turned to Cody. "Has he not been fully briefed?"

Cody took another huge bite out of his quickly disappearing triple decker. "Since he was hired from the private sector, we thought it best to keep his privity to a minimum—at least until he had a need to know."

Hutch stabbed a finger in the commando's direction. "You know, I'm getting awfully tired of this 'need to know' crap. If this thing is dangerous, I want to know about it before I get myself nuked."

"I gave you a Geiger counter, didn't I? I figured—"

"Goddamn it, you should have told me what the hell I was dealing with." Hutch's fist bobbled like the head of a pigeon chasing bread crumbs. "Hard radiation can produce irreversible damage at the very least, and kill at the most. Maybe when I bring it back, you'd like to sit on it for a few hours."

Cody rolled his eyes, and sighed. "Look, I thought—"

"No, that's just it. You didn't think. You put my life in jeopardy without letting me know the hazards of exposure to that—that thing."

"But, I didn't have all Kung's data at the—"

"You knew enough to know it was radioactive. You knew enough to have a special underwater case built for a Geiger counter."

"Yes, but I—"

"Gentlemen. Gentlemen, please. If you will allow me to intrude." Kung held out his hands as if he were holding back two boxers in the ring. "First, I insist on full disclosure. That is why I made available my photographs and my notes. Have you read any of my material yet, Mr. Hutchison?"

Hutch shook his head. "I didn't get that far ... "

"Then, please, allow me to explain the circumstances. Second, the artifact is not radioactive in the way that we perceive radioactivity. When Dr. Chang Wung Su first discovered the cylinder, he handled it without an awareness of the destructive potential of its being. But when he brought it to me, and I saw his condition, I knew that he was suffering from contact with some as yet unknown, unearthly power. Even when he died from the wasting disease, no one recognized the symptoms of radiation sickness. It was not until after I saw victims of the Hiroshima and Nagasaki atomic bomb explosions that I understood its grave import.

"As time passed, Dr. Chang's coworkers were afflicted with unusual pathological conditions of various degrees: pustules, loss of hair, infections, and internal disorders. Those who survived later exhibited mutagenic effects in their children: they were born deformed, or dead."

Hutch again stabbed the air with a stiffened index finger. "And you were going to send me into that nuclear furnace without telling me."

"Come on, you can't even settle down in a stable relationship, much less think about having kids."

"That's not the point! Whoever touches that thing becomes stale Crispy Critters."

"I swear, I had no idea it was dangerous. You saw the pictures we had. They were smuggled out by a disgruntled digger. They don't show any signs of radioactivity. Now, granted, we had some indication of this light beam. That's how we got onto the idea it was still active. But we figured the cylinder's some kind of focusing control, or power module. Hell, I never thought it was a goddamn box of compacted neutrons. And I don't even know what that means."

"You also never thought about turning me into fried rice. But if you had *told* me some of this in the beginning at least I could have taken some precautions to save my lower case jewelry.''

''Mr. Hutchison, I comprehend now as I did at the time that one must treat this alien artifact with great caution. However, let me further explain. I experimented with animals. I soon discovered that the mere presence of the artifact did not harm them. Only if they were placed in the emitted energy beam did they become sick and die. Otherwise, the cylinder can be handled with completed impunity. I myself have touched it many times, with no ill aftereffects.''

''Yes, well, I still don't like it. If this guy had the decency—''

''I said I'm sorry, and I meant it.'' Cody engulfed the last bite of meat and cheese. ''Believe me, I want you to live through this mission as much as you do—Well, almost as much. So we'll get you a lead lined jock strap. As long as you stay out of the beam, you'll be okay.''

''Cody, you're as bad as those outer space characters. If they'd had any basic humanity, they wouldn't have left behind something so deadly. I wonder how many Peking men died carrying or rolling this thing into their cave.''

Ronnie said, ''The aliens might have had attitudes not much different from ours. Look how we pollute our atmosphere with industrial waste, and pour hazardous chemicals into the ground, and use the ocean as a toxic dumping station. Do we care about the fish at the bottom of the sea?''

''But they're more technologically advanced than we are. Shouldn't they also be more civilized?''

''Technology and culture don't necessarily evolve at the same rate. Look out our own society. We can send a man to the moon, but we can't feed all our indigents. We can control the atom, but we can't restrain our own base desire to unleash its power on others. Hutch, we ourselves are a paradoxical race. Can we expect any better from others?''

''Not only that,'' Cody added. ''But they may not even be living creatures—in the way we think of life. Maybe they're some kind of machine people. Robots. Mechanical counterparts. And maybe their spaceship just crashed, so they're not responsible for any of this.''

Kung shook his head. ''No, my friends, there was no crash. The artifacts we found showed no signs of fire, or breakage, or any kind of cataclysmic destruction. All the evidence points to purposeful abandonment of unwanted property. Jetsam, as opposed to flotsam. However, if you will allow me to digress from this admittedly intriguing philosophical discussion, I would like to direct our conversation toward the more important issues at hand. Cody, did you inspect the underwater search and locater equipment?''

''I've got to hand it to you, Kung, you do things in style: side-scan sonar, sub-bottom profiler, *two* proton magnetometers. If your gunboat is anywhere on or under the ocean floor, the *Pegasus* is the boat to find it.''

Kung's smile shone a little brighter as he gave a curt bow. ''Thank you.

Let us hope that the wreck has not already been found, and looted.''

Hutch humphed. "We have a saying in archaeology: a looter is someone who took something you would have taken if you had found it first.''

Kung laughed. "Quite true, Mr. Hutchison. Quite true. You have an offbeat sense of humor.''

"Try spending a couple months with him,'' Cody grumbled. "After a while, offbeat tends to off*end*. And his awful jokes become offal.''

Kung laughed harder. "With such companionship, I believe this cruise will be quite an adventure.''

"Just keep an eye on this guy.'' Hutch pointed a finger at Cody. "Every time he gets near a boat, bad things happen to it.''

"Just coincidence,'' the commando scowled.

Ronnie said, "Kung, I think I should check in with HQ. You know, to let them know where we are. If we want backup within patrolling distance—''

"Pardon me, Lieutenant, but I prefer that we remain incommunicado unless absolutely necessary. My strategy is to let no one know where we are. When the faucet is disconnected, the tap cannot leak.''

"Of course. I understand.''

"So, enjoy the hospitality. Chou will soon be serving lunch. In anticipation of your Western tastes, I have had the freezer stocked with a large supply of hamburger. However, I suggest that you try the Chinese delectables. Cody, would you help me set up the towing cables and check out the transducer? We will not arrive until after midnight, but I would like to start scanning at once.''

"With a captain, mate, and engineer running the show, there's not much else for me to do.''

"Good. We will set it up on the back deck so that we can drag the towfish while we are trolling. We might catch some quite sizeable tuna—''

The engine roar came and went as the pair left the cabin. Hutch picked up a photograph at random, and stared at it.

"Honey, would you like something for your nausea?''

Hutch pursed his lips, and shook his head. "Dimenhydrenate won't cure what I've got. I'm not seasick. I'm nauseated by all this Saturday matinee serial stuff: the killing, the double crossing, the charades. I just want to do anthropology.''

"Honey, we all have things we'd rather do. But when other people try to prevent you from doing them, you have to take a stand.''

"How, by knocking them off? That's not how people are supposed to act.''

Ronnie was quiet for a long time. Finally, "You know, for all your sophistication you have a broad streak of naivete. You think that just because you're a righteous, upstanding citizen, everyone else is, too. That's a rather simplistic view of the world, and an abnegation of reality.''

"Cut the twenty-five cent words."

She placed her had on his. "Honey, the world is full of big bad wolves."

"So? Maybe they should be penned."

"That's easy to say; not so easy to do. Sometimes, you have to kill the leader of the pack so the rest get the message. Even a pacifist has to recognize that, or he's nothing but a slave to the first person who comes along and orders him about."

"We have government to—"

"Right. But freedom begins on an personal level. You first have to have the integrity to stand up for yourself. Then, when you band together with others who think the same way, you create a trenchant, spiritual gestalt. If you hide under the guise of government protection, without doing your part, you're nothing but a parasite on society: willing to let others go out and do your fighting for you, while you stay home and talk about peace."

"All right, I know what you're saying. I'm no flower child. But this cold blooded—"

"So! That's what's got you so glum."

Hutch snickered like a startled horse. "Ronnie, I—I just saw you shoot down a man like he was a cardboard target at a carnival shooting gallery. My god—"

"And I'd do it again, only faster if I could. Hutch, that man was out to kill me, and for that he deserved to die. But even worse, he was trying to take away someone I love, someone who means more to me than life itself. That brings out maternal instincts that are genetically bonded with family and survival of the species. You should know more about that than I do. You figure out the cause, all I know is the effect: I do whatever is necessary to protect me and mine. There's nothing wrong with that response. If there were, I could never live with myself."

*   *   *

"I don't believe this. All these fancy electronics aboard, and we're *dragging* for the wreck."

Kung kept the binoculars glued to his face. "And using land ranges instead of sensitive positioning equipment. Sometimes, the old ways are best. That spike on the depth recorder is too tall to represent a hundred and fifty foot long gunboat, Mr. Hutchison, yet we seem to be in the right area. You understand, of course, that I left the *Ting-Yuen* rather hastily, and did not have time to take accurate sightings."

Hutch attached a Chinese regulator to the short, stocky tanks. "This doesn't exactly look like Grand Central Station. I would think that an anomalous reading couldn't be anything *but* the *Ting-Yuen*."

"You are probably correct. Our distance from the island seems about right, but the trees and rocks I used for triangulation are different."

"Trees have a nasty habit of growing through the decades."

Cody shouted down from the flying bridge. "We're over it right now!"

Ronnie emerged from the cabin, rubbing her eyes. "What's happening?"

"I'm going diving. Enjoy your nap?"

"I stood a watch last night so the others could catch up on their sleep. They'd been running the boat for over twenty-four hours. Are you having trouble there?"

Hutch fumbled with the unfamiliar gear. "I can't figure out how to get this thing facing the right way."

"Must be Allsdivers disease: too much time decompressing. Here, let me." Quickly she set up the regulator and hoses. "I've done lots of diving with this equipment."

"It's hooked!" Cody shouted.

Hutch peered through the cabin glass and saw the mate and engineer wrapping the anchor line around the windlass. As the boat took up a strain on the rope, it pivoted on the grapnel.

"Okay, hot stuff, get ready to go down." Cody climbed down the ladder and jumped the last rung to the deck. "You, not her."

Kung let the binoculars hang by the strap. "Mr. Hutchison, I am uncomfortable with your going into the water under these conditions. I am so unsure: although this appears to be the right spot, the relief is too high."

"So, I'll check it out. That's what I'm here for."

"Do be careful, Honey."

"Do be careful, Honey." Cody did a squeaky voice imitation of Ronnie. In his normal, base voice, "The current's pretty bad. A couple of sea gulls floated by so fast they had wind burn. How about if I tow you up to the bow?"

Hutch pulled up his beaver tail and snapped it in place. "Sounds good to me. But if it's really that bad, you'd better keep an eye out for me in case I get swept off the wreck or run low on air. I don't like diving without backups, especially without a pony bottle."

"Hey, you take what you can get."

"I'll pop a bag as a marker if anything goes wrong."

"I'll keep my eyes peeled." Cody tousled Hutch's dirty blonde hair. "I wouldn't let anything happen to you—but I haven't forgotten about that crocodile on Borneo."

"And if you find the artifact, don't get in front of it." Ronnie helped him slip into the tank harness. "I wouldn't want you sterilized."

Cody clipped a spare dive light to his tank lanyard. "Yes, please take care of the equipment."

Hutch slung on the weight belt, snapped it in front, and adjusted it on his hips. His mesh bag hung from a weight snap. "I'm glad everyone's so concerned about my health. Kung, do you see what I've had to put up with. And I was drafted for this mission."

"You Americans play as hard as you work," Kung laughed. "Would you like a last look at the plans, Mr. Hutchison?"

"No, I've got them memorized." Hutch stuck the regulator in his mouth and gave a few test inhalations. The diaphragm pressure was triggered by the slightest intake, and air was practically forced into his mouth. He was pleased with the efficiency of the Chinese manufactured equipment. "The goods are in the magazine."

"In a wooden box lined with lead sheet."

"Got it." He held out his hand, and Ronnie slipped the main light lanyard over his wrist. "Okay, let me get out of here before I sweat to death."

Cody handed him a nylon loop. "Have a good one."

Hutch closed his fingers on the rope, nodded, held his mask to his face, and rolled overboard. The water was cool as it seeped up the sleeves, cuffs, and neck of his wetsuit. When he bobbed to the surface, he was strung out on the line like a flag in a gale. He kicked his fins, but was sure that he was doing nothing to counteract the stiff current. Water rushed past his face as Cody hauled him like a limp fish to the bow. It took several minutes to travel the length of the boat, and he was exhausted when he got there. Still, Cody could not pull him around the anchor line, since it angled forward past the bowsprit. Hutch would have to kick the rest of the way.

He flung off the loop, ducked his head underwater, and kicked like mad. He made long, even strokes that did not seem to propel him any closer to the white line; he felt as if he were barely keeping his own. The bow of the *Pegasus* plunged down and slapped his tanks; with his feet touching the fiberglas hull he was not able to kick. He gulped down as much air as the regulator would feed him, and pushed off to the side. He was nicked in the shoulder by the rounded edge, but not hurt.

He kicked harder. His arm was outstretched, his fingers cluthcing. The anchor line was close one second as the boat dipped into a trough, then far away as the *Pegasus* rode the crest of the following wave. It took every ounce of strength and all his power of will to not give up, to keep kicking his weary legs. Finally, his fingertips brushed the line; he lunged, and managed to grasp the rope during a downsweep. Then it jerked him completely out of the water as the boat rose high. For a few precious seconds, Hutch's shoulder was wrenched in its socket as he was alternately dragged down, then up, then down again. He caught on with his other hand, went through several more gyrations, then managed to pull himself below the surface. At five feet he realized he was fighting the buoyancy in his compensator. He struggled to let out air. Then he sank, still being jerked around, and was forced to stop to catch his breath at ten feet.

Several minutes passed before he could continue his descent. At thirty feet, he paused to check his gauges. He had used an inordinately large amount of air, considering that his dive had not even started yet. Already, his arms ached as he fought to hold onto the heaving line and pull himself down at the same time. At fifty feet the surface pounding was no longer noticable, although the current was just as strong. His forearms burned. He was afraid of being torn off the line and swept away. At one hundred feet he paused to rest again.

Slowly, he descended. Hand under hand, he reached down the anchor line, each fistful of rope advancing him another six inches. Because of the seas, the captain had let out a large amount of scope. Each foot of rope was less than half that in depth. There was over four hundred feet of anchor line laid out. Below one hundred fifty feet, it soared about the sandy bottom almost horizontally.

Hutch pulled himself along, breathing hard. The muscles in his arms were weakening fast. Finally, the water ahead became a shade darker. A dim silhouette took form. The grapnel hung precariously in the gunboat's starboard rail. With each topside surge the iron piping bent and stretched, and threatened to break. The tension on the anchor line was incredible: enough to play a tune on it. He could not possible move the grapnel to a more secure position.

The *Ting-Yuen* was sitting upright, and nearly perfectly intact. Except for the thin veneer of deep water encrustation, blobs of anemones shrunken into balls because of the current, and long fans of coral waving like banners, it might have been sitting in drydock. The bow gun stood on its mount, the barrel slightly elevated. The top part of the wheelhouse, constructed of thinner metal, had collapsed. Most of the superstructure bulkheads were gone, leaving a skeletal framework of beams like the studs of a house not yet sheetrocked. Although it was dark because most of the lowlying sunlight reflected off the surface instead of penetrating downward, the water was extremely clear: Hutch could see more than half the wreck.

A tremendous gash carved through the hull just below the bridge area: the point of collision with the destroyer. The cut went straight down to where the keel was buried in the sand. Jagged pieces of metal were folded into the wreck. Aft of this, a crosshatched design hung over the hull, draped over the remaining superstructure, and arced upward for forty feet: a green, swaying mass of seaweed and marine growth. It was a trawler net. Some time in the past, a Korean fishing boat had dragged across the *Ting-Yuen* and lost its gear. Glass floats held it up, giving the wreck the unusually high relief spotted on the depth recorder.

When Hutch at last clutched the rail, his strength was about to give out. He pulled himself along the twisted iron pipe until he reached the superstructure. He crept into the walkaround deck in the lee of an upright bulkhead. The current was blocked. Only inches over his head, fish and plankton raced by as if on a waterborne escalator. He checked his gauges while he caught his breath: one hundred eighty feet, and one third of his air gone.

By the time he was breathing more or less normally, he had decided that to swim above the hull against the current was out of the question.

Instead of dropping down the stairwell in the superstructure, he thought he could enter the wreck through the breach in the engine room. He slipped over the rail, dropped down, and shone his light into the black cavern within.

A mangled mess of iron pipes, copper tubing, and electrical cables barred the way, but Hutch waded into the opening and squirmed through the wreckage. His hoses hung up several times, as did the mesh bag hanging from his weight belt, but he pushed through into the inner spaces where there was more room.

The starboard engine had shiften off its bedplate, and lay at an angle with its forward end touching the port engine. Several feet of silt covered the deck so the lower half of both engines were buried in a thick, brown ooze on which grew tiny, filigreed anemones. Wires half stripped of their insulation lay over the whole like a collapsed spider web.

Hutch aimed his light at the overhead. He wove through the hanging debris until he reached the lip of the skylight. He rolled over on his back, pulled himself under the coaming and up into the opening. The forward bulkhead was nonexistent. He could see directly into the officer's mess. The starboard side was crushed inward. The port table stood on its twin stanchions and, oddly, a mug sat on the very edge, as if placed there by a departing sailor.

The light swept the room. Hutch took notice of the shattered ports, the broken benches, the debris littering the deck. A lighting fixture dangled from its wires, with the bare light bulb unimploded by the pressure of depth. Already, his exhaust bubbles raced along the overhead, dislodging rust and accumulated silt. He moved fast across the room, but kept his fintips well above the mud.

A doorway led forward into the tiny galley. A porthole on either side let in two green circles of light. An endless stream of silvery baitfish charged through the port side porthole, sucked in by the current, and dashed madly across the room and exited through the starboard porthole. When Hutch reached the middle of the room the current hit him like a battering ram. He was swept sideways before he managed to grasp the leading edge of the other doorway. He pulled himself into the crew's quarters. No. A bulkhead was missing, and so was a ladder. The companionway he was looking for actually merged with the crew's berthing space.

The overhead hatch was ajar, and light seeped in around the edges. Hutch shoved upward. The hatch moved an inch, then jammed. The marine encrustation was thick, and prevented further progress. Below, another hatch was missing. Hutch made himself vertical, aligned his feet over the opening, and slowly slid into the lower deck level.

The handling room was completely dark. It had no portholes, no openings aft into the machinery spaces, no circulation of water. No fish lived in this dead zone, and only a few hardy anemones managed to eke out a living in the decomposing muck. Two hoists were exposed in the forward bulkhead. One had a projectile in it, waiting these many years to be lifted topside for removal by that long dead gun crew. Empty shell casings littered the deck, protruding half out of the mud, where they had been hastily thrown after being dropped down the scuttle. They would never be repacked.

Each end of the handling room had a door facing forward. The port side was the small arms room where pistol, rifle, and machine gun ammunition was stored, along with gunpowder and miscellaneous explosives. Hutch headed to starboard, for the shell room. As he neared the open door he saw a green glow emerging from the opening, as if outside light were pouring in. Unless the magazine was open to the sea, no ambient light should be visible.

Hutch placed his light against his chest. He peered around the metal jamb—and saw it.

Emerald radiance flooded the magazine with a steady, all-encompassing sheen. Every corner was softly illuminated; there were no shadows. Hutch's own white light was stark and intrusive in that alien glow of warmth. He switched it off.

One entire bulkhead was lined from deck to overhead with a rack of gun shells, stacked nose to butt in alternating rows. Much of the wooden storage cases were eaten away by wood borers, exposing the armor piercing tips and the brass bases with their primers.

Hutch's astonished eyes followed a thin beam of intense green down to the deck. Lying amid a jumble of loose shells and a pile of gunpowder—black, cigarette filter sized stubs with fine holes bored through their lengths—was the artifact.

The cylinder with tapered ends did more than glow—it coruscated. It did not appear to have a true surface. It was like looking at a neon tube whose capacitor leads were fed through a cycling rheostat: the power surges caused an indefinite, constantly changing output. So charged was the artifact that Hutch could even *feel* a deep thrumming through the water, through the metal of the ship.

It lay at an angle, cocked upward as it rested on the edge of a stack of lead sheathing. All signs of the box which contained it were long since gone. Hutch pushed slowly into the room. He was careful to stay out of the direct beam. When he held his hand over the cylinder, beams of light scintillated between his fingers. He pulled off one cotton glove, and placed his hand near the artifact.

There was no heat, no sensation. But he could feel the—antiquity. He sensed the awesome power. Genty, fearfully, he forced his hand closer. The refulgent light continued to flow outward, and through the skin along the edges of his fingers. He *touched* it.

The cylinder seemed to vibrate. It thrilled him, running electrically through his hand, up his arm, into his shoulder, and encompassing his brain. Fighting off the narcotic effect, he wrapped his fingers around it. He saw the digits disappear into the outer coruscation, but felt no pain. The surface was not smooth. He never felt anything so—indefinite. It was like touching a penny arcade foot vibrator. When he brought his hand away, his fingers were still whole.

He grasped the artifact again, and wrenched as hard as he could. It did not budge. Kung was correct: it was heavier than the platinum counterfeit on the *Gremyashchi*. It would take quite a bit of lift to move it. He pulled back his hand.

He should go. He should check his gauges, calculate his time. But he was captivated by the alien artifact. He was astounded to find, after months on the quest, that it was not a delusion, not a figment of imagination, not a phantom of mass hysteria. It was with great difficulty that he accepted the fact that it actually existed.

Hutch forced himself to back out of the room, out of the influence of the alien aura, away from the comfort of uncertainty, and into the pain of reality. Numbed by the fantastic actuality, he switched on his cold, unfeeling dive light. He worked his way back through the handling room, up into the companionway, aft through the galley and officer's mess, down the engine room skylight, and out the vertical gash.

It was not until he rose above the deck level, and the current hit him full tilt, that he recovered his senses. He fought to hang on to the railing, to pull himself along the bent, twisted stanchions. The rude awakening actually occurred when he reached the rail that should have held the grapnel—and found that it had been ripped out bodily.

The anchor line was gone. He had no emergency ascent line. His tanks were almost empty, and he had no backup supply. Without a decompression computer, he had to rely on calculations based on the Navy Air Decompression Tables.

He let go of the wreck. Instantly, he was swept away like a leaf blown off a tree in an autumn storm. But current, once he was no longer fighting it, ceased to be a problem. He no more felt the lateral movement than a shopper on an escalator. Hutch went with the flow. He puffed some air into his BC, and stared at his depth gauge to monitor his ascent.

Despite the recommended rate of sixty feet per minute allowed by the Navy Tables, Hutch performed his own interpolations. He had left the bottom at seventeen minutes into his dive, shorter than he had originally allowed. He watched his ascent rate as closely as he could, considering he had no anchor line on which to check his speed. At approximately thirty feet per minute, it would take five minutes to reach his first decompression stop. The toughest part was letting air out of the BC as it expanded due to decreased pressure. He rose too fast, let out too much air, started dropping, put air back in, rose again too fast, and let air out. But somewhere about five minutes later, he reached his first ceiling.

He had only a couple hundreds pounds of air left—much less than what he needed to do a forty-five minute decompression.

A strange feeling of aloneness overcame him. The bright blue ocean extended out in all directions as far as he could see. Nothing was below him except the gradual darkening of water. There were no fish, no sharks, nothing of iminent danger. Yet above him lay instant death—invisible, unseeable, but all too real.

Even as he thought, death formed in his bloodstream. Seventy-eight percent of the air he breathed was nitrogen. The body could not use it. Normally, it was exhaled at the same rate at which it was inhaled. But under pressure, the diatomic molecules were forced into solution in the blood, carried throughout the body, and sequestered in the tissues. Now, those same molecules were striving to come out of the tissues, back into the bloodstream, to get out of the body. But if too many came out of solution at once, the bloodstream could not handle the overload. They bunched up, especially at the strictures where the vessels bent around the joints. As the innocuous solitary molecules agglutinized into bubbles too large to pass those tight junctures, they formed a block which stopped the flow of blood, and the flow of oxygen. Everything beyond that point began to die.

Depending on where the bubbles stuck, the result could be felt as intense pain, pins and needles, or total numbness. If the damage was severe, death could follow. If the nervous system was affected, permanent paralysis could ensure. Nerves did not heal readily; usually, once they died, they stayed dead. A victim, if he survived, might never walk again.

The horror of the situation raced through Hutch's mind as he looked up at the surface thirty feet overhead. He could see the sun and clouds through the clear water. Except for the wave tops, the world seemed so placid, so peaceful. Yet he was staring at uncompromising death, with no weapons to fight it off except the dwindling air supply in his tanks and his frantic skip breathing. It was a fate which held more fear for Hutch than the largest great white shark. The bends were a realistic possibility, here and now; sharks were an overrated dramatization simply because they had corporeality in the human imagination.

So, Hutch hovered at his artificial ceiling. Staying neutrally buoyant was using up air faster than he could afford. If he let too much air into his BC, he would soar to the surface out of control. If he let too much out, he had to kick his fins to overcome his descent. Staying perfectly neutral was impossible: every deep inhalation expanded his lungs and added balloonlike buoyancy; every exhalation squeezed out that reserve buoyancy and made him sink into the blue depths.

He pulled out the liftbag, tied a small leader to it, purged his regulator under the opening, and let the liftbag rise to the surface. The twenty-foot line brought him past the thirty foot stop which, he hoped, could be dispensed with by now. He made himself heavy and hung onto the end of the line. His capillary gauge placed him at twenty-five feet. Then he took out the plastic card on which was printed the outdated Navy Tables, and used it to interpolate the more conserative Buhlman tables on which his computer simulation was based. He kept an eye on his watch and depth gauge. If he could stretch out his air, he might make it through this.

With the strong westering current Hutch was floating off into the sunset. Even with twelve hours of daylight, since he was no longer in a stationary position, and somewhat in the clutches of the vagaries of the wind pushing the liftbag, those on the *Pegasus* might never find him. They, too, were floating somewhere off the wreck, more a slave to the wind because of hull exposure. Each of them was probably sailing in different directions—and how visible was this old-fashioned, white liftbag when it looked like a cresting wave?

Hutch still had twenty minutes to decompress at ten feet when the regulator showed signs of tightening up. Each breath became more difficult to draw. The pressure gauge was pegged on zero: there was not enough air in the tanks to register movement of the needle. The chill that coursed along Hutch's spine was not caused by the water, which was as warm as a sauna. He looked up at that barrier only ten feet away, with a fear that had no substance beyond the intellectual capacity of understanding his potential vulnerability. This was worse than being left alone in the middle of the ocean, since rescue would not save him from paralysis or death.

Then he heard the noise. At first it was a faint, humming sound audible only when he inhaled, when the rumble of bubbles passing his ears allowed him to hear. He held his breath, now more to listen than to conserve air. It was louder, definitely coming his way. He spun around, not knowing in which direction to look. Underwater, sound traveled much faster than in air because of relative density. The vibrating molecules hit both ears with such speed that the auditory nerves were not sensitive enough to measure the time delay.

The sleek, white hull was on him suddenly. There was a momentary slowing of engines, a splash and a froth of bubbles, and a descending diver in a black wetsuit. The boat kept going, but the diver spun around, dropped below the surface, and kicked directly toward Hutch. One single tank was harnessed behind, another was cradled in the arms. The extra tank was being held out, and a spare regulator dangled off the manifold. Hutch took but a fleeting glance at the diver before spitting out his own regulator and fumbling to get the other in his mouth.

It was Cody!

Hutch could have kissed him at that moment. But he was too busy sucking in air, making up for the deficiency he had been suffering while skip breathing and breath holding. The air poured into his lungs with a vitality that revived him from the imagery of death. He breathed, and breathed, and breathed some more. He had been starving himself for air for the past fifteen minutes, and was close to passing out because of it. Now, he had an unlimited supply, so he made up for what he had missed.

He felt reincarnated.

Cody held onto the line next to him. He poked Hutch on the shoulder to get his attention. He touched thumb to index finger, and made the okay sign. Hutch smiled, pointed down with his finger, than signaled with the thumb up. Cody went wild. He responded first with a balled fist and flexing arm, then he hugged Hutch tightly and kissed his mask. Cody's eyes glistened the remaining ten minutes, until Hutch calculated his decompression was over. Slowly, he ascended the last then feet to the surface.

"Cody, am I ever glad to see you."

"Boy, you sure—" A wave washed over the commando's face. He sputtered, spit water, and coughed. "You sure gave me a fright, pulling—" This time he closed his mouth before the spume slammed into him. "Pulling a disappearing—I thought you were defecting to China."

"What the hell are you doing here? I thought you hated the water?"

"What else was I gonna do? The Chinks don't dive, and I was afraid she couldn't handle the current. I had no choice."

"You could have let me drown."

"No way. I knew you'd come through for us."

"Don't thank me. Thank Kung."

"I will, as soon as he gets back here with the goddamn boat."

The *Pegasus* approached from down current. The captain kept the engines in gear, but moved ahead slowly so the two men would drift down the starboard side. The boat had no ladder. The mate tossed a tire over the side. It was lashed short so it hung just out of the water.

Cody stuck his arm through the rubber circle and hung on. "What the hell did you do, go for a cruise?"

Ronnie leaned over the gunwale. "Get aboard fast. We've got company."

Hutch grabbed Cody's outflung hand, and pivoted into the fiberglas hull. "Help me with my tanks."

The mate and engineer held onto the manifold while Hutch released the quick release snaps and squirmed out of the shoulder straps. He reached up high, got a firm grip on the low rail, and pulled himself over the gunwale and onto the deck.

Cody dumped his tanks and clambered aboard at the same time. "What is it. Who's coming?"

Kung peered down from the flying bridge. "I can see it only on radar, twelve mile scale, but it is approaching fast."

"All right, get the hell out of here." Cody ripped off his wetsuit top. "Clear the deck for action."

The dive gear was dragged into a corner. Cody climbed up the ladder and took a look through the binoculars.

"Honey, are you all right?"

"I am now." Hutch threw his arms around Ronnie, and gave her a resounding smack on the cheek. "I found it, exactly where Kung said it would be. God, it's awesome."

"Hey, cut the chatter," Cody shouted. "Get to battle stations. I don't know what the hell's going on, but that blip is in sight already, and coming on like a hydrofoil.''

The *Pegasus* skipped along with the bow banging against the waves and sending sheets of water over the cabin. Hunching low for support, Hutch followed Ronnie inside. The mate was down below in the gun locker, taking out high powered rifles and boxes of ammunition. He passed them to the cook, who handed them up to the engineer.

Ronnie took one of the Chinese assault rifles, and sat down on the bench to load it. "Help me, Hutch. Start pushing shells into the magazine, like this. The banana clip will hold thirty rounds.''

With all the ammunition spread out on the table, Hutch tore into the cardboard boxes and did as he was told. "This isn't my idea of scientific exploration or progressive anthropology. Why do I feel like a soldier of fortune? I think I prefer the vicissitudes of academia, and being sniped at by my archaeological competitors.''

A whistling sound filled the air. It dropped in pitch as it grew louder. A whoosh was followed immediately by a waterspout off the stern, and a thunderous roar.

Cody hit the deck without touching a single rung. He let go the sliders and crashed through the cabin door. "I think they mean business.''

"Jesus Christ! I thought they were supposed to fire a warning shot over the bow, or something.''

"You know what you're problem is? You read too much.'' Cody flung the binoculars at Ronnie. "See if you recognize any markings.''

"What is it, a patrol boat?''

"It sure as hell ain't a tug. Here, give me them rifles.''

Cody took a handful of weapons and put them on the deck. He stepped aside as the mate and engineer climbed up carrying a fifty caliber machine gun between them. They took it out onto the open deck. It was but a moment's work to pull the fighting chair off its mount, and set up the gun in its place. It fit with a perfection that was part of its design.

Hutch recognized the warning whine of an approaching gunshell. Another shot exploded off the port side. Something like hail rattled against the hull. "Hey, I came on this trip to *study* dead men, not become one.''

Cody shouted out the cabin door, "Evasive maneuvers!''

The *Pegasus* veered sharply to starboard, heeling over with the sudden, high speed change of direction. The mate and engineer rushed back inside, went down below, and started unpacking steel ammunition cans. The next whine was so loud that Hutch swore the projectile was coming right through the cabin. It missed the boat, but exploded so close to the starboard side that the *Pegasus* was lifted right out of the water. The jabbering below became a scream of pain, followed by an awful moaning. The mate stumbled out clutching his side. He collapsed in a pool of blood. Hutch hurried through the forward door into the smoking cauldron below.

The wind that hit him in the face was blowing in through a door-sized hole in the hull. The galley had been where water now gushed in through splintered fiberglas. The engineer lay against the port bulkhead, in a pandemonium of still falling pots and pans. If he was not dead, Hutch prayed fervently that he would not recover consciousness, for there was not enough to piece together into a recognizable human being.

The short cook had become shorter by a foot. He writhed on the deck, swinging his stump uselessly. Hutch swallowed hard, climbed down below, grasped the man under the arms, and dragged him out of the debris and up to the upper cabin.

He stared wide-eyed at Ronnie. "What the hell is going on?"

Ronnie did not answer. She slammed a full magazine into the breech, pulled back the bolt, and chambered a round. Cody ducked back in long enough to pick up a handful of rifles from the deck and carry them back outside. Hutch looked out the starboard window in time to see the oncoming gray hull spout flame from its single bow gun.

At the same time, Kung manned the machine gun. The injured mate crouched by his side, feeding the belt into the mechanism as Kung pulled the trigger. Red tracer rounds arced out over the sea, far off the gunboat's stern. Kung quickly adjusted his aim, and walked the stream of lead up to the steel hull. He raked the superstructure once, then concentrated his fire on the forward gun crew.

Two loaders were whipped completely off the hull, to crash into the sea on the other side of the boat. The gunner folded up in the middle, was slammed against a bulkhead, and slid down to the deck like a broken doll.

The deck gun was silenced, but a machine came on line from a sponson above the bridge. With unerring accuracy the return fire enfiladed the *Pegasus* from the stern, ripped up the after deck, and gouged into the cabin. Hutch ducked as the glass blew in. Bullets pounded through the rear bulkhead and chewed up the forward bulkhead. Tape decks, speakers, navigational equipment, and the television monitor exploded into electronic components. Paneling and upholstery were torn to shreds.

Hutch was still lying on the deck when Cody leaped off the flying bridge and charged into the shambles of the cabin. "The captain's gone."

Ronnie leveled her rifle out the rear window. She emptied a clip in a matter of seconds.

"Get out there and help Kung!" Cody shouted.

Hutch crept up to his hands and knees. He was shaking from fear, but managed to scramble out on all fours. The mate was lying huddled in a corner, knees to chin. His body was a froth of blood, and this time he would not recover.

"Mr. Hutchison, do you know how to clip on the links?"

"N-n-n-n-no."

Kung leaped to the right side of the machine gun. "Then you shoot."

Hutch gulped. He turned around and stared at Cody. He was standing by the lower steering station, spinning the wheel rapidly from side to side.

Ronnie's gun was poked out the cabin door. "Hurry, get that gun on line."

Hutch looked at the nearing gunboat. He saw a man in the upper sponson pull a limp body away from the gun, and take his place. Fireflies leaped out of the black muzzle, danced across the waves, and cut a zigzag path toward the *Pegasus*. At the same time, half a dozen sailors lined the rails with hand held weapons. This tremendous fire power was directed at the slowing sportfisherman.

Hutch gulped again, held his breath, and squeezed the trigger. The gun leaped in his hands. He felt the brutal, frightful power within his grasp. His own line of tracers sped over the rear deck and into the water not fifty feet astern. Bullets richochetted in a fanlike pattern that showered the steel hull. Not one shell hit the gunboat, but so wild and erratic was his fire that the top gunner hid behind his shrapnel shield, and the sailors ducked for cover.

"Raise the barrel," Kung said, calmly and with infinite patience. He strung out the belt and let it feed straight into the breech.

Hutch zeroed in on the gunboat, now practically on top of them. He pulled the trigger, and never let it go. He just spun the machine gun on its swivel mount, and swept his tracers up and back the hull. They bounced off the armor plating with a shower of sparks. He saw the machine gunner knocked off his perch, but it was like a movie reel: Hutch was merely a spectator, and had nothing to do with what was being shown on the silver screen. One sailor on deck level rebounded off the shielding, and pivoted over the rail and into the water. Others crawled along behind the metal gunwales, taking occasional, one-handed pot shots.

By the time the gunboat veered away, most of the glass ports in the navigating bridge were shot out. Hutch continued to shoot as the distance between the two boats increased. The gunboat was swinging around for another pass, but the fantail of the *Pegasus* was rising above Hutch's line of sight.

"*We're going down!*"

Hutch released the trigger and swung around toward Cody. The boat was sinking by the head—fast.

Cody grabbed Ronnie by the arm and dragged her out of the cabin. He tossed lifejackets at Hutch and Kung. "Get that thing off. It's full of holes."

Hutch realized he was still wearing his BC. It was completely deflated. When he ran his hands over his chest, he felt hot, sharp metal fragments and wood splinters sticking out of the rubber. He shrugged off the BC, stood up to don the lifejacket, and promptly fell down as he slipped and rolled over a listing deck full of spent shell casings. He lay in a tangle with Kung, and would have laughed at his predicament if it had not been so serious.

The bow knifed under, and waves washed over the forward deck and into the shot-out windows. The engines had died out; in the ensuing silence

Hutch heard a far off whupping that was not the gunboat's diesels. He searched the sky for the sound, then saw an olive drab speck heading his way. The helicopter started spitting orange, and tongues of flame darted ahead toward the hulk of the *Pegasus*. With the boat dead in the water, there was no way the rocket fire could fail to hit it. Yet, miraculously, the missiles zoomed overhead and exploded closer to the gunboat than to the sportfisherman.

"Here come the Marines!" Cody shouted.

The second fusillade of rockets was more accurate. They impacted against the steel hull in great balls of flame that boiled skyward. The chopper zoomed by overhead, following up the rocket attack with gatling gun fire that hit the water with so many projectiles that the ocean looked like it had been inundated with a local rain squall. The gunboat's magazine must have gone up next, for the titanic explosion that followed sent steel splinters so far into the air that they rained down on the sinking *Pegasus*. The helicopter banked sharply to the side and barely avoided the fiery cauldron.

On the steeply tilting deck, Hutch could not maintain his balance. He and Kung slid into the cabin bulkhead at Cody's and Ronnie feet.

Cody grinned down at him. "I think it's time to abandon ship." He tossed Ronnie overboard bodily, then reached down for Hutch.

"The first good advice I've heard from you all day." Hutch scrabbled among the cartridges, and reached the gunwale on his belly. A windstorm was spouting out the cabin as water rushing into the hole now below the waterline forced air through the forward cabin door. Hutch squirmed over the rail and into the sea.

The stern rose high, and the propellors came out of the water. Cody helped Kung over the side. With increasing speed, the boat nose-dived under the water. Cody got off with only seconds to spare. The *Pegasus* knifed down as thousands of gallons of water gurgled out of the hull along with the trapped air. The final plunge took less than five seconds, then it was gone. A last spurt of air and water exploded upward like a fountain, the sea bubbled, the ripples spread outward, floating debris foamed to the surface. Then the ocean became calm.

Five of them drifted with the flotsam. The mate lay face down, dead. The engineer and the cook had been dragged down with the boat. The captain was nowhere to be seen.

"Chou was still alive!" Hutch shouted.

"Yeah, he didn't get out. I saw him trying to go through the forward window. Thought he would make it." Cody grabbed Hutch's hand and pulled him close. "Listen, we all gotta stick together so the chopper can pick us up."

The foreign gunboat was gone—utterly. The four of them held hands as the helicopter veered around for another pass. As it slowed and hovered, Hutch felt the deep thrumming of the downward deflected prop wash. It whipped the sea to a froth. A cable lowered from one side as the crew chief guided the rescue ring into the group of survivors.

"Cody, I'm getting awfully tired of being blown out of the water."

"I know. It gets old after a while." Cody grabbed the horse collar and slipped it around Ronnie's shoulders. "But like you said, you can't get an experience like this off the boob tube."

The *Ting-Yuen*

"When this is all over, I'm going to park my rear in a recliner and become a couch potato."

"You love it, and you know it." Cody plopped himself on the wardroom table. His fatigues were cleaned and pressed. "You've got a definite aptitude for this kind of business."

"Don't confuse the necessity of my actions with enjoyment." Hutch stretched his lanky body along the length of the plastic cushioned couch. He wore khaki work clothes only because no civvies were available from stores. "The only thing I like about this whole deal is the laboratory. Do you know, the whole time we were gone the *Morton's* technicians performed just about every test known to man on those remains—and input the whole works on computer. Then *it* went ahead and correlated everything. There's enough information for an encyclopedia on Peking man."

"Just remember when you write your papers, it's got to have my approval."

"I know, you're afraid I might give away some valuable military secret."

Cody humphed. "No, I just want to check your spelling. Ah, here they come."

Ronnie led Kung into the room. She was back in uniform. "Cody, you surprised me—calling a special meeting *before* we eat."

"Yeah, well, some things can't wait. Kung, where'd you get that outfit?"

Kung smoothed his dress whites. "It has been a long time since I have been in unifrom. I cannot say that I like the memories it conjures up. The executive officer was kind enough to lend it to me, although I do not think that Commander Petrie approves.''

"There's very little he does approve, except—well, speaking of the devilfish ... ''

Petrie flung open the door and charged into the wardroom. The expression on his face could have scared off a school of barracudas. "Cody, what's this about your ordering my ship turned around and headed for the Yellow Sea?''

Cody spread his hands, palm up. "Sounds self explanatory to me. What's to understand?''

"This ship has a cruise plan which specifically forbids it to enter the territorial waters of any nation, enemy or otherwise. If we get caught on the surface, the international repercussions will be—''

"Commander, commander, commander. Believe me, I want this thing handled as clandestinely as you do. I have no intention of surfacing at any time. The entire operation will be carried out underwater.''

Commander Petrie's mouth worked silently. When he finally found his voice, it was somewhat cracked. "Wha—how can—how do you propose to do that?''

"It's her plan, so I'll let her explain.''

Ronnie stood a little straighter. Her eyes glanced around the room at the various participants to the conference. "Well, uh, Commander, the purpose of this mission is to recover a—an object—whose exact description I am not at liberty to disclose. It is so long, and—''

"Lieutenant Wakefield!'' Petrie boomed. "Isn't it bad enough that I have to maintain station while you go galivanting around the ocean, monitoring radio channels, and sending a helicopter to go and pluck you out of the sea? Now you want to use my submarine to retrieve your belongings. This is preposterous—''

"Commander, please. Just let her finish,'' Cody said.

"Cody, I know you throw a lot of weight, but—''

"Then you can understand that this is not just a simple salvage operation.'' Holding his hand out toward Ronnie, "Please continue.''

She cleared her throat. "Well, as I was saying, this object contains— intelligence—of vital interest to the United States. It was sunk intentionally to prevent that intelligence from reaching foreign powers. It is extremely heavy, weighted so that it's, uh, information cannot be easily recovered.''

Petrie was impatient. "What is it? Some kind of black box, with flight recordings?''

"I'm not at liberty to say.'' Ronnie now spoke with more conviction, and less intimidation. "It was Mr. Kung, here, who showed us where it went down. Mr. Hutchison verified that the object was there, but, as you know, our boat was sunk before salvage could be attempted. With the approximate position known to subversive factions, it is necessary that we reclaim the object without making our presence known.''

"That's going to be rather difficult in a nuclear submarine. Our cavitation is like a signature. The Russians can decipher our propellor noise with such accuracy they can tell not only what ship this is but what I'm having for breakfast."

Ronnie raised an eyebrow. "Cody?"

He nodded.

"Commander, we're not concerned here with Russians, but with certain third world nations without underwater detection capabilities. May I continue?" She waited a moment while the commander grumbled. "What I propose is that you place the *Dudley Morton* alongside the wreck so that the object can be transferred without ever breaking the surface."

"But, the water in that position is two hundred feet deep. My divers can't lock out at that depth."

Cody interrupted. "Don't worry about it. We have our own talent."

"We don't have the equipment. You need hoses, and hook ups—"

Cody jerked a thumb at Hutch. "He can do it on scuba."

"But, it isn't safe."

"It isn't safe for a three year old to cross the street on his own. But when he grows up it's a different story. Would you let her finish? It gets better."

Commander Petrie scowled.

Ronnie paced the room as she explained the situation. "Okay, so, Mr. Hutchison will exit through the lock out chamber, swim to the wreck, attach a lifting device to the object, and tow it back to the *Morton*. Now, we've already checked out the chamber with one of your divers, and found that because of the decking and the physical constraints of the hatch, it will be impossible to get the object inside that way. It's too heavy to be handled without mechanical advantage. And we can't leave it rattling around outside the pressure hull. Therefore, we have to bring it in through one of the missile tubes."

Petrie's scowl faded into disbelief. His jaw dropped halfway to his chest. "You—you—you people are out of your minds. You think I have a conveniently empty missile tube to use as a storage compartment?"

Cody flashed his characteristic grin. "Of course not. But you can clear one."

"Trident missiles weigh sixty-three tons, and they're forty-four feet long. They can't be unloaded at sea. We'd have to go back to Washington to have it extracted."

"I'm sorry, but this is a rush job. We can't wait that long. Besides, I know you can evacuate a tube at the push of a button."

Petrie stared at Cody. "Sure, I can drain the tubes into the bilges and pump the water overboard. I've got more ballast capacity than the weight of an entire World War Two submarine. But you can't drop a heavy object on the top stage of a missile. It'll damage the nuclear warhead."

Cody turned to Ronnie. "Go ahead. Spell it out for him."

Without hesitation, she said. "Commander, I propose that you *launch* one of the missiles, and leave the tube flooded so we can drop the object inside it. That way, if we need to bring it aboard, we can haul it in through the guidance control inspection plate. But I see no reason not to just leave it where it is until we—"

"*You're sick*! All of you! And especially you—" Commander Petrie leveled a shaky finger at Cody. "—for thinking I'd go along with a harebrained scheme like this. You know damned well I can't fire as much as a peashooter without Presidential sanction. And if you think I'm going to call the Oval Office and make a recommendation like this, you're out of your fu—"

"You don't have to. I've already done it." Cody grinned smugly.

Ronnie rushed on. "The only thing you have to do is open the access panel to the fusing section, disarm the detonator, tighten a few bolts—and presto! With a six thousand mile range, you can drop it anywhere in the Pacific Ocean. Shallow, for later retrieval; or, in the bottom of the Marianas Trench."

Cody added, "Even if they could find it, the Russians'll never get it up from thirty-six thousand feet."

"And besides, you'll still have twenty-three Tridents as a nuclear deterrent. The loss of one little missile won't affect—"

"*That does it!*" Commander Petrie pulled the wardroom door practically off its hinges. It banged against the bulkhead and knocked the notice board off its hanger. Thumb tacks clattered and pieces of paper fluttered all over the deck. "I *am* going to call the President—to tell him you've gone off your rocker. You need psychiatric evaluation. All of you. Don't think I'm going to let you take over my ship so you can traipse all over the world picking up old bones for this—this—"

The slamming door knocked down two cardboard sketches and jolted a fire extinguisher off its mount.

Hutch sagged deeper into the couch. "Whew, whoever said that Australopithecus was extinct?"

Ronnie wandered around the table until she stood in front of the grinning commando. "Cody, why did you make *me* give the explanations? You could have done it with a lot less emotional strain."

He tilted his head. "To prove whose side you're on."

Ronnie squinted. "What? What do you mean by that?"

Cody slid off the table, took Ronnie by the shoulders, backed her into a chair, and sat her down. "This isn't going to be easy—for any of us. A few mistakes have been made, some sensitive information has been disclosed, but I think we can still save the situation. But it's going to take your full cooperation, because if you screw up now, it may mean *his* death, failure of the mission, and irretrievable loss of the artifact for all of mankind. Do I make myself clear?"

Ronnie looked first at Hutch, then at Kung, and back to Cody. Cody said "No, I don't think you do." Then he looked at Hutch. "And I *know* you don't."

Hutch sat up a little straigher. "What the hell are you getting at?"

Cody took a deep breath. He stared intensely at Ronnie as he said, "She's been doing a little dealing on the side. It took me a while to figure out what was going on. I trusted her. Like my own wife, I trusted her. And she let me down." Cody shrugged. "Well, it happens in this business. It's all part of the game, I guess. But it sure doesn't make me feel any better."

Ronnie rubbed her palms on her skirt. "Cody, I—"

"Wait a minute. Are you accusing her of double-crossing us?"

Cody sighed. "Not exactly. I'm simply saying that she's been— indiscreet. You see, counterintelligence is a complicated ploy with many functions: on one hand, it collects genuine information; on the other hand, it leaks out false information; and in the middle, it tries not to let the other side know which is which. It gets confusing after a while. There's no line of demarcation, no black and white—just various shades of gray: a complicated equation with an infinite number of variables. Ultimately, there's never a simple solution, and no such thing as a right answer."

"Is this a philosophy course?"

Cody gestured with his hands. "Sometimes we do the right thing but for the wrong reason. Sometimes, we do the wrong thing for the right reason. Every once in a while, we get really lucky and do the right thing for the right reason. Then we pat ourselves on the back and say how smart we were."

Hutch rolled his eyes. "Indeterminism. Get to the point."

"She—" Cody pointed at Ronnie, fidgeting in her seat. "—has done something, and for a reason. The validity of her reasoning is arguable from many different sides: there is no omniscient means of perception. I have my viewpoint, she has hers." Cody paused for a breath. "We've been tracked on this mission every step of the way. That chopper in Newfoundland was as much a shock to me as it was to you. Well, maybe not *quite* as much. So was the Chinese gunboat on the *Awa Maru*, and the napalm attack off Borneo. Then there was that little altercation on the docks at Chilung. Now, an unmarked assault ship off Korea. Of all these incidents, the only one explainable was the Chinese gunboat which, after all, had a right to patrol its own coast. And Kung saw to it that all they did was check us out. The other episodes were more serious. I didn't have to be hit on the head with an apple to deduce the presence of an unknown force.

"The real poser wasn't who was against us, but how they were procuring their information. We've got pretty tight security, and I trust implicitly everyone in our organization. Our people can't be bought: not with money, not with power, not with position, and certainly not with politics. There's only one way we can be gotten to, the most basic human threat: not to life, but to family.

"So, as soon as I boarded the *Charles Lockwood* I started an internal investigation in that direction. It turned up a lot of interesting facts, even about my own parentage. But that's not the issue. I can live with the fact that my father—the man who raised me—might not be my biological sire. I'll never know, but it doesn't change anything. But it wasn't until we got to Taiwan that the pieces started to fall into place."

Cody held out his hand toward Kung, by way of introduction.

The Chinaman stepped forward stiffly, hands clasped behind his back. "Thank you, Mr. Cody. Lieutenant, I realize this is difficult for you. In China, too, we hold kinship in high regard. Relationships are sacred, parents are honored, children are loved, friendships are inviolable. In your behalf, I can state that you were deceived as much as I. My trusted and valued servant betrayed me—not for family, but for gain. As a way of opening negotiations with certain antagonistic governments, and in return for pecuniary rewards, he distributed some of my confidential documents through the underground market, thus precipitating this entire chain of events and eventually forcing my hand to initiate defensive measures before permanent damage could be effected.

"Information found upon the remains of—this spy—led me to suspect infiltration into your organization. I did not know who, only how. In each case, prior to an attack, a coded, eight character message was transmitted on a specific frequency: latitude and longitude refined to the minute. After bringing you all aboard the *Pegasus*, I held a private conference with Mr. Cody who, I reasoned, since he was the mission leader, and always on the receiving end of the munitions, could not be a participant in the plot."

Cody took over. "Call me blind, or simple, but my suspicions weren't aroused till I noticed how oddly Buching looked at you, and took you to his side. He may have been senile, but during his moments of lucidity he recognized you. Or, at least, you looked familiar to him. I ignored it until I heard about the omnispy. So, I laid a trap. I warned HQ to expect a coded message, and on what frequency, and told them if they picked it up, they'd better send help pronto. You must have told them our general direction, so they dispatched a patrol boat to the vicinity. According to the *Dudley Morton's* log, the signal went out during your watch."

"I swear, I had nothing to do with it. I don't know how they were tracking us, but it wasn't from me." Ronnie gripped the arms of the chair so tightly that her suntanned hands turned white. "I—I—It's true that I was—" She looked at Hutch, whose jaw was agape, and tears streamed down her cheeks. "I had to give them information or—or they would have—"

She cried into her palms, choked, and cried some more. Cody handed her a tissue. She got control of herself, dabbed her cheeks, and stared up at the commando. "My—my mother ran off when I was only a little girl. Daddy raised me. He was the only one I had—the only one I *ever* had. I could always rely on him. The other men—well, they never wanted me. Just what I could give them. So, when they said—when they told me they had him—"

"Come on, now. You're a smarter intelligence officer than that." Cody leaned forward, and bent at the waist to bring his face closer to hers. His voice was commanding. "That's the oldest trick in the book. They find someone whose father or son is reported missing in action, and they say he's a POW. Just because your old man disappeared in the Bermuda Triangle doesn't mean *anybody's* got him. How could you fall for such an obvious fraud?"

"I had—no choice," Ronnie cried. "He's—my—my—father."

Kung placed a paternal hand on her heaving shoulder. "The ties run strong with her. Her motivation is pure. She is not to blame."

"Goddamn it, if you had only come to me when this whole thing started, I could have checked it out. I could have investigated—"

"But you couldn't be sure!" Ronnie screamed. "And I know you. You'd just tell me what I wanted to hear. Or whatever suited your purpose best."

"That's not true. I've never lied to you."

"No, but you have a habit of telling only that part of the truth which is applicable to your needs. You're right, I *am* a good intelligence officer. Good enough to know that I had to see this through my own way. Without your misguided help."

"If you're so goddamn good, why didn't you figure out that your informer was passing the information along to the OPEC conspiracy. Did you really think he was a Russian agent who just wanted to know that the artifact existed, and was recovered. Did you really believe that nonsense about 'knowledge of a technological innovation is just as important as the technology itself, because with that knowledge the eventual development is only a step behind.'?"

"*Yes!*" Ronnie screamed. "Yes! I believed it. I had no choice."

"And you believed the information he had was from personal war correspondence from your mother, Catarina Kardova?"

"Yes!" She was crying again. She looked at Hutch with pleading eyes. She held out her hands to him. "Oh, Hutch, I didn't know it would turn out like this. I thought they only wanted to know what was going on. The Soviets are not bad people. They want this—this energy source—as much as we do. But I didn't know about the subterfuge, the OPEC connection. I swear it. I just didn't know."

Kung was still holding onto Ronnie's shoulder. "When the full moon shines down from the heavens, it obscures the light from nearby stars."

"Yeah, well, I guess if it had been my wife, I'd have reacted a little differently." Cody brushed his hands through his short hair, and rubbed his scalp. He turned to Hutch. "How about you?"

Hutch had been watching the proceedings almost as an outsider, not comprehending most of what was going on, disbelieving what was really happening. His mind was in utter turmoil at the turn of events. He pushed himself up off the couch, disdaining to make even the slightest eye contact with Ronnie.

"I say take her out and shoot the bitch."

*   *   *

"Are you sure you know how this thing works, now?"

"We've gone over it enough times." Hutch swung shut the inner door of the lock-out chamber. The parallelogram hinge aligned the gasket with the hatch, and a quick turn on the breech ring latched it shut. "Of course, you can always come with me."

"No way, man." The Navy diver wiped his hands on his white t-shirt. The sleeves were rolled up, revealing large, red and blue tattoos on each shoulder. "You wanna surface, have me check the hull for dings, I'm your man. But you ain't gettin' me out in two hundred feet o' water."

Mounds of diving gear were spread all over the deck. Hutch waded into the mess of tanks, regulators, hoses, and gauges. "I want these doubles pumped up to thirty-five hundred p.s.i. And did you find me a pony bottle?"

"Yes, sir. I took one of the emergency oxygen bottles out of the medical kit. All I gotta do is hose clamp it on."

"Good." Hutch picked up a decompression computer manufactured specifically for the Navy. "I've never used this kind before. But the instructions seem pretty clear."

"I don't trust any of 'em. Even if I *did* get bent a few times usin' the Tables."

"Hell, man, why do you think Christ walked on water? They told him he'd have to decompress on Navy Tables if he got wet."

"Yeah, well, you say whatchu want, man. 'Lectronics is 'lectrohnics, an' likely to conk out on ya any time. You keep this card witchu jus' in case." The diver handed Hutch a plastic printout with the decompression stops and times printed in bold type. "When you get back in the chamber and set your depth, if that thing goes floozy you always got this to fall back on."

"Thanks." Hutch slipped it into the pocket of his wetsuit.

"I'll top off these tanks—give you a nice cold fill."

Cody appeared as the diver left for the compressor room. "So, how goes it?" He wore a set of camouflage fatigues. The only adornment was a radiation film badge where the name tag should have been. "You ready for the big dive?"

"As ready as I'll ever be. Everything set from your end?"

"Couldn't be better. She made the transmission with the fake coordinates, just like I asked. Some place in the sea of Japan. That'll keep the A-rabs off our beavertail long enough to get this hunk of neutronium aboard. Speaking of which, professor, what the hell *is* neutronium?''

"In simple terms?''

"I'm a simple man.''

"You know about the atom consisting of a nucleus of protons and neutrons, surrounded by spinning electrons?''

"I had highschool chemistry. I know that protons and electrons can combine to *form* neutrons, and that neutronium is nothing but pure neutrons without any additives. But what does that mean?''

"The first thing it means is it's very heavy. What makes an atom so light is that it's mostly empty space. Just like the solar system, with the planets revolving around the sun, is mostly empty space. Even the sun is mostly empty space, because it's made up of atoms of hydrogen and helium. But if you reduced the sun to neutrons, you'd end up with an object with the same mass, but only ten miles across. A thimbleful of that material would weigh over a hundred million tons.''

"Impossible, of course.''

"No, actually not. Naturally, you're not going to crush an atom without an incredibly strong outside force, any more than you can crush a pingpong ball in your hand. Uh, you can't, can you?''

"No.''

"Good. But if you hit it hard enough with, say, a sledge hammer, you could flatten the pingpong ball. By the same token, with enough pressure you can crush atoms into neutrons. But it would take an explosion on the supernova level to create those conditions. In fact, it's theorized that when a star blows up, the outer shell is vaporized into an expanding gas cloud, and the inner core left behind is tightly compressed neutronium: a neutron star.''

"Not something that can be checked out in the lab. But, if this thing has that much neutronium, it would weigh . . .''

"No, it's not solid neutronium. Kung thinks it consists of an infinitesimal neutronium core whose only purpose is to generate the massive gravitational field that holds the whole thing together. The cylinder is actually a pressure chamber that contains ionized gases: not atoms, but the fragments of atoms.''

Cody squinted, and raised an eyebrow. "Is this possible?''

"Oh, research in plasma physics has been going on for decades. It's beyond my ability to understand, much less than explain, even though Kung has gone over it with me pretty thoroughly these past few days. It's all tied in with fusion reactors: like the sun, converting hydrogen to helium. If this artifact is really a magnetic bottle for confining the fourth state of matter, we're talking about a fuel cell that can produce power practically forever and almost for free. No more wasteful uranium fission plants that convert water to steam, but a particle accelerator that can produce slow fusion—like controlled atomic bombs. And with no moving parts. It's a self-contained energy unit, and probably interchangeable in any number of output modes. The only thing is, you'd think if it had a full plasma charge, it would be a lot heavier."

"Good thing it's not, or we wouldn't be able to move it without a goddamn Navy salvage team. And we'd like to study it before the Ruskies *invent* it. How close are you to being ready?"

Hutch swept a hand over the dive gear. "I'm just waiting for the go ahead from the captain. Sorry. Commander. We're parked in the right spot, but the current was a little stiff. As soon as it dies down, I'm out of here."

"You seem eager."

"Anxious is the word. I just want to get it the hell over with. I have a weird feeling about this mission. We've lost every boat we've used so far."

"If the *Dudley Morton* is a ship, as Commander Petrie so delicately mentioned, we've got nothing to worry about. Except—how do you feel otherwise?"

Hutch turned away, and fiddled with his gear. "I'm just staying out of her way."

"She cares about you, you know."

"Cody, I've been over this a thousand times in my head. She almost got us killed—more than once—she might even have blown the mission, and you keep making excuses for her. I don't buy it. I don't like being—lied to, or deceived."

"She only deceived herself. Sometimes, you believe what you want to believe."

"Yeah, well, she made a pretty big chump out of me. I believed in her. I thought she was—special."

"She is."

"Yeah, she's special—a special agent. And unpredictable."

"That she is."

"You never know who's side she's on."

"We all have to make compromises."

"*I* don't. And anyway, how safe do you think we are, after being betrayed to the enemy...?"

"All right, I know the route to this point has been a little—circuitous. But this is where we are now. This is where we have go from. Through a brilliant tactical maneuver, she's got the other guys bumping up against the Ruskies, and *that'll* keep them both busy while we sneak in and pick up the goods. I'll write a recommendation for her intelligence work, HQ will never learn about the, uh, errors of her ways, and she'll come out of this operation wearing captain's bars. I know you can't accept that, but that's the way it is. You have to give and take in all sides of life, not just in counterintelligence. Besides, if she hadn't convinced her father to turn over the Kardova letters—"

"If it were up to me, I'd have her keelhauled in a thousand feet of water and—"

"What's this about keelhauling?" Commander Petrie boomed. "Cody, if you're volunteering, let me tie the ropes."

Cody grinned. "Just a philosophical discussion. Are you here to wish us well, or just playing messenger boy?" He plucked the paper out of the commander's hand.

Petried fumed, and his face went into contortions.

"Ah, tidings from the Pres." Cody handed the missive to Hutch.

Hutch squinted at the strange code. "ARMPOXWELL?"

Cody took the message back, and reread it. "Oh, that's a note from my wife. Just telling me the kids're okay. Read the one below it."

Under the heading Cody/Wakefield/Hutchison was printed one sentence: "May the work of today light up the future of mankind." It was signed by the President of the United States.

"Wow."

"Cody, I still don't like you or your attitude." Commander Petrie turned to Hutch and held out his hand. "Mr. Hutchison. The best of luck to you. If there's anything else I can do ..."

Hutch shuffled his rubber-coated feet. "Just don't leave without me."

The Navy diver returned with the tanks. "All pumped up, sir, just like you said. I just hope the seals don't blow." He put the regulators on the orifices and screwed them down tight.

"The tide is dead slack," Petrie said. "You'd better be going."

"And the missile bay?"

"Open and waiting. I just hope all this is worth it."

Cody clicked his tongue, and winked. "We'll know in about twenty minutes."

Hutch slipped into the tank harness the Navy diver was holding up for him. After tightening the weight belt, he pulled the mask onto his forehead and picked up his fins.

Kung and Ronnie entered the diver preparation room. Ronnie hung back, but Kung came forward and placed both hands on Hutch's shoulders. He was a full head shorter, so he had to look up to peer into his eyes. "Bring home the cow, Mr. Hutchison, so we can milk it together."

Despite his feeling of discomfort at Ronnie's presence, he managed a weak smile. "I'll bring it back to the barn, but you can pull the udders." The Navy diver opened the hatch. Hutch sat down on the lip, squeezed into his fins, and rolled his legs into the tiny lockout chamber. The filler tank was already in there, with a pry bar and a hammer lashed to it with thick rubber bands.

Just before the hatch closed, Cody knelt by the opening. He gave the thumbs up sign. "Have a good one."

"Thanks, Cody." Hutch adjusted the mask over his face. "Hey, Cody. I just happen to think. Do you—do you have a first name?"

Cody winked. "Yes." He slammed the hatch shut.

Hutch went through the procedures the way he had been shown: opening flood valves and increasing air pressure in such a way as to simulate a normal descent. He monitored the gauges on the bulkhead as he cleared his ears. He crouched uncomfortably in the tiny chamber. Slowly, the water welled up around him. When the red globe lights submerged, the room took on the ethereal quality of a drowned darkroom.

He left the intake valve open a few seconds after equalization: the positive internal pressure would make it easier to open the outside hatch. He released the dogs, spun open the wheel, and shoved. It was pitch dark under the deck grating.

After pushing out the single aluminum eighty, Hutch rolled forward and through the opening. He closed the hatch behind him, and dogged it down. He switched on his dive light. He was outside the pressure hull, but still under the steel skin. He released the overhead gate, shoved the filler tank out over his head, and climbed out behind it. Curious silversides swam in lazy patterns above the submarine's sleek, black hull.

Because of the gargantuan size of the nuclear vessel, the depth to the hull was only one hundred fifty feet. Hutch could see the white, pearly sand some fifty feet below. He inflated his BC, checked his gauges and gear bag, and kicked forward dragging the extra tank with him. He did not have to go far along the submarine's five hundred sixty foot length before he spotted the bow of the *Ting-Yuen* about seventy-five feet off the port side.

He kicked against a mild current until he reached the opened missile silo. He felt like an ant looking down the dark barrel of a twelve gauge shotgun. The circular rim was scorched from the flames of the solid rocket propellent. From there he took an angled course across the intervening space that intersected with the gunboat's deck gun.

He kept his elevation above the *Ting-Yuen's* deck: there was no reason to dip to two hundred feet unnecessarily. It seemed as if he were kicking forever before he noticed any nearing of his goal. When he finally settled down in a cloud of silt, he was breathing hard. Even without current, dragging all the equipment was quite a chore.

He let go the extra tank and removed the hammer and pry bar. He spent several minutes banging coral off the hinges of the deck hatch and from around the lip. Then he inserted the three foot pry bar under the open edge, planted his fins on the encrusted deck, and pried upward with the powerful muscles of his legs. The hatch moved, and stopped. He got a new grip, repositioned his feet, and stood up against the chromed steel bar. The hatch moved another inch.

There was nothing to do but go back to hammering. This time, Hutch took a twelve inch chisel out of his mesh bag, and chipped away at the thick, rainbow colored coral bases. Every time he got ready to swing, the slight current shoved his body around so that he missed the chisel completely. He managed to bang his hand a couple times before he knew he had to stabilize himself. He stretched out along the deck, pushed his feet against the gun mount, and leaned one shoulder against the tilted hatch. By crooking his wrist, he was able to hold the chisel against the coaming.

By this time he was surrounded by quite a menagerie of tropical fish whose identities were obscured in Latin names. Hutch waved his hammer at them, but they took no notice and kept nipping at the chunks of coral and floating debris. This was a feast created for them by a large, bubble blowing protector.

When Hutch uncovered the hinges, and saw that they were locked in place, he worked with the chisel for several minutes to sheer them off. Then he went back to the pry bar. This time the hatch moved up to about a forty-five degree angle before stopping solid. Fighting for equilibrium, he took a vertical stance, slipped his legs down into the opening, bent them so they wedged against the coaming, and placed his shoulder against the lid. He tried with all his might to straighten his body. Something snapped, and the hatch jerked another fifteen degrees. His wetsuit was also shredded by the sharpened bits of coral.

He took another survey of the back of the hatch, and under the powerful beam of his light was able to distinguish between marine growth and steel. A mechanical stop was welded to the back of the hatch cover, preventing it from opening any more than sixty degrees. It would be impossible to chisel it off. Resignedly, Hutch dropped the filler tank down the opening, and followed it down feet first.

He was in the corridor between the galley and the crews quarters, with another hatch leading below. Again, he followed the tank into the handling room. Down in the darkness his dive light illuminated the wreckage, the split open powder cannisters and dislodged shells, and the shell hoists. He dragged the tank along the narrow corridor to the starboard door. The green glow was there to meet him as he neared the powder magazine. He switched off the light: when it dangled freely on its lanyard it spun around annoyingly, blinding him as its beam lanced into his eyes. The artifact supplied more than enough light to work by.

A chill passed through Hutch's body when he saw it again, this time with a greater comprehension of its sheer power. The soft radiance soon warmed him. The outworldish glow emitted a calming, hypnotic effect that put Hutch at his ease. Awe was still uppermost in his mind, but it was no longer a fearful omnipotence. Instead, he thrilled at the promise the alien artifact held for mankind. It was only with great difficulty that he dragged his eyes away from the gleaming emerald surface, and concentrated on the task at hand.

Hutch opened his mesh bag and dumped out all his tools. The cylinder lay half out of its lead-sheathed box, one end of it crushing a gunshell with its spectacular weight. As his hands neared the cylinder's ethereal outer surface, that part of the object which passed for physical corporeality, an electrical jolt leaped into his palms and made all his hair stand on end— despite the clinging wetsuit. His head felt as if balloons were being rubbed all over it. His spine tingled with—anticipation?

Slowly, reverently, he threaded a stretched stainless steel basket through the space between the cylinder and the underlying debris. He was careful to stay out of the pencil thin beam that stabbed through the water like a fine neon tube. The braided wires spread like a child's version of a Chinese handcuff, offering two inches of surface area for contact with the artifact. To each end of the basket was welded a D-ring of different size. He pushed the smaller through the larger, pulled and snugged it tight, and made a choker which would tighten up under the weight of the cylinder when it was raised.

Although the plan called for a straightforward lift, Hutch entertained the eerie thought that the artifact might not *want* to be moved.

He took out the liftbag. The rubberized plastic unrolled stiffly. He clipped the brass snap ring from the lifting shrouds to the choked D-ring. When he had the spare bottle positioned properly, he jammed the exhaust orifice into a corner of the liftbag, and cracked the valve. Full pressure air hissed out quickly, some of it pouring around the edges of the bag. Hutch shoved the tank in tighter so that no air escaped. After a few seconds at full blast, the bag unfurled the rest of the way and took on an inverted teardrop shape.

Compressed air continued to inflate the liftbag until it was a great orange ball, its sides as taut as steel sheet. When it was half full, Hutch checked the connections: the choker had cinched tight, and the basket was imbedded in the green coruscation so that it was hardly visible in the brighter glow. Perfunctorily, he checked his gauges.

The compass was at a spin. The needle rotated slowly, sometimes reversing its direction, pointing aimlessly. Worse, the decompression computer displayed a blank screen, with no readings for depth, time, or decompression schedule. Neither was the digital watch functioning. Only the spring-loaded mechanical timer gave any indication of reliable operation.

Hutch shrugged it off, and returned to the job at hand. He continued inflating the liftbag until the seams bulged menacingly. He was half afraid the five hundred pound liftbag had insufficient capacity, when the cylinder shifted poisiton. He instantly shut off the valve. When he shook the liftbag by the shroud, it did not even budge. He opened the tank valve again, and watched closely as air escaped into the plastic balloon.

Finally, the cylinder shuddered, and one end of it came free. Hutch closely monitored the air so the bag would not overinflate and soar up into the overhead. If the top should be punctured, he would have to return to the ship and start all over again. He offered a last jet of air, just enough so if he yanked hard the cylinder rose up out of the debris, and settled back down again when he let go.

With a jumping, pogo stick motion, he pulled and hauled, inching the ancient artifact toward the doorway. Even though the buoyancy was effectively neutralized, the mass was the same. Getting the momentum going was like pushing a stalled car uphill. When he got it to the sill, he added a little more air by holding his pony bottle regulator under the opening and pushing the purge.

The top of the bag scraped the lintel, and the cylinder hung up on the sill. Together, they were taller than the opening. Hutch had to let the cylinder settle into the silt, then pull the top of the bag through, and wrestle the heavy weight up and over the steel lip. Moving something that heavy, and that bulky, taxed his strength and overburdened his breathing. In seconds, his air consumption had risen to double his nonworking rate.

Once in the handling room, he added more air in order to make it easier to move the cylinder among the fallen girders and I-beams, and the conglomeration of collapsed piping, cables, and electrical wiring. He tugged on the shroud, jumping the cylinder along the debris-filled deck. When he reached the middle of the room, he added enough air to the bag to let it rise up through the hatch.

The bag was billowed out so wide that its sides scraped against the squared edges. The whole thing hung there like an umbrella in a chimney. He pulled himself under the bag, and shoved in the sides, working the material bit by bit through the opening. He had to get it through, because if it remained stuck in the only exit, there was no way for him to get out of the wreck.

His heart was palpitating as he worked around the bag, shoving and gouging. Suddenly, it went through. The cylinder passed quickly by his eyes as it rose up to the overhead of the next deck. The room became dark. He climbed through the hatch, and lay on the deck to catch his breath. The emerald glow shone down from above like the light of God.

Because the other hatch was offset, Hutch had to drag the bag across the overhead. The top scraped along sharp encrustations and rusted metal protrusions, which threatened to puncture the rubberized mateiral. He squeezed his hand over the top of the bag and worked his fingers toward the relief valve. When he pressed it, a thin stream of air escaped. As soon as the bag began to sink, he stopped. Then he aligned it with the outer hatch, stuck his backup regulator under the bag, and added enough air to get it positively buoyant again. It rose up until it lodged in the opening the same way it had stuck in the lower hatch.

Again, he poked and prodded the material, and worked it through the opening. But no matter how hard he pushed, it would go no further than halfway. When he tried to pull it back down, it refused to move. The portion of the liftbag above the rim was filled with air, and expanded sideways so that it no longer fit through. It remained firmly stuck.

Hutch switched on his light as he kicked his way aft, through the galley, the officers mess, and the partially remaining bulkhead separating the engine room. He dropped down between the engines, located the collision hole by the light streaming in through it, and pushed through the torn, ragged hull. Once outside, he kicked forward along the starboard side until he rounded the bridge wreckage.

The liftbag was held in place by the half opened hatch. A thin stream of bubbles escaped from a pinhole on top of the bag, but the leak was not serious. Hutch hugged the solidly inflated ball of air, trying to wrestle it through the opening. The liftbag offered no handholds, no way to grip the material. He made a fist and slammed the bulging sides as if it were a punching bag. His efforts had no effect.

He wedged the pry bar between the liftbag and the angled hatch. With his feet braced on the deck, he pried the billowing material away from the steel constraint. After a few tries, he felt sure that the bag was moving outward and upward. He kept at it, pushing, pulling, and prying with his entire body. He was overbreathing his regulator, and felt the insufficiency in his lungs. But he kept working, kept trying to break it free.

With an unexpected lurch the hatch hinge snapped off and the hatch fell backward onto the deck. Immediately, free of the barrier, the liftbag floated out of the opening and headed for the surface. The glowing cylinder passed by like a shot. Hutch dodged the needlelike radiation beam, and grabbed onto the shroud. His buoyancy was practically neutral, so he had no way to stop the quickly rising liftbag: it just dragged him along with the artifact.

As they soared upward, Hutch climbed up the side of the liftbag and jammed his finger into the release valve. Air cascaded out through the gasket, but not at a rate excessive of the increasing internal expansion due to the lessening of pressure as the depth decreased. Still, there was nothing more he could do but hold on, and keep the valve open. It seemed like an eternity before he noticed a slackening of motion. As the rate of ascent stabilized, he also held his BC hose over his head and pushed the purge, thus making his own body heavier. Finally, the liftbag and its precious cargo came to a halt, reversed direction, and sank back down into the clear blue water.

Hutch looked below him. He could see nothing but an endless expanse of ocean. Neither the *Ting-Yuen* not the *Dudley Morton* were in view. As they descended, and the ambient pressure became greater, the air in the liftbag was compressed. Hutch felt like a skydiver as the rate of fall increased. He held onto the shroud as the cylinder plummeted toward the bottom.

He saw a shadow to one side: it was the sail of the *Dudley Morton*. Then he saw the huge bulk of the submarine. He spun around, peering past the liftbag, and saw the gunboat lying serenely on the other side. Then he passed between them both, and a moment later crashed full speed into the white sand.

Hutch pushed himself away at the last second. As the cylinder buried itself in the upper layer of silt, he landed on his heels and rolled over backward in slow motion, like a training acrobat wearing a safety harness. He was not hurt, just disoriented. He stood up above the billowing cloud of silt. When he tried to haul the cylinder out of its burial pit, its incredible weight held it in place as if it had been shackled to the bottom. Again, he placed his spare regulator under the opening and purged air into the liftbag, but only until it showed a hint of buoyancy. Then, lying heavily on the sand, with one hand on the nylon shroud, he crawled along the bottom toward the submarine.

Instead of kicking, he gouged his heels and fingers into the sand and pulled himself along. His head was buzzing from the depth, a combination of nitrogen narcosis and hyperventilation. Gasping from the exertion of the last several minutes, he dragged the precious artifact in leaping bounds as it alternately came up out of the sand, went forward a few inches, and dropped back down again. With his mind in a fog, kaleidoscopic images revolved in front of his eyes. He was straining with every ounce of strength.

When at last he reached the five story high steel wall that was the hull of the *Dudley Morton*, he lay on the bottom and gasped for air. He allowed himself a full minute of deep breathing before he rolled up to his knees. He added enough air to his BC to neutralize his buoyancy. Once more, he stuck his spare regulator under the liftbag opening and allowed air from his pony bottle to purge into it. Slowly, the cylinder lifted up off the sand. The orange material of the liftbag scraped along the smooth side of the submarine's outer skin.

As soon as the cylinder passed the bulge of the circular hull, Hutch kicked and tugged at the shrouds, designing a course along the curve toward the flattened deck above. The immense weight of the artifact and the large profile of the liftbag contrived to hold him back. He struggled against the massive opposition, breathing rapidly.

Then he realized he was fighting more then lateral resistance. This far off the bottom, as it had before, the air in the liftbag was expanding at an ever increasing rate. Once more, the artifact was getting away from him, pulling him slowly upward. He was being dragged off the hull, and there were no protrusions for him to hold onto. He let the air out of his BC, to make himself heavy. He pulled down on the shroud. He was able to counteract most of the buoyancy. His fin tips bent as he tried to walk on them and grab traction on the hull.

He felt himself being lifted off the steel skin. The liftbag was again taking him for an elevator ride to the surface. It was moving slowly this time, but inexorably. Hutch was about to work his way up the rubberized material and stab in the purge when his regulator slowed down to almost nothing.

Instantly, he knew he had run out of air, and that at this depth he might get only two or three breaths before he ran out completely. With his free hand he grappled for his pony bottle regulator. He spit out his main and shoved in the spare. By this time he was definitely on his way to the surface.

A glint of steel passed by his eyes. A knife blade stabbed through the lower edge of the liftbag. Air surged out. The uncontrolled ascent was halted, and the weight of the cylinder started pulling the liftbag back down. Hutch saw the diver on the other side of the bag, saw a gloved hand on the other shroud. Together, they pulled the artifact toward the missile silo. The cylinder clunked down just short of the flattened deck, and its ponderous weight started to take it down along the curve. Hutch dug in his heels, and the other diver did the same.

The wetsuited figure had skillfully placed the slit low enough so that only part of the air could escape. The two of them fought, hauled, clawed, and dragged the cylinder against the force of gravity, until at last, gasping and exhausted, they reached the level deck. Still breathing hard, Hutch managed to look up from his horizontal position and give the okay sign.

Lieutenant Veronica Wakefield signaled back the same.

There was no time for thanks, no time for recriminations. Hutch ignored the turmoil within his mind, within his heart, and concentrated on the task at hand. He pointed to the missile silo. Ronnie nodded in understanding. They each took one of the liftbag shrouds, and tugged the emanating cylinder along the hull plates.

At the open maw they stopped. Hutch got behind the liftbag, gave one last shove, and tipped the artifact over the lip into the maw. It fell promptly into the seven-foot-diameter tube. The liftbag hung up for an instant on the edge of the hole, then it was swallowed up by the tube like a chewing gum bubble inhaled by a ten year old. Hutch looked down the silo, saw the green glow descend to the bottom, and come to a halt with a clang.

He signaled immediately, then turned and kicked toward the lockout chamber. Ronnie was right behind him. He went only a few feet before his pony bottle chugged, offering more resistance than it should. He had used so much of its air in repeatedly filling the liftbag that it was almost empty. The chamber was in sight when it stopped delivering air altogether.

Hutch spun frantically, spat out the useless regulator, and drew his finger across his throat. Ronnie responded by taking out her mouthpiece and shoving it in Hutch's face. He wrapped his lips around the soft rubber, drew in two good, deep breaths, and handed it back. He took off again for the lockout chamber with Ronnie's hand in his.

She offered him more air, and he took it. Buddy-breathing while they kicked along the hull, they finally reached the open deck granting. Hutch took a breath, let Ronnie's regulator go, and motioned for her to descend first through the hatch. She stood vertically, letting her feet slip into the opening, then paused before ducking her head below the deck level and let Hutch have another breath. He followed her in head first.

While he closed the deck grating, Ronnie backed her fins into the lockout chamber. She paused until Hutch faced her. He took another breath from her regulator, nodded, and pushed her backward. Wearing only a single tank, she slipped into the tiny compartment easily. Hutch pulled himself inside. He bent double, reached behind, slammed the hatch, and spun the wheel that tightened the mechanism against the gasket.

Something was wrong. The wheel would not turn because the hatch was not seated properly. Holding his breath, Hutch pushed Ronnie aside so he could see what was preventing it from closing. His own fin tip was caught in the opening. Choking, with his throat burning, he tried to pull in his foot. They were so crammed in the chamber that he could not move, could not signal the trouble to Ronnie, could not even ask for a breath of air. He swallowed hard. In another second, reflex was going to made him inhale water.

He felt rubber against his face. Ronnie shoved the mouthpiece between his lips. He took another breath from her regulator, then a second and a third. He fought hard to keep down his panic. When he felt as if he could hold his breath for a few seconds, he twisted around, rotated the hand wheel counterclockwise, shoved open the hatch, pulled in the errant fin, slammed the hatch tightly, and locked it in place.

Desperately, he twisted the inlet valve. Air hissed into the chamber, music to Hutch's ears. As it came in, he activated the suction pump. The water was drawn out through a drain and injected into the bilges. As soon as there was an air pocket overhead, he jammed his face against the overhead and gratefully sucked in lungsful of air. After a few breaths he noticed Ronnie doing the same. The tank was in front of her, and in her hand she held the second stage of the regulator. When she pushed the purge, only a tiny tickle of air emerged.

"Thanks," he gasped. His voice sounded strange, not only resonating in the small chamber, but thickened by compressed air. "You're a sight for sore eyes—and sore lungs."

"Are you okay?"

"As long as I'm breathing, I'm okay."

Hutch kept his eyes glued to the internal gauges until the ambient pressure was reduced to sixty pounds per square inch: the equivalent of one hundred feet of sea water. He leaned back and shrugged out of his tank harness. There was not enough room to take them off, and already he and Ronnie crouched knee to knee. The last of the water trickled out. It continued to rain inside as the overhead, the gauges, and the valve wheels dripped.

"Omigod." With his decompression computer among the dead, Hutch stared at his timer. "Thirty-three minutes. No wonder I ran out of air."

Ronnie smiled. "You don't give up, do you?"

"It turned out to be harder than I thought."

"That's what I like to hear."

Hutch could not prevent a smile from touching his lips. But it only touched. A moment later he wiped it off. He pulled out the plastic card with the Navy Tables, and started calculating.

"So, what made you decide to come after me."

Ronnie shrugged. "It seems like you always let me come first."

Hutch rolled his eyes. If he was going to have to spend an hour and a half in close confinement with her bantering, he would never hold out in serious mein.

"Hey, I leave you two alone for a minute, and already you're back at it." The intercom rattled raucously, with a grating static. "How'd it go, Hot Shot?"

"It had its ups and downs."

"It's gonna get worse when you get inside. The Old Man's ready to blow a rivet. Your stellar prize blew out every solid state circuit within a fifty foot radius. All three decks. Fried the electronic circuitry on more than half the missiles—and the ship besides. He's gonna get you for assault on a battery."

"One joker's enough, Cody."

Ronnie held her hand over the waterproof microphone. "Hutch, we have to talk. Seriously. I know how you feel, but—"

Hutch held up his hand. Aloud, "Cody, I've got troubles with another celestial body. I'll get back to you." He flipped the switch. His face was no more than a foot and a half from Ronnie's. "Okay, I can't get away this time. And after what you did out there, I guess I owe you that much."

He glanced at his timer, then at the Navy Tables, and siphoned air out of the chamber. He was under more pressure here than he had been at two hundred feet. But at least in here he could breathe. He stretched out his cramped legs as best he could. Ronnie did the same, and they sat facing each other with their arms and legs mingling like love-torn earthworms. It was a long way to the surface.

*　　*　　*

"So, did you two kiss and make up?"

Hutch pulled on a pair of khaki pants, and buckled them around his waist. He tucked in the tail of his shirt. "Not exactly."

Cody sprawled across his bunk. "What's your hang-up?"

"I don't have any hang-ups!" Hutch shouted. "I just don't like being lied to. I don't like being deceived. I won't stand for it."

"Seems to me, I recall reading in your file, you once dumped a gal because she broke a date because she was going out of town, and forgot to tell you. I'd call that a hang-up."

"See, that's how much your silly investigations are worth. She lied to you, too, and you don't even know it. She had some childish belief that lying was defined as stating in words something specifically contrary to the truth. She rationalized that as long as she didn't tell me she was spending the weekend with another guy, and she never said anything about it, it didn't count as a lie. What you don't say, when it's intended to deceive and make someone believe something you know isn't true, is just as much a lie. But in her own thwarted little mind, she couldn't see that. At least, not when it was to her advantage. Your problem is you're so used to imposture you accept it as a way of life."

"There are two sides to every story."

"Come on, Cody. Wise up. She's been playing both of us for fools ever since this thing began. Doesn't that bother you?"

"Not when I understand her rationale. Look, just because you hated your father doesn't mean everybody does. Call it a weakness in her personality if you want, but she was merely acting on her emotions."

Hutch ran the towel over his face and hair. His beard was getting ragged, and his hair stood out at obtuse angles. "Do you know how ridiculous that sounds, coming from someone who's almost an android? My god, do you know what the world would be like if everyone used such an irresponsible excuse as 'acting on emotions'?"

"I know what it would be like if we didn't *have* emotions. It's a necessary evil, part of the human make-up, one of the things that differentiates us from the animals. Without emotion there's no drive, no ambition—just a programmed response, without diversity."

"Doesn't *anything* bother you?"

Cody placed his hands behind his head, and leaned up against the back of the bunk. He crossed his feet. "Of course. I'm concerned about where we're going now that we've found this thing."

"We won't be going anywhere for a long time. You don't think they can mass produce those cylinders like gas tanks, do you? Hell, the technology's *way* ahead of us. We're no closer to it now than we were back in the Pleistocene, when those supersophisticated extraterrestrials used Earth for a dumping depot." He stabbed a finger at Cody. "You know what that thing is, don't you? It's rubbish."

"One man's trash is another man's treasure."

"Cody, how the hell can you be so smug about it? Doesn't it bother you that our ancestors were trash pickers, rummaging through scrap piles?"

"It doesn't change who I am, or what I've developed myself to be. You've got to get off your elevated eohippus and look at the big picture."

"Yes, well, that's what scares me. I've got too much re-evaluating to do." Hutch sat down and pulled on his socks and shoes. "A year ago, a deadeye dredged up by a fisherman sent me out on the most significant archaeological quest of the century—well, maybe the decade. Now, whether or not the Norwegians reached America before Columbus is totally meaningless. This—this isn't simply the most important find in the history of mankind: it's the *cause* of the history of mankind. You think that flask is *going* to change the course of human events, but it did that already. When the Australopithecines had been conceeded by Nature as a dead-end development, and were on their way to extinction, along comes a family of prehuman pack rats who—''

A light tap came at the door. It swung open, revealing Kung and Ronnie in the corridor. Ronnie smiled, ''Hi. Can we come in?''

Cody vaulted up to a sitting position on the edge of the bunk. ''Anything to get this negativist off my rumble seat.''

Kung smiled profusely as he closed the door behind him. ''Mr. Hutchison, I would like to congratulate you on a job well done. You have succeeded admirably in, how do you Americans say it, bringing home the bacon.''

Hutch scowled. He avoided looking at Ronnie. ''Or a pig in a poke. Kung, you've known for a long time about the mutagenic effects of radiation caused by the artifact. Have you given any thought as to what it must have done to the early hominids who got in the path of that beam? Of what it implies about our ancestry?''

''I have studied its possible consequences for many years. It is indeed strange that through a hole only one atomic nucleus in diameter should come the seeds of change. But remember, Mr. Hutchison, that mutation is a natural process. Technically, any creature that does not *perfectly* imitate its parent, is a mutant—''

Hutch interrupted. ''That's like saying a week old embryo is nothing more than a tumor.''

''Perhaps. But, at that stage of its development a baby more closely resembles a cancerous growth than a human adult. And although it has the biological potential of growing into human form, it is cultural and environmental circumstances which endow upon that conglomerate of splitting cells the stamp of humanity. Radiation does not change evolution, Mr. Hutchison. It merely hastens it.''

''But we're not talking about slow adaptation through physical change. We're talking about a quantum leap in the genetic structure of the species, and an enormous and complex alteration in the workings of the brain: the sudden emergence of intelligence, of cognitive awareness, of a level of consciousness not previously in existence. And you know what's so ironic about the whole thing? It wasn't by design, it wasn't even by accident. We're not the progeny of some benevolent galactic race.

''Do you know what the cylinder really is? Do you know why it's so light? Because for all practical purposes, it's empty. It's like a goddamned throwaway propane bottle. Instead of refilling it, you junk it and take another one out of stores. *That's* the extent of the alien technology of half a million years ago. *That's* what's got the world in such an upheaval today. And *that's* what made man what he is. In the most derogatory sense you can imagine, all that we are came about because some retarded ape fell into somebody's sewage. Our entire existence is a joke—nothing but one big lie.''

Cody clicked his tongue. ''No, you're being too harsh. You're saying that a kid out of the ghetto is still a nobody when he becomes a millionaire businessman. What's important in life is not where you came from, or what you started out with, but who you become. Whatever our parentage, we got where we are today by our own intitiative. And species can accept a helping hand the same as individuals taking out a student loan.''

Hutch glared. Another fact had just emerged from his file.

"Maybe *we'll* get the chance to return the favor some day.''

Ronnie said, "Remember, you have to look at the overall fabric, not just a single thread. Like human relationships, the purpose of the Universe cannot be divined without the overview of time and space.'' She shrugged her delicate shoulders. "Besides, who knows how *they* achieved their civilization. Before you make any hasty judgments—about anything—you have to make allowances for the limitations of your point of view. It might make a difference in your mind, as well as in your heart. At least, you ought to give it a little thought.''

Hutch shuffled awkwardly, and stared down at his feet. One cheek twitched. He looked up at the faces of his companions; all eyes were upon him. He took in a deep breath, grateful for the moment that there was plenty of air to breathe. Ultimately, all perspectives began with life, and that much, for the moment, he had.

"All right, I'll think about it, and give it some rational emphasis. But for now, I'm going to give in to my emotions.'' He inhaled deeply again. "It's so goddamned great to be alive. Let's all go get stinking.''

Author's Note

The basic premise of *The Peking Papers* is one of historical record. All the people and incidents involved in the discovery and excavation of the Peking man fossils, including the exhibition and study at the Peking Union Medical College and the probable course of events leading to the loss of the crated remains, are depicted in Christopher Janus's book, *The Search for Peking Man*.

It is true that the fossils were last seen on a train headed for the Marine barrack at Camp Holcomb, that the Marines defending the base were captured by the Japanese and held as POWs until the end of the war, that the Japanese secret police interrogated people in China during the war years in an attempt to recover what was considered to be one of China's greatest national treasures. It is true that the manifest of the *Awa Maru* listed three crates of Peking man fossils, and that the hospital ship was torpedoed by the U.S. submarine *Queenfish*. Also, the People's Republic of China conducted extensive salvage operations on the wreck of the *Awa Maru* during the late seventies, primarily to recover bullion worth a fortune on today's market.

Immediately after President Nixon opened peaceful negotiations with Red China in 1972, Christopher Janus was called in under mysterious circumstances to institute a search for the fossil remains. He was never able to account for the fossils, but the political intrigues he unearthed were as thick as the fictional intrigues of *The Peking Papers*, involving both the People's Republic of China and Nationalist China. The CIA also investigated all the people who contacted Janus with information supposedly leading to the fossils' rediscovery.

Janus tracked rumors that the fossils had been taken from Shanghai to Yalta by the Russians, in 1946, and that the Chinese Nationalists had absconded with them during their retreat from the mainland in 1949, but was unable to substantiate either claim. If any country actually got away with the fossils, that country is still keeping their existence a secret. *The Peking Papers* picks up all the historical threads where they terminated, then extrapolated the possibilities from there.

The castings of the 175 fossils found prior to the war are available for study at the Museum of Natural History, in New York City. Further excavations at the original site have produced a few more fossils, but none that are as complete as the initial finds.

In the present volume the contemporary spelling of traditional Chinese place names has been used in order to avoid the confusion brought about by the new wave of Anglicization. While Peking will be seen on modern maps as Beijing, the name of that city has not been changed; rather, the phonetic symbols used in transliteration have been converted to a different combination of letters in order to better represent local pronunciation. In spoken Chinese twang, the "P" in Peking is a sound that falls between the English "B" and "P": a slight variation of the formation of the lips. Today's newscasters are burdened with the additional task of simulating sounds for which their tongues are untrained.

Similarly, Choukoutien may sometimes be seen as Chou Kou Tien, while in the modern spelling system it is translated as Zhoukoudian. Peking man, however, is still spelled and pronounced in English as Peking.

Today, after decades of controversy, Sinanthropus pekinensis has been reclassified so that it falls into the genus of Homo erectus—humanity's true ancestor in the direct line of evolution.